THEMES IN DRAMA

Themes in Drama is a journal which brings together articles and reviews about the dramatic and theatrical activity of a wide range of cultures and periods. The articles offer original contributions to their own specialized fields, but are presented in such a way that their significance may be readily appreciated by non-specialists.

Themes in Drama

An annual publication

Edited by James Redmond

15

MADNESS IN DRAMA

Editorial Advisory Board

SUBSCRIPTIONS The subscription price to volume 15, which includes postage, is £45 (US $81.00 in USA, Canada and Mexico) for institutions, £26.00 (US $51.00 in USA, Canada and Mexico) for individuals ordering direct from the Press and certifying that the annual is for their personal use. Airmail (orders to Cambridge only) £7.50 extra. Copies of the annual for subscribers in the USA, Canada and Mexico are sent by air to New York to arrive with minimum delay. Orders, which must be accompanied by payment, may be sent to a bookseller, subscription agent or direct to the publishers: Cambridge University Press, The Edinburgh Building, Shaftesbury Road, Cambridge CB2 2RU. Payments may be made by any of the following methods: cheque (payable to Cambridge University Press), UK postal order, bank draft, Post Office Giro (account no. 571 6055 GB Bootle – advise CUP of payment), international money order, UNESCO coupons, or any credit card bearing the Interbank symbol. Orders from the USA, Canada and Mexico should be sent to Cambridge University Press, 40 West Street, New York, NY 10011–4211.

BACK VOLUMES Volumes 1–14 are available from the publisher at £40.00 ($75.00 in USA and Canada).

MADNESS IN DRAMA

CAMBRIDGE
UNIVERSITY PRESS

Published by the Press Syndicate of the University of Cambridge
The Pitt Building, Trumpington Street, Cambridge CB2 1RP
40 West 20th Street, New York, NY 10011–4211, USA
10 Stamford Road, Oakleigh, Melbourne 3166, Australia

First published 1993

Printed in Great Britain at The Bath Press, Avon

British Library Cataloguing in publication data
Themes in Drama, 15
1. Drama – History and criticism – Periodicals
809.2′005 PN 1601

Library of Congress catalogue card number 82–4491
ISSN 0263–676x
ISBN 0 521 44376 8

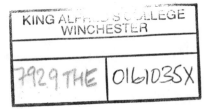

Contents

Themes in Drama volumes

The series has come to its conclusion, and the list of volumes is now complete

Illustrations

Contributors

Rob K. Baum, *University of California, Santa Barbara*
Marcia Blumberg, *York University, Toronto*
Ipshita Chanda, *Comparative Literature, Jadavpur University*
Karin S. Coddon, *Comparative Literature, Brown University*
Mimi Gisolfi D'Aponte, *Graduate School, City University, New York*
John J. Flynn, *University of California, Los Angeles*
Dominique Froidefond, *Department of French, Indiana University*
Abiodun Goke-Pariola, *Department of English, Georgia Southern University*
Dianne Hunter, *Department of English, Trinity College, Hartford, Conn.*
Kaarina Kailo, *Concordia University, Montreal*
Elizabeth Klaver, *English Department, Southern Illinois University*
Amelia Howe Kritzer, *West Virginia University*
Arthur L. Little Jr, *Department of English, University of California, Los Angeles*
Oluremi Omodele, *English Studies, Osaka University*
Mark William Rocha, *Department of English, California State University, Northridge*
Christian Rogowski, *Department of German, Amherst College*
Elizabeth Schafer, *RHBNC, University of London*
A. Velissariou, *Department of English, Aristotle University, Thessaloniki*
Elizabeth Hale Winkler, *Department of English, Texas Tech University*

The Duchess of Malfi: tyranny and spectacle in Jacobean drama

KARIN S. CODDON

The untenability of the mad tragic subject in early seventeenth-century English drama suggests a significant rift between interiority and unreason. For while Jacobean drama is noteworthy for its ubiquitous lunatics, the disordered *subjectivity* that so marks the later Elizabethan and early Jacobean tragic hero tends to be eclipsed, if not outright effaced, by representations of madness almost impenetrable in their exteriority, their theatricality.[1] The corruption of the courts in which tragic madmen move is duplicated rather than opposed in the morbid declamations of the melancholy malcontent who is at once emblem and effect of his disordered world. The contamination of subjectivity by an exterior-ized mad discourse heralds the exhaustion of the trope of madness, as the problematic subject of absolutist authority gives way to an increasingly rational and privatized subjectivity enabled by operations of authority less and less centered in the power of sovereignty.

The individual – and individuated – mad tragic subject is displaced by emblematic madmen whose 'out of fashion melancholy' no longer signifies internalized contradictions in a disruptive dialogue between subject and authority: it now signifies the external, manifestly public effects of that disruption. No Jacobean melancholic is more vituperative and morbid than Tourneur's Vindice – nor less individuated, as his morality-play name suggests.[2] The ostensible content of his madness – corrupt power, lechery, physical decay – is also the content of Hamlet's and Lear's tirades, but with a significant difference: Vindice's speeches have a strikingly literal, even reportorial quality whose excesses are matched, even subsumed, by the material circumstances of the play-world. Vindice's melancholy is engaged in these very material circumstances, not unlike the macabre but eminently *functional* prop of Gloriana's skull. In *The Revenger's Tragedy* as in *The Duchess of Malfi*, madness's alignment with representation becomes its explicit function: madness is emphatically identified with outwardness, with costume, disguise, playing. Like the spectacular body,[3] the exteriority of madness in Jacobean tragedy marks a disjunction between inwardness and materiality. If madness can be excluded from inwardness, its externalization enables confinement if not containment; the notion of a wholly 'private' self necessarily excludes the unreason that traverses indistinct boundaries between inward and outward, psychic and political. The privatization of subjectivity, then, de-politicizes as well as stabilizes the interior space.

If Elizabethan madness serves at once to subversively demystify the myths of absolutism and to contain such interrogations wtihin the marginality of unreason, the relentless Jacobean deflation of absolutist mythology effaces the transgressive space from which madness speaks.

> Surely, we're all mad people, and they
> Whom we think are, are not – we mistake those;
> 'Tis we are mad in sense, they but in clothes

comments Vindice (III, v, 78–81),[4] and to an extent he articulates the structural reformulation of madness in Jacobean tragedy. Disclaiming any authority to speak that within which passes show, madness is no longer the medium of disordered, potentially transgressive subjectivity. Madness is confined, almost literally, to mere playing, 'seeming', spectacle. The concentration of madness in the spectacular body enables its objectifica-tion as a pathological phenomenon; madness is thus something that is observed in a clinical, proto-empirical sense as well as in the realm of theatricality. And, as I have argued elsewhere in reference to *Macbeth*,[5] from such observation madness enters into the discursive order of diagnosis, wherein the language of reason may define, dissect, and silence that of unreason. If its 'wild and whirling words' are madness's excess that evades the containment – the discipline and/or punishment – imposed on the lunatic's body, the literal objectification of madness (i.e., its constitu-tion as an *object* of discourse and knowledge) is bound up in the erasure of any possible or liminal position from which madness might speak. The displacement of the mad subject from the tragic center in Jacobean drama is, then, no less politically interested a narrative restructuration than the shift in the late 1590s from king to tragic subject.[6]

Thus in such plays as *The Revenger's Tragedy* and *The Duchess of Malfi*, madness neither defers nor mediates the disclosure of subjectivity. The madness of Hamlet or of Marston's Antonio speaks the contradictions of early modern subjectivity, the conflict between post-Reformation inward-ness and the microcosmic subject of sovereign power. But the madness of Macbeth or Vindice, Bosola or Flamineo, is more mirror than mask, its object the spectacle itself. The exteriority of such madness recalls but is not necessarily a throwback to the sensational Senecan fury in which excessive passion is nonetheless accommodated within narrativity. Rather, Jacobean madness is inscribed almost haphazardly among a variety of characters and theatrical effects; so the dramas become themselves strangely useless, foregoing even the perfunctory claim to edification or affirmation of 'moral order'. Jacobean tragedy is distinctive, however, not only for the pervasive and explicit ethical anarchy that misrules the plays of Tourneur and Webster, but also for its almost self-parodic theatricality, what Francis Barker has called 'the innocent foregrounding of [the theatre's] own device'.[7] The 'theatricality of this theatre'[8] is perhaps nowhere better exemplified than in *The Duchess of Malfi*, with its pageant of Bedlamites, mutilated wax figures that 'plague in art', and overt plot manipulations (e.g., the dropped horoscope, the Cardinal's bizarre instructions that his cries for help be ignored). It is as if the notion of inwardness is beginning to retire from the publicity of the spectacle, the mutilated bodies that bloody the Jacobean stage suggestive of the violent unreason that will be exiled from the realm of a private and unseen 'self'. This disciplining and displacement of the violence within is a necessary condition for the emergence of the reasoned resistance that will make revolution – and regicide – feasible in seventeenth-century England. Yet the tragic madman of late Elizabethan and early Jacobean tragedy comes to the representational foreground touched by emergent as well as residual cultural elements.[9] The mad tragic hero articulates and embodies untenable contradictions in an anachronistic ideology, not the overthrow of 'subjectification' but rather a tacit perception of the inadequacy of the dominant in fashioning subjects.[10] But if madness speaks the breakdown of the relation of inwardness to its enabling authority, it posits no alternative discourse. The inchoate construction of an alternative – the private, rational subjectivity – signifies the tragic madman's obsolescence. To some extent, however, tragic madness has been engaged in the production of the reasonable individualist subjectivity that will exclude unreason from the discourses of contestation. By exposing the conflicts between inwardness and authority, and in the spectacular medium wherein power was not only represented but *reproduced* (i.e., proliferated), tragic madness plays both a liminal and a productive role in the crucial reformulation of the seventeenth-century English subject.[11]

But the melancholy malcontent is less frequently the tragic hero of Jacobean drama than he is a kind of embodied emblem, an overt stage device.[12] Such figures as Flamineo and Bosola in Webster's plays are narratively as well as socially marginalized, serving a narrative structure as ruthless and unaccommodating as the courtly power structure it represents. Instrumentalized and contaminated by this narrative/political structure, they are ultimately contained by it as well. 'We are merely the stars' tennis-balls, struck and bandied which way pleases them,' Bosola surmises (v, iv, 54–5)[13] in a play in which coincidence, accident, and apparently inexplicable plot manipulations dominate tragic action. Moreover, the Jacobean emphasis on the material, economic conditions of the malcontent's melancholy is not only topical,[14] but also allows for the construction of inwardness outside of melancholy, which is represented as a political guise rather than a 'private' and subjective malaise. In *The Duchess of Malfi* Bosola's melancholy is chiefly emblematic and instrumental, bound to visible strategies of corrupt political practices.[15] But this overt appropriation of madness by the authority to which it is ostensibly antagonistic does not structurally efface the space of transgression. Rather, it opens up a different, but significant, site for contestation as well as for subjectivity: the private and domestic sphere that the resolutely sane Duchess and Antonio strive to occupy.

Indeed, in *The Duchess of Malfi* madness is an instrument and metonymy of the public, spectacular world that constantly encroaches upon the private, the subjective, the sane. No longer located in the equivocal, ambiguous space between interiority and exteriority, subjectivity and subversion, madness *seems* rather than *is*; it is explicitly but an action that a man might play. Like political power in the play, madness is as fragmented itself as it is fragmenting, dispersed among the dramatis personae.[16] But rather than destabilizing subjectivity, madness itself is unstable, a habit or livery that aptly is put on. Thus Bosola deflates Ferdinand's boast that

> He that can compass me, and know my drifts,
> May say he hath put a girdle 'bout the world,
> And sounded all her quicksands

(III, i, 84–6)

by advising the Duke 'That you Are your own chronicle too much, and grossly Flatter yourself' (lines 87–9). Like Bosola's own melancholy, Ferdinand's unfathomable distraction functions chiefly as a mode of self-representation equivalent to the part he plays. In a similar fashion Antonio will debunk the authenticity of Bosola's melancholy, identifying it with a manifestly political strategy:

> Because you would not seem to appear to the world
> Puffed up with your preferment, you continue
> This out-of-fashion melancholy.

(II, i, 91–3)

Mechanistic and depersonalized, madness in the play becomes a material instrument of an equally disordered power; as Bosola and the Bedlamites are to the perverse will of Ferdinand, so all are the 'creatures' of a spectacle that overtly disclaims any other dramatic or didactic purpose than to 'plague in art'.

The world of *The Duchess of Malfi* is one in which the macro-microcosmic mythology of order, centered in the body and blood of the monarch, is honored only in the breach. Where *King Lear* dramatizes the degeneration of the sovereign's mystical body into the naked and battered body of unaccommodated man, *The Duchess* takes as its point of departure the vacuity of the organic paradigm.[17] The mystical political body which incorporates immutable sovereign authority is displaced by 'a rotten and dead body [that] we delight / To hide . . . in rich tissue.' Antonio's early speech in the first act gives lip-service to the conventional ideal of the body politic, but only as it points up the discrepancy between a distant political ideal and an immediate political reality. He admires the French court because

> In seeking to reduce both state and people
> To a fixed order, their judicious king
> Begins at home, quits first his royal palace
> Of flattering sycophants, of dissolute
> And infamous persons, which he sweetly terms
> His master's masterpiece, the work of Heaven,
> Considering duly that a prince's court
> Is like a common fountain, whence should flow
> Pure silver drops in general, but if't chance
> Some cursed example poison't near the head,
> Death and disease through the whole land spread.
>
> (I, i, 5–15)

The possibility of a topical reference to the actual state of things in France is less significant than the location of order well outside the realm in which the dramatic action takes place. As has been often noted, not only the troubled court of Malfi but the equally troubled court of James is none too subtly evoked in Antonio's speech. James's penchant for 'flattering sycophants' and 'dissolute and infamous persons', of which Robert Carr and George Villiers were two of the more notorious, was a character flaw far more typical of the King of England than of either of the fictive dukes of Malfi.[18] Indeed, the speech seems almost pointedly addressed to the courtly world outside rather than within the play. As J. W. Lever has remarked,

> At the time when [*The Duchess of Malfi*] was being written, James I had dispensed with . . . chief minister Cecil, and placed the entire control of the state in the hands of his young favorite Robert Carr. The Privy Council had become a mere rubber stamp for arbitrary personal rule. Honours were openly bought and sold; marriages and divorces were steps to political influence.[19]

The ideal body politic is thus markedly excluded from the spectacle, as distant from the court of James as from the court of Malfi. Significantly, the spectacle cannot *show* the ideal but only narrates it, for representation is itself implicated in the corrupt world of dissembling but opaque appearance.

Accordingly, then, Antonio becomes as good as a chorus, providing the gloss for each of the emblematic actors who appear onstage to people the court of Malfi. The lofty speech on the French court is negatively punctuated by the immediate appearance of the malcontent Bosola vainly suing the Cardinal for advancement. Notably, both authority and malcontent are characterized by the idiom of poison and disease; in fact, Antonio's description of the Cardinal is more evocative of the conventional idiom of treasonous melancholy than is his description of Bosola. Of Bosola, Antonio comments, 'This foul melancholy / Will poison all his goodness' (lines 77–8), suggesting a faint tension between an essentialist 'self' and the politically inscribed suit of woe. Antonio's remarks about the Cardinal are far more damning:

> . . . observe his inward character: he is a melancholy churchman; the spring in his face is nothing but the engendering of toads; where he is as jealous of any man, he lays worse plots for him than ever was imposed on Hercules, for he strews in his way flatterers, panders, intelligencers, atheists, and a thousand such political monsters.
>
> (lines 166–72)

For the Elizabethans it was usually the melancholy subject, the malcontent, who was 'a brocher of dangerous Matchiavellisme, and inventor of strategems, quirkes, and policies';[20] here the malcontent is almost literally but the extension of a corrupt and corrupting distraction inscribed in authority itself. If the Cardinal is especially sinister for his identification with the anti-Christ papist church, Ferdinand, possessed of a 'most perverse and turbulent nature' (line 179), is even more the embodiment of the mad *actor*; the Duchess's twin, he also doubles the Cardinal and Bosola in opaque dissemblence: 'What appears in him is merely outside' (line 180).

Hence, the play seems to question any significant distinction between princely authority and politic disorder. However, the tragedy does posit an alternative, in the person of the Duchess. Antonio praises her in terms of her personal, 'essential' qualities, and the opposition of the highly individuated, virtuous subject to impenetrably mad and theatrical authority comprises a major conflict in the drama. The conflation of prince and traitor indicts a power structure here exposed as degenerate and unable to sustain its enabling distinctions; the constitution of opposition in the space of the private and individual opens up a different structural possibility that obviates the function of the mad subject. Thus the ruler and the malcontent are crudely aligned against inwardness. Ferdinand commissions Bosola to infiltrate the Duchess's privacy, to 'live i' th' court here, and observe the duchess; / To note all the particulars of her havior' (lines 261–2). The task that Ferdinand requests is more than a little voyeuristic, as it involves the visual penetration of a private, female space. But Ferdinand's interest in the government and constraint of the

Duchess's sexuality cannot be taken as normative, patriarchal self-assertion, for it is deeply implicated in incest and madness. But again, it is a madness externalized, delegated in fact to Bosola. Bosola apparently recognizes as much: 'It seems you would create me / One of your familiars' (lines 267–8), he comments, adding shortly afterwards, 'I am your creature' (line 297). The notion that authority enables the subject's agency is parodied and literalized in the compact; Bosola becomes the instrument of corrupt though legitimate authority.

Similarly, melancholy becomes an actual guise, a role, in the service of princely authority attempting to disrupt the construction of the private. Ferdinand bids Bosola to

> Be yourself;
> Keep your old garb of melancholy; 'twill express
> You envy those that stand above your reach,
> Yet strive not to come near 'em: this will gain
> Access to private lodgings.

(lines 287–91)

Specifically aligned against rather than with inwardness, melancholy is explicitly ideological, even its conventional association with thwarted ambition engaged in the performance of the very political power it ostensibly threatens. The malcontent is indeed the prince's creature. Webster's relentless exploration of the instrumentalization of identity is historically rather than humanistically informed; in Jacobean England the wholesale commercialization of social status persisted in blatant disregard of the fixed social hierarchy of contemporary propaganda.[21] The notorious title-mongering of the Jacobean court, in divorcing blood and social status, would ultimately work against the interests of those who most profited from the sale of titles in the short run. Ironically, it is the purity of royal bloodlines that ostensibly impels Ferdinand's outrageous response to the Duchess's marriage, but his complicity in the debasement of blood as a basis for nobility is signified not only by his madness but also by his perversion of patronage. 'Say, then, my corruption / Grew out of horse-dung', Bosola sardonically concludes (lines 296–7); the prince's bounty degenerates into a mutually contaminating transaction.

Significantly, the compact is followed shortly by another transaction, though one of a markedly contrasting variety. The audience is given a window into the 'private lodgings' of the Duchess yet to be penetrated by the 'politic dormouse' Bosola. That the Duchess summons Antonio under the premise that she is 'making [her] will' (I, ii, 84) is more than a portent of the violent end to which her marriage dooms her. Perhaps more than any other legal document, the will is a token of *individualism*, a literal inscription of the subject as a possessor and distributor of objects that, conversely, constitute his or her *self*-possession.[22] Here, the unorthodox

self-assertion of the Duchess's courtship of her steward further underscores the pun of her 'will'. Certainly, according to common contemporary notions of social hierarchy, the Duchess is transgressing natural order,
not only as a woman courting a man, but a prince courting a commoner.[23]
However, to assume, as many critics have, that the Duchess is thus
'responsible' for her tragic fate is to overlook Webster's explicit identification of the social values and political practices of the dominant with
dissemblance, corruption, even madness. Disorder in the play is overly
aligned with those figures who embody and articulate strict enforcement
of hierarchy and degree – Ferdinand and the Cardinal. Christopher Hill
has gone so far as to argue that 'Webster clearly approves of the Duchess
of Malfi's marriage beneath her, though it horrifies her court'; Hill con-
tends that Webster, like Middleton, had a strong allegiance to so-called
'city values'.[24] Whether or not the play actively endorses the Duchess's
marriage is, I believe, deliberately ambiguous; what is clear is that the
ideology by which her deed is constituted as transgressive is virtually
indistinguishable from a madman's perverse obsession. Antonio may
initially demur from the Duchess's proposal with a solemn invocation of
hierarchy and degree, but given the contamination of these by their intersection with madness, his conservative position seems more nostalgic than
prescriptive. Just as his early speech of act I, scene i pays self-conscious
homage to a conventional icon – the idealized body politic – that is
travestied both in the text and context of the play, Antonio's response to
the Duchess's overtures articulates the conventional, indeed, the 'official'
position on ambition and madness that has just been thrown into confusion in the previous scene between Ferdinand and Bosola:

> Ambition, madam, is a great man's madness,
> That is not kept in chains and close-pent rooms,
> But in fair lightsome lodgings, and is girt
> With the wild noise of prattling visitants,
> Which makes it lunatic beyond all cure.
>
> > (lines 125–9)

But ambition in the play is *not* 'a great man's madness'; for the madness of
Ferdinand, the most flamboyant and obvious distraction in the drama, is
bound up in authority and punishment, not in the excessive ambition that
is so typically their object.

Thus, the Duchess counters with a notion of desert that is resolutely
private and individualistic. She discards her public role as freely as an
actor stepping out of character, subordinating 'representation' to the
'authenticity' of a privileged essentialist subjectivity:

> What is't distracts you? This is flesh and blood, sir;
> 'Tis not the figure cut in alabaster
> Kneels at my husband's tomb. Awake, awake, man!

I do here put off all vain ceremony,
And only do appear to you a young widow
That claims you for her husband, and, like a widow,
I use but half a blush in 't.

(lines 157–63)

The Duchess's 'will' to discard the values of an ideology centered in public ceremony and fixed hierarchy in favor of values centered in individual merit and desire is yet premature; Ferdinand, of course, does succeed in imposing by violence the tyranny of blood upon his would-be bourgeois individualist sister. But the Duchess's very articulation of subjectivity based on markedly 'private' criteria points up the decadence of the 'public' values of Malfi. Similarly, her playful invocation of *legalese* in securing Antonio's acquiescence to marriage anticipates the crucial movement in early modern England to a contractual society rather than one centered in the body and blood of the monarch, a movement whose culmination enables the execution of a king in the name of the very state the sovereign was once purported to incarnate. So the Duchess's clandestine marriage to Antonio resonates with implications beyond the realm of the purely domestic: in the world of Ferdinand and the Cardinal, it is a patently subversive act. The Duchess explicitly privileges the private negotiation over the institutional sanction: 'We now are man and wife, and 'tis the Church That must but echo this' (lines 192–3). If the gesture of rebellion against 'the [Roman Catholic] Church' accords with Anglican as well as Puritan marriage theory, the exclusion of institutional authority from the realm of subjectivity rests at the heart of the English Revolution as well as the Reformation.

Alan Sinfield has remarked that '[the Duchess] asserts her own will, but she seeks merely domestic happiness'.[25]. But I would suggest that the domestic context of the Duchess's defiance of her brothers' wishes does not efface its subversive implications. Nor should Cariola's commentary at the scene's end be taken as authoritative. As in Antonio's conventional rhetoric of ambition, Cariola offers a self-consciously facile identification of madness with social transgression:

Whether the spirit of greatness or of woman
Reign most in her, I know not, but it shows
A fearful madness; I owe her much of pity.

(lines 204–6)

As a kind of summary statement, Cariola's speech is rather incongruous, for the behavior to which it refers manifestly does *not* show 'a fearful madness'. Indeed, as the audience has just witnessed, the Duchess has conducted her courtship of Antonio with an air of legalistic calm and practicality. Her love for Antonio is plainly not the distracted passion of amorous melancholy nor the frivolous and irrational affection identified with 'the spirit . . . of woman', as the Homily on Marriage (1547) describes it:

> . . . the woman is a weak creature not endued with . . . strength and constancy
> of mind; therefore they be the sooner disquited, and they be the more prone to
> all weak affections and dispositions of the mind, more than men be, and
> lighter they be, and more vain in their phantasies and opinions.[26]

Cariola's declaration puts forth a parodically simplistic formula – the Duchess transgresses authority, *ergo* the Duchess is mad (and 'fearfully', at that). Implicit in Antonio's speech about ambition, explicit in Cariola's comments, the referent of 'madness' is clearly at odds with its sign. Again, the possibility of contestation that is *not madness* at once heralds the emergence of oppositional individualism and the deterioration of the sign of madness into but a sign. In *The Duchess of Malfi* madness participates in a maze of semiotic and spectacular confusion, about which Franco Moretti has remarked:

> In Webster, meaning does not deceive, but rather dissolves: into appearance
> ('methinks'), indeterminacy ('a thing'), and inexplicable detail ('arm'd with a
> rake'). Nor is the problem how to interpret such signs, but, more basically, to
> determine whether or not they are in fact signs.[27]

The madness that Cariola and Antonio invoke is, like the organic sovereign body of act 1, scene i, a trope invested in a symbology fallen into incoherence in the world of the play.

Thus madness and contestation serve as mighty opposites, the former contiguous with the tyrannical power that has produced it, the latter bound up in an individualistic self-assertion that cannot be contained by the discourses of madness. This opposition is metaphorized by two antithetical images of the body – one emblematic, spectacular, and semiotically dissembling, the other the site of private contracts, essentialism, secrecy. Bosola's morbid denunciation of the 'outward form of man' is not only a conventional, overtly theatrical set-piece; it is a 'meditation' (II, i, 52) whose referentiality is wholly circumscribed, confined to the public and spectacular, deflected and contradicted by the private and individuated body of the Duchess:

> What thing is this outward form of man
> To be beloved? We account it ominous,
> If nature do produce a colt, or lamb,
> A fawn, or goat, in any limb resembling
> A man, and fly from 't as a prodigy:
> Man stands amazed to see his deformity
> In any other creature but himself.
> But in our own flesh, though we bear diseases
> Which have their true names only ta'en from beasts –
> As the most ulcerous wolf and swinish measle –

Though we are eaten up of lice and worms,
And though continually we bear about us
A rotten and dead body, we delight
To hide it in rich tissue: all our fear
Nay, all our terror, is lest our physician
Should put us in the ground to be made sweet.

                                        (lines 53–68)

This corrupt, grossly material yet essentially specious body will become literally the body of representation, prefiguring not only the mutilated wax dummies of Antonio and his children, but also the metamorphosis of Ferdinand into an 'ulcerous wolf', mad with lycanthropia. In a sense, Bosola's speech formulates a response to Antonio's idealized but absent body politic, the malcontent's version of the *Realpolitik* of the court of Malfi borne out by the spectacle itself. But if the 'rotten and dead body' of Bosola's speech contradicts the healthy body politic of Antonio's paean to France, it is itself contradicted by the Duchess's body, the 'rich tissue' of her 'loose-bodied gown' concealing not corruption but fecundity. As Bosola turns his attention to the Duchess's body and the possibility of her pregnancy, he necessarily undermines his own 'meditation' on the sterility and morbidity of the flesh. The Duchess's condition thus deflates any ostensible claim to inwardness put forth in Bosola's bitter discourse; the speech becomes but another piece of self-conscious theatricality, at jarring odds with any narrative referent. The Duchess's body, while concealed, is nonetheless the site of essentialist authenticity; the body whose 'outward form' is impenetrable – the spectacular body as well as the body in which madness is inscribed – is a sign whose referent is almost literally nothing.

Similarly, Bosola's comment that the Duchess's gown is 'contrary to our Italian fashion' (line 75) points up the degree to which her disregard for 'outward form' is engaged in her particular transgression. She bids the ever-orthodox Antonio to keep his hat on before her, noting that

    'Tis
    Ceremony more than duty that consists
    In the removing of a piece of felt.

                                        (lines 131–3)

It is important to note that it is not 'duty' but 'ceremony' that the Duchess is questioning; she is more a proponent of Protestant individualism than of egalitarianism. She is not challenging hierarchy per se, only its ceremonial, public model. For it is, after all, Antonio, not Bosola, whom she urges to disregard courtly protocol, and by virtue of their secret marriage, he is *her* lord. That the observation of public hierarchy conflicts with 'duty' to a private, domestic hierarchy heralds the displacement of the macro-microcosmic model of social relations by a significant stratification for seventeenth-century England. As Jean Elshtain has observed,

All social ties and relations suffer as the split between public and private widens into a gap and then a chasm. Within the domain of *Realpolitik* intractable terms like 'power, force, coercion, violence' structure political action and consciousness. On the other side of the chasm, softness, compassion, forgiveness, and emotionality are allowable insofar as they do not intervene with the public imperative. The private world is called upon to 'make up' for the cold (but necessary) inhumanity of the public.[28]

In *The Duchess of Malfi* the private and domestic as yet do 'intervene with the public imperative'; but their tension nevertheless anticipates the full emergence of the 'public/private' dichotomy by which early modern European capitalism will be constructed and sustained.

The spectacular but ultimately specious function of madness in the play is exemplified in the double-torture that Ferdinand contrives for the Duchess: the mutilated wax figures of Antonio and the children, and the pageant of Bedlamites. In both instances, opaque theatricality serves Ferdinand's madness precisely as the melancholy Bosola does. All three – the waxen corpses, the Bedlamites, and the malcontent – literally embody Ferdinand's corrupt power; their materiality give his madness local habitation and a name, but, significantly, displaces inwardness as the site of distraction. Like Bosola, the artificial corpses and the madmen are crudely instrumental devices designed to break down the pales and forts of the Duchess's inward resolve, her subjectivity. 'Her melancholy seems to be fortified With a strange disdain', Ferdinand observes (IV, i, 11–12); not even physical confinement is sufficient to disrupt her *self-possession*, indeed, her 'will'. The Duchess's sanity is even enabled by the spectacles of madness Ferdinand imposes upon her. Briefly, however, Ferdinand's perverse ploy seems to achieve its end, when the Duchess, devastated though deceived by 'the sad spectacle' of the waxen corpses, weakly grants theatricality the tyrannical efficacy with which the duke – if not the playwright – wishes to invest it: 'I account this world a tedious theatre, For I do play apart in 't 'gainst my will' (lines 80–1). The subordination of agency ('will') to power's spectacle comprises one important foundation on which pageants of power rested in Elizabethan and Jacobean England. But Webster's play demonstrates this structure primarily to interrogate and parody it. By the end of the play it is Bosola, the self-identified 'creature' of a mad tyrant, who invokes the 'world-as-stage' topos to account for his subjection to lunatic authority, referring to himself as 'an actor in the main of all, / Much 'gainst my good nature' (V, v, 87–8). Theatricality comes to trope – and demystify – the determination of the subject by an absolute power unable to sustain the coherence of its own illusions.

Ferdinand's anticipation that his sister will 'needs be mad' (line 123) because of his deceptive spectacle assumes, like Hamlet's faith in playing to 'make mad the guilty and appall the free', a dramatic effectivity that much of late Elizabethan and early Jacobean tragedy calls into question. Thus the Duchess may nonetheless assert, 'I am not mad yet' (IV, ii, 22); in fact, it will be the very 'tyranny' (line 3) of the madmen's masque that will 'Keep [her] in [her] right wits' (line 6). The Duchess's recognition that her sanity is deeply engaged in the constitution of an *external* madness counters Ferdinand's attempt to impose his 'tyranny' (here, literally identified with madness) wholly upon the world of the play, to distort the boundaries between spectacle and subjectivity, public and private. The Duchess's resistance not only deflects madness, but situates it in a maze of antic self-reflexivity on the margins of subjectivity's discourse. Here madness may be the material instrument of power, but the Duchess's response (or lack thereof) points ahead to the emergence of *reason*'s sovereignty that will relegate unreason to a distant realm of otherness against which the rational will construct and define itself. In many ways *The Duchess of Malfi* is a consummately Jacobean play, but Foucault's commentary on madness in 'the classical age' (not coincidentally, *l'âge du raison*) seems almost uncannily appropriate to Ferdinand's perverse stagecraft – and to Webster's:

> Thus madness is no longer considered in its tragic reality, in the absolute laceration that gives it access to the other world, but only in the irony of its illusions. It is not a real punishment, but only the image of punishment, thus a pretense; it can be linked only to the appearance of a crime or to the illusion of a death . . . Madness is deprived of its dramatic seriousness; it is punishment or despair only in the dimension of error.[29]

So the appearance of the Bedlamites represents playing at its most purposeless, madness literally in the employ of a power that yet cannot secure a stable ideological effect. As Frederick Kiefer has noted, the Bedlamites serve no 'readily discernible purpose: the dancers' appearance before the Duchess is completely unexpected; it fails to advance the plot; and it seems to reveal little, if anything, about the characters onstage'.[30] Precisely; but rather than to seek a covert rationale for the lunatics' pageant, it is more useful, I think, to attend to its very narrative inutility. Stephen Orgel has remarked that '[m]asques are the expressions of the monarch's will, the mirrors of his mind';[31] the masque of madmen, commissioned by Ferdinand, travesties the ideological investment of the spectacle. The madmen embody tragic representation at its most ineffective and irrational, the furthest point possible from the didactic *de casibus* model of early Elizabethan tragic theory. Collective rather than individuated, spectacular rather than interior, the madness of the Bedlamites is manifestly *not tragic*. A testimonial to the unintelligibility of spectacular representation, the madmen are but poor players who perform their 'dismal kind of music' before a subjectivity 'chained to endure [their] tyranny'[32] but notably indifferent to it. The Duchess ostensibly observes the grotesque pageant,[33] but there is no direct interaction between her and the madmen. Their several but undistinguished mad speeches have markedly no reference to her particular situation – or to that of the play. Nor is there any suggestion that madness contaminates the Duchess's subjectivity: 'I am the Duchess of Malfi still' (line 142). The resilience of her self-possession emphasizes the estrangement of madness and subjectivity; if there is any bridge between the two it is Bosola, whose participation in the antic disguise of the pageant reiterates the subordination of his 'good nature' to the irrationality of a spectacle determined and contaminated by corrupt power. His assumption of the role of Death augments the scene's parody of tragic form itself. 'The end is death and madness', Hieronymo proclaims in *The Spanish Tragedy*; the achievement of this 'end' in *The Duchess of Malfi* is self-consciously theatrically contrived. The externalization of both madness and death, that they may all but literally vanquish the subject, is reminiscent of the emblematic *ars moriendi* tradition,[34] but its anachronism is offset by the refusal to naturalize the represented event – the Duchess's murder is no morality play allegory but a deed expressly ordered by a mad tyrant.

The swiftly ensuing estrangement of the instruments of the Duchess's death – Ferdinand and Bosola – from their agency in her murder metaphorizes the estrangement of tragic form and tragic purpose. Unlike Hamlet or Lear, Bosola and Ferdinand may act, but their wills and fates do so contrary run. Both explicitly disclaim any authority for what has occurred, openly disavowing its enactment. There is no reason in madness because it has been displaced by a yet deeper polarity, a division of agents from their actions; will, or subjectivity, becomes wholly irrelevant to the deed's performance and effects. Bosola's apparent inability to allow his compassion for the Duchess to impede his complicity in her torture and murder, Ferdinand's castigation of Bosola, his 'creature', for obeying him ('By what authority didst thou execute / This bloody sentence?', IV, ii, 296–7), are not simply refusals to accept moral responsibility for the deed. Rather, these self-contradictions work to deflate any illusion of subjectivity that has been at least metonymically suggested by the one's madness, the other's melancholy. The sole representational possibility that the play has offered for coherent subjectivity has been the Duchess; with her extinction, the space of inwardness is wholly effaced by brutal theatricality, the very spectacular violence that has executed her. The structural homology between the tragedy and public executions[35] is parodied as the spectacle becomes almost the literal means of the heroine's torture and death. The proposition that Webster seems to be implying is striking: if theatre is but one public manifestation (executions would be another) of the violence monopolized by tyrannical power, to what extent is the play itself a 'creature', a crude instrument, of tyranny?

So the fifth act of the play is virtually given over to theatricality that can do little more than call parodic attention to itself. The onset of Ferdinand's lycanthropia is sensationalistic, more reminiscent of the bestial furor of Hieronymo and Titus than of the madnesses of Hamlet and Lear. The burlesque business with the Cardinal and his instructions that his cries for help be ignored is as self-consciously contrived as the 'echo' that warns Antonio of his wife's death. And, perhaps most memorably, Bosola accidentally slays Antonio, as an overt plot manipulation mocks and engulfs his professed will. As Moretti has noted, 'At the heart of Jacobean tragedy we find a consciousness devoid of autonomy, an agency devoid of freedom'.[36] Indeed, the tragic is violently displaced by 'accidental judgments and casual slaughters', by 'purposes mistook Fallen on th' inventors' heads'. In fact, the plot summary so glaringly inadequate to closure in *Hamlet* could quite accurately serve as epilogue for *The Duchess of Malfi*. This is not, however, to suggest that Webster's tragedy is an anachronistic reversion to the less equivocal madness and mayhem of the theatre of the 1580s. What is most equivocal – and most Jacobean – about *The Duchess* is that its conviction of the estrangement between spectacle and signification is rigorously articulated in the very medium whose authority it disclaims. For the authority of spectacle is contaminated by a madness and tyranny that are mutually indistinguishable; hence contestation may be constructed only in a space outside the publicity of the spectacle. The Duchess's murder *by* the spectacle as much as *within* it effectively removes subjectivity and its contestatory possibilities from the stage. But the exclusion of the transgressive subject pointedly does not simultaneously exclude madness; rather, the tragic spectacle itself degenerates into the semiotic opacity of unreason. For Hamlet or Lear, madness cannot be recuperated or effaced: it can only be silenced. In *The Duchess of Malfi*, the purpose of playing itself is given over to madness, as if in anticipation of a forthcoming silence. The figuration of authority rather than subjectivity as irrational suggests the conditions under which opposition is generated and legitimized – that is, rendered *reasonable*. The realization of these conditions in Jacobean and Caroline England testifies to the drama's productive role in pre-Revolutionary as well as post-Reforamtion English society.

NOTES

1 On the interplay of the disordered subjectivity and the unruly political subject, see my essay '"Suche Strange Desygns": Madness, Subjectivity and Treason in *Hamlet* and Elizabethan Culture', *Renaissance Drama* 20 (1989), 51–76.

2 Cf. Catherine Belsey, *The Subject of Tragedy* (London: Methuen, 1985), pp. 31–3.

3 I refer, of course, to Francis Barker's still provocative *The Tremulous Private Body: Essays on Subjection* (London: Methuen, 1984).

4 I am citing the New Mermaids Edition of *The Revenger's Tragedy*, ed. Brian Gibbons (New York: W.W. Norton, 1967, 1989). Compelling discussions of Tourneur's play may be found in C. Belsey, *The Subject of Tragedy*, pp. 31–3; Jonathan Dollimore, *Radical Tragedy* (Chicago: University of Chicago Press, 1984), pp. 139–50.

5 Karin S. Coddon, 'Unreal Mockery: Unreason and the Problem of Spectacle in *Macbeth*', *ELH* 56 (1989), 485–501, p. 498.

6 Franco Moretti, *Signs Taken for Wonders*, trans. Susan Fischer, David Forgacs and David Miller (London: Verso, 1983), p. 74.

7 Barker, *Tremulous Private Body*, p. 18. Cf. Dollimore, *Radical Tragedy*, p. 65.

8 Barker, *Tremulous Private Body*, p. 17.

9 I use the terms 'dominant', 'residual', and 'emergent' with indebtedness to Raymond Williams's enlightening discussion of the 'dynamic interrelations' of cultural processes in *Marxism and Literature* (New York: Oxford University Press, 1977), pp. 121–7.

10 For a concise definition of 'subjectification', see Michel Foucault, 'The Subject and Power', *Critical Inquiry* 8 (Summer 1982), 777–81, p. 781.

11 As Louis Montrose remarks, 'To speak, then, of the social production of "literature" or of any particular text is to signify not only that it is socially produced but that it is socially productive – that it is the product of work and that it performs work in the process of being written, enacted, or read' ('Renaissance Literary Studies and the Subject of History', *ELR* 16:1 (Winter 1986), 5–12, pp. 8–9).

12 Belsey considers the emblematic tradition as it pertains to *The Duchess* in her fine essay 'Emblem and Antithesis in *The Duchess of Malfi*', *Renaissance Drama* 11 (1980), 115–34.

13 All references are to the AHF Crofts Classic Series Edition of *The Duchess of Malfi*, ed. Fred B. Millett (Arlington Heights, IL: AHM Publishing, 1953).

14 See Frank Whigham's essay 'Sexual and Social Mobility in *The Duchess of Malfi*', *PMLA* 100 (March 1985), 167–86.

15 Ibid., pp. 167–86.

16 Charles and Elaine Hallett assert that 'Webster has transferred the madness from the hero-revenger to the villain [both Bosola and Ferdinand]' (*The Revenger's Madness* (Lincoln: University of Nebraska Press, 1980), p. 291), but do not account for the passing identification of the Duchess and Antonio with madness (see I, ii, 125 and I, ii, 204–6).

17 Irving Rabner characterizes Webster as 'a dramatist who can no longer accept without question the postulates of order and degree so dear to the Elizabethans' (in *The White Devil and The Duchess of Malfi*, ed. R. V. Holdsworth (London: MacMillan, 1985), p. 118). While I have reservations about *which* Elizabethans Ribner believes were so enamored of 'order and degree', his observation about Webster is acute.

18 M. C. Bradbrook comments extensively on the possible significance of the Robert Carr–Frances Howard scandal for Webster's artistic development in *Artist and Society in Shakespeare's England* (Brighton: Harvester Press, 1982), pp. 56–7.

19 *The Tragedy of State* (London: Methuen, 1971), p. 87.

20 The description of the malcontent is that of minister Thomas Walkington (quoted in Lawrence Babb, *The Elizabethan Malady* (East Lansing, MI: Michigan State University Press, 1951), p. 80).

21 Stone *The Crisis of the Aristocracy* (New York: Galaxy, 1967), pp. 37–61.

22 On the evolution of the will from spiritual to secular (and individualistic) document, see Philippe Ariés, *The Hour of Our Death*, trans. Helen Weaver (New York: Knopf, 1981), pp. 188–201. Inga-Stina Ekeblad also notes the pun on 'will', 'playing, of course, on the two senses of "testament" and "carnal desire"' (*John Webster: A Critical Anthology*, ed. G. K. and S. K. Hunter (Harmondsworth: Penguin Books, 1969), pp. 220–1).

23 According to James Calderwood, for example, the Duchess's courtship of Antonio demonstrates her 'reckless inattention to social degree' (Hunter, ed. *John Webster*, pp. 266–80).

24 *Collected Essays, Volume One: Writing and Revolution in Seventeenth Century England* (Brighton: Harvester Press, 1985), p. 7.

25 *Literature in Protestant England 1560–1660* (London: Croom Helm, 1983), p. 103.

26 Quoted in Doris Stenton, *The English Woman in History* (New York: Schocken Books, 1977), p. 105.

27 *Signs Taken for Wonders*, p. 80.

28 *Public Man, Private Woman: Women in Social and Political Thought* (Princeton: Princeton University Press, 1984), p. 99.

29 *Madness and Civilization*, trans. Richard Howard (London: Tavistock, 1967), pp. 32–3.

30 Frederick Kiefer, 'The Dance of the Madmen in *The Duchess of Malfi*', *Journal of Medieval and Renaissance Studies* 17:2 (1987), 211–33.

31 *The Illusion of Power* (Berkeley and Los Angeles, University of California Press, 1975), p. 45.

32 Ibid., p. 58.

33 Kiefer identifies the Duchess's apparently impassive response to the madmen with the medieval iconographic tradition of Dame World witnessing the dance of the Seven Deadly Sins ('The Dance of the Madmen', pp. 211–33).

34 '*The Duchess of Malfi* . . . is a play poised, formally as well as historically, between the emblematic tradition of the medieval stage and the increasing commitment to realism of the post-Reformation theater' (Belsey, 'Emblem and Antithesis', p. 115).

35 For examinations of the peculiar, spectacular relation between theatrical scaffolds and the scaffold of punishment, see Karin S. Coddon, 'Unreal Mockery: Unreason and the Problem of Spectacle in *Macbeth*', *ELH* 56 (1989), 485–501; Steven Mullaney, 'Lying Like Truth: Riddle, Representation and Treason in Renaissance England', *ELH* 47 (1980), 32–7; Leonard Tennenhouse, *Power on Display* (London and New York: Methuen, 1986).

36 Moretti, *Signs Taken for Wonders*, p. 79.

'Transshaped' women: virginity and hysteria in *The Changeling*

ARTHUR L. LITTLE, JR

So Woman has not yet taken (a) place. The 'not yet' probably corresponds to
a *system of hysterical fantasy* but/and it acknowledges a *historical condition* . . . She
is never here and now because it is she who sets up that eternal elsewhere
from which the 'subject' continues to draw his reserves . . . She is not
uprooted from the earth, but yet, but still, she is already scattered into *x*
number of places that are never gathered together into anything she knows of
herself.[1]

Critics generally agree that virginity and madness are the two principal
subjects of Middleton and Rowley's *The Changeling* (1622), but many of
these critics disregard the physical body as the sight/site of these subjects
and move instead to abstract the play's religious, moral, or topical meanings, transforming the play all too quickly from a dramatic piece of
literature into an allegory about evil and damnation.[2] The play's vocabulary is unquestionably invested in religious terminology – note, for example, the frequent use of such words as 'creation', 'devotion', 'holy'. Several
critics have taken the characters' use of religious terms as impetus for
defining the play as a religious or allegorical exemplum. At least discur-
sively, the characters seem to imagine that their lives are informed or
structured by religious paradigms, the edenic story being the most pronounced. It does not necessarily follow, however, that the play itself is a
grand religious allegory. Frequently, these interpretations end with the
bodies onstage being almost if not entirely eradicated by the allegorical
rubrics through which they are contemplated.[3]

Considering that virginity and madness are particularly relevant to
cultural constructions of femininity, it perhaps would be more critically
beneficial to investigate how the play succeeds finally in giving meaning to
the physical, female body. This essay assumes more than it argues that
women are allowed access to the patriarchal community through the
transformation of themselves into physical or theatrical objects.[4] While
readings of virginity as a 'religious ideal' or of madness as signifying
sinfulness are not irrelevant, this essay is concerned more with virginity
and madness as they contribute to our understanding of the politics of
corporeality at work in Middleton and Rowley's play.

When critics do discuss the interconnectedness of virginity and madness, the propensity is towards an essentializing of them as binary opposites: virginity is good and madness is evil. Such oppositions allow the audience to become empathic participants and know all too well the cultural constructs that speak of sexuality itself as a kind of madness.[5] Instead of commenting further on this particular binarism, I wish to look more textually at the relationship between virginity and madness, and to argue that the patriarchal community in the play demands to see the virgin's madness as a way of either exorcising it from her or condemning (or sacrificing) the virgin because of its presence. This essay is most sympathetic towards those critics who at least hint at the political and gender dynamics of this play about madness.[6]

This essay argues that the investigated and textualized madness in *The Changeling* is hysteria, a madness which cultural thinkers from Plato through Robert Burton through Freud thought to be of an especially sexual and female kind. Hysteria, especially through the eighteenth century, has been defined as a disease caused by the woman's uterus which floats about her body attacking her; the wandering of the uterus usually signified some aberration in the woman's sexual constitution. This definition of hysteria is not dissociated from the more recent psychoanalytic and feminist readings of hysteria as a physical body at odds with its psychic self.[7] Hysteria – this disease of the free-floating uterus or of the woman divided against herself – often signified for the male voyeur the woman's sexual instability and was thought to be curable by the woman's proper initiation into the patriarchal community through marriage and family.[8] From division to cure, *The Changeling* makes a fetishistic investment in hysteria.

I

Both Beatrice in the main plot and Isabella in the sub-plot perform physical signs of madness during the play, Beatrice enacting the convulsive, symptomatic behavior called for by the virginity test and Isabella pretending to be a madwoman in order to protect the sanctity of her marriage. Isabella desires to teach Antonio a moral lesson about the relationship between one's inward character and one's outward appearance. Diaphanta, the only other named woman in the play, takes the virginity test and actually experiences the convulsive behavior that Beatrice will only mimic. The stories of virginity and madness come together in all three women.

Concerning the two most central women, we should not rush to differentiate between them simply because the first is condemned by her madness and the latter exorcised from it. This play is not merely interested in

THE
CHANGELING:

As it was Acted (with great Applause)
at the Privat house in D r u r y L a n e,
and *Salisbury Court*.

Written by {THOMAS MIDLETON,
and
WILLIAM ROWLEY.} Gent'.

Never Printed before.

L O N D O N,
Printed in the Year, 1653.

1 *The Changeling*, title page

the patriarchal acceptance or rejection of these women but with how the masculinist community of the play demands their madness, irrespective of the individual woman's innocence or guilt in any essentialist sense. Whether one feigns madness to deceive one's lover/husband or to 'cure' him, the reconstruction of the community demands madness. Attempts to discern a polarity between the madnesses of these two women frequently result in the obliteration of Isabella's madness. Bawcutt argues, for example, that 'Beatrice becomes entangled in her own intrigues and is destroyed; Isabella retains her sanity and integrity through her own strength of character.'[9] Joost Daadler goes so far as to insist that Isabella 'is neither foolish nor mad in any sense'.[10] And Penelope Doob acknowledges some similarities between their madnesses, but her unguarded claim that 'one may justly laugh at the perpetrators of both human follies and crimes to the extent that the doer's own deeds reduce his stature and make him ridiculous' elides the fact that the virginity test (to which she most specifically refers) forces the virgin and not the sexually experienced woman to display physical signs of madness.[11] Even while insisting upon their opposition to each other, Doob herself parenthetically observes that 'the gaping and violent laughter [of Beatrice during the virginity test] are, after all, not far removed from the asylum'.[12] Hysteria emerges, as it so frequently does in masculinist literatures, as the always already present sign/symptom of a female self.

The Changeling works towards Beatrice's confession of her infirm (female) self. Hysteria demands this particular self-betrayal. Jacqueline Rose makes this point quite succinctly when she writes that

> [In] a case of hysteria, in which the symptom speaks across the body itself, the feminine is placed not only as source (origin and exclusion) but also as manifestation (the symptom). Within this definition, hysteria is assimilated to a body as site of the feminine, outside discourse, silent finally, or, at best, 'dancing'.[13]

From Beatrice's concern about her feminine body to her 'talk of modesty' being intercepted by DeFlores to her dance during the virginity test to her death, we find evidence of her hysterical disposition. Beatrice as origin, exclusion, and symptom is evident in the play and is repeated in the criticism, which so often, instead of attempting to contextualize Beatrice's evilness or madness in the social milieu of the play, castigates her for the play's shortcomings.[14]

Whether we wish in criticism to condemn or vindicate Beatrice, we should at least be cautious about the ease with which her every act seems ready to indict her. Lisa Jardine, who does not write about hysteria but about patriarchal assumptions in *The Changeling*, says about such women as Beatrice that in the eyes of the Jacobean audience they are above all *culpable*, and their *strength* – the ways in which they direct the action, scheme and orchestrate, evade the consequences of their impulsive decisions, and ultimately face resolutely the final outcome – need to be seen in this context.[15]

Jardine's argument attempts to resist blindly repeating those fictions perpetrated by the characters of Middleton and Rowley's drama. She questions the naturalness of patriarchy, unlike Christopher Ricks who argues that 'the morality against which Beatrice is broken is the morality of Nature',[16] suggesting that her 'broken' or hysterical disposition is apposite to some universal scheme. T. S. Eliot, who is frequently referenced by *Changeling* critics, also makes no such effort to resist. 'Beatrice is not a moral creature', Eliot writes. 'She becomes moral only by becoming damned. Our conventions are not the same as those which Middleton assumed for his play. But the possibility of that frightful discovery of morality remains permanent.'[17] The play is haunted throughout by a Beatrice who does not become a (subjective) self until she is damned. Eliot posits that within *The Changeling* Beatrice comes into her actualization as a moral self only through the damnation or destruction of that same self. By substituting the word 'patriarchy' for Eliot's 'morality', we begin to discern how patriarchy and morality are implicated the one in the other. What remains most frightful perhaps is the possibility of Beatrice's disclosure of patriarchy's own mythologized self.

Less in a moral sense than in a patriarchal sense, *The Changeling* is a 'tragedy of damnation'.[18] Beatrice is not so much the moral subject as she is the patriarchal object. In fact, her immorality is entangled in her desires for a male subjectivity (II, ii, 107–9). The court world of this play comes together to *return* Beatrice to her hysteria, her objectification. As Sara Eaton argues, Beatrice 'becomes the focus of the dramatic action, organized to get her off the stage, because she is designated this hell's source',[19] and the play effects her removal by transforming her body into something unhealthy and then turning that body against her more ideal feminine self. The play's repatriative objectives depend upon the on- and offstage audience's complicity and belief in the deformation of Beatrice. The play 'transshapes' her by dividing her body from her virginity.[20] Nicholas Brooke is right to argue that 'Beatrice's madness is built on a strange obsession, a total assumption of the twin values of her aristocratic world: Honour, and Love',[21] even though I would put it differently by speaking of virginity [honor] and the virgin's body [love] as the twin values of early seventeenth-century, patriarchal culture. The play also maintains that the woman's deformation is not explicitly related to her participation in illicit sexual activity; this is made apparent by the play's transshaping of Isabella.[22] Whatever else Middleton and Rowley's play is about, it is also about patriarchy's attempt to recover its idea of an original, paradisiacal order which necessitates the exorcism or condemnation of things feminine, and this includes Isabella.[23]

Her story of virginity and hysteria mimics and parodies Beatrice's story. Although *The Changeling* and several other plays of this period 'include contrasted female stereotypes, one saintly, submissive, faithful, forgiving and silent, and the other predatory, dominating, usually lustful, destructive and voluble',[24] the mere fact of this female pairing does not decide how the audience is supposed to read the relationship between them. Bawcutt's reading of the relationship between the main plot and the sub-plot may also be taken as paradigmatic of the relationship between Beatrice and Isabella: he observes that 'all the situations which parallel the main plot are turned to comic effect, and certain points in the sub-plot almost suggest a deliberate parody of the main plot'.[25] Because Isabella acts as Beatrice's parodic counterpart, however, we should not take this as a hint to set them in opposition and stop there.[26] The most telling difference between them is in their sexual choices. Beatrice consciously or romantically chooses Alsemero, and subconsciously or concupiscently DeFlores who is more interested in her body than in her disembodied self. Isabella has – if not before the play, certainly by the end of the play – made the choice of Alibius, a much older, dull-witted, and perhaps impotent man whose ownership of a madhouse only further underscores his buffoonery. He is the *senex iratus* of the fabliau displaced into seventeenth-century tragedy without much apology but with a lot of masculinist, sexual paranoia. He is never convincing as a concupiscent or romantic choice.

However, we do take seriously, and perhaps even more seriously because of Alibius, the effectiveness of Isabella's patriarchal inculcation.[27] Even though the fabliau tradition would allow her adultery, she refuses and chooses madness instead – a choice that has more to do with ideology than biology. Before the play ever begins, Isabella's sexual desires have already been subsumed by the *enclosure* of a mad, patriarchal ideology, an enclosure dramatized quite literally by Alibius' incarceration of her in his madhouse.[28] Isabella does not only mimic Beatrice's seriousness but is her parodic alternative. Isabella is the satirized good woman, a parodic Griselda. The characterization of Beatrice does not eminently depend, however, on the parodic caricature that is Isabella. In enacting her alternative role, Isabella signifies the parodic that is always already potentially present in a masculinist idealization of woman. Throughout, the men – Vermandero, DeFlores, Alsemero – along with Beatrice, transshape Beatrice's seriousness into parodic and grotesque representations. Beatrice's virginity (but not only hers) is subjected to this kind of transformation. Virginity, for Beatrice especially, is 'both an object of ironic scrutiny and a factor contributing to tragedy'.[29] Beatrice comes scripted with her own ironic reading; Isabella is her counterpart, not her opposite.

From one end to the other, the play advocates a thorough investigation of the woman's hymen, the original locus of her congenitally hysterical self. In any event, the woman's hysteria remains much less important than whether she evinces it through a closed or opened hymeneal self. Irrespective of her sexual experiences or lack thereof, as feminine body the woman is implicated in the drama of hysteria. The play progresses towards the sight/site of its hysterical origins; it moves from the secrets of the castle in the opening scene to the secrets of Beatrice's physical body, most aggressively from the fourth scene of act III to the end of the drama. The play continues to focus in until the audience on and off stage are not simply made privy to but become the speculum that stares into Beatrice's hymeneal self.

Alsemero begins this probing into Beatrice's secret self with his mythic reading of her virginal body. As Eaton says, 'Alsemero expects Beatrice-Joanna to be a chimerical representation of female sexuality. She functions as a vaginal pathway back to an edenic world that he would also test in this one.'[30] In the opening speech of the play, he soliloquizes about the first two times he sees her:

> 'Twas in the temple where I first beheld her,
> And now again the same; what omen yet
> Follows of that? None but imaginary;
> Why should my hopes or fate be timorous?
> The place is holy, so is my intent:
> I love her beauties to the holy purpose,
> And that, methinks, admits comparison
> With man's first creation, the place blest,
> And is his right home back, if he achieve it.
> The church hath first begun our interview,
> And that's the place must join us into one,
> So there's beginning and perfection too.
>
>   (I, i, 1–12)[31]

As frequently noted, Alsemero's words allude to Adam's first sight of Eve and signify his belief that he can reclaim paradise through the bond of marriage.[32] He does allude here to Eve but to Dante's Beatrice and Petrarch's Laura as well: Eve as *prototypical* woman, Beatrice as the woman who leads Dante *back* to paradise, and Laura (first seen by Petrarch in a church) as the woman through whom Petrarch *rediscovers* the original Platonic immortality of his soul. Here, Beatrice represents Alsemero's amalgam of these women: nonetheless, she unifies their prelapsarian, mythic identities more so than they are incorporated into her physical body.

Without teasing out these various intertextual presences in Middleton and Rowley's Beatrice, and whether seriously or parodically, her character evokes these women. By being drawn into a comparison by Alsemero, Beatrice's ontological status is posited somewhere among the biblical, the visionary, and the poetic. The woman Alsemero dreams of here is mythic. When we take into account the often disillusionary function of the *locus amoenus* (the lovely place) during the early modern period, it is perhaps all too easy to argue that instead of depicting Alsemero as a 'holy man' who dreams of the concomitant duo of marriage and paradise, the play sets him up first and foremost as one who is placed somewhere 'outside normal human experience'.[33] As a man ensconced in myths of perfection as opposed to the physical world of political bodies, Alsemero is counterpoised to and no less extreme than the quintessential world of imperfection represented by the madhouse community. The play submits Alsemero's vision to a disillusionment and replaces these more biblical, visionary, and poetic women with the tangible body of Beatrice who transshapes these mythic women into physical bodies.

DeFlores both impels Beatrice to and assists her in these transformations. When DeFlores enters the opening scene, for example, Beatrice and Alsemero's ethereal musings about eyes and judgment forcibly change to an exposition on physical ailments. His presence (with his diseased face) works instantly to recall Beatrice and Alsemero from their musings. DeFlores's message to announce the arrival of Beatrice's father is actually assisted by Beatrice who attempts to interrupt him:

> *DeFlores.* Lady, your father –
> *Beatrice.*   Is in health, I hope.
>
>   (line 93)

The completion of each other's lines becomes one of their dramatic signatures. Here also is Beatrice's own attention to the physical body, her thinking upon her father's health which stands in contradistinction to the sickness of DeFlores. Moreover, when DeFlores in an aside makes known his lust for Beatrice, the audience finds Beatrice dichotomized by two extreme responses to the female body. For Alsemero, she is something mythic; for DeFlores, she is so much a physical body that her mere physical presence amounts to a kind of orgasmic experience.

The woman's entrapment between these cross-purposed readings of her existence is not uncommon in sixteenth- and seventeenth-century tragedy. In Thomas Kyd's *The Spanish Tragedy* (1587), revenge tragedy's prototypical example, Bel-Imperia is caught in a similar dilemma with the more ethereal Balthazar and the more physical Horatio. This kind of division is especially prevalent in seventeenth-century tragedy, where these choices are inevitably made to collapse into each other. Othello exemplifies as much throughout *Othello* (1603/4) and especially in the murder scene in which he at one and the same time apotheosizes and demonizes Desdemona. Middleton dramatizes a similar breakdown in his *Women Beware Women* (1613): the adulation of Bianca's husband for her and the rapacious duke's lust for her become almost interchangeable. Like Eve, Dante's Beatrice, and Laura, these women – or at least the chimerical ideal of these women – figure also in the intertextual construction of Beatrice. The beginning of Middleton and Rowley's play positions Beatrice between the patriarchal ideals of virginity and whoredom but abruptly shifts attention from the mythic disembodiment of the first to the physical embodiment of the latter.

After the departure of DeFlores, the conversation between Beatrice and Alsemero changes into the subject of health and illness, and Beatrice speaks of DeFlores as her 'infirmity' and 'deadly poison' (lines 109, 112). And once Alsemero pontificates on the commonness of man and woman's allergic imperfections (lines 116–126), admitting to his own allergic reaction to cherries (line 128), he and Beatrice betray their entanglement in physical sexuality. Their dispositions are seemingly the same: both are allergic to sexual things. The sexual nature of Beatrice's allergy to DeFlores is scripted into DeFlores's name which refers either to 'defloration' or more pointedly to 'deflowerer'. Alsemero focuses his sexual infirmity on cherries.[34] His allergy to sexuality is further accentuated by his choosing aphrodisiac objects, when he casually and extemporaneously tries to name some of the allergic imperfections found in the population more generally: roses, oil, and wine (lines 118–23). His sexual subtext is The Song of Songs: 'O that you would kiss me with the kisses of your mouth! For your love is better than wine, your anointing oils are fragrant, your name is oil poured out; / therefore the maidens love you' and 'I am a rose of Sharon, a lily of the valleys. / As a lily among brambles so is my love among maidens' (1.1–2, 2.1–2). The Song (as subtext or intertext) betrays the sexual underpinnings of the conversation here between Beatrice and Alsemero.[35] The physical is also allowed to invade this scene through Diaphanta and Jasperino, Beatrice's waiting-woman and Alsemero's friend. They are engaged in a conversation about Jasperino's claim that he is a 'mad wag', and Diaphanta attempts to recommend him to a doctor whom she knows can 'cure' him (lines 137–51). Their seductive raillery foregrounds the easy conceptual commingling of madness, disease, and sexuality. In effect, their conversation repeats and perhaps parodies the dialogue between Beatrice and Alsemero who seem to stand in moral opposition to the physicality of the sexual body.

Notwithstanding the complicity of both Alsemero and Beatrice in this disembodied sexual fantasy, the ideology which will allow Alsemero to be rendered as something other to the physical and sexual will demand that Beatrice be seen as always already constructed as a physical and sexual subject. Alsemero evinces a patriarchal manliness throughout: he is husband, male gynecologist, and finally Tomazo's new brother and Vermandero's new son. His body comes into its birth, its newfound identities, in the closing moments of the play. Beatrice comes into her identity as a body whose death is demanded by the chief personages of the court. Her prizing of her virginal self is not the same as Alsemero's prizing of her virginal self; the play is about the difference, and the affecting of this difference through Beatrice being finally transshaped into the figure of Alsemero. In other words, Beatrice's wish that she had been formed a man comes true in a way that she herself had probably never suspected.

Like many women in seventeenth-century tragedy, Beatrice is not simply a virgin. She has a very defined and problematic relationship to her virginity. This also becomes clear in the opening scene of the play. Shortly after Vermandero enters, he announces that Beatrice must quickly prepare for her upcoming marriage to Alonzo. Beatrice responds,

> Nay, good sir, be not so violent, with speed
> I cannot render satisfaction
> Unto the dear companion of my soul,
> Virginity, whom I thus long have liv'd with
> And part with it so rude and suddenly;
> Can such friends divide, never to meet again,
> Without a solemn farewell?
>
> (lines 191–7)

And Vermandero dismissively protests this valuation of her virginity, 'Tush, tush, there's a toy' (lines 197). Beatrice makes this plea because she wishes, of course, to forestall her impending marriage to Alonzo so that she can be free to marry Alsemero. Nevertheless, she predicates her hesitancy on more than either of these marriages. Once she loses – or is divided from – her virginity, Beatrice realizes not only that her *enclosed* hymeneal self cannot be recovered but that she loses all power of sexual negotiation. Given the valuation placed on female, corporeal enclosure, the rude and sudden loss of her virginity would signify the first and last gesture of her patriarchally idealized self.

Moreover, instead of the terms 'part' and 'divide' being mere euphemisms, they connote what will literally happen to Beatrice's hymen. We may also compare her to Desdemona who speaks of her 'divided duty' (I, iii, 179),[36] and who remains essentially divided between her father's earlier reading of her as an enclosed patriarchal territory and Othello's knowledge or assumption of her body's penetrability. The division to which Beatrice refers is no less implicated in the story of father and husband. This patriarchal divide becomes, in effect, erased or normalized when the father transfers his daughter to her husband. The division from her virginity also replicates the parting from her father.[37] When the father does not give his real approval, as in *Othello*, or the father is, unbeknownst to him, duped into compliance with his daughter's will which would (if all were known) be in opposition to his own, then instead of the ideological erasure of this divide, the divide stands out in relief. True, Beatrice's concern for her virginity may be 'the object of the play's most trenchant irony', but we need not suspect Beatrice's seriousness about this virginity that becomes a primary object for DeFlores, Alsemero, and her father. And her father's response is in no way a momentary detraction from the significance he seems elsewhere to put on her virginity.[38] Vermandero can satirically dismiss Beatrice's virginity as a trifle for at least two related reasons. First, Beatrice's virginity is a 'toy', a thing that (for patriarchy) means everything and nothing – 'nothing' also being another name in the sixteenth and seventeenth centuries for female genitalia. Her virginity stays secondary to the male power structure whose social interchange is guaranteed by its presence. Second, Vermandero evinces his confidence, his unshaken assurance in the inviolate and inviolable constitution of his daughter's virginity. His dismissal announces his patriarchal assuredness more than it acknowledges the actual presence of his daughter's virginity. In his remark, Beatrice's virginity exists as both a serious and parodic thing.

II

Female hysteria is also read as something serious and parodic. It represents both the seriously essentialized female body and the essential male body that her body seems constantly to parody. The emerging deformity of Beatrice's body is the result of her failure to recreate 'the unity which' Mary Jacobus argues, 'the hysteric yearns to recreate on the site of her body,'[39] or of what Eaton sees as the inability of Beatrice to resolve the 'inherent contradictions in male perceptions of women'[40] that she (Beatrice) has internalized. Beatrice is not enclosed or unified but divided; her body comes into its patriarchal identity through its being broken, made mad, silenced.

   The opening scene prefaces the change (or easy slippage) of Beatrice from the mythic into the physically horrific. The scene begins with Alsemero seriously ruminating over his vision of Beatrice's perfect paradisiacal body and ends with DeFlores thrusting his fingers into the 'sockets' of her gloves (lines 233–4), quite sardonically mimicking the division or scattering of her hymeneal self.[41] While not as overt, the hymeneal story of the first act is part of the subtext of the second act. In the first scene of this two-scene act, Beatrice reasons that because any demonstration of nuptial improprieties would force her father's blessings to be 'transform'd into a curse[,] some speedy way / Must be remembered' (lines 20–5), meaning that she must find a way of changing her allegiance from Alonzo to Alsemero without offending her father. The language of transformation and the sense of expedience remind the audience of Beatrice's plea not to be parted so quickly from her virginity, but the transformation of her virginal self is inevitable once (in the next scene) she speaks of curing DeFlores by washing his face with her own hands (lines 83–7). By doing so, Beatrice takes the audience back to the opening scene, where DeFlores thrusts his hand into her glove. All of this culminates in act iii, scene iv, when DeFlores brings Beatrice the dis-severed finger of Alonzo still toting Beatrice's ring of which she says, '’Tis the first token my father made me send him' (line 33).

From DeFlores's hand to Alonzo's finger, Beatrice seems always represented as a penetrated self. This 'first token' also wittingly or unwit-tingly recalls those hymeneal first tokens in certain other choice late sixteenth- and early seventeenth-century texts, namely the handkerchief in *The Spanish Tragedy* and that in *Othello*.[42] In *The Changeling* Beatrice's 'first token', that is, the giving of her virginal self,[43] has all the makings of a scattered anatomy: Alonzo anticipates being first, DeFlores actually is, and Alsemero thought he was. Summarily, the instant she gives the ring to DeFlores as partial payment for his murdering Alonzo, she completes the exchange begun in the opening scene, where (presumably in disgust) she gives DeFlores not only the glove he touches when he stoops to retrieve it for her but the other one as well.

Beatrice's hymeneal story becomes salient in the fourth scene of the third act, where DeFlores demands her 'perfect' hymen as payment for his murdering of Alonzo. This episode is often noted for its strong allusions to edenic matters – Beatrice as Eve and DeFlores as the serpent[44] – its reenactment of the fall. As far as Beatrice does represent Eve, this postlap-sarian intrigue is, however, as much concerned about the birth as it is about the fall of Eve. In fact, through Beatrice the birth and fall of Eve become one and the same. This scene, in which Beatrice is made several times to 'remember' her origins, emerges as one of the misogynistic cen-terpieces of early modern drama: before the eyes of the audience, she comes into her birth as a fallen woman. When she attempts to speak to DeFlores about her modesty, her virginal self, he responds 'Push, you forget yourself! / A woman dipp'd in blood, and talk of modesty?' (lines 125–6). Beatrice represents the woman divided between paternal expec-tation, i.e., modesty, and the immodesty or excess that is signified by the existence of any female voice – *talk* of modesty? As Catherine Belsey argues,

> To speak is to possess meaning, to have access to the language which defines, delimits and locates power. To speak is to become a subject. But for women to speak is to threaten the system of differences which gives meaning to patriarchy.[45]

Belsey's observations are especially relevant here where DeFlores attempts to strip Beatrice of any vestiges of subjectivity (as Vermandero tries to do in his dismissive response to her plea for her virginity), and here where Beatrice is born as patriarchal difference. DeFlores demands an emblematic silence.[46] Here and elsewhere Beatrice is not a patriarchal ideal: she is not 'patient in her reserve, her modesty, her silence, even when the moment comes to endure violent consummation, to be torn apart, drawn and quartered'.[47] In DeFlores's undisguised and violent patriarchal reading of her body, the blood of which he speaks belongs not only to the murdered Alonzo. Beatrice's being dipped in blood amounts to her holy, moral, and patriarchal baptism into femininity – birth, menstruation, devirgination. Her immodesty is indubitably evinced by her willful complicity in the evocation of her feminine blood.

She tries also to insist on a social distinction between her blood and DeFlores's blood (lines 130–1), not realizing that in this scene blood is transformed from a code of social differentiation to a sign of physiology. The transformation becomes most apparent when DeFlores protests against Beatrice's evocation of their social differences:

> Push, fly not to your birth, but settle you
> In what the act has made you, y'are no more now;
> You must forget your parentage to me:
> Y'are the deed's creature; by that name
> You lost your first condition, and I challenge you,
> As peace and innocency has turn'd you out,
> And made you one with me.
>
> (lines 134–40)

Beatrice is figured not only as someone who has been turned out or expelled from an edenic world but as someone newly created apart from it. As the 'deed's creature', Beatrice is not simply expelled but created again. DeFlores challenges and rewrites her origins. Her last words in the scene affirm as much: 'Was my *creation* in the *womb* so curs'd, / It must *engender* with a viper *first?*' (lines 165–6).[48] Beatrice becomes in this scene newly engendered and newly gendered. The murdering of Alonzo allows Beatrice to reach her moment of patriarchal truth by pointing not, as she expects, towards her manly self who would presumably be capable of committing bloody deeds (II, ii, 107–9), but towards her womanly self whose blood is already understood to be about her – i.e. Eve's – original deed.

To the extent that Beatrice is surprised by this unwelcomed violation of her virginity, this scene also acts as a parodic moment. Her insistence upon her modesty and blood are used by DeFlores as invectives against her. We see this also when Beatrice urges DeFlores to take flight and he argues that it is not 'fit we two, engag'd so jointly, / Should part and live asunder' (lines 88–9). His words mock Beatrice's earlier insistence on not being so abruptly parted from her virginity. Instead of the momentous occasion being her departure from her virginity, it should be, DeFlores suggests, her departure from him. His suggestion or threat that they should 'stick together' (line 84) points to his desire not only to be beside but inside her. The playful way in which DeFlores mimics Beatrice's words exemplifies the parodic throughout this scene in which DeFlores mocks Beatrice's failure to grasp the violent sexual fantasies provoked by her 'perfect' virginity. It is not her sexual self but her virginal self that has aroused DeFlores. The mockery she endures from DeFlores resembles the suspicion she endures from critics. Bawcutt, for example, rebukes her for rebuking DeFlores 'as self-righteously as any blameless heroine'.[49] DeFlores's parody does not simply divide the virgin from her virginity but sets them in opposition.

This division found at the roots of hysteria receives its most elaborate pronouncement during the virginity test. The dramatic use of the test begins in the first scene of act IV, when Beatrice discovers Alsemero's physician's closet and finds inside a book supposedly by Antonius Mizaldus called, 'The Book of Experiment, / Call'd Secrets in Nature' (lines 24–5). Along with this she finds two glasses of liquid: one marked 'M' to test whether a woman is still a maiden, and the other marked 'C' to test whether a woman is with child. Shortly into this scene, Beatrice hires the virginal Diaphanta to take her place in bed on her wedding night and then gives her some liquid from glass 'M' to assure herself of the physical reactions the liquid promises to affect in a virginal woman. Diaphanta demonstrates the symptoms as scripted in the physician's text: ''Twill make her incontinently gape, then fall into a sudden sneezing, last into a violent laughing' (lines 48–50). On Beatrice and Alsemero's wedding night (in the next scene), Alsemero submits Beatrice to this test, and she, having learned the virgin's symptoms, performs them to Alsemero's satisfaction. The virginity test ends with Alsemero's patriarchal and territorial enclosure supposedly rewarding Beatrice for her virginal enclosure: 'Thus my love encloses thee' (IV, ii, 150).

The virginity test is somewhat more intricate to the construction of Beatrice's role in the drama than most critics allow. When dismissive, critics have read Beatrice's virginity test as 'preposterous'; when appreciative, as befitting the woman who has 'committed herself to evil'.[50] And while it is perhaps useful to explore the seriousness of virginity tests during the sixteenth and seventeenth centuries, as does Dale B. J. Randall, who argues (supported by numerous examples) that 'throughout the seventeenth century the testing of virginity continued to be taken seriously not merely by popularizers but also by scholars and physicians',[51] *The Changeling* is concerned not only with mimetic representation but with using the virginity test as a way of further delving into Beatrice's virginity which is always already a divided thing. Randall's argument is a very informative and convincing one for our understanding the unapologetic dramatization of the virginity test, but his claims are finally more interested in historically validating the scientific authenticity of the virginity test than studying its broader, interpretative implications in the play.

The virginity test literally forces the woman to display her madness; the woman's reactions during the test are easily recognizable as manifestations of hysteria. As Barbara Ehrenreich and Deirdre English note in their study of women's illnesses, 'Hysteria apeared, not only as fits and fainting, but in every other form: hysterical loss of voice, loss of appetite, hysterical coughing or sneezing, and, of course, hysterical screaming, laughing, and crying.'[52] In order to prove herself worthy of patriarchal enclosure, the woman must physically prove her hysterical disposition. The woman, in effect, confesses to being sexually experienced or impure, if her body remains unresponsive to the test – this test which supposedly exorcises (mad) sexuality from the virgin's body. Rather than simply evoke images of Beatrice as polluted, we need to think about the ways in which she comes into a pollution which her male audience knows to be ever present. The virginity test presents the woman with two choices: either she is mad in her purity or sane in her pollution, which amounts to one and the same thing. It should not be assumed, therefore, that Beatrice's being deflowered is in some way a necessary antecedent to her 'hysterical annihilation',[53] which begins (at the latest) the moment Alsemero first sees her in the temple. Before accepting Beatrice, Alsemero must first demand her madness as proof of her virginity. The other women must undergo a similar initiation into patriarchal enclosure: Diaphanta actually submits to the test and Isabella (in the scene following Beatrice's) dons a mad disguise in order to prove the enclosure of her virginal and patriarchal self.

Rather than compare Beatrice's and Isabella's sexual statuses, we should, it seems, think more about their particular relationship to madness, since here they seem more alike than different. Beatrice, like Isabella, fakes her madness, but this does not distract from the seriousness of Beatrice's mad display during the virginity test. Doob, thinking about the difficulties many critics have with this scene, suggests that reading it emblematically removes many of the difficulties critics have with it. Doing so, she argues, 'Two aspects of the scene are striking: first, the actions that Beatrice must feign – gaping, sneezing, and violent laughter – are extremely grotesque and ugly; second, they are potentially quite comic.'[54] She goes on to say that even though Beatrice is a 'tragic and heroic figure' her physical 'deformity' attests to her sinful nature.[55] Arguably, Beatrice's symptoms are grotesque and potentially comic, but the transshaping of Beatrice's hymeneal self has been present since the opening scene. This

scene pushes the transshaped Beatrice to the fore. The hysterical deformity that Beatrice exhibits in this scene is quite parodic, not only because
of her exaggerated physical display but because she is pretending. It
becomes difficult to decide, however, whether the reins of parody belong
to Beatrice or to the onstage and offstage male audiences examining her.

Her madness acts as both her parody of Alsemero's science and that
science's parody of woman. Perhaps the most exacting reading we can do
here argues that the scene is both a serious and parodic display of female
virginity. Beatrice's parody does have much comic potential, but such a
reading does not work against her tragic or heroic status but seems doubly
to emphasize it. Despite what some critics have argued, Beatrice performs
this grotesque trick not because she is evil – indeed this grotesque display
is the fate of every tested virgin – but because she wishes to protect the
patriarchal validation of her virginal self. At least from the vantage of the
twentieth century, this scene at best provides a comic pathos which works
not to alienate our sympathies from Beatrice but to draw her firmly into
them.[56] Instead of reading the scene emblematically, we need to focus
more analytically on the harsh representation of corporeality. This scene
repeats the voyeuristic and parodic attention to Beatrice's hymeneal self
that begins in the opening scene. What we have here in the first scene of
act 4 is a more climactic and demonstrative focus upon this self.

The mad or divided virgin receives her most destructive and inevitable
reading in the last scene of the play. Several times during this scene,
Alsemero speaks of Beatrice's 'deformity', this deformity which he finally
admits has been in his fears ever since he first saw her in the temple (v, iii,
72–6). The body which is en/gendered in act iii, scene iv, reaches its
horrific and misogynistic pinnacle in this final scene. Alsemero's procla-
mation – about 'the temple / Where blood and beauty first unlawfully /
Fir'd their devotion, and quench'd the right one' and 'the bed [which]
itself's a charnel, [and] the sheets shrouds / For murdered carcasses'
(lines 73–5, 83–4) – announces the destruction of Beatrice's hymeneal
enclosure.[57] Sexual death is transshaped into mortal death.

As Alsemero begins his final exploration into his suspicions about
Beatrice, he is told by his friend Jasperino, ''Tis not a shallow probe /
Can search this ulcer soundly, I fear you'll find it / Full of corruption' (lines 7–
9). Bawcutt compares Jasperino's words to *The Defence of Poesy* (1580),
where Sir Philip Sidney writes that both 'the right use of comedy . . . [and]
the high and excellent tragedy . . . openeth the greatest wounds, and
showeth forth the ulcers that are covered with tissue'.[58] Beatrice seems
both the embodiment of the 'high and excellent tragedy' and the tragedy's
cathartic sacrifice. Because she figures as source and symptom (see the
earlier quotation from Rose), her body also must consequently represent
what such a tragedy finds necessary not simply to expurgate but obliter-

ate. The probing of the corrupt ulcer in Middleton and Rowley's play indeed invites comparison to this ulcer in Sidney's *Defence*.

The relationship between the female anatomy and the wound is not a casual one. Culturally, this link is quite common. An affinity between the wound and womb is prevalent in the psychoanalytic studies of Freud and Luce Irigaray as well as in Hoffman R. Hays's anthropological work. Hays has observed, for example, that

> women by their recurring supernatural wound [i.e., their vulva] are set apart as aliens from the male norm. Sensitivity to contact and contagion is aroused and the symbol of the whole complex is blood, the powerful magic liquid on which life depends.[59]

The play has made its way to the sight/site of its contagion; it has moved from the mythic woman imagined in the temple in the first act to the woman's blood in the third act to the woman's wound here in the fifth act. The play finds its original pollution in the body of woman; its original health – *the* moment of cultural origin – in the body of man. A 'wounded' Beatrice speaks to this en/gendered difference when she says or perhaps rehearses what Bawcutt claims are the most famous lines in the play:[60] 'Oh come not near me, sir, I shall defile you: / I am that of your blood was taken from you / For your better health' (lines 149–51). Beatrice's *disclosure* of her supposedly self-fashioned and self-inflicted, wounded identity, resonates with a familiarity that resists reading her disclosure as being exclusively about her body. Among other cultural references, Beatrice is like the menstruating woman who must live in isolation and is obliged to cry out if approached, presumably to prevent the infection of others, 'I am unclean.'[61]

Despite and because of the simulated exorcism of Beatrice's (mad) sexuality in the third act, here she incarnates and is transformed into that pollution which her onstage audience thought had been eradicated. In her feminine contagion she stands in contradistinction to her father's healthy body. The purging of Beatrice's blood also rewrites the myth of Eve's being created from one of Adam's ribs. (This point is further underscored by DeFlores who immediately before Beatrice's speech refers to her as 'that broken rib of mankind', line 146.) Here woman is born as the physiological blood ejected from the male body. More than identifying Beatrice's blood as feminine, the play indicts femininity as being a disease, a contagion. It is an infirmity whose convulsive display and sexual conspicuity have transshaped the female body in all its original illness into both a tragical and theatrical spectacle.

As we muse over the dead and wounded body of Beatrice and the court's embracement of Isabella, perhaps the play asks the audience to inquire into the difference between deformity celebrated and then condemned and deformity celebrated and then exorcised. The court is secure with the death of Beatrice and with the presence of Isabella who is not only a woman from a parodic tradition but has in turn made mockery of that tradition. Whether condemned or exorcised, this putting of deformity *back* in its cultural place by licensing the play to return to its fantasy of its paradisiacal origins, ostensibly allows the patriarchal court to cure itself of its hysterical otherness. Bawcutt says as much when he argues that 'the normal tenor of life has been interrupted by a sudden crisis; at the end of the play the crisis is resolved and normality finally reasserts itself'.[62] The normality he speaks of is presumably that *reasserted* by Alsemero in the play's epilogue in which Alsemero responds to the forlorn brother of the murdered Alonzo as well as Alsemero and Vermandero and those in the audience: 'Your only smile have power to cause re-live / The dead again, or in their rooms to give / Brother a new brother, father a child; / If these appear, all griefs are reconcil'd' (lines 224–7). Alsemero's celebration of a homosocial enclosure presumably provides the on- and offstage male audience with the original, paradisiacal vision it has fantasized about all along. This dramatization of a sudden crisis, a presumed disruption of patriarchal normality, endeavors to prove, repeat, and mythologize the woman's hysterical or wounded virginity as the original sight/site of both her imperfect self and the imperfections of patriarchal culture.

NOTES

1 Luce Irigaray, emphasis in text, *Speculum of the Other Woman*, trans. Gillian C. Gill (Ithaca: Cornell University Press, 1985), p. 227.

2 There are numerous examples of religious and moral readings of *The Changeling*. Two essays the reader may wish to consult for some sense of these are Penelope B. R. Doob's 'A Reading of *The Changeling*', *English Literary Renaissance* 3 (1973), 183–206, and Joost Daadler's 'Folly and Madness in *The Changeling*', *Essays in Criticism* 38 (1988), 1–21, respectively. These and other such critiques will occasionally be referenced in this essay. The topical story which sometimes figures into readings of the play involves the infamous divorce trial between the Count and Countess of Essex in 1613. Two years after the divorce, it was discovered that Sir Thomas Overbury, who attempted to bar the divorce, was clandestinely murdered. For an example, see J. L. Simmons, 'Diabolical Realism in *The Changeling*', *Renaissance Drama* 11 (1980), 135–70, esp. pp. 153–63.

3 For some examples, see N. W. Bawcutt's introduction to his edition of Thomas Middleton and William Rowley's *The Changeling*, The Revels Plays (London: Methuen & Co., Ltd.), pp. lvi–lvii. Also, Douglas Duncan, 'Virginity in *The Changeling*', *English Studies in Canada* 9 (1983), esp. pp. 26–7 and 33–4, and Doob, 'A Reading', esp. pp. 184–6.

4 See Sara Eaton, 'Beatrice-Joanna and the Rhetoric of Love in *The Changeling*',

Theatre Journal 36 (1984), 371. Eaton pursues the physical and theatrical readings of women found in the courtly love tradition and argues that in this
tradition women could be transgressive but they must not *seem* so. Her essay
examines Beatrice's body through courtly love rhetoric. My essay agrees with
the direction of Eaton's but assumes that the physical body is the most likely
place to see such readings being put into cultural practice; also, Eaton's essay is
not interested in madness in these physical and theatrical constructions. Madness, this essay argues, is *the* trope.

5 See Susan Mayberry, 'Cuckoos and Convention: Madness in Middleton and
   Rowley's *The Changeling*', *Mid-Hudson Language Studies* 8 (1985), 21–2.

6 See Mohammad Kowsar whose reading is interested in the presence of
   Kristevan abjection within institutional discourse. His essay is in sympathy
   with my argument, but he is more interested in discursive form as opposed to
   corporeal form even though these forms are ultimately inseparable: 'Middleton
   and Rowley's *The Changeling*: The Besieged Temple', *Criticism* 28 (1986), esp.
   pp. 145–7, where Kowsar most succinctly outlines his argument that 'the
   consecration of the undefiled female body has unavoidable juridico-political
   repercussions'. Also, Jonathan Dollimore, *Radical Tragedy: Religion, Ideology and
   Power in the Drama of Shakespeare and His Contemporaries* (Chicago: University of
   Chicago Press, 1984), where he discusses Beatrice's social fall and argues that
   blood and birth are 'myths in the service of historical and social forms of power,
   divested of which Beatrice becomes no more than what "the act" has made
   her', p. 178. And also, Lisa Jardine, who attempts to understand these 'strong'
   and 'manipulative' women of the Renaissance within their socio-historical
   context: '*The Duchess of Malfi*: A Case Study in the Literary Representation of
   Women', *Teaching the Text*, ed. Norman Bryson and Sussane Kappeler (London
   and Boston: Routledge & Kegan Paul, 1983), pp. 208–9.

7 Trying to determine the meanings of this division between the woman's physical and psychic selves often highlights the theoretical division between
   psychoanalysis and feminism. For an informative, brief discussion of femininity
   and hysteria consult Charles Bernheimer, 'Introduction Part One', *In Dora's
   Case: Freud – Hysteria – Feminism*, ed. Charles Bernheimer and Claire Kahane
   (New York: Columbia University Press, 1985), pp. 5–12. For an example more
   contemporaneous with the play, see Robert Burton, 'Symptoms of Maids',
   Nuns', and Widows' Melancholy' section in *The Anatomy of Melancholy*, ed.
   Floyd Dell and Paul Jordan-Smith (New York: Farrar & Rinehart Inc., 1927),
   2.4, pp. 353–7; also Lawrence Babb's discussion of Burton in *Sanity in Bedlam: A
   Study of Robert Burton's 'Anatomy of Melancholy'* (New York: Greenwood, 1977), p. 11.
   For more attention to the socio-political dynamics, see Barbara Ehrenreich and
   Deirdre English, *Complaints and Disorders: The Sexual Politics of Sickness*, Glass
   Mountain Pamphlet, 2 (New York: The Feminist Press, 1973), pp. 14–44.

8 Bernheimer, 'Introduction', p. 5.

9 Bawcutt, 'Introduction', p. lxvii.

10 Daadler, 'Folly and Madness', p. 2.

11 Doob, 'A Reading', pp. 200–1. She also neglects to think through these seemingly effortless, cultural associations between madness and ridicule or between
   madness and punitive discourses. See, for example, Michel Foucault's chapter

on incarceration in his *Madness and Civilization: A History of Insanity in the Age of Reason*, trans. Richard Howard (New York: Vintage Books, 1973), pp. 38–64.

12 Doob, 'A Reading', p. 201.

13 'Dora – Fragment of an Analysis', *Sexuality in the Field of Vision* (London: Verso, 1986), p. 28.

14 The madness or 'evil' nature of the court is often made to belong most directly and innately to Beatrice. See, for some examples, Simons, 'Diabolical Realism', pp. 149–50; T. S. Eliot, 'Thomas Middleton', *Selected Essays, 1917–1932* (New York: Harcourt Brace & Co., 1932), pp. 142–3; Daadler, 'Folly and Madness', p. 7; and Doob, 'A Reading', pp. 187–8.

15 Emphases in the text, 'Case Study', p. 208.

16 Christopher Ricks, 'The Moral and Poetic Structure of *The Changeling*', *Essays in Criticism* 10 (1960), 303.

17 'Thomas Middleton', p. 142.

18 Helen Gardner, 'The Tragedy of Damnation', *Elizabethan Drama: Modern Essays in Criticism*, ed. Ralph J. Kauffman (New York and Oxford: Oxford University Press, 1961), pp. 320–41.

19 'Beatrice-Joanna', p. 381.

20 The term 'transshape' is from IV, iii, 21. My reading of Beatrice as a trans-shaped woman is further supported by Simmons who draws an association between Beatrice and certain demons from the Hebraic tradition who 'can transform themselves, like witches, into other shapes; or, more precisely, they can give the illusion of transformation', 'Diabolical Realism', pp. 148–9. Also see Dale B. J. Randall, 'Some Observations on the Theme of Chastity in *The Changeling*', *English Literary Renaissance* 14 (1984), 350–1, who quotes from John Rider's *Dictionarie* (1640) the definition of 'lamiae' – another meaning of 'changeling' – as 'Women or devils in shape of women'. More theoretically supportive is Iragaray who writes about patriarchy's reading of woman as 'deformed and formless', *Speculum*, p. 167.

21 *Horrid Laughter in Jacobean Tragedy* (London: Open Books, 1979), p. 79.

22 The mapping out of the relationship between madness and sexuality often leads to conclusions such as those made by Mayberry who argues that Isabella's self-preserving, mad performance is intended to exemplify 'the madness and ugliness of passion', 'Cuckoos and Convention', pp. 28–9.

23 There is a common agreement in criticism that the play moves towards some kind of paradisiacal vision. For some examples, see Bawcutt, 'Introduction', pp. lvi–lvii; Duncan, 'Virginity', pp. 26–7; and Doob, 'A Reading', pp. 187–94. In contradistinction to these critiques, this essay figures the 'paradise' of Middleton and Rowley's play not, most profoundly, as a biblical but a patriarchal construct – a world of innocence without the guilt presumably ushered in by femininity.

24 Catherine Belsey, *The Subject of Tragedy: Identity and Difference in Renaissance Drama* (London and New York: Methuen, 1985), p. 165.

25 Bawcutt, 'Introduction', p. lxv. For further demonstration of how critics have analyzed the relationship between the two plots, see Richard Levin who argues for 'a negative analogy built on direct moral contrast', *The Multiple Plot in English Renaissance Drama* (Chicago and London: University of Chicago Press,

1971), esp. pp. 34–8. Also consult William Empson, *Some Versions of Pastoral* (London: Chatto & Windus, 1950, first pub. 1935), pp. 48–52, and Bawcutt, 'Introduction', pp. lxiii–lxiv.

26 Doob's argument, for example, contrasting Beatrice's deception through madness to Isabella's cure through madness, takes the difference between their madnesses to signify the opposition between their moral dispositions, 'A Reading', p. 201.

27 We may relate Isabella's patriarchal inculcation to that of seventeenth-century women more generally. According to Peter Stallybrass's 'Patriarchal Territories: The Body Enclosed', William Whately in his conduct book, *A Bride-Bush* (1617), suggests a rigorous program of 'education' [Whately's word], supported by violence. Speaking of and quoting from Whately's text, Stallybrass writes, 'Woman is a horse to be broken in, only properly trained when "shee submits herselfe with quietness, cheerfully, even as a well-broken horse turnes at the least check of the riders bridle, readily going and standing as he wishes that sits upon his backe', *Rewriting the Renaissance: The Discourses of Sexual Difference in Early Modern Europe*, ed. Margaret W. Ferguson, Maureen Quilligan, and Nancy J. Vickers (Chicago and London: University of Chicago Press, 1986), p. 126. (See the discussion of the virginity test on pp. 32–3.) Understanding Whately's comment (as Stallybrass does) to be more typical than anomalous, we may read this *breaking* of woman through education and her subsequent quietness and cheerfulness as arguing that the gendered and manneristic 'education' of women refers predominantly to the hysterical trans-shaping of women.

28 The significance of this imprisonment is articulated quite well by Alibius and Lollio (I, ii, 69) and by Isabella herself (III, iii, 1–18). The fact that Isabella is not seen by the offstage audience until the penultimate scene of the third act underscores the effectiveness and thoroughness of Alibius' enclosure of her. The term 'enclosure' here and elsewhere in this essay is indebted to Stallybrass who has said that 'the "unruly woman" presided over the destruction of literal and symbolic enclosures alike', 'Patriarchal Territories', p. 142. Throughout his essay Stallybrass discusses the valuation of the female body as a symbolic and political enclosure. He is especially interested in the ways the female body is made to signify a *hortus conclusus*, a garden fortified against intruders, ibid., pp. 123–42.

29 Duncan, 'Virginity', p. 26.

30 Eaton, 'Beatrice-Joanna', p. 374. To make a distinction that Eaton does not make, the imaginary representation of feminine sexuality includes the essential differentiation between the woman's virginal and vaginal selves. Also see Brooke's use of female genitalia imagery in his discussion of DeFlores and Alsemero's descent into the dark pathways of the castle, *Horrid Laughter*, p. 85.

31 All *Changeling* quotations are from Bawcutt's Revels Plays edition.

32 Duncan, 'Virginity', pp. 26–7.

33 A. Bartlett Giamatti, *The Earthly Paradise and the Renaissance Epic* (Princeton: Princeton University Press, 1966), p. 16. Giamatti attends to both the desire to 'return' to paradise and the inability of doing so. See esp. pp. 3–7, 15–16, 123–4, and 356–60.

34 On the subject of cherries, A. R. Braunmuller has referred me to Thomas Dekker, John Ford, Rowley et al., *The Witch of Edmonton* (1623): 'Well, I'll have a witch. I have loved a witch ever since I played at cherry-pit', *Three Jacobean Witchcraft Plays*, ed. Peter Corbin and Douglas Sedge (Manchester and New York: Manchester University Press, 1986), III, i, 18–19. It has been suggested that there is the possibility of a connection between 'cherry' and female genitalia, because in the child's game known as 'cherry-pit' the 'cherry-pit' was the name given to the hole in which the pits were tossed. See Thisbe's line to Pyramus in *A Midsummer Night's Dream*, 'My cherry lips have often kiss'd thy stones' (v, i, 192), which plays with images of sexual intercourse and oral sex – the former is relevant to my argument here: The Signet Classic Shakespeare edition, ed. Wolfgang Clemen (New York and London: New American Library, 1963). Also see 'cherry-pit' in *OED* and *Webster's Third New International Dictionary*. The latter defines 'cherry' as hymen and virginity, def. 5.

35 The New Oxford Annotated Bible, Revised Standard Version, 1973. The Song of Songs may also be considered an appropriate choice for Alsemero, since the physical eroticism of the Song is often marginalized by or made secondary to more allegorical exegeses. Such allegorizing conveniently allows Alsemero to talk about/through sexuality without ever really naming the subject itself.

36 All *Othello* quotations are from the Signet Classic Shakespeare edition, ed. Alvin Kernan (New York and London: New American Library, 1963).

37 The play is replete with images of parting and dividing, with especial reference to Beatrice's self or to Beatrice's relationships with others.

38 Duncan, 'Virginity', pp. 27–8.

39 *Reading Woman: Essays in Feminist Criticism* (New York: Columbia University Press, 1986), p. 206.

40 Eaton, 'Beatrice-Joanna', p. 372.

41 On the subject of female scattering, see Nancy J. Vickers' study of the Diana/Acteon myth as it pertains to Petrarch's depictions of Laura in his *Rime Sparse* [*Scattered Rhymes*]: 'Diana Described: Scattered Woman and Scattered Rhyme', *Writing and Sexual Difference*, ed. Elizabeth Abel (Chicago and London: University of Chicago Press, 1982), pp. 95–109.

42 See both plays: I, iv, 47 and III, iii, 290, respectively.

43 Doob points out that whoever has Beatrice's ring is entitled to Beatrice's virginity, 'A Reading', p. 204; Doob insists on Beatrice's knowledge of this sexual proprietary. This essay assumes that the audience is aware of the ring's significance but Beatrice is not.

44 For some examples of critics reading 3.4 in relation to the edenic fall, see Bawcutt, 'Introduction', p. lvi; pp. Duncan, 'Virginity', 31–2; and Doob, 'A Reading', pp. 191–2.

45 Belsey, 'Subject of Tragedy', p. 191. See chapter, 'Silence and Speech', pp. 149–91, esp. pp. 178ff.

46 Writing about what she understands to be Petrarch's (and Acteon's) linguistic power over Laura (and Diana), Vickers observes that 'silencing Diana is an emblematic gesture; it suppresses a voice, and it casts generations of would-be Lauras in a role predicated upon the muteness of its players', 'Diana Described', pp. 107–9.

47 Irigaray, *Speculum*, p. 227.

48 Emphases added.

49 Bawcutt, 'Introduction', p. lv. Also see Duncan, 'Virginity', pp. 26–7.

50 For a very good grasp and summary of critical responses, see Randall, p. 353; Doob, 'A Reading', p. 199; and Bawcutt, 'Introduction', p. lvii.

51 'Some Observations', p. 357.

52 *Complaints and Disorders*, p. 40.

53 Simmons argues that Beatrice's hysteria is the consequence of her being deflowered, 'Diabolical Realism', p. 148.

54 Doob, 'A Reading', pp. 199–200.

55 Ibid., p. 200.

56 Doob argues that the virginity test gives the audience a 'comic detachment' from Beatrice and helps prepare the audience for Isabella's role in the 'moderately happy ending' of the play, 'A Reading', p. 201.

57 In a problematic marriage and consummation, Hymen, the god of marriage, seems to focus his energies on blood as opposed to the unity of disembodied souls. These problematic instances seem to expose the woman's hymeneal self. In a proper marriage and consummation, on the other hand, Hymen seems to deflect attention away from the hymen and towards the unity of souls. Alsemero's depiction of Hymen's marriage torches as being extinguished with blood is obviously a sign of an improper marriage and consummation: his marriage conjures up the image of the body not of the soul. For exemplification of these observations see Ben Jonson, *Hymenaei, or the Solemnities of Masque and Barriers at a Masque* (1606) in *Ben Jonson: The Complete Masques*, The Yale Ben Jonson, ed. Stephen Orgel (New Haven and London: Yale University Press, 1969), esp. lines 1–25. Also, Kyd's *The Spanish Tragedy*, ed. Philip Edwards, The Revels Plays (London: Methuen, 1959), where Revenge explains a dumbshow to the ghost of Andrea says: 'The two first, the nuptial torches bore, / As brightly burning as the mid-day's sun: / But after them doth Hymen hie as fast, / Clothed in sable, and a saffron robe, / And blows them out and quencheth them with blood, / As discontent that things continue so' (iii, xv, 30–5).

58 *Selected Prose and Poetry*, ed. Robert Kimbrough (Madison: Madison University Press, 1983), p. 129. Also see Bawcutt's editorial gloss for v, iii, 7–9.

59 Hays, *The Dangerous Sex: The Myth of Feminine Evil* (New York: Pocket Books, 1964), p. 32. See especially Freud's 'Mourning and Melancholia' in the *Standard Edition of the Complete Psychological Works of Sigmund Freud*, ed. James Strachey et al. (London: Hogarth Press and the Institute of Psychoanalysis, 1957), 14, pp. 251–3, where he compares melancholia to an 'open wound', and then see Irigaray who discusses the relationship of Freud's 'wound' to the female body, this sick body whose lost, original health can be traced back to the little boy the little girl once was, *Speculum*, pp. 70–4.

60 Bawcutt, 'Introduction', p. xli.

61 Hays, *The Dangerous Sex*, pp. 39–48. Hays speaks here of Surinam women, but (as he himself argues and illustrates) such taboos are widespread, not exclusive to this part of South America. For some other examples, see Mary Douglas, *Purity and Danger: An Analysis of the Concepts of Pollution and Taboo* (London and New York: Routledge & Kegan Paul Inc., 1988, first pub. 1966), pp. 147, 151,

176–7. Especially see Janice Delaney et al., *The Curse: A Cultural History of Menstruation* (Urbana and Chicago: University of Chicago Press, 1988, rev. and expanded from 1974 edn), pp. 7–8, 13, 18–27. Both works may also be consulted more generally for further analysis of the cultural associations between women and pollution.

62 Bawcutt, 'Introduction', p. lxviii.

The confined spectacle of madness in Beys's *The Illustrious Madmen*

DOMINIQUE FROIDEFOND

Characters afflicted by madness are in no short supply in French pastorals. And in the tragicomedies which follow in the 1630s, madness becomes a veritable leitmotiv. In 1660, Corneille in his 'Examen' of *Mélite ou les fausses lettres* (1630) admits that he decided to incorporate madness in the play in order to appeal to the taste of his public.[1] *L'Hospital des fous* (*The Asylum*) by Charles Beys performed in 1634 occupies a unique place since it marks the first occasion in the history of French theatre on which the action of a play takes place in an insane asylum. It enjoyed such great success that he reworked it three times, which culminated in 1653 in a new version entitled: *Les Illustres Fous* (*The Illustrious Madmen*).[2] Having understood that he owed the success of the play to his mad characters and not to the banal love story, he consequently simplified the plot and gave larger parts to the madmen.

In the first version, the scenes in the hospital have an important role in the first act, in the last scene of Act II, and in the third act, after which the insane disappear totally. In the version of 1639, they are present in more than a quarter of the thirty scenes and in *The Illustrious Madmen* in half of them. What is interesting in the last version is that characters endowed with reason and others who have lost it exist side by side since the plot takes place almost entirely in the hospital. This division is actually too simplistic given the fact that among the characters endowed with reason, some of them are going to lose it and others are going to pretend that they've lost it. We are thus confronted with three different representations of madness that we are going to examine in order of increasing importance: temporary madness, faked madness, and in contrast to the first two, 'true' madness, 'true' being the adjective used by Dom Alfrede.

There is nothing original about temporary madness; on this score, Beys follows his predecessors. Luciane, thinking her lover is dead, faints and comes to 'confused by what she thinks and what she sees' (p. 84). The excessive nature of her pain has caused her to lose her reason.[3] When Dom Alfrede sees her in the asylum, she does not recognize him and mistakes him for the head of the band of thieves responsible for their separation.

Madness disrupts her senses of perception. It immerses her in a world of error and illusion. It gives rise to visions and induces her to be mistaken about the identities of others.[4] Then she believes that her lover is 'dead and covered with blood' (p. 81). In desperation, she faints once again, thinking that she's dying. This second fainting spell causes her to regain her senses, at which point she leaves behind 'those false objects' and recognizes her lover. As in countless other plays of the period, madness is brought on by a misconception, an error which causes someone to hold as true something that is false and vice versa.

Because it's only a question of making a mistake, reason can always return to correct it, which means that madness is a temporary and thus curable condition. Reason reassumes its triumphant reign.[5] Beys is not interested in this representation of madness which for him belongs to the past. He is content to imitate a model which had become commonplace. Temporary madness is no longer even an 'ornament' here; it is rather an excuse that allows Beys to place Luciane in the hospital, after which it will be necessary to devise a way to get her out. This situation gives rise to the more original representation of feigned madness.

Luciane's lover decides to pass himself off as a madman.[6] He hopes to be reunited with his mistress. To be admitted to the asylum, he must pretend that he has lost the notion of his own identity, which forces him to act as though he sees himself other than he really is.[7] Most of the 'real' mad people correspond to this definition, as we shall discover.[8] Dom Alfrede's madness is catalogued right away. Since he thinks that he is Jupiter, the Concierge, the head of the establishment, tells his employees: 'Tie up this gentleman, he is mad with love' (p. 97). This type of madness demands confinement.[9] Dom Alfrede achieves his goal. He is locked up next to 'someone who thinks he is a girl' (p. 99) and who is none other than Luciane still disguised as a man. (She donned this disguise to escape with Dom Alfrede from her father.)[10] When Tirinte decides to leave for Madrid with one of the mad persons, the Concierge offers to show him Dom Alfrede and Luciane, of whom he says: 'He is a young boy/ With a pleasant personality and good manners./ He thinks that he is a girl./ One of the others committed here caresses him,/ Even thinks that he is a girl/ And takes him for his mistress' (p. 118). Dom Alfrede and Luciane exhort each other to play the comedy in front of Tirinte, the Concierge, and his valets: 'You have to pretend well', says Dom Alfrede, to which she answers: 'But so do you.'

It's paradoxical play acting, however, because Luciane must pretend that she's a girl and that she loves Dom Alfrede, and Dom Alfrede must pretend that he loves her. Their illusion is to say the truth about their sexual identity and feelings. But since everybody thinks that Luciane is a boy, their discourse reveals their homosexuality which is considered a type of madness.[11] This artifice developed to be able to stay together is going to work against them because Tirinte decides to take Luciane /Fernand with him on his trip to be entertained. Dom Alfrede thinks that he only has to say that it was a trick for everything to be set aright: 'Let's reveal our ruse/ And put a stop to their efforts' (p. 121). But because there is no feint, or more precisely because the feint was the truth, he can only repeat that he loves his mistress and does not want to be apart from her, which for the Concierge is proof that he 'is even madder' and must be 'locked up even more securely than before' (p. 122). Dom Alfrede discovers in a long scene added in *The Illustrious Madmen* (scene iv of Act III) that the discourse of the madman has, for the reasonable man, no credibility. Like everybody else, the Concierge thinks that madmen can't speak the truth because truth and madness are incompatible. The insane live in a world of fiction and, therefore, of lies: 'Madmen say that they are reasonable,/ Which they all pretend to be/ To get away from their slavery' (p. 140).

This remark of the Concierge brings us to 'true' madness, which occupies center stage and gives the play its originality. On the one hand, Beys lets madmen locked up in an asylum speak, which allows us to apprehend their madness. On the other hand, all the characters involved in the love story visit the hospital at one time or another for various reasons. Upon seeing the madmen, they give their appraisals of madness. There is a play within a play: at the beginning, the audience is the sole spectator and all the characters are actors. But as soon as the characters who are not mad enter the hospital, they also become spectators of the 'comedy' which is played out before their eyes. This unique situation is of particular value since the questions, opinions and judgments expressed by these new spectators reflect the manner in which madness was perceived in the middle of the seventeenth century.

What Foucault says in *Histoire de la folie à l'âge classique* about the administration of the General Hospital, which was created in Paris in 1656 and gave rise to what he called 'the great confinement', can be applied to the asylum as it was conceived by Beys: the General Hospital, says Foucault, 'is not a medical establishment. It is rather a semi-judicial structure, a kind of administrative entity' (p. 60). In Beys's play, we are told in effect that the madmen have been placed in the hospital 'by force' (p. 152) and that 'for the most part, it is their creditors' (p. 100) who have put them there. We are dealing, therefore, with an *economic* and not a medical reason. Being unemployed and having spent their entire fortune, they disturb 'the ordering of the social sphere'[12] just as do those who were confined in the General Hospital.

It is not an accident if in *The Illustrious Madmen*, Beys includes a portrait of a ridiculous marquis. He refuses to abide by the new edicts which forbid the wearing of clothes with gold and silver trim. Moreover, such members of the aristocracy are idle and for that reason alone deemed guilty since they have lost their fortunes: 'But having no more money to fatten up their hides, their stomachs are as empty as their minds' (p. 100). An obscure cause-and-effect relationship is established between the dilapidation of fortune, debts, poverty and madness: 'Their debts incurred in the past and the little credit that they have now have deranged their minds' (p. 100). These marquis who don't respect the law are henceforth excluded from the aristocracy.

Moreover, we learn that whereas it is easy to have a mad person committed, it is hard to get him out. Dom Gomez is aware of this: 'To extract them from here, one encounters great difficulties (p. 84). It is not a doctor who chooses to commit a person, nor can one discharge him. Only 'the favor dispensed by a powerful person' (p. 85) – and even he must appeal to the Magistrates – can accomplish this, proving once again that confinement is a question of a judicial structure and not a medical one.

In this institution, reason, which desires order, has succeeded in ordering disorder. Thus each madman is checked in and 'all their names are recorded in alphabetical order' (p. 167). The types of madness are also catalogued so that the 'Concierge' can remember them easily: 'Every type of madness has its own apartment, whose name is written on the door in plain view.' Several types of madness are presented: the one brought on by literary identification in the case of the Musician, the one induced by an obsession with gambling, and delusions of grandeur with the Astrologist, the Alchemist, the Philosopher, the Poet and the Actor. They are not all conceited – for example, the Lawyer, the Gambler and 'the people who became politically involved' (p. 124). But all of them represent an imminent danger to the extent that they neither *can* nor *want to* be integrated into society. Therefore, as in the General Hospital, those susceptible to moral and social disorder are brought together.

Numerous details in the play are dedicated to the way in which the madmen are treated in the asylum. This does not mean that this description coincides with the way that madmen were really treated at that time, but it does allow us to analyze the manner in which society interpreted, imagined and judged madness in the middle of the seventeenth century. Although these men are in an asylum, they don't receive any medical treatment. The sole remedy that the Concierge proposes to Dom Alfrede is '*Ellébore*', a plant whose roots were thought to cure madness (cf. Erasmus in his *Praise of Folly*, Montaigne in his essay 'On Coaches' and Rabelais in his *Tiers Livre* for Panurge). They are subjected to an imprisonment which is two-fold: already cut off from society once they are placed in this asylum, they are locked up in 'cells' that they are permitted to leave for only an hour a day (p. 72), a completely circumscribed freedom since they cannot leave the hospital. Regarding the size of their rooms, the Valet alludes to the 'Little Houses' ('les Petites-Maisons', an asylum on the rue de Sèvres in Paris which got its name from its tiny cells.) They sleep on a floor covered with straw, like wild animals in the zoo. During a visit to this establishment, Dom Gomez is horrified by the poor quality of the food since they receive for their supper 'some herbs in vinegar' (p. 98). Their bad treatment can be improved if the jailer receives money from their family or friends, but those who are not supported in this way can't hope for any amelioration of their condition (p. 99).

Among the inhabitants of the hospital we never see are both inoffensive and dangerous madmen. The Valet mentions the 'furious' madmen on only two occasions: they either want to commit a murder or to kill themselves. They never leave their cells, and to prevent them from getting violent, they are placed in irons or 'tied up in the darkest places' (p. 142). In this respect, this hospital resembles once again the future General Hospital which will contain 'detention cells and a security ward'.[13] The characters involved in the love story who enter the asylum don't hesitate to associate it with a prison and substitute the word 'prisoner' for that of 'madman' without shocking anyone. This substitution reveals the condition of the mad person who is deprived of freedom but, more importantly, it gives rise to an implicit comparison between the madman and the criminal: both are marginal and transgress the norms of society. It is not at all surprising that the Concierge compares the conduct of a madman to that of a criminal: 'Just as criminals claim to be innocent, madmen say that they are reasonable, which they all pretend to be to get away from their slavery' (p. 140).

The manner in which madmen are treated can be explained by the way in which men judge them. According to Luciane, a madman does not remember what has happened to him nor is he conscious of what can happen to him. He has no memory and is a stranger to the notion of time. Above all, he has no awareness of death, which allows him to be peaceful. This description is not new. It can also be found in Erasmus' *Praise of Folly*.[14] But the way in which the madman is perceived has changed drastically. Until the seventeenth century, he alone had the freedom to do and say anything with impunity because he was under the protection of God.[15] In his delirium, he could have access to the truth. Thanks to his unusual position of both being and not being of this world, he also had the ability to predict the future.[16]

Now the madman no longer possesses these sacred capabilities. He has lost his former power and prestige. Madness is condemned by reasonable men. When Dom Gomez and Dom Alfrede are in the hospital listening to the musician speak, Dom Gomez does not reject him. He thinks that 'No matter how insane he is, he deserves our compassion' (p. 76). The mad

Philosopher agrees with him: 'We must have more pity for these troubled souls/ Than we do for decrepit, deformed, mutilated bodies:/ The mind is the part to which everything pays homage,/ On which the gods have imprinted their Image,/ And whoever makes fun of its deformities/ Makes fun of Divinity' (pp. 74–5). But Dom Alfrede refuses to have pity and answers coldly: 'those whose fault brought misfortune upon them are worthy of mockery and not of sympathy' (p. 75).[17] The insane are not considered innocent since they are *responsible* for and guilty of their madness. It is the indelible stain of their fault. This moral condemnation is also a *justification* of 'reasonable' men: universal mockery replaces respect. One can laugh at the madman with a clear conscience because he *deserves* it.

For reason, madness has become a form of entertainment as the Philosopher states: 'People can laugh at the effect of this illness, and they come here as if they were going to the theater' (p. 75). All of the characters of the love story will at one time or another be in the asylum, and they will all be amused by the show that the madmen put on for them. People go to see them as if they were a rare species of animal: 'Let's be entertained in this hospital, I've been told that I had to go see one of these miserable creatures' (p. 64). In this regard, Beys is not making anything up. In the seventeenth century, mad people were locked up and exhibited. Until the Revolution, Bicêtre was open to the public. Although admission was not free, it was a popular attraction visited by more than 2,000 people on a good day![18] The Concierge of the *Illustres Fous* gives guided tours to anyone who is willing to pay: 'I will pay you, let this mad couple out' (p. 102), and Tirinte with the help of a tip enjoys himself immensely: 'Pleasant madness', 'O pleasant caprice!' (p. 105). Dom Alfrede also visits the asylum on the advice of his friend. It becomes a tourist attraction. Julie and Luciane are not exceptions to the rule when they hide there to escape Tirinte: 'One can't get bored in this hospital./ It's so entertaining!' (p. 153).

Madness could become a form of entertainment for reason only from the moment that reason excluded and imprisoned madness. Even if 'the great confinement' occurred three years after the *Illustres Fous* with the creation of the General Hospital, it is certain that a desire for order was already well developed in France, which is reflected in Beys's play: the addition of scenes with madmen and the introduction of new insane characters nineteen years after the first version of the play can be explained by an awareness of the necessity to draw clear lines between the worlds of reason and madness. This is probably why Beys's hospital prefigures the General Hospital in so many respects.

We must not forget that between the first and last versions of this play, France was divided by the civil conflict of *La Fronde*. In its aftermath, bourgeois society felt more than ever the need for order and stability. Not surprisingly, in 1653, one year after the end of *La Fronde*, Beys alluded to this uprising in his final version. 'The people who became politically involved', whom the Valet has just admitted to the asylum, are considered mad because they upset the order of the State: 'the earth is so fertile in this type of insanity/ That it will be necessary to intern everyone in this place./ We see at every turn little freaks/ Forming armed squads on every street corner,/ Doing whatever is necessary to right all the wrongs,/ Without ever really changing the state of affairs' (pp. 124–5).

The madman has been found guilty by bourgeois society which demands order and advocates hard work. Madness has become a *fault*, or, in other words, a failure to live up to bourgeois moral standards. It is worth noting that contrary to the characters of the love story, whom we can recognize by their first or last name, the madmen don't have a true identity since they are designated only by their profession or their status in life. It's not a coincidence. Beys emphasizes the function that madmen fulfilled when they were still integrated members of society. Nearly all those who have lapsed from their former professions or statuses are punishable for bourgeois society because none of them is productive.

Formerly reason *spoke with* madness. Now reason *speaks about* it. All possibility of a dialogue between reason and madness has disappeared, which explains why in Beys's play the love story really has nothing to do with the conversation between the madmen.[19] These two elements function independently. Reason comes to listen to the insane who talk only to each other. Their discourse has become a source of entertainment and commentary.

What Foucault has called 'a critical consciousness of madness' is likened to the comedy of manners. We can laugh at the inhabitants of the asylum with a clear conscience and at the same time benefit from a moral lesson. The Concierge admits that 'everybody is a little crazy' and that 'it is just a question of degree' (p. 139). But the distinction between the two is clearly established: those who recognize this tendency are of 'strong mind' and like the Concierge can be the guardians of order, and those who don't recognize it are the 'truly' mad and must be shut out from the mainstream of society. As Foucault says, it is a question of a

> critical consciousness which pretends to be so rigorous as to perform a radical critique of itself, and to risk itself in the absolute of an uncertain combat, but which also secretly saves itself in advance by recognizing itself as reason by virtue of the fact of accepting the risk. In one way the engagement of reason is total in this simple and reversible opposition to madness, but it is total only insofar as a secret possibility of a complete disengagement is posited from the beginning.[20]

In conclusion, we might ask ourselves why French comic theatre of the seventeenth century was a privileged space of representation of madness.

Let us briefly recall the powers of madness: it thrusts people into a world of illusion; it makes them forget their own identity in favor of a new one which exists only for them. Thus it induces them to take people for what they are not, to mistake death for life and lies for the truth. It takes them in by its 'powerful charms'. And yet, how is the theatre any different?[21] For the duration of a performance, it thrusts the audience into the most complete of illusions. No one better than Scudéry in his 'Prologue' to *La Comédie des comédiens* (*The Comedy of actors* [1632]) has expressed this close relationship between madness and the theatre:

> I don't know (gentlemen) how to describe the outrageous behavior of my companions, but it is so much so, that I am forced to believe that some spell has made off with their reason, and what's worse is that they are trying to make me lose mine and you, yours. They want to persuade me that I am not on a stage; they say that we are in Lyon, that it is actually an inn and that over there is a tennis court where actors we both are and are not are performing a pastoral. These insane people are working under assumed names and believe to be unknown to you. They want you to think that you are on the banks of the Rhône and not of the Seine, and without leaving Paris, they have the gall to pass you off as inhabitants of Lyon; these gentlemen from the Little-Houses want to persuade me that metempsychosis is real . . . Isn't it risky for them and doesn't it offend you? But that's not all, their madness extends even further; for the play they are performing lasts only an hour and a half, but these insane people are sure that it lasts twenty-four hours, and these deranged minds [*esprits déréglés*] call that adhering to the rules [*règles*].[22]

It is striking to what extent we find in this text all the attributes that madness possessed at that time. The theatre is an *initiation* to madness. In this sense, 'the critical consciousness of madness' found in the theatre its privileged space of representation 'in the absolute of an uncertain combat', since to attend a theatrical performance is to agree to lose one's reason. But at the same time, this theatrical performance is the proof of reason's disengagement. This critical consciousness is willing to lose its reason because it knows that neither the risk nor the fight exists. The madness in question is actually a false madness; it is temporary and above all, it is regulated and respects a pre-established code. Therefore, we can let ourselves be taken in by the disorder of the theatrical performance since it's only after all an ordered disorder: 'these deranged minds call that adhering to the rules'. And we know, according to the last sentence of the play uttered by the Concierge that: 'Madness which is shortest is always best' (p. 173).[23]

NOTES

1 'Eraste's madness is not in the best taste. In my mind, I always condemned it, but since it was a theatrical ornament which never failed to please and was often admired, I willingly affected these fits of derangement' (*Oeuvres complètes*, vol. i, ed. Georges Couton (Paris: Pléiade–Gallimard, 1980), p. 6). All translations from the French are by Dominique Froidefond and John Gregg.

2 *Les Illustres Fous*, ed. Merle I. Protzman (Baltimore: Johns Hopkins University Press, 1942); all citations are from this edition. Since Henry Lancaster discussed Beys's *L'Hospital des fous* in his *History of French Dramatic Literature in the Seventeenth Century* (Baltimore: Johns Hopkins Press, 1929), vol. ii, pp. 553–4 and 556, surprisingly only two articles have been devoted to this play: V. Pompejano, 'Il tema della follia ne *L'Hospital des fous* di Charles Beys', *Il teatro al tempo di Luigi XIII*, Quaderni del Seicento Francese, i (Paris: Nizet, 1974), pp. 137–50, and G. J. Mallinson, '*L'Hospital des fous* of Charles Beys: The Madman and the Actor', *French Studies* 36: 1 (1982), 12–25. Jean Rousset mentions it in *La Littérature de l'âge baroque en France* (Paris: José Corti, 1954). John D. Lyons refers to it briefly five times in the first chapter, 'The Woman as Man', of his book *A Theater of Disguise: Studies in French Baroque Drama (1630–1660)* (Columbia: French Literature Publications, 1978). Even more surprising is the total absence of research on *The Illustrious Madmen* given the richness of the representations of madness found therein.

3 *L'Hypocondriaque*, Rotrou's first play (1628), has the same plot. Cloridan thinks that his mistress is dead and passes out from grief. When he regains consciousness, he is mad. In Pichou's *Les Folies de Cardénio* (1629), Cardénio thinks that his mistress has married another man and becomes crazy. In *Agarite* (1633) by Durval, the king loses his mind when he thinks the woman he loves is dead. In *Cléomédon* (1634) by Du Ryer, Cléomédon becomes mad because his mistress Célanice must obey the orders of the king and marry another man. In *La Folie du sage* (1644) by Tristan, Ariste thinks his daughter is dead and on account of the excessive degree of his suffering loses his reason. Madness in Corneille's *Mélite* is slightly different. Believing himself responsible for the death of the two lovers, Eraste is stricken by remorse. He faints and like Cloridan loses his mind when he wakes up. (In these examples, we have restricted ourselves to tragicomedies.)

4 In *L'Hypocondriaque*, Cloridan, thinking himself dead and in the Underworld, 'runs after Perside whom he imagines seeing' (*Oeuvres*, vol. i (Paris, 1820), p. 55). He confuses identities: he takes Cléonice for Perside and imagines that Cléonice's father is his rival. Similarly, Eraste mistakes the Earth for Hades and thinks that Cliton is Charron, that Philandre, whom he betrayed, is Minos, and that the Nurse is Mélite. He also imagines that the Furies are pursuing him. Cardénio thinks that he sees enemies ready to attack him and mistakes the Barber for his mistress. Ariste talks to Plato, Aristotle, Socrates, and many others whom he angrily dismisses.

5 This is also what happens in all the tragicomedies mentioned above. Death is a

false death, the contents of a letter are untrue, and the madman sees only 'false images'. Reason always succeeds in making the madman aware of his error, and madness disappears instantly.

6 There is also a faked madness in *La Pélerine amoureuse* (1632–3) by Rotrou. In this instance, a woman pretends to be mad so as to avoid a marriage.

7 In the French pastorals and tragicomedies which portray temporary madness, whereas the madman was always mistaken with respect to the identity of others, he never was with respect to his own.

8 Desmarets is undoubtedly indebted to Beys for this representation of madness in *Les Visionnaires* (1640).

9 In the version of 1634, Beys was more specific: 'By love and furor his heart is possessed.' Interestingly, in the seventeenth century, the word 'furor' was, as Foucault has noted, 'one of the most frequent words that can be found in the registers of confinement. It signifies an ill-defined region of disorder – disorder of conduct and of the heart, disorder of morality and of the mind' (*Histoire de la folie à l'âge classique* (Paris: Gallimard, 1972), p. 125).

10 The disguise of women as men in pastorals, tragicomedies, comedies and tragedies is also a leitmotiv of this period. Lyons counts at least sixty-one plays between 1630 and 1660. (See his list, *Theater of Disguise*, pp. 58–9.) He states that 'the insistence on such episodes or main plots of disguise seems evidence that temporary transformation of sexual identity is not simply a device but a theme in itself, a mysterious convention of the period, a myth of the baroque imagination' (p. 45).

11 'The disparity between dress and the other codes results in a failure of identity or madness. For example, in Beys's *Hospital des Fous*' (Lyons, *Theater of Disguise*, p. 43).

12 Foucault, *Histoire de la folie à l'âge classique*, p. 76.

13 Ibid., p. 63.

14 '. . . these folk are free from all fear of death – and this fear, by Jove, is no piddling evil! They are free from tortures of conscience . . . they are not blown up with hope of future good. In short, they are not vexed by the thousand cares to which this life is subject' (*The Praise of Folly*, trans. Hoyt Hopewell Hudson (Princeton: Princeton University Press, 1941), p. 48).

15 'Thus it comes about that, in a world where men are differently affected toward each other, all are at one in their attitude toward these innocents; all seek them out, give them food, keep them warm, embrace them and give them aid if occasion rises; and all grant them leave to say and to do what they wish with impunity . . . They are indeed held sacred by the gods' (Ibid., p. 48).

16 See Michael Screech, *Rabelais* (London: Gerald Duckworth, 1979), pp. 259–63, and 277–81.

17 This is one of the reasons for the success of Desmarets's *Les Visionnaires*. Like *The Illustrious Madmen*, his visionaries are 'worthy of mockery'.

18 It was not only in France that madmen were an attraction. As late as 1815 in England, according to Foucault: 'the hospital of Bedlam exhibited the madmen for one penny every Sunday. The annual income from these visits was nearly 400 pounds, which translates into the very high number of 96,000 visits per year' (*Histoire de la folie à l'âge classique*, p. 161).

19 Merle Protzman notes: 'the parade of *fous* is simply well woven into this plot but is extraneous to it and does not further the action' (*Les Illustres Fous*, p. 41).

20 *Histoire de la folie à l'âge classique*, p. 183.

21 J. G. Mallinson emphasizes the parallel 'between the madman and the actor. The art of the *comédien* is seen to lie in the replacement of his own identity with that of another ('*L'Hospital des fous*', p. 22), and 'The process of acting itself becomes something of a "folie" which makes him doubt his own sanity' (p. 23).

22 Georges de Scudéry, *La Comédie des comédiens* (Exeter: University of Exeter Press, 1975), p. 8.

23 In a note concerning the origin of this sentence, Protzman states: 'Richelet quotes this verse as a proverb . . . *Le Cochon mitré* cites it from Beys; O. Guerlac, *Les Citations françaises*, Paris 1931, also quotes it from Beys and says that it is found in P. Charron's *De la sagesse* (1601), Liv. I, chap. xxxviii.' He adds: 'I have been unable to find this last reference' (p. 173). It is indeed in Charron, but in chapter xxix of his first book: 'To say that one must always go to extremes without any reservation or respect is a very pernicious doctrine: and the opposite proverb says it all, madness which is shortest is best' (*De la sagesse*, 3 vols. (Geneva: Slatkine Reprints, 1968), p. 265).

The male gaze in *Woyzeck*: re-presenting Marie and madness

ELIZABETH SCHAFER

Many accounts of 'the birth of modern drama' accord Georg Büchner's play *Woyzeck* a seminal status.[1] Given this privileged position, it is crucial that feminist critiques of *Woyzeck* intervene and compete with the dominant (non-feminist) discourse on the play.[2] Such intervention is particularly vital because the climactic act of *Woyzeck* – the murder of Marie for unchastity – can easily create space for misogyny directly in proportion to the extent of a reading's or a production's bid for sympathy for Woyzeck. Indeed the narrative of Marie has inspired quite startling misogyny in some criticism of the play in English. Ronald Hauser argues of Marie that 'the beast within her makes her become untrue to her mission as Woyzeck's woman'.[3] Claiming glibly that Woyzeck's experience 'transcends gender', Richard Gilman comes close to blaming Marie for her own murder, stressing her 'treachery', and commenting that 'in this drama of elemental consciousness about oppression by the nature of things, Maria (sic) has already "murdered" Woyzeck by destroying their unity'.[4] Most obnoxious of all however is Tom Haas's vision of Marie with a 'roaring furnace between (her) legs', getting 'the ultimate sexual satisfaction as the steel knife tears apart her hot pleading flesh'.[5] In opposition to such readings, I want to propose a feminist reading of the play, a reading which uses the structure of the 'male gaze' for its focus, and which sees *Woyzeck* as a text which obtrusively foregrounds the gaze as an instrument of power and aggression.

The gaze, as E. Ann Kaplan comments, is 'not necessarily male (literally), but to own and activate the gaze, given our language and the structure of the unconscious, is to be in the "masculine" position'.[6] Kaplan discusses 'three explicitly male looks or gazes' which operate in relation to film:

> the look of the camera (which) . . . while technically neutral . . . is inherently voyeuristic and usually 'male' in the sense that a man is generally doing the filming: . . . the look of the men within the narrative which is structured so as to make women objects of their gaze; and finally . . . the look of the male spectator . . . which imitates (or is necessarily in the same position as) the first two looks. (p. 30)

Of course there is no camera gaze in *Woyzeck*;[7] however, Kaplan's second category of gaze 'within the narrative' appears in *Woyzeck* in several scenes which are structured so that they display characters in the act of gazing on, and objectifying, another character. Kaplan's third look, that of the 'male' spectator, is also under scrutiny and is problematized as the text foregrounds acts of reading and misreading – something which can implicate the audience (as well as the characters and playwright) in an obnoxious gaze system.[8]

The gaze appears in several forms in *Woyzeck* and one of the most overtly problematized of these forms is the diagnostic gaze – a gaze closely associated with the debate over whether or not Woyzeck is 'mad'. As the dispute about the historical Woyzeck was diagnostic, it is not surprising that this debate is implicit in Büchner's play.[9] What is interesting is the way in which that debate is set up. From the very opening scene the audience are confronted with a series of startling images of psychic disturbance, and they then have to process these images, in effect to make a diagnosis of what these images mean. The text encourages the audience to diagnose the hero as mentally disturbed because of the way in which it offers a series of plausible suggestions as to how mental instability may have occurred; the pea diet (causing Woyzeck to hallucinate?); the oppression of Woyzeck by his social superiors, the Captain and the Doctor (both of whom appear somewhat unstable themselves); the pressure building up as 'One thing after another' (4,14) goes wrong. However, if the audience participate in this diagnosis, they then find themselves positioned uncomfortably close to the diagnosis-loving but obnoxious Doctor. The theatrical convention whereby the audience gaze on and analyse both Woyzeck's 'symptoms' in particular and the physical and visual action of the play in general is unsympathetically imaged by the Doctor, on three occasions (scenes 4,8 (see also 2,6); 3,1; and 2,7), when he gazes on and then callously 'reads' Woyzeck. When the Doctor is specifically looking for evidence of an 'aberratio mentalis partialis' (4,8) the act of reading, or diagnosing Woyzeck – of asking the question is he mad? and concomitantly what is madness? – is particularly problematized by its association with this overbearing and oppressive character.

The strength of the diagnostic impulse in *Woyzeck* is implicitly acknowledged by translators and adaptors who have added a diagnostic post-mortem scene to the text.[10] This theatrical tradition complements the critical fashion for finding post-mortem precision and objectivity in Büchner's work in general and for locating in *Woyzeck* a scientific presentation of the neutrally observed 'facts' of Woyzeck's symptoms to the audience.[11] The play however, undercuts the whole notion of the 'objective', scientific gaze simply because the primary 'objective', scientific observer within the text is the Doctor, a grotesque caricature who may insist on the import-

2 Albert Steinrück as Woyzeck in the first production of the play, Munich 1913

ance of the 'question of the relationship of subject to object' (3,1), but who is more interested in objectification than objectivity. The objectification of Woyzeck reaches an extreme in the scene (3,1) where the Doctor diagnoses Woyzeck for his audience of students, instructing these students in the power of their gaze as scientific experts – they can not only 'look' on

Woyzeck as an object, but they can also man handle him – the Doctor urges them to 'Feel him, gentlemen, feel him'. In this scene, as in 4,8, the Doctor appears in a position of power gazing down on the action from an 'attic window'. The Doctor then descends in order to interrogate, oppress and diagnose Woyzeck. On both occasions the Doctor at his window offers an image of power and surveillance which has the potential to reflect harshly both on the surveying gaze of the audience and the surveying perspective offered by the play text itself which, in displaying the tragedy of Woyzeck's decline into 'madness' for an audience, can be seen to be exploiting 'Woyzeck' almost as clinically as the Doctor exploits him for his demonstration class.[12]

However uncomfortable it may be, some diagnosis of Woyzeck's relative state of sanity or insanity has to take place in performance and the director's/performer's answer to the question how mad is Woyzeck? has radical implications for the representation of Marie. With a Woyzeck who is clearly mad, Marie is more likely to be seen as even more significantly oppressed than Woyzeck – and killing a woman for unchastity is identified as a mad gesture because it is the voices of Woyzeck's madness which tell him that an appropriate response to Marie's unchastity is to 'Stab, stab the bitch to death' (4,12). By contrast, with a sane Woyzeck, A. H. J. Knight manoeuvres into dangerous territory. When Knight proclaims 'Büchner's Woyzeck knows perfectly well what he is doing, and his ideas on good and evil, or right and wrong, are acute, and on the whole sensible' he appears to be endorsing the murder of Marie as the action of a 'sensible' man.[13] I would maintain that with this line of argument, the male oppression Marie suffers in the play is continued in twentieth-century criticism.

The gaze structuring in *Woyzeck* also affects the representation of Marie by drawing attention to the fact of Marie's subjection to the male gaze, something which prefigures her subjection to male brute force despite, and because of, her attempts at rebellion. Marie is introduced into *Woyzeck* in a scene (4,2) where her role as receiver of the 'gaze' is highlighted, as she appears onstage focussed, framed by a window – framed that is both for the passing Drum Major and for the audience. Later in the play Marie (4,16) is again framed for the audience by a window when she is reading about and attempting to roleplay the archetypal penitent whore, traditionally identified with Mary Magdalen. Marie squirms under what she sees as the oppressive, accusing gaze of God ('My God, my God! Don't look at me'), and opens the window, complaining of the heat of her room. Büchner often places characters at windows when they are in crisis.[14] However, the framing, liminal window also helps to define part of Marie's problem as the window/picture-frame evokes the notion of women subjected to, limited by, and indeed trapped by the male gaze in high art. The high art reference seems particularly appropriate given that Marie's framed appearance on both these occasions evokes two of western art's most popular icons – the penitent Magdalen is complemented and complicated by the framed Marie and baby of 4,2 evoking images of the Virgin and child.[15]

The representation of Marie as receiver of the gaze also raises the question of voyeurism. This is at its most conspicuous in the very suggestive moment (4,11) when Woyzeck gazes through a window frame at Marie dancing in the tavern. The barrier of the window frame of course underscores the separation of Marie and Woyzeck – picking up on something suggested as early as 4,2 where a window frame also divided them. However, 4,11 also offers a challenging and troubling image of the audience/performer relationship. This relationship is imaged several times in *Woyzeck* – for example 4,3, where the crowd/audience at the fair gazes at the exhibition of the astronomical horse or the two scenes (4,14, and 1,17) where the tavern crowd plays audience to Woyzeck in distress. However in 4,11 Woyzeck gazes on and is stimulated by Marie's performance (as dancer) while the 'performer' remains unaware that she has an audience. Hence the audience/performer relation is imaged as clearly voyeuristic. Voyeurism (and the related subject of fetishism) is also represented in the play when the Captain explains how he enjoys gazing at 'white stockings as they go tripping down the street' (4,5), and when the Doctor evokes a Biblical narrative of voyeurism (David and Bathsheba) as he comments on the sight of 'underwear on a clothesline in the garden of the girls' boarding house' (3,1). The Drum Major's gaze in 4,3 also has strong voyeuristic elements as he gazes on the unaware Marie, constructing her as something to sire drum majors upon. There is even an element of voyeurism as Woyzeck, having quite literally objectified Marie by rendering her a corpse, gazes on her when she is dead, assessing the oblivious Marie in terms of her appearance, her hair and gruesomely her 'necklace' (1,19).

The murder of Marie takes place in the open fields, the space where Woyzeck's madness is most vivid, most poetic and most lethal (4,1; 4,12 (see also 1,12); 1,15; 1,19). This is the opposite space to Marie's cramped home where she feels confined and oppressed (4,4; 4,16), dreams of escape to gypsyland (4,4) and tries to escape through her affair with the Drum Major. In between these two extremes in *Woyzeck*, spaces exist where distinctions between interior and exterior become blurred; 4,2; 4,3; and 4,11 all take place in spaces which are both interior and exterior at the same time.[16] This blurring, this confusion over boundaries (something which is particularly pointed by the use of the liminal window frames in 4,2 and 4,11), is strongly associated with acts of transgression and rebellion by Marie. However, the gaze structuring in these scenes also clearly

signals that Marie's transgression and rebellion will be contained by the
male order. Thus in 4,11 Marie (inside the tavern) dances with her lover
the Drum Major but is contained by the voyeuristic and malevolent gaze
of Woyzeck (outside the tavern). In 4,2, Marie (inside) flirts with the
Drum Major (outside), behaviour which is bold enough for Margret to
comment on it but which also of course positions her as the object of the
Drum Major's gaze. In 4,3, the fair scene, exterior and interior merge as
Marie, Woyzeck, the Drum Major and the Sergeant move from the fair-
ground into the show tent. The context of the fair is particularly suggestive as here traditional hierarchies are turned topsy turvy, a monkey is the
equal of a soldier, a horse the equal of a university professor and the
showman's wife wears trousers. Here Marie acts disruptively – 'This I've
got to see' and pushes to the front of the (onstage) audience. However,
Marie's assertive behaviour here (as in 4,2) also confirms her containment
because even as she is acting asertively, she is simultaneously being objectified by the Drum Major's reductive gaze, which constructs her as 'Good
enough for the propagation of cavalry regiments and the breeding of drum
majors.'

Marie also attempts subversion on two occasions when she becomes the
gazer (4,6 and 4,7) and although neither subversion is ultimately successful, her rebellion is significant. These attempted subversions are prepared
for by 4,4, a scene where Marie suggestively plays with a broken mirror
(to create the 'sandman' running along the wall) and plays with her gaze,
appreciating her own image, if not the image of her surroundings which
the mirror reflects back at her.[17] Woyzeck's entrance, however, presents a
different sort of gaze, one which clearly disconcerts Marie as she attempts
to hide the earrings from that gaze by covering her ears with her hands.

Marie becomes more assertive in 4,6 when she persuades the Drum
Major to subject himself to her gaze, asking him to parade around her
room for her entertainment and visual pleasure:

> Go march up and down the room for me. – A chest like a bull and a beard like
> a lion. Nobody else is like that. – No woman is prouder than me.

In Kaplan's terms Marie is now the male gazer – however, her enjoyment
of the gaze is short lived. The Drum Major demands sex from Marie; she
resists but, despite the fact that she has the 'devil' in her eyes, her refusal
is ineffective. In a scene which contains elements of rape as well as
elements of seduction games, Marie seems to give in – 'What does it
matter?'. If she gives in unwillingly, then she has travelled a long way, in a
short time, from her enjoyment of the power of her gaze at the beginning
of the scene. In the next scene (4,7) a similar power exchange is
highlighted by a transfer in aggressive gazing. Here Marie is confronted

by the hostile and unstable Woyzeck who gazes fixedly at her, looking for visible signs of her unchastity in her appearance:

> Hm! I don't see anything, I don't see anything. Oh, I should be able to see it; I should be able to grab it with my fists.

Here Marie outgazes Woyzeck, something made most explicit in the second draft (2,8) where Louise (Marie) expands on her ability to outgaze a man:

> Don't you touch me, Franz! . . . When I was ten years old, my father didn't dare touch me when I looked at him.

The power of Marie's gaze is acknowledged as Woyzeck is unable to strike her when she gazes boldly back at him. However, as with the Drum Major, Marie's temporary resistance to or subversion of the male gaze here is short lived and this time instead of sex it leads to murder.

Marie's attempts at subversion and/or escape are commented upon most bleakly in the Grandmother's story.[18] A large number of commentators and translators claim this story solely as a parable for Woyzeck's experience; David Richards, in *Georg Büchner and the Birth of Modern Drama*, offers a particularly male-centred reading of the tale; 'The poor orphan in the Grandmother's tale . . . is analogous to Woyzeck and his child' and 'in its loneliness and isolation the child represents not only Woyzeck and Woyzeck's child, but also Danton, Leonce, Lenz, and *man* in general' (my emphasis).[19] The omission of Marie from this list is startling for the story links tellingly and precisely with Marie's history. Marie, like the child, attempts escape – through her dreams of gypsyland, through the Drum Major and through God. In 4,16, Marie, like the child, searches for life and hope; and, like the child, she finds that everything is 'dead'.[20] The Grandmother's parable speaks of defeat, prefiguring the final defeat of Marie in the following scene (1,15). 1,14 assembles three generations of women – the girls, Marie and the old woman, the wise witch figure. The scene is another liminal one, with Marie and the girls framed by the 'house door', and it is redolent with the passing on of received wisdom, with the archetypal structures of the fairy tale dooming humanity to endless repetitions of the child's defeat. However, reading the play through the structure of the male gaze at least emphasizes the reality of Marie's rebellion even though, in drawing particular attention to her oppression, it does run the risk of constructing her primarily as a victim. To compensate for this danger it is important to acknowledge that Marie's moments of joy and sensuality are also emphasized when we are attentive to the gaze structuring of the play.

Given that both her rebellion and her joy are ultimately contained in the play's narrative by a violent and in some ways insane male order, Marie's story can seem a dismal one. But the self-consciousness of the gaze structuring of the play encourages a stringent critique of the power plays involved in her suppression and at the same time offers the audience a confrontational opportunity to gaze at and assess images of their own gaze and processes of understanding.

NOTES

1 See e.g. David G. Richards, *Georg Büchner and the Birth of Modern Drama* (Albany: State University of New York Press, 1977); Richard Gilman, *The Making of Modern Drama* (New York: Farrar, Strauss & Giroux, 1974); *The Beginnings of Modern Drama* (section on *Woyzeck* written by Susan Khin Zaw) (Milton Keynes: Open University Press, 1977). The text of *Woyzeck* used in this paper is from *Georg Büchner: Complete Works and Letters*, ed. by Walter Hinderer and Henry J. Schmidt, trans. Henry J. Schmidt (New York: Continuum, 1986). All references are thus to draft number and then scene number within that draft.

2 Although we deal with very different material in offering feminist accounts of *Woyzeck*, I am very much in sympathy with Kerry Dunne's reading of the play in 'Woyzeck's Marie "Ein schlecht Mensch"? The Construction of Female Sexuality in Büchner's *Woyzeck*', *Journal of Germanic Studies* 26: 4 (November 1990), 294–308. I would like to thank Kate Rigbey of Monash University German Department for drawing my attention to this article.

3 Ronald Hauser, *Georg Büchner* (New York: Twayne, 1974), p. 125.

4 Richard Gilman, *The Making of Modern Drama*, p. 39.

5 Tom Haas, 'A Director's Notes After a Performance of *Woyzeck*', *Yale Theatre* 3: 3 (1972), 91–8. Kerry Dunne discusses two other particularly 'disquieting' performances of Marie's murder in her article 'Woyzeck's Marie "Ein schlecht Mensch"?', p. 294.

6 E. Ann Kaplan, *Women and Film; Both Sides of the Camera* (London: Methuen, 1983), p. 30. Kaplan makes clear her debt to Laura Mulvey's discussion in 'Visual Pleasure and Narrative Cinema', reprinted in *Visual and other Pleasures* (London: Macmillan, 1989). The notion of the gaze owes much to Lacan and Freud – see, e.g., Toril Moi's discussion of the gaze in *Sexual/Textual Politics: Feminist Literary Theory* (London: Methuen, 1985), p. 134 and Gayle Austin's discussion of Mulvey's work in *Feminist Theories for Dramatic Criticism* (Ann Arbor: University of Michigan Press, 1990), ch. 5, 'Feminist Film Theory: "Man as Bearer of the Look" and the Representation of Women'.

7 The directional gaze of the playwright offers the closest analogy to the gaze of the camera.

8 In discussing 'the audience' in this paper, I am solely concerned with the audience in their conventional capacity in the theatre, positioned as gazers, auditors and interpreters of the action.

9 I am in complete disagreement with critics who claim Woyzeck's 'madness' is not an issue; for example, A. H. J. Knight, *Georg Büchner* (Oxford: Basil Black-

well, 1951), p. 136, comments 'Woyzeck is not insane, and no one supposes him
to be so'; Margaret Jacobs, introduction to her edition of *Woyzeck* (Manchester:
Manchester University Press, 1954), p. xxiv, states 'Büchner does not intend us
to consider Woyzeck as insane'. Jacobs's confidence over the author's intentions here is hard to reconcile with the fact that so much of Büchner's work,
fictional and otherwise, is concerned with the subject of nervous disorders and
madness.

10 For examples of autopsy scenes see *Büchner: The Complete Plays*, edited and
introduced by Michael Patterson (London: Methuen, 1987), pp. 162, 164, 174.

11 Julian Hilton, *Georg Büchner* (London: Macmillan, 1982), p. 17, quotes a much
cited letter from Büchner's contemporary Karl Gutzkow, who identifies an
element of 'autopsy' in everything Büchner writes. Hilton himself comments on
Büchner's use of the 'objective precision of medical research' in his drama (p.
16). Compare also Maurice Benn, *The Drama of Revolt: A Critical Study of Georg
Büchner* (Cambridge: Cambridge University Press, 1976) who comments (p.
200) of *Lenz* 'Though madness had often enough been treated in literature
before Büchner, it had never been studied with this cool clinical precision, this
tenacious and unflinching objectivity.'

12 Hilton, *Georg Büchner*, p. 129, feels that Büchner's 'love' 'answers' the charge
that he as playwright is exploiting Woyzeck.

13 Knight, *Georg Büchner*, p. 136.

14 See Hilton, *Georg Büchner*, pp. 65–6, 124 and G. Bell, 'Windows: A Study of a
Symbol in Georg Büchner's Work', *The Germanic Review*, 47 (1972), 95–108. The
truncated *Woyzeck* in *All the World's a Stage*, written and directed by Ronald
Harwood (BBC, 1983), suggestively features a disembodied window/frame.

15 Reinhold Grimm in *Love, Lust, and Rebellion: New Approaches to Georg Büchner*
(Madison: University of Wisconsin Press, 1985), p. 105, comments on Büchner's play with Biblical associations in the naming of both Marie and Marion
in *Danton's Death*. See also Michael Ewans, *Georg Büchner's 'Woyzeck': Translation
and Theatrical Commentary* (New York: Peter Lang, 1989), p. 86.

16 Ewans, *Georg Büchner's 'Woyzeck'*, p. 134, comments that the 'violent transition
from private to public' becomes 'central' to the 'dramatic impact' of *Woyzeck*.
See also Hilton, *Georg Büchner*, pp. 124–5.

17 The mirror image seems particularly suggestive given Luce Irigaray's medi-
tations in *Speculum of the Other Woman*, trans. Gillian C. Gill (Ithaca, New York:
Cornell University Press, 1985). Richards, *Georg Büchner and the Birth of Modern
Drama*, pp. 91–2, discusses mirror imagery in Büchner's work.

18 Benn, *The Drama of Revolt* (pp. 232–3) rightly stresses that this scene is crucial to
the interpretation of the whole play.

19 Richards, *Georg Büchner and the Birth of Modern Drama*, p. 193. Other examples of
critics who ignore Marie in their interpretation of the story include Gilman, *The
Making of Modern Drama*, p. 43; Ronald Hauser, *Georg Büchner*, p. 117. For the
source story see Benn, *The Drama of Revolt*, p. 233 and Michael Ewans, *Georg
Büchner 'Woyzeck'*, pp. 144–5 – the latter also comments on how many translators have ignored the neuter case of 'das Kind' and made the 'child' into a
boy. Werner Herzog's film of *Woyzeck* (1979) stresses the application of the
story to Marie's plight by cutting the grandmother and having Marie herself

tell the story to the children in a way which suggests that her story is wistfully reflecting on her life.

20 Precisely the same phrase is used in the German – 'Alles todt'. Woyzeck has experienced a similar emotion in the opening scene of the play but Marie's more recent experience is likely to be freshest in the audience's memories.

Mental illness and the problem of female identity in Ibsen

A. VELISSARIOU

Femininity in Ibsen's plays has traditionally been a controversial area of dramatic criticism. Critics, faced with the challenge of unorthodox female behaviour, betray at best a certain puzzlement before the task of the smoothing over of contradictions into a neat logic. However, in Ibsen, female psychologies and the concomitant practices have proved to be exceedingly resistant to any attempt to assimilate them into prevalent notions of femininity. Over the years they have displayed a remarkable tenacity in their defiance of a number of tenets underlying dominant assumptions about gender roles. The easiest way out of the impasse to which critics have been led seemingly by the unreasonable behaviour of Ibsen's heroines, but in reality by their own logic, is offered by the category of 'the abnormal'. This specific term has the great advantage of encompassing a wide range of manifestations, from simple irregularities and eccentricities to downright criminal or insane behaviour. Moreover it conveniently collapses the social and the psychological into the category of the morally reprehensible without being totally identifiable with either. The very term 'abnormal' also suggests the pathological, and implicitly, the problematic area of mental health. As a pseudo-medical term therefore, it lends itself to the objectivity of scientific discourse, concealing thus its heavy reliance on received morality. Under the guise of impartiality it effectively combines the notion of illness with that of social aberration while obscuring the crux of the matter – the problem of gender.

A brief account of John Northam's analysis of *Hedda Gabler*, for example, can illustrate the above point. For all its perceptiveness his reading does not steer away from ingrained assumptions about gender. In realizing that the female protagonist's behaviour challenges them to the core he resorts to the category of the abnormal. Having drawn attention to Hedda's complaints about the sunlight and the flowers which brighten the set in the opening scene, as well as to her repulse of Miss Tesman's affection, he remarks that she is a woman 'who is unable, for some reason, to accept and enjoy what seems naturally enjoyable'.[1] Northam finds Hedda's rejection of what he calls 'naturally' or 'normally attractive'

shocking, 'strange', and on the whole extremely unsettling.[2] His bewilderment over her behaviour increases in the face of her abhorrence of pregnancy, which he considers the most serious symptom of her general
distaste for what is natural in life:

> Hedda's distaste for what is naturally attractive is more than superficial. To
> hate pregnancy, as she seems to, suggests a radical abnormality; and the
> violence of her reaction shows that it is an abnormality that can place her
> under acute stress.[3]

The association of the hatred of pregnancy with abnormality leaves no
doubt as to the fact that what is at stake here is Hedda's failure to fulfil the
'natural' and 'normal' role ascribed to her by her gender. That motherhood and fertility provide the crucial definition of femininity is suggested
through the comparison that Northam draws between Thea's emotional
and physical 'richness of being'[4] and Hedda's sterility. It is irrelevant that
the one woman is physically sterile and the other is not. What counts for
Northam, and for a number of critics, is that Thea, for all her silliness and
'faint hysteria',[5] is finally vindicated by simply being feminine; that is, she
has thoroughly internalized and endorsed her feminine role of providing
the receptacle for male seed, albeit spiritual. In the light of this, Hedda's
suicide comes most appropriately at the moment when Thea is in the
process of conceiving a new child/book, this time by Tesman. Her death
marks her defeat as a woman placed against a background of infinite
female reproductiveness.

Her radical abnormality, as Northam says, releases 'acute stress'; or, as
Caroline W. Mayerson declares, Hedda is neurotic (but not psychotic).[6]
What underlies both statements is a tendency to medicalize unconventional female behaviour. Critical discourse gives way to medical language
precisely at those points in which female characters react in unexpected,
that is, not stereotypical ways. Critics therefore, momentarily borrow the
voice of psychiatrist and transform dramatic heroines into case studies. It
is not surprising that this fate has befallen most of Ibsen's heroines. The
medicalization of critical discourse is not a new phenomenon. It dates
back to the contemporary reception of Ibsen notably in England. It is
worth quoting at length from an unsigned notice on *Hedda Gabler* (*The
Times*, 21 April 1891) as a paradigm of such critical discourse:

> Ibsen does not say in so many words that he is giving us a study in *névrosité*.
> He allows the case to explain itself, and . . . in a short time we are content to
> resign ourselves to what is really a demonstration of the pathology of mind,
> such as may be found in the pages of the *Journal of Mental Science* or, in the
> reports of the medical superintendents of lunatic asylums . . . The author is
> satisfied with bringing Hedda Gabler's insanity very plainly before us. It is
> suggested in her inconsequent actions, in her callous behaviour, in her aim-
> less persecution of all around her, and it is finally proved by her motiveless
> suicide . . . Hedda Gabler is manifestly a lunatic of the epileptic class.[7]

The above passage is written as a pseudo-medical report wholly unconcerned with the dramatic value of the piece. The judgement that the critic/doctor passes on the play is that it constitutes 'a study in *névrosité*'. Hedda is a pathological case, so the diagnosis goes, and as such she displays a number of symptoms. That the anonymous critic conflates more specialized medical vocabulary (*névrosité*, epilepsy) with generic terms (insanity, lunacy) might cast doubt on the extent of his 'specialized' knowledge; it does not, however, undercut in the least the forcefulness of his argument. On the contrary, the critic amplifies its effect because by borrowing terms from medical discourse, he also borrows some of its prestige. The combination of 'scientific' terminology and complacency obviously had its merits judging by the large number of similar approaches to the play appearing in the contemporary British press. The play 'made its melancholy way'[8] to England to present a woman who 'suffers from the hopeless complication of maladies – anaemia of the affections, with hypertrophy of the aesthetics'.[9] This 'sane lunatic' and 'reasoning madwoman'[10] is yet another of 'Dr. Ibsen's emancipated heroines' whose 'morbid imagination' managed to contribute to the 'drama of disease' a new 'study of insanity' far exceeding even its predecessors.[11]

Contemporary criticism of other Ibsen heroines ran along the same lines. Ibsen is attacked on the grounds that his plays are studies in morbid heredity, with Rebecca West, Ellida and Hilda Wangel, and Aline Solness exemplifying their creator's disordered intellect. So Ellida Wangel, is considered 'a victim of the insane temperament',[12] Hilda Wangel 'a specimen of Norwegian girlhood imaginative to the point of madness' which the ingenious critic calls 'aeromania',[13] while in a notice on *The Master Builder* the reviewer is at a loss to attach any name to Mrs Solness's 'special form of insanity'.[14] Nevertheless, behind the attempts to categorize those unconventional heroines as insane[15] lie preconceived ideas about femininity. This becomes clear in its crudest form in the following statement of Ellida's 'insanity': 'After a few years of married life Ellida Wangel, who is a wife of a highly respectable, devoted noodle, develops alarming symptoms of "baulked individuality", as the consecrated phrase is.'[16] The idea is that marriage should be enough for women's self-determination; therefore, any quest for individuality outside marriage can only be a symptom of an inexplicable illness that for want of a better name could be called 'madness'. One might argue that we are worlds apart from the category of the 'abnormal' and, moreover, that there can be no possible connection between contemporary criticism and the bulk of openly prejudiced and hostile receptions of Ibsen's plays in his own time. Yet, what underlies the use of both the notion of mental illness and of abnormality as explanations of 'aberrant' female behaviour is the universalization of male-specific terms; consequently, the unquestioned assumption that they constitute the only available means of defining the right and the normal. In this context, female 'madness' can only signify difference from the male norms.

The main concern of this paper will be to examine the conflicts, traumas and impasses that a number of Ibsen's heroines experience when confronted with socially sanctioned definitions of femininity. It will also be to show that psychological reactions regarded as manifestations of psychic disorder are in reality a form of revolt against the roles that these female characters would have to assume to comply with the prevalent notions of femininity. In this context, symptoms of mental disorder are the indirect expression of unresolved conflicts vis à vis their gender identity, or the results of their failure to conform to the norm. Female mental illness in Ibsen functions as a means by which the dramatist 'contains' and expresses his heroines' dissatisfaction with the requirements made of them. There are two premises upon which this argument rests. The first concerns the refusal to accept as universal terms which are gender specific. In this sense, words such as madness or insanity, when applied to resistance or subconscious reaction to traditional roles, can only obscure the conflicts involved in the heroines' relationship to their gender identity. At the same time the unproblematic appropriation of the category of mental illness presupposes its opposite, 'mental health', which is in itself a debatable term. The second premise requires the discarding of the notion of abnormality which, likewise, implies the highly suspect idea of normality. Consequently, the challenge that Ibsen's female characters have presented us with does not pertain to our assessment of their mental 'health', but is of a different kind. It concerns their violation, conscious or not, of expectations and codes of behaviour deriving from the prevalent ethos, and the resultant traumas. It is ultimately, therefore, a question of the mental and emotional penalty they have to pay for being different.

Ellida Wangel (*The Lady from the Sea*), Beata Rosmer and Rebecca West (*Rosmersholm*), Hedda Gabler and Aline Solness (*The Master Builder*):[17] 'insane' female characters will be treated in the context of the above argument. The grouping together of such diverse female figures is not accidental. All of them are involved in a problematic relationship with their own identity as women and with the concomitant commitments and duties. All of them seem to be suffering as a result of the construction of that identity by others, outside and beyond their personal needs and desires. Extreme stress, nervous tension, delusion, melancholy, and consuming guilt are manifestations of their tormented effort to negotiate their female state. Finally all of them, except for Ellida, pay the price of their 'incomplete' femininity through self-destruction, be it suicide (Hedda, Rebecca, Beata), or living death (Aline). Ellida is the only one who survives and fully integrates herself into the social sphere, but to the cost of her individuality. Central to their traumatic relationship to their femininity is the harrowing presence of the absent child, never born (Beata, Hedda), or irrevocably lost (Ellida, Aline). Frustrated or unwanted motherhood, therefore, becomes a powerful catalyst of emotional instability and mental strain and in certain cases the very source of devastating guilt.

Stephen Heath, commenting upon the first appearance of the word 'sexuality' – in its present sense of 'possession of sexual power, or capability of sexual feelings' – in a set of lectures on the 'diseases of women', remarks that both the date and the context are significant. The date (the second half of the nineteenth century) marks an era in which the family, at least the middle-class family 'that serves as the overall standard for recognised public morality and social values', was organized on the basis of the patriarchal power of the father; an era in which ideological and economic discourses had become increasingly concerned with the individual and the notions of private fulfilment in love, individual experience etc.[18] Second, the word sexuality appears within a medical context. Therefore it arose as a problem to be accounted for within the context of medical discourses and practices belonging in the area of disturbance of the individual. Furthermore, it was connected to women. The association between femininity and sexuality constituted an implicit recognition that women did possess sexual feelings, an awkward 'fact' in the face of the prevalent assumption that they were devoid of them. However, the refusal to acknowledge the disturbing reality of women as sexual beings was 'resolved' through the 'diagnosis' of female sexuality as 'the manifestation of something wrong, an illness'.[19]

Heath's argument clarifies considerably many aspects involved in Ibsen's construction of disordered femininity. Ibsen's heroines are presented as being caught in the middle of arising notions of individuality, something, however, denied them by virtue of their gender. At the same time they experience their sexuality as an illness or a disorder for which they are held responsible. The reason is that they are denied the terms by which they can acknowledge its existence as anything other than a mental disturbance. Ellida and Beata are offered as illustrations of the contradictions deriving from their need to acknowledge their sexual desire and the social demand to repress it. In both cases the existence of desire manifests itself as madness and its repression takes the form of delusion, fixation, and morbid guilt.

Ellida's madness is constructed by two different but interwoven discourses: a medical one, structured by her husband who is, significantly, a doctor, and a language of passion voiced by Ellida herself. Ellida is pronounced mentally ill by Wangel and his daughter Hilda. In the opening scene, Wangel, talking to Arnholm, an old friend of the family, says of his wife's 'condition':

> She's not exactly ill, but her nerves have been very bad – on and off, that is – these last few years. I really don't know what to make of it. But do you know, once she gets into the sea she's perfectly well and happy.[20]

What precedes this statement, however, is Wangel's reference to the loss of her baby which roughly coincides with the deterioration of her nerves. The death of the baby is indirectly identified by him as the date marking Ellida's collapse into illness, thereby implying it to be the very cause of it. The linking of his wife's 'disorder' and childbearing seems to be a fixation at least for the husband-doctor. He attributes to frustrated motherhood Ellida's 'mental unrest', thus locating it in the area of the biological. So, when later she confesses to him that her long-forgotten desire (her madness) for the Stranger awoke in her while she was expecting the child, he readily interprets it as evidence for his theory. 'Now I'm beginning to understand so many things' (p. 271) says he. As his wife's protestations to the contrary make clear, Wangel is simply under the illusion that he knows. In reality what he thinks he understands is just a reflection of his female-biology-as-the-source-of-insanity theory. Wangel's collapse of the mental into the biological also underlies his final synopsis of Ellida's case. In a move typical of his confidence in his own authority and of his disregard of Ellida's opinion, first he casts doubt on her ability to assess her own condition; second, he proceeds to his own diagnosis of her mental unrest linking it again to her pregnancy:

> *Wangel.* When she heard . . . that Johnston . . . was on his way home in March three years ago, she evidently convinced herself that her mental unrest started at that time.
> *Arnholm.* But didn't it?
> *Wangel.* Not at all. Signs of it were noticeable before. It's true that she did – quite by chance – have a rather severe attack in March just three years ago.
> *Arnholm.* Well, then
> *Wangel.* But the circumstances – her condition at the time – would easily account for that.
>
> (p. 300)

In a medical discourse the idea that 'a rather severe attack' occurs by chance strikes one as somehow odd. And yet Wangel quickly fills in the gap of his scientific logic by locating her mental unrest in her pregnancy, the very thing that Ellida had refused to do. It is clear that in the face of Wangel's authority Ellida's 'irrational' belief that her fascination for the Stranger lies at the root of her problem can only lose ground.

The text offers medical discourse as a possible context within which female 'irregular' behaviour might be explained while demonstrating its failure to function as such. Wangel treats Ellida as a mentally ill person in need of special care. This attitude to Ellida also characterizes Hilda. Hilda flatly declares that she would not be surprised if Ellida went 'raving mad' precisely like her mother who died mad (p. 262). Thus heredity, invoked as the ultimate cause of madness, appears as the second explanation for disordered behaviour. Ellida's heredity and biology inscribe her in late nineteenth-century discourses on insanity.[21] Yet the text keeps a distance from such discourses. It shows that the medicalization of Ellida's behaviour by her doctor-husband is in reality a way of coping with female difference by ultimately subjugating it to 'normality'. Not accidentally Ellida's 'illness' is assessed on the basis of her suitability to perform female roles prescribed by conventional notions of femininity. Both Wangel and Boletta seem to have accepted with resignation Ellida's inability to perform her household duties – Boletta: 'she isn't able to do all the things that Mother did so well' (pp. 278–9), – to take care of the girls – Wangel: 'I really can't expect her to attend to things like that' (p. 297), – and be a real wife – Wangel: 'Then why, all this time, have you not wanted to live with me as my wife?' (p. 271). Ellida appears to be a failure both as wife to the doctor and as a mother to his daughters. Yet the very same reasons for her failure, namely, her physical estrangement from her husband and lack of care for the girls, signify her distancing from, and implicit rejection of the self-sacrificial archetype of mother-wife. At the same time they are the unmistakable signs of an individuality which could only strike the others as odd or peculiar in so far as female individuality was literally unthinkable. In this sense her relationship to the sea which, as Wangel admits, is the only thing that makes her happy, is considered obsessive and thus, implicitly, proof of a sick mind.

Female individuality, expressed in terms of withdrawal from traditional roles into a private world of personal needs, arises as a problem for the men of the play. Wangel resolves it by turning Ellida's desire for privacy and autonomy into a symptom of insanity. Her 'irresistible longing for the sea', as she puts it, exemplifying precisely this need for autonomy, typically arouses the male and scientific authority in him: '[*Putting his hand on her head*]. That's why this poor sick child shall go back to her own home again' (p. 265). As a doctor and a father to his own wife (p. 298), Wangel provides guidance and medicine. Significantly it is Boletta, the substitute wife and mother to her little sister, who draws attention to the fact that Wangel often gives her medicine while expressing doubts as to the rightness of such treatment (p. 279). Boletta rejects the word 'ill' or 'mad' for the word 'strange' to describe Ellida, thus differentiating herself from her father and sister. Precisely like her step-mother, she feels trapped in her patriarchal family, and in her assigned duties. As Ellida feels that she has 'obligations' to herself, so does she think that she has a 'duty' to herself. She will finally be manoeuvered into a marriage in which she will also try 'to negotiate a narrow zone of self-determination'.[22] As Elinor Fuchs makes clear in her brilliant gender reading of the play, for Arnholm and all the other men in it, female autonomy is inconceivable. In so far as 'there is no such thing as an unmediated freedom by birthright for a woman',[23] then the men of the piece feel they have to act as mediators in the women's relationship to their own freedom. Marriage in this respect, is offered to men as the ideal means of regulating women's freedom. This explains the striking fact that 'all men hold inflated narcissistic views of male power in marriage';[24] not even the 'weak' Lyngstrand is exempted. Both Arnholm and Wangel, much older than their women, guarantee for them in a gesture of fatherly benevolence a 'zone of self-determination'; however wide by contemporary standards, this zone proved to be too restrictive for Ellida, and it is very likely that it will be equally so for Boletta. The female tragedy in this play, as in most of Ibsen's plays, is that women are led to marriage for the lack of alternatives by which they can feel whole alone. Women, trapped in a patriarchal family in which they are denied what men enjoy, their individuality, internalize their oppression. Ellida, like Mrs Alving, Aline, and Beata, feels guilty for the incomplete fulfilment of her roles as a wife and mother. Furthermore, she also treats her quest for individuality as an illness while deferring to her husband's medical authority for its cure.

What lies at the centre of that very same quest is her passion for the Stranger which she explicitly identifies as 'madness'. Ellida, having assimilated the denial of the female right to desire, constructs her own madness by speaking the language of passion. The discourse of medicine and that of the irrational alternate with each other in a process by which the patient talks and the doctor thinks that he listens. In reality he 'helps' Ellida by imposing a kind of speech control.[25] In her account of her 'illness', her fascination for the sea is explicitly associated with her infatuation with the Stranger (p. 290). Time and again she describes her adventure with the Stranger as 'utter madness' (p. 249), their marriage to the sea as 'mad' (p. 269), and her passion for him as 'an inexplicable power that he has over [her] mind' (p. 271) which frightens and yet fascinates (p. 308). Wangel's stereotypical response is to treat Ellida's passionate discourse of desire as a symptom of insanity. The word 'cure' recurrently appears in an absurd effort to find a remedy for an illness which he is unable to diagnose. 'And now we must try another cure for you' (p. 270), says he, using 'we', and thus implicating Ellida too in the medical game. And yet when she talks to him of her fear of the Stranger he becomes utterly convinced that she is mad. 'Good lord – you're more ill than I thought. More ill than even you realize, Ellida' (p. 273). Passion 'as the meeting ground of body and soul' has long been suspected of madness; it was actually held responsible for it in that it was seen as containing its very seeds.[26] Fear, fascination and irresistible longing permeate Ellida's language of passion bringing her close to the borders of delusion just as when she thinks that her baby had the eyes of the Stranger (p. 274). The sea and the Stranger merge into the mystery of the eyes of a child which, in Ellida's imagination, was the fruit of her desire for that man. Wangel's rational voice is silenced by her passionate cry. Unable to come to terms with the madness implicit in passion, he can only interpret her talk as raving.

Yet Ellida herself is also caught in the same medical discourse of insanity. While recognizing that her longing for the sea is the expression of her attraction to the Stranger, she is unable or unwilling to accept that at its root lies her relationship to her own sexuality. Her fearful attraction to the sea in fact signifies the fascination and fear that her sexuality exerts on her. The sea as a symbol of the boundless and the unknown has long been associated with the irrational and the feminine. More specifically it has been related to female biology through water which represents woman's fluidity (blood, milk, tears).[27] This makes clear Ellida's association of the Stranger with the sea: both figures overlap precisely because they represent her unsettling but deeply compelling relationship to her sexual desire. The 'inexplicable power' that the Stranger has over her and the sea's hold over her senses are manifestations of a repressed, but existing sexuality. Because of the lack of a socially acceptable outlet, her sexual being can only surface as insanity. Consequently its manifestations are seen as symptoms of illness, also by Ellida, who for that reason seeks her husband's medical support. The scream 'Wangel – save me from myself' (p. 289) reverberates throughout the text. The self she wants Wangel to save her from is her sexual self. He is invited therefore to do what she has been unable to do – resolve the contradictions arising from her own ambivalent relationship with her sexual identity. As he admits 'this is no ordinary illness . . . for an ordinary doctor – or any ordinary medicine' (p. 297). Interestingly, however, his own attraction to Ellida lies in her symptoms: her changeability, instability, that is, her fluidity which makes her so much like the sea. Wangel, fascinated by and frightened of his wife, finally arrives at an understanding of her. As has been noted, the process by which he learns is extremely painful for Wangel.[28] For the first time he had to learn to listen to Ellida's speech instead of simply dictating to her what she needs or desires.

Wangel will renounce his authority as a man and a doctor and will let her decide for herself. This, however, far from marking his defeat, confirms his victory over Ellida. Schechner remarks that in her confrontation with the Stranger it is with herself that she is face to face. Her rejection of him, therefore, signifies her conquering of her 'daemonic urge to wander'.[29] Yet, to put Ellida's struggle with herself in metaphysical terms is equal to losing sight of the real nature of her conflict. This stems from her rejection, but also the simultaneous acceptance of the social norms which consider female desire unthinkable. The same applies to Ellida's 'wishes' as typified by the Stranger.[30] It is important to define these 'wishes' as sexual desire. Thus, there is nothing daemonic about her wandering which is simply an attempt to flee from prescribed roles into her individuality. In this sense her decision to stay with Wangel and integrate herself into the family confirms the defeat of her search for individuality in which her sexuality played the crucial part. Ellida's 'sanity' will be restored by Wangel who, as she says, has found 'the right remedy' (p. 329) for her. That this is her freedom within marriage makes even more visible the limits of the 'narrow zone'. As Ballested very appropriately remarks at the end 'human beings . . . can acclam – acclimatize themselves' (p. 330). Ellida acclimatizes herself to land, with a considerable loss, that of her sexuality. Her de-sexualization is represented by her severing of her link with the sea. The mermaid dies and from her ashes rises a new Ellida, a proper wife and mother. Ellida has truly come to her senses: she has now become a sane woman. In the clash between Wangel (the scientific mind) and Ellida (nature, the sea), the man wins.[31] For all his attraction to the lady of the sea standing for the irrationality and unpredictability of nature, he ends up taming her. The play ends with 'responsibility' sealing the victory of the rational.

The Lady from the Sea is one of the few Ibsen plays with a happy ending, and for that reason one of the most ambiguous. Ellida's survival is the other side of her final full adaptation to the social requirements of femininity. She is certainly a unique case amongst Ibsen's mentally 'unstable' heroines in that, having taken a trip into her own private world of fantasies, she manages to escape from it. Yet precisely like all the others, she enters the same world of self-denial, by renouncing a substantial part of herself. For Beata Rosmer, however, self-denial acquires its literal meaning, namely, suicide. Beata, the dead wife in *Rosmersholm*, is the real protagonist of a play predicated upon madness and death, guilt and retribution. As a figure of female insanity she resembles Ellida in three important respects. First, she has also been deprived of a child which, however, she was unable to conceive in the first place. Beata experiences childbearing as a debt she owes her husband, and her sterility in terms of a self-consuming guilt which finally drives her to self-destruction. Second, being faced with her sexuality which, in contrast with Ellida, she does not repress, she feels equally unable to contain it within socially acceptable limits. Sexual passion, even for one's husband, is clearly out of place within the patriarchal family identifying female sexuality solely with reproduction. In the context of such a family which recognizes a single dimension for women, i.e. motherhood, Beata is a failure, too. Third, precisely like Ellida, she is also pronounced mad by her own husband for similar reasons: her childlessness and her sexual desire. The difference is, though, that sexual desire in Ellida's case was not named as such but it was metaphored in terms of the sea/Stranger mysterious attraction. In this play, it is explicitly stated as the very source of Beata's 'insanity'. In the following dialogue between Rosmer and her brother Kroll, concerning the reasons for her suicide, the construction of a female 'madness' in terms of a woman's sexual being is sharply brought into focus.

Rosmer. . . . Can you ask for reasons for what an unhappy, irresponsible invalid may do?
Kroll. Are you certain that Beata was completely irresponsible for her actions? The doctors, at any rate, were by no means convinced of it.
Rosmer. If the doctors had ever seen her as I have often seen her, for days and nights together, they would have had no doubts. . . . . . . I have told you of her wild frenzies of passion – which she expected me to return. Oh, how they appalled me! And then her causeless, consuming self-reproaches during the last few years.
Kroll. Yes, when she had learnt that she must remain childless all her life.
Rosmer. . . . Such terrible, haunting agony of mind about a thing utterly beyond her control – . How could you call her responsible for her actions?[32]

Rosmer proceeds in two moves typical of the ways whereby he constructs his wife's insanity throughout the play. He starts by certifying the authority of his own conviction of her insanity in the face of evidence to the contrary. At this point he disregards medical opinion as well as Kroll's reliance on it. Later on, when Mortensgard, the editor of a radical newspaper, confronts him over the letter sent by Beata before she died to the effect that there were 'malicious' people at home wishing her husband's injury (p. 990), he dismisses again the journalist's suggestion that there was nothing wrong with her. He reasserts himself as the only authority capable of assessing Beata's stability, linking it again to her supposed lack of responsibility for her deeds (p. 991). Rosmer, by appropriating medical authority for himself and by rejecting other people's opinions, places himself in the position of the sole arbiter of Beata's moral accountability. Interestingly, for all his dismissal of the doctors' opinion, he relies on familiar medical tenets holding female biology as responsible for madness. Rebecca, echoing Rosmer, declares what only remains implicit in his account of his wife's 'madness'. In a similar attempt to prevail upon Madam Helseth's doubts over her mistress's insanity, she reasserts childlessness as the thing 'that unsettled her reason' (p. 1003). Psychiatrists at the time claimed that the end of a woman's reproductive cycle caused a tremendous mental upheaval accompanied by 'paroxysms' and 'extreme delusions'.[33] The ending of Beata's reproductive cycle, let alone its 'incompletion' for want of a child, directly inscribes her in the female biology-as-mental destiny discourse. This, by disconnecting psychic symptoms from the social context within which they appear, employs the biological as the only explanation for socially determined manifestations of disorder. In the light of the biological determination of the female mind, Rosmer's lack of understanding of his wife's traumatic experiencing of childlessness is not surprising. Yet even so, his rationale sounds particularly chilling and insensitive. He fails to see that Beata's depression and melancholia were forms of a socially determined sense of inadequacy as a woman. Trapped in marriage, the institution that has par excellence generated a female identity centred on motherhood, she is unable to cope with her situation as a childless wife. This she experiences as a structural contradiction within her own female-ness for lack of an alternative definition outside motherhood. Therefore, her fixation on her childlessness, rather than being proof of a sick brain, is a sign of an internalized compulsion to motherhood. Childbearing being impossible, Beata conceives of her place in her marriage as no-place, and of her self-destruction as a penalty for not having been a proper wife (p. 1019).

The second step that Rosmer takes in 'producing' his wife's insanity is the displacing of his own sexual problem. In a classic 'blame the victim' tactic he charges her for being too sexual while in fact he is not sexual enough. Typically again, in line with psychiatric attitudes of the time treating uncontrolled sexuality as the major symptom of female insanity,[34] he medicalizes his wife's physical needs. Borrowing directly from the vocabulary of madness, he calls her passion a wild frenzy, thus thinly disguising his own impotence in the face of female desire. Beata's sexual demands, safely consigned to the realm of aberration and irrationality, remain unsatisfied for no other reason than that they cause fear. Rosmer's dread of his wife's sexuality is concealed in the distorted picture of their relationship. There, sexual coldness is masked as idealism whereas her desire is presented as 'incontinence'.[35] The familiar polarity between man as spirit and woman as body is however undercut by a text which focusses on man's inability to enjoy the physical aspects of life. 'The Rosmer view of life' ennobles by killing happiness and women, in particular. It sublimates sexual desire by transforming it into spiritual vocation, while victimizing women for embodying it.

Rosmersholm marks the beginning of Ibsen's late drama, which revolves around the clash between the physical needs of life as represented by the female characters and the idealistic notion of one's calling to which the male protagonists adhere. Rosmer, Borkman, Allmers, Solness and Rubek see the female demands of love, affection and joy as inimical to their spirit; thus they come to associate women with the threat that the body poses to the spirit. For those male neurotics women, identified with sex (the death of the spirit), have either to efface or literally destroy themselves on the altar of male ambition. More emphatically than any other play, *Rosmer-sholm* shows the cruelty of male egotism, however 'idealistic'. Rosmer's sublimated sexuality demands the sacrifice of female desire to the 'higher' ideal of duty. It has condemned Beata to a life-denying existence and has killed Rebecca's passion for him. Their suicide is the ultimate gesture by which both women renounce their desire while at the same time purge 'the Rosmer view of life' of the stain of passion. However, Rosmer's self-destruction is not offered in atonement for his victimization of female desire. Opposite to the long enduring association of woman-as-sex-leading-to-death,[36] Ibsen establishes man in connection with death. For his denial of sexual gratification, man becomes a figure of death and as such haunts all Ibsen's late plays.

The Master Builder is predicated upon the same motif of man as death-dealing by virtue of his willingness to sacrifice the emotional and physical aspects of life in order to realize his amibitions. In so far as women represent the private world of warmth and affection they are profoundly injured by male life-denying ideals. Aline falls victim to a major contradiction that Solness faces: that between his search for happiness and his dedication to his calling as an artist. This is ultimately a conflict between the demands of the private and the public, experienced by him as completely irreconcilable. His choice of the latter results in the crushing of his wife, who, permanently fixed inside the private realm, is unable to compete with the claims that the public sphere makes on him. Typically, however, Aline internalizes Solness's inability to cope with private needs and projects it as her own. As a result of this, she withdraws into the personal world of guilt and self-reproach overwhelmed by a tremendous sense of inadequacy.

Aline, precisely like Ellida and Beata, considers herself a failure as a woman, an awareness similarly manifested as illness. The phantom of the dead child(ren) arises again as the apparent cause of what is clearly a case of melancholia. At first sight, frustrated motherhood seems to be Aline's fixation and the source of a constantly renewed sadness, providing another link with Beata. Yet, the similarity stops here because the death of her children *is not* that fixed idea which feeds her melancholia as Aline herself makes clear. While talking to Hilda about her misfortunes, she hastily corrects the young girl's impression that the loss of the two boys is her worst plight. Characterizing it as 'a dispensation of providence' to which 'one can only bow in submission',[37] she impatiently asks her not to talk any more about it. The two boys are 'happy' now, says she, and surprisingly focusses on 'the small losses in life' as the cause of her grief. It is the burning of the portraits, the old dresses, the jewels and then of the dolls that has retained a powerful emotional hold on her. The memory of the burnt dolls chokes Aline with tears. In a broken voice she tells Hilda the astonishing story of her nine dolls from which she never parted even after she had married, 'so long as he did not see it' and which 'no one thought of saving' (p. 363):

> For you see, in a certain sense, there was life in them too. I carried them under my heart – like little unborn children.
>
> (p. 363)

Yet what appears simultaneously with her odd yearning for the lost dolls is a resignation to the righteousness of divine punishment for what she calls her lack of fortitude in misfortune (p. 362). One is under the impression that a terrible guilt weighs upon Aline, the exact nature of which becomes clear in association with the story of the dolls.

Even from early on, in Solness's dialogue with Dr Herdal over the cause of Aline's sadness, the death of the children has been played down in comparison with the effect that the burning of her home had had on her. Solness implicitly acknowledges that this was definitely the worst blow for her. The burning of her home usurps the place that the death of her boys might have had, by right, in her depression; it has become the fixed idea around which a melancholic universe of bitterness, isolation and moral rigour has built up to trap her in. Her guilt therefore, stems from what she herself perceives as an obsessive attachment to her old home:

> *Mrs. Solness.* . . . I had duties on both sides – both towards you and towards the little ones. I ought to have hardened myself – not to have let the horror take such a hold upon me – nor the grief for the burning of my old home.
>
> (p. 330)

Guilt appears as the major symptom of her awareness that she had fallen short of the roles of a wife and a mother by improperly having stuck to her past from which she 'ought' to have cut herself off. As a married woman and a mother she 'ought' to have assumed a different identity, and repressed her girlhood. In this sense, her attachment to her dolls, significantly continuing even after her marriage, can be seen as a sign of an 'incomplete' transition to womanhood.[38] Young Aline's attachment to her dolls functioned as a substitution of girlish behaviour for that of an adult woman, whereas elderly Aline's emotionality is a form of regression:

> Regression is not a natural falling back into the past; it is an intentional flight from the present . . . But one can escape the present only by putting something else in its place; and the past that breaks through in pathological behaviour is . . . the factitious imaginary past of the substitutions.[39]

But what was that present that Aline wanted to escape from by holding on to her girlhood? It was her new identity as a married woman that she took flight from when carrying her dolls under her heart. The dolls, as a metaphor for a childhood that she had to relinquish, became central to a game of substitutions by which the woman-mother was replaced by the girl-mother, and the real children by simulations. The burning of the old house marks the end of substitutions, and consequently Aline's traumatic entry into adulthood. Elderly Aline speaks of motherhood and marriage in terms of duty, a word upon which her speech obsessively rests. Duty, and not love or affection, is the word that she chooses to describe her relationship to husband and children; this betrays the way in which even now she experiences adult femininity: a painful commitment to roles in patent incongruity with her real needs. 'It is only my duty to submit myself to him', says Aline about her husband, and continues: 'But very often it is dreadfully difficult to force one's mind to obedience' (p. 361).

There are times when her mind flies back to 'the small losses in life', and the heart grieves over the burnt dolls. Yet most of the time the elderly Aline manages to harness intellect and feelings into the yoke of female duty. Still, early in her married life, and at the critical moment, after the burning of her home, she had failed to repress her childish self. Childhood attachments though, turned into illness, and the mechanical commitment to a motherhood that she obviously did not enjoy, turned against her boys. Aline insisted on nursing them despite the fact that her milk was affected by fever. 'It was her duty, she said' (p. 339).

The little boys did not survive their mother's sick milk; they die 'poisoned' by their own mother who has been affected by her excessive depression over the loss of that part of her life which she could no longer claim. No wonder that in this chain of transgression and retribution Aline sees the hand of Providence, and her present misery as an atonement for her crime against her children. The three empty nurseries, standing for the three weeks the babies remained alive, stay there as the masochistic reminder of her failure as a mother. At the same time, however, they demonstrate that the borders between moral and social guilt and insanity are often difficult to discriminate. A rigorous sense of what her duty as a mother ought to be had compelled her into the insanity of breast-feeding when she was sick. Morbid guilt, in which the death of the children is superseded by her grief over her home, traps her into the discourse of melancholia. That, orchestrated by the word 'duty', is, however, meant as a gesture not only of self-reproach but also of aggression towards Solness. She annihilates his implicit demand for joy by constantly reminding him of what he is already painfully aware of: his debt to her. The burning of her home which gave him his life opportunity, fixed her once and for all into the state of a wife. Depression, withdrawal and illness appear, therefore, as forms of protest against prescribed roles. These blindly implicate man and woman in a guilt trip in which causes and effects, wrongdoers and victims, collapse into the same insane world of duty.[40]

With Hedda Gabler and Rebecca West, women's relationship to

received notions of femininity acquires a new dimension. Both of them react differently from Ellida, Beata and Aline, to their allotted identities. The latter have fully internalized their difference as mental illness, thus implicitly adhering to those very principles that constructed that 'illness'. In contrast with them, Hedda and Rebecca seem to revolt against feminine roles, and emphasize, with spectacular energy, their difference from them. The word 'madness' appears nowhere in association with them and yet both are inscribed in the discourse of mental disorder by virtue of their difference. However, as in his other plays, and in *Hedda Gabler* in particular, Ibsen keeps critical distance from such a discourse while giving its terms. He achieves this by concentrating on the social context which engenders female insanity; he makes it emphatically clear that the latter is a convenient socal category for what constitutes a resistance to familiar stereotypes.

Hedda and Rebecca appear to fall victim to their confusion over gender positions. This is obvious in the case of Rebecca, who is described by Kroll as an emancipated woman with the woman-as-a-man prejudice attached to it. The same idea is suggested through Hedda's upbringing as a boy and her handling of the pistols. Their divergence from the submissive stereotype of self-effacing femininity is marked by their relationship to power and their will to have their share of it. Both of them, faced with self-sacrificial women (Thea, Aunt Tesman, and Beata), display the same unwillingness to self-denial. As a result of their adherence to their individuality and of their defiance of gender expectations, they are forced into the area in-between masculinity and femininity, reason and unreason. Both resort to suicide; self-destruction in both cases demonstrating the limits of their resistance and the impasses of a quest for individuality fraught with contradictions.

Hedda and Rebecca typify Ibsen's conviction that women find themselves excluded from the social spheres of action, decision-making and power which are unquestionably men's territory. The tragic irony is that they are equally subjected to the middle-class rhetoric of individuality proclaiming the individual's right to freedom, to which, however, they are denied access. So their share of the world of freedom is limited to responsibility and duty without the concomitant prerogatives. In so far as femininity becomes synonymous with the lack of self-determination then its denial confirms, for the two heroines, their will to freedom. At the same time it asserts their individuality in the face of female conformity to established norms.

Hedda Gabler peers through the windows at the outside world of a freedom that only men are entitled to enjoy. Insomuch as freedom is a masculine prerogative she can have her share of it only by encroaching beyond the borders of femininity. Trapped in idleness and boredom by the constraints of her gender position first as a daughter and then as a married woman, she fantasizes the forbidden pleasures of masculinity; hence her intimate discussions with Lovborg and Brack. These enable her to gain vicarious access to the male realm of power, and, significantly, of sexual pleasure. Fantasy, 'the product of repressed sexuality, boredom and vacuity',[41] shields her from the painful awareness of her gender limits but only partly so. Caught between her fantasy existence as a substitute man and her female reality, she 'resolves' the contradiction by two interrelated gestures: she denies motherhood which would irrevocably bind her to femaleness, and she attempts to gain power control. Both moves, however, are self-defeating because they are already inscribed in the domain of personal relationships; they operate in the very same context of the private that has deprived her of self-determination. Devoid of any reference to the social, Hedda's 'revolt' is doomed to failure to the extent that it increasingly entraps her into the female yoke which she wants to escape. With pregnancy admitted at last to Tesman and her part in the Lovborg affair revealed to Brack, Hedda finds herself compelled to accept the roles of a mother and a mistress. Refusing to lay herself open to Tesman, Brack and her child-to-be, she kills herself. Her last words to Brack before withdrawing to the inner room, are a confirmation of her will to a freedom that she has to surrender to him now that he is in control:

Hedda. . . . So I am in your power, Mr. Brack. From now on you have a hold over me . . . At the mercy of your will and demands. And so a slave! A slave! . . . No! That thought I cannot tolerate. Never![42]

Yet that will to freedom was in fact the impossible demand of Hedda's self-determination within an institution which operated on the basis of female self-effacement. Hedda believed that she could benefit from the social and economic security of marriage while ignoring the attendant commitments. Having thoroughly accepted women's determination in and by marriage, and having embraced the expediency of its economic aspect – 'And since he insisted with might and main on being allowed to support me, I don't know why I shouldn't have accepted the offer' (p. 300) – she, however, tries to hold on to an individuality already refuted by the very premises of that same institution. That structural contradiction in her identity as a woman remains unresolved since the two aspects of herself, Hedda as the individual and as the wife, are felt to be diametrically opposed and, therefore, irreconcilable. Hedda does not wish their reconciliation precisely because she values her individuality as circumscribed by her maiden past, over her present identity as Tesman's wife. The presence of the inner room with the portrait of General Gabler and her old piano, as well as of her father's pistols, confirms her will to retain her individual space amidst foreign territory. Insomuch as the possession of a room and objects of her own reasserts her adherence to a past clearly defining her individuality, any trespassing upon it is seen as violation of her independence.

Hedda's desire for privacy, her odd habits such as shooting, and her withdrawal from the Tesmans' society, draw the portrait of an introverted and an essentially unsocial 'unit'.[43] These very same features were treated by the psychiatry of the time as the typical characteristics of female insanity. Central to this view is the threatening figure of a woman as an individualist who is engrossed in self-concern and refuses care for others. The individualist woman, for her lack of altruism and devotion to others, is thought to be both unnatural and insane. Female egotism, considered a major sign of insanity, relegates the 'selfish' woman to the area of hysteria and neurasthenia. In the context of prescribed gender roles and of medicalization of their aberrations Hedda's egotism can only appear as monstrous and insane, for what it really is: an inadequate, almost pathetic, means by which she safeguards her independence from the intrusion of familial relationships to which she is bound through marriage. Hedda's repulsing of Aunt Tesman's affection marks her unwillingness to let the others have a share of herself. Physical and emotional intimacy are threatening to the extent that they can break into the private self and crush it under the weight of personal demands for care and commitment. Her sexual coldness towards her husband, and her loathing of her pregnancy signify her refusal to open up and let herself be invaded by an alien body. That body, be it her husband's or her baby's, would deprive her, as it does, of her individuality in that it would subsume her under the type of self-sacrificial mother and devoted wife. So when Brack suggests motherhood as something that would be 'a serious claim' on her and 'one full of responsibility' she curtly answers: 'I have no gift for that kind of thing, Mr Brack. Not for things that make claims on me' (p. 306).

However, for lack of social forms which could accommodate her protest against feminine behaviour, Hedda's reaction is manifested as 'illness'. Neurosis appears as a result of the irreconcilable conflict btween woman's quest for individuality and the internalized demand to fulfil the ideal of a submissive femininity.[44] Yet the ineffectualness of female illness as a form of revolt against woman's estate was never clearer than in Hedda's case. Hedda, deeply divided by the above conflict, finds destruction as the only available means by which she can claim her individuality. The burning of the manuscript, Thea's and Lovborg's child, has been interpreted as a sign of Hedda's inferiority complex with regard to Thea's rich femininity. The spiritually sterile woman takes revenge upon her emotionally fertile rival, who, though barren, gives birth to a 'child', the product of a free union between two emancipated individuals.[45] The opposition between sterility and fertility, the physical child and the intellectual child, serves here as a metaphor for proper and improper femininity; hence value judgements as to the superiority of Thea's 'rich' femininity over Hedda's physical and emotional poverty. By the same token, the rebirth of Thea's 'child' from the rescued notes can be seen as the triumph of a female essence synonymous with everlasting fecundity, over 'destructive' forms of resistance to it.

Yet Ibsen is careful not to attach value judgements to his two female characters. Instead, he emphatically draws attention to a male world in which women survive only in passivity. For all her defiance of public opinion, Thea is equally a victim of female stereotypes. Through her and Aunt Tesman, Ibsen exposes the opposite effects of women's subservience to men. Both women are devoid of a self precisely because they exist as supports to male aspirations. The book, rather than the product of the equal union of two free individuals, stands for the opposite: it exemplifies Thea's passive position in a creative process to which she simply provides the inspiration. Apart from *being* Lovborg's inspiration she *does* little. She puts down what he dictates to her while making sure she provides for his needs. Lovborg uses the word 'need' very appropriately to refer to her position within a relationship that he is the one to dictate. One could argue that he chooses his words carefully in order to impress upon her the necessity of their parting. Later on, he acknowledges their common contribution to the book but, significantly, it is Thea who calls it a child, associating the intellectual process with female reproductiveness and the idea of life (p. 342). Since Thea's 'rich' femininity endows her with an infinite reproductive capacity, no wonder that she will finally restore herself to the same position of inspiration and helper, vis à vis another man this time. Thea will do her 'best' to inspire Tesman laying herself open to his intellectual insemination.[46]

In this context the burning of the manuscript by Hedda acquires a different meaning. Far from signifying her envy for a fecund femininity it is meant as a gesture of annihilation. What she seeks to annihilate through a form of sympathetic magic is Thea's influence over Lovborg. When he admits to that influence – 'it is the courage to live, and to challenge life, that she has broken in me' – she expresses both her envy and wonder at such a thing: 'That pretty little fool has played her part in a human being's fate' (p. 342). Thea's real contribution to the production of that book lay not so much in its writing as in her reforming Lovborg. Thea's role was to impose discipline on a creative energy so far dissipated, and channel it towards 'proper' productive purposes. By doing so she managed to destroy what Hedda most admired in Lovborg: his courage for living, his passion for life. The book therefore is for Hedda living proof of Thea's power over another human being, that she feels she is devoid of. To see the burning of the book only as a substitute child-murder is to inscribe again Hedda's behaviour in the fecundity–sterility discourse. As she makes clear to Thea it is power that she is after: 'I want, for once in my life, to have power over a human being's fate' and then she adds:

> . . . Ah, if you could only realize how poor I am. And here are you, offered such riches! [*Throwing her arms passionately round her.*] I think I shall burn your hair off, after all.

> (p. 324)

That scene has been interpreted in terms of Hedda's jealousy of Thea's femininity as symbolized by her abundant hair. Yet it follows directly Hedda's attempt to gain control over Lovborg by making him drink; abstinence from drinking marking his reformation and thus Thea's power over him. So the riches that Thea is offered refer to her experiencing of power and not of the physical and emotional aspects of her relationship with Lovborg. Hedda's revulsion at 'that sentimental word', love (p. 299), underscores her distancing from the feminine world of emotionality, and her affiliation with the masculine realm of power. She asks Lovborg agonisingly twice whether she has any power over him (pp. 316, 320), brushing aside his tentative suggestion that after all there must have been love 'at the bottom' of their past relationship. No doubt she has proved that she has an enormous capacity for passion, but not of the physical kind. Her real aphrodisiac has always been power; yet her relationship to power has been deeply contradictory.

As a woman who prefers the passionate and energetic life of men to female passivity, she has tried to ignore differences by assuming a 'male' identity. Being raised by her father as a boy in a home where the position of the mother is vacant, she engages in riding and shooting. Furthermore, through her intimate conversations with young Lovborg she is offered 'a glimpse of a world . . . that one isn't allowed to know about' (p. 317). Yet her 'hunger for life', that is for free and pleasurable activities, as already mentioned, is satisfied through substitutes. Having essentially accepted the necessity of substitute action for real action, she derives from the external signs of masculinity the illusion of power. Thus her threatening of Brack and Lovborg with her pistols is meant as a gesture rather than truly wielding power. As Mayerson notes, Hedda does not even shoot straight until her suicide.[47] At the same time, however, her handling of the pistols signifies her willingness to enter into competition with men over power. Not accidentally the two men that she threatens are Brack and Lovborg, those whom she sees as holding, or potentially acquiring, some kind of power over her. Still she fails to shoot in both cases precisely because she does not dare to convert her will to power from gesture into action. The ineffectual nature of her gesture is underscored by Brack's description of her shooting as the playing of a game (p. 296). Precisely as Hedda plays the role of a man in her fantasies of male revellings so does she play at being the aggressive competitor of 'other' men in a game of power.

With Brack and Lovborg the fight was for her own control; with Thea, the competition is over Lovborg, power in this case, taking for her the more feminine form of 'influence'. Her will to power, being void of any social dimensions, turns into the obsessive demand to determine a human destiny; therefore, it identifies Hedda's relationship to power as strictly private. In this sense, the burning of the manuscript is an act exemplifying the a-social and insular character of the pathology of the personal. It is the crossing over of the borders of reason and sociality at the same time. It also represents the climax of a range of deviant practices from spying on Thea and Lovborg and prying in their affairs, to downright lying and naked manipulation. Her ultimate destructive move was to send Lovborg to what she imagined would be his death. So next to Hedda's other 'sick' characteristics 'moral insanity' could be added as the finishing touch to this portrait of female disorder. 'Moral insanity', a Victorian term, is 'a morbid perversion of natural feelings, affections, inclinations, temper, habits, moral dispositions, and natural impulses, without any remarkable disorder or defect of the intellect'.[48]

'Moral insanity', an extremely wide concept encompassing all kinds of deviations from standard practices rather than medical symptoms, clearly illustrates the social need to medicalize aberrant behaviour. Ibsen refrains from doing so in Hedda's case, too. What he does in *Hedda Gabler* is to indicate the failure of society to give the notion of sexual difference a non-oppressive meaning for women. At the same time he displays the tragic implications for a woman's inner life of her refusal to accept difference in its association with oppression; ironically, he also suggests that the implications would be equally tragic, though of a different order, if she accepts it. Hedda finding it at last impossible to disentangle herself from her feminine position, will finally use her pistols, those symbols of her individuality, against herself. 'Male' Hedda kills the pregnant Hedda asserting thus once and for all the individual over the mother. Through death she achieves what she was incapable of while alive: the ceasing of her oscillation between accepting and resisting her position as a woman. Her suicide is a supreme gesture of defiance on the part of the individualist Hedda towards her conformist self. At the same time, as a form of child-murder, it confirms her 'egotism': the child will be sacrificed to the mother, rather than the mother to the child. Hedda manages at last to 'resolve' her conflict.

Yet women's conflict with their identities in Ibsen's drama is never truly resolved. Death simply gives an end to a tortuous awareness of not fitting into gender stereotypes; by no means does it constitute a resolution. On the contrary it is the ultimate form of self-abnegation reinscribing the Ibsenian individualists into the very same sphere of female self-efface-ment which they had resisted. Even Hedda's suicide, essentially an act of self-assertion, is a tacit avowal of defeat. Hedda collapses under the weight of contradictions intrinsic to her unsure position with regard to femininity. The same applies to Rebecca West who, having equally dis-played a ruthless egotism, resorts to self-destruction after having openly acknowledged defeat.

One might wonder why Rebecca is included in this consideration of mental disorder in Ibsen's heroines. There is nothing in *Rosmersholm* to suggest that Rebecca is merely a representation of a robust consciousness of the type of Hilda Wangel; at least this is how Rosmer hails her: as the quintessence of mental health. That would be the case if there were not a strange passage worth quoting in detail. Kroll accuses Rebecca of using her influence over his sister so as 'to get a footing at Rosmersholm':

> *Rebecca.* You seem utterly to have forgotten that it was Beata who begged and implored me to come out here?
> *Kroll.* Yes, when you had bewitched her to. Can the feeling she came to entertain for you be called friendship? It was adoration – almost idolatry. It developed into – what shall I call it? – a sort of desperate passion. – Yes, that is the right word for it.
> *Rebecca.* Be so good as to recollect the state that your sister was in. So far as I am concerned, I don't think any one can accuse me of being hysterical.
> *Kroll.* No; that you certainly are not. But that makes you all the more dangerous to the people you want to get into your power.
>
> (p. 1010)

Interestingly the word 'hysterical' seems to pop out from nowhere. Nobody has accused Rebecca of being hysterical and yet the word surfaces in her speech for no apparent reason. Yet, the language that Kroll uses to describe her influence on Beata draws in fact the portrait of the hysterical woman; Rebecca's denial of being hysterical is an acknowledgement of Kroll's implicit point. He immediately denies that he has suggested that, yet the point has been made. Kroll charges her with having 'bewitched' Beata making her feel 'adoration', 'idolatry' for her, the 'right word' being 'passion'. So Rebecca has inspired passion in Beata, not friendship. Pas-sion sounds odd in the context of a female 'friendship'; it carries a faint air of homosexuality. Yet, not only does she arouse passion in others but she is victim of her own passion, too: a 'wild, uncontrollable passion' for Rosmer, that came upon her as 'a storm on the sea' and caught her in a whirlwind (p. 1026). At the same time, Kroll refers to her will to power that makes her dangerous. Passion and power merge in that picture of unorthodox femininity which by contemporary standards would be sub-sumed under the category of 'hysteria'. In an account of female hysteria, it was noted that hysterical girls were energetic and passionate, 'exhibiting more than usual force and decision of character, of strong resolution, fearless of danger . . . having plenty of what is termed *nerve*'.[49]

Indeed Rebecca is presented as fearless and energetic, passionate and resolved; in other words, she appears to straddle the borders of sexual difference. Precisely like Hedda she is her father's daughter. Mother is somewhere in the picture, yet her position in Rebecca's life has also remained vacant. Rebecca may not have been brought up as a boy by Dr West. However, she has been infiltrated by his emancipated ideas about individual freedom and rights irrespective of gender. As a woman she has reached her thirties without getting married and having children. The liminality of her position within the context of fixed gender roles is underscored by her living in a triangular relationship to the Rosmers without filling the familiar space of a mistress. Furthermore, Rebecca displays a singularly 'unfeminine' energy and initiative. She fights 'a life-and-death struggle' (p. 1026) with Beata over Rosmer using a series of ruthless tactics to gain control. First, she breaks her will by exerting a tremendous influence on her, and then she drives her 'crazy' by implanting into her mind the obsessive idea that she is redundant. Beata's suicide is the outcome of the cold-blooded plan to conquer Rosmer, conceived and callously executed by Rebecca. As Rosmer admits, Rebecca was stronger than Beata and him together (p. 1026). What arises from that reversal of sexual positions by which the woman becomes the man through her association with power and desire is the figure of the hysterical woman:

> What does psychoanalysis listen in hysteria? A problem of sexual identity in phallic terms: the hysteric is unsure as to being woman or man, 'the hysterical position – having or not having the phallus' . . . She is in trouble with her position as a woman, simultaneously resisting and accepting the given signs, the given order.[50]

The problem however, with this type of definition is that it seeks to explain a psychic situation on the basis of the very same logic that has produced it. The assumption is that a woman wants to possess the phallus, that signifier of power and desire, but, being trapped into her gender, she cannot have 'proper' access to it; as a result of that she becomes 'ill'. Yet what remains unexplained are the social conditions which made possible the attaching of that signification to the phallus, and determimned sexual difference in terms of having it or not. So our concern cannot be whether Rebecca was hysterical or not. The crucial thing is that she could be considered so in terms of standardized ideas about sexual difference; even more importantly, that she had obviously internalized them to the extent that she wonders about her being hysterical. Precisely like Hedda she is torn between her adherence to her individuality as demarcated by current morality, and her increasing recognition of the power implicit in the latter. In this sense, Kroll's suggestion of an

incestuous affair between her and Dr West[51] was decisive in her rapid
conversion to moral principles which she had consciously fought.

Heredity as the cause of moral insanity – as Kroll puts it 'the moral
antecedents' that determine her 'whole conduct' (pp. 1011–12) – makes its
impressive entry into a consciousness already on the verge of collapse.
Rebecca's slow erosion by the ethics of the Rosmer view of life resulted in
the loss of her power long before her suicide. That power, described by her
as a fearless will that 'knew no scruples' (p. 1026), was broken down: 'I
have lost the power of action' (p. 1027) she says, thus pinpointing the very
nature of her difference from the stereotypes of passive femininity. That
her loss of power and thus of her individuality was synonymous with the
erasing of that difference becomes clear when she talks of 'the great self-
denying love' (p. 1028) for Rosmer. Self-denying love supplanted her wild
passion by 'ennobling' it. In reality passion was sacrificed to Rosmer's
'noble', that is a-sexual, view of life. Only by sexually 'mutilating' herself
could Rebecca fulfil his major, yet implicit demand on her: the surrender-
ing of her second mark of individuality, her uncontrollable passion to his
higher 'ideals'. Brendel's heavily symbolical speech brings into focus
Rebecca's sexual 'mutilation' as the absolute precondition for loving him:

> The woman who loves him shall gladly go out into the kitchen and hack off
> her tender, rosy-white little finger . . . Item, that the aforesaid loving woman –
> again gladly – shall slice off her incomparably-moulded left ear.
>
> (p. 1033)

This has been interpreted as the sacrifice of sexual gratification to the
idea of mission, the finger standing for the symbol of the male organ,
whereas the ear stands for the female.[52] Yet the text is firm on this point:
the finger belongs to Rebecca. As for the sacrifice, it is far from mutual:
Rosmer was never endowed with any desire to deny. Consequently the
demand for the castration of desire is wholly addressed to her. If, however,
we accept the phallic symbolism of the finger, then what is required of her
is the relinquishing of power and desire, and ultimately her 'feminization'.
Indeed Rebecca takes up her position in the ranks of self-abnegating
women once she relinquishes the signs of her difference. With these gone
she becomes like Beata and she goes the same way that she went. Furthermore, she finds 'a horrible fascination' (p. 1035) in Rosmer's suggestion of suicide thus wholeheartedly embracing the woman-susceptible-to-
life-denial stereotype. Rosmer after all was the strongest of all.

Rebecca follows Hedda, Beata, Aline and Ellida on the same path to
self-destruction. The fact that Ibsen presents her revolt as a conscious
reaction to dead ideas makes its outcome all the more tragic. The reason is
that it brings into focus the contradictions intrinsic to the search for a
female identity outside the constraints of gender. All these women, living

in a society which required uniformity in the face of strictly defined notions of femininity, were victimized for being different. Their psychic and mental world collapsed as the result of the pressure of roles either conceived outside their real needs (Hedda, Ellida, Aline), or creating those needs (Rebecca, Beata). All of them, having found it impossible to surrender themselves to the prescribed roles, became 'mentally ill' and finally destroyed themselves. Ibsen, using mental illness as a metaphor for female revolt, demonstrates its ineffectualness before the dominant logic of institutional practices such as marriage and family. However, his tremendous insight into their operation makes it also emphatically clear that a society that confronts the challenge of difference by resorting to the category of 'illness' is itself 'sick'.

NOTES

1 John Northam, *Ibsen. A Critical Study* (Cambridge: Cambridge University Press, 1973), p. 150.
2 Ibid., pp. 150, 151.
3 Ibid., p. 150; same emphasis on Hedda's dislike of pregnancy as a symptom of abnormality (p. 155).
4 Ibid., p. 169; see also pp. 162, 167.
5 Ibid., p. 152. See also Stein Haugom Olsen, 'Why Does Hedda Gabler Marry Jorgen Tesman?', *Modern Drama* 4 (December 1985), 597, and Caroline W. Mayerson, 'Thematic Symbols in *Hedda Gabler*' in *Ibsen. A Collection of Critical Essays*, ed. Rolf Fjelde (Englewood Cliffs, NJ: Prentice-Hall, 1965), pp. 132–4, for the same contrast between Thea's rich femininity as symbolized by her abundant hair and Hedda's sterility. Both critics, while conceding Thea's insignificance and passivity, stress her courage to break with social convention in order to fulfil herself as a woman. Mayerson (p. 133), implicitly comparing her with Hedda, even calls her 'the most emancipated person in the play', a feature that seems to her in radical opposition with Thea's 'palpitating femininity'.
6 Mayerson, 'Thematic Symbols', p. 132.
7 *The Times*, 21 April 1891, cited in Michael Egan, *Ibsen: The Critical Heritage* (London: Routledge and Kegan Paul, 1972), pp. 218–19.
8 *Saturday Review*, 25 April 1891, ibid., p. 223.
9 'An Ibsen Success – *Hedda Gabler* at the Vaudeville', *Pall Mall Gazette*, 21 April 1891, ibid., p. 220.
10 From a review by Clement Scott, *Illustrated London News*, 25 April 1891, ibid., p. 227.
11 *Observer*, 26 April 1891, ibid., p. 230.
12 *The Times*, 12 May 1891, ibid., p. 246.
13 From an unsigned notice, by Clement Scott, *Daily Telegraph*, 21 February 1893, ibid., pp. 270, 271.
14 *Evening News and Post*, 21 February 1893, ibid., pp. 274–5.

15 'Unchastity may *à la rigueur* be held to result from a neuropathic condition' says the anonymous critic with reference to Rebecca West finding it, however, an inadequate explanation of her behaviour (*The Times*, 24 February 1891, ibid., p. 164).

16 *Referee*, 17 May 1891, ibid., p. 250.

17 Irene, in the *When We Dead Awake*, obviously belongs to the same category. However, she is not included in this article because she exists more as a symbolic projection of Rubek's repressed self than in her own right. Therefore, she belongs more in the area of male psychic problems and especially of those related to men's relationship to the 'female' part within themselves, synonymous with physical gratification, or 'the joy of life'. Irene, the repressed female self of Rubek, returns to destroy the male Rubek, the artist.

18 Stephen Heath, *The Sexual Fix* (London: Macmillan, 1982), pp. 7–12.

19 Ibid., p. 25.

20 Henrik Ibsen, *The Lady from the Sea* in *Ibsen: Plays*, trans. Peter Watts (Harmondsworth: Penguin, 1978), p. 244. All references to the play cited in the text by page number are to this edition.

21 For psychiatric Darwinism see Elaine Showalter, *The Female Malady: Women, Madness and English Culture, 1830–1980* (London: Virago, 1987), pp. 101–20, and for the organic etiology of mental illness, Michel Foucault *Mental Illness and Psychology*, trans. Alan Sheridan (1976; rpt. Berkeley: University of California Press, 1987), pp. 1–14. Showalter's is an excellent study of the medical and social discourses and institutional practices within which female mental disorder was inscribed, produced and reproduced; I am indebted to Showalter.

22 Elinor Fuchs, 'Marriage, Metaphysics and *The Lady from the Sea*', *Modern Drama* 3 (September 1990), 438.

23 Ibid., p. 437.

24 Ibid., p. 438.

25 Ibid., p. 463. Ellida's language is a language with no response, which becomes clear in Ibsen's directions (p. 282) that she gazes into the pool 'now and then talking to herself in broken phrases'. She talks to an imaginary interlocutor who is herself.

26 Michel Foucault, *Madness and Civilization*, trans. Richard Howard (1965; rpt. New York: Vintage Books, 1989), pp. 85–8.

27 Showalter, *The Female Malady*, p. 11.

28 Fuchs, 'Marriage, Metaphysics', p. 439.

29 Richard Schechner, 'The Unexpected Visitor in Ibsen's Late Plays' in *Ibsen. A Collection of Critical Essays*, p. 161. Alfred Schwarz, *From Büchner to Becket* (Athens, Ohio: Ohio University Press, 1978), p. 198, also refers to the 'daemonic' will of Rebecca West, Ellida, and Hedda Gabler, using, precisely like Schechner, a metaphysical term for the female quest for individuality.

30 Schechner, 'The Unexpected Visitor', p. 160.

31 For the sexualization of science as masculine and of nature as feminine in western scientific and philosophical athought see Evelyn Fox Keller, 'Gender and Science' in *Discovering Reality: Feminist Perspectives on Epistemology, Metaphysics, Methodology, and Philosophy of Science*, ed. Sandra Harding and Merill

B. Hintikka (Dordrecht, Holland: D. Reidel Publishing Company, 1983), pp. 187–92.

32 Henrik Ibsen, *Rosmersholm* in *Eleven Plays of Henrik Ibsen*, trans. H. L. Mencken (New York: The Modern Library), p. 979. All the references to the play cited in the text by page number are to this edition.

33 Showalter, *The Female Malady*, p. 59.

34 Ibid, p. 74.

35 For Rosmer's sexual coldness as resulting from his philosophy of life see Arthur Ganz, *The Realm of the Self* (New York: New York University Press, 1980), pp. 160–1; also Leo Lowenthal, 'Henrik Ibsen: Motifs in the Realistic Plays' in *Ibsen. A Collection of Critical Essays*, pp. 148–9, for the problematic area of sexual relationships in Ibsen.

36 For the association of woman with death through sex as established by Christianity and assimilated by western culture see Beth Ann Bassein, *Women and Death. Linkages in Western Thought and Literature* (Westport, CT: Greenwood Press, 1984), pp. 18–43.

37 Henrik Ibsen, *The Master Builder* in *Eleven Plays by Henrik Ibsen*, p. 361. All references to the play cited in the text by page number are to this edition.

38 Schechner, 'The Unexpected Visitor', p. 162, reads the dolls as Aline's lost love and innocence, sacrificed to male aspirations. Ganz, *The Realm*, p. 158, sees the nine dolls as standing for the months of pregnancy, and signifying the destruction of life that the putting of male ideals before the family entails.

39 Foucault, *Mental Illness*, p. 33.

40 In the text 'duty' clearly arises as the symbol of 'the sickly conscience' (p. 348) that the Solnesses possess and which both of them experience as illness (insanity). That is also Hilda's view of them, who, as the representative of a 'robust conscience', throws into relief by her mere presence the sickliness of their minds.

41 Showalter, *The Female Malady*, p. 64, draws attention to women's dependence on their inner lives as a result of passivity and boredom. Their engrossment in the personal makes them victim to depression and mental breakdown.

42 Henrik Ibsen, *Hedda Gabler* in *Hedda Gabler and Other Plays*, trans. Una Ellis-Fermor (Harmondsworth: Penguin, 1985), p. 362. All references to the play cited in the text by page number are to this edition.

43 My account of those features which, at the time, were held to characterize female hysteria and neurasthenia has been taken from Showalter, *The Female Malady*, pp. 132–4.

44 Ibid., p. 144.

45 Northam, *Ibsen*, pp. 165–9, and Mayerson, 'Thematic Symbols', pp. 132–3.

46 Kay Unruh Des Roches in 'Sight and Insight: Stage Pictures in *Hedda Gabler*', *Journal of Dramatic Theory and Criticism* 5 (Fall, 1990), 64, underscores Thea's lacking of character by focussing on Ibsen's directions concerning the use of lighting in the closing of scene: 'She now shines again, albeit by a reflected light. This, that Tesman and Thea do not shine by their own light, is as close as Ibsen comes to a condemnation of them. Yet it is enough.'

47 Mayerson, 'Thematic Symbols', p. 136.

48 Eric T. Carlson and Norman Dain, as quoted in Showalter, *The Female Malady*, p. 29.
49 F. C. Skey, as quoted ibid., p. 132.
50 Heath, *The Sexual Fix*, p. 47.
51 Thomas R. Whitaker, *Fields of Form in Modern Drama* (Princeton, NJ: Princeton University Press, 1977), p. 44, refers to Freud's conviction that actual incest took place between Dr West and Rebecca who, after discovering it, is driven to suicide. An earlier draft of the play was clearer on this point; yet the final text also vaguely suggests such a possibility.
52 Ganz, *The Realm*, p. 161.

Representing mad contradictoriness in *Dr Charcot's Hysteria Shows*[*]

DIANNE HUNTER

Jean-Martin Charcot (1825–93) was an important figure in the legitimizing of secular power as philosophical and medical positivists gained control of administrative centers in nineteenth-century France. Though Charcot had made significant contributions to medicine before 1870, when he became director of the Salpêtrière, the Paris public asylum for women, he is remembered by feminists primarily for his work on hysteria at the Salpêtrière, where he advanced his career by staging spectacular demonstrations of his ability to hypnotize and control patients. Charcot's widely publicized contributions to the hysteria diagnosis, which increased dramatically during his tenure as hospital director, were for him and his followers a way of attacking demonic possession and religious ecstasy, and of getting institutional control of hospitals and schools taken away from the Catholic Church. That is, Charcot's work on hysteria contributed to an anticlerical campaign promoting the triumph of positivism.[1]

In his obituary of Charcot, Freud describes him as a *visuel*, someone for whom sight is the dominant mode of knowing; and Freud reports Charcot's supreme satisfaction in naming and classifying clinical facts.[2] As part of his positivistic method, Charcot commissioned draftsmen to make sketches of hysterics in action on the Salpêtrière wards; and he founded a photographic studio at the hospital. Charcot's disciples Paul Régnard and Desiré Bourneville produced two journals, the *Iconographie Photographique de la Salpêtrière* (1875–77), and the *Nouvelle Iconographie de la Salpêtrière* (1888–1918), disseminating a visual record of hysteria.[3]

This historical drama in which priests and positivists contested administrative power at the site of the female body, and in which the winner was a man with a powerful gaze, a magnetic personality, the authority and space to exhibit and interpret unruly women, and the technology to mechanically reproduce their images was the starting point for what evolved into four separately produced versions of a dance theatre performance titled *Dr Charcot's Hysteria Shows*. This essay will describe

[*] A draft of this paper was presented at the *Themes in Drama* Conference held at the University of California, Riverside, in February 1991.

aspects of the genesis of the piece, some of the thinking behind it, and the staging strategies of the first production, a work-in-progress performed at Trinity College, in Hartford, Connecticut, in 1988; and of the third production, performed at the Ohio Theatre in New York City in 1989. I was coauthor of and a performer in these productions, for which I also served as dramaturg.[4]

I

The genesis of the work was in a research project on gender and creativity carried out by a faculty group at Trinity College: Performance artist Lenora Champagne, dancer and choreographer Judy Dworin, dance historian Katharine Power, and I, a psychoanalytic feminist literary critic, shared an interest in the theme of the female body in performance and in doing research via our own bodies. Hence when I brought reproductions of photographs of the Salpêtrière hysterics to this group, we decided to physically enact the postures we saw represented in the photographs and then try to describe and analyze the postures on the basis of our subjective impressions. Though we saw the Salpêtrière hysterics as other than ourselves, I also felt that I could recognize in their situation precursors of elements foregrounded in twentieth-century feminist theory, especially film theory and psychoanalytic feminism. Influenced by the idea that the fascination exercised over late twentieth-century feminists by the great hysterics of the nineteenth century takes root in their suggestiveness as metaphors or threshold figures for the women's liberation movement, of which they are the inverse, we acted on the basis of the theoretically unfashionable notion of a transhistorical female body whose positioning and expressivity could be decoded through subjective identifications. I regard the idea of using physical replication to get in touch with the meanings, energies and latent intentions of the Salpêtrière hysterics as our enabling fiction; perhaps it can be described in retrospect as an example of the role of illusion in symbol-formation. As a feminist, I was attracted to the idea of reclaiming the hysterical body from its enclosure in fixed images, and of seeing where the energy and power I felt in the Salpêtrière poses would go if it were free to move. I wondered about the significance of the word 'movement' in the phrase 'women's movement' and how that significance might be related to hysterical movement.

In the spring of 1986, Champagne, Dworin, Power, and I met with movement-analyst Brad Roth to investigate the iconography of hysteria at the Salpêtrière. Since most people in this group were interested in movement, we started with pictures that form parts of sequences, for example the set photographed by Albert Londe called 'Sense Suggestions in the Cataleptic Period of Grand Hypnosis' (figures 3 and 4). Ignoring the title, we simply analyzed the first four positions as if they were part of a dance. The woman lifts up her arms, but she is either getting up from her chair or about to sit down, and she is half holding her arms down. Next she is seated and prays, but her body is twisted off-center. Still seated, she lifts her skirt to reveal a contortion of her legs in an effect of genital closure, which creates, however, an opening at her ankles. Then she is standing with her hands protecting her genital area while drawing attention to it.

We next turned to Paul Richer's chart of the sequence of postures he saw comprising what Charcot believed were the four phases of a regular attack of grand hysteria (figures 5 and 6). We focused on Row J for enactment. What we found in the first position in Row J elaborated on the tension we saw in the contra-lateral pose 2 in the Londe set, a tension, as we saw it, between spirituality and sexuality expressed in a contradiction between the upper and lower body. In pose 1 below the line in Richer's Row J, the attitude is one of prayer, but the petitioner has her body arranged as if she is searching uncertainly with her upper body for the addressee of her prayer, while her lower body pulls in a different direction; her knees point one way, her torso and arms another. In the next posture, the body reclines with head facing in one direction, while the knee is bent on that side and turned away as if to protect the genitals. The figure looks toward and pulls her lower body away from a fixed point in space, as if in response to someone who has come into the room where the figure reclines. In the next position, she holds her arms over her breasts while twisting her lower body as if her upper body were detached from the accessibility of the lower body. Upon enactment, this third posture seemed to us to be acting as though one were giving in to penetration while at the same time not giving in, through detaching and protecting the upper part of the body from what is happening to the lower part.

In the next position in this sequence, pose 4, the figure points in a fashion that suggested to us accusation, and with her other hand displays a fist. This is followed by enactments of postures suggesting withdrawal of energy into the self, backing away and then standing up while backing away, which is however, in turn, reversed in the next pose by an opening out into a wide movement, legs apart, mouth open, arm extended in a way that suggests Delacroix's 1830 painting, *Liberty Leading the People*. In the final two positions in this sequence, the figure extends her hand as if to be kissed, then draws it away in a sudden refusal, her gaze extending, however, toward the implied addressee of her gesture.

Though we had initially intended to try for strictly dance notation and anatomical description of this movement sequence, and indeed, had invited Brad Roth to join our group because of his training in Labanotation, we soon began talking about seduction and agreed that the final part of Row J of the Richer sequence represents a caricature of feminine

Pose 2

Pose 1

Pose 4

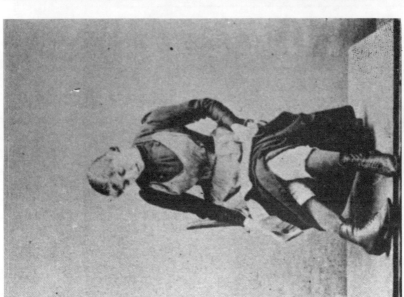

Pose 3

3 and 4 Photos: Albert Londe, 'Suggestions par les sens dans la periode cataleptique du grand hypnotisme' (1891), from an article by Guinon et Wolke, *Nouvelle iconographie de la Salpêtrière*; reproduced from Didi-Huberman, *Invention de l'hystérie*, p. 226

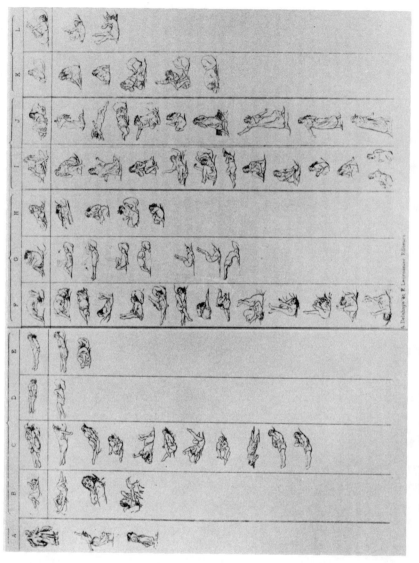

5 Paul Richer, *Etudes cliniques sur la grande hystérie*, 2nd edn (Paris: Delahaye & Lecrosnier, n.d.)

role playing. The figure poses as the object of a powerful gaze while playing subversively with her pose. What Charcot classified as the 'passionate attitudes' phase of hysteria, we interpreted as poses in an angry game miming a contradictory drama of submission, seduction and retreat. We felt that a spectator was built into the movements, and that the represented figure signaled a desire to communicate, but wished to baffle her observer. In the first three positions of Row J in particular, we felt a secret was being staged that put the observer into the role of a voyeur, subject to covert sexual excitement. As the sequence continued, we felt that the figure accused, withdrew, advanced, and then became frustratingly seductive, mocking the role of being the sexual object of another's gaze, acting instead as a fascinatingly repulsive subject/object who disconcerts her viewer by suddenly saying no.[5]

With this interpretation we felt we had the starting point for a scenario about patriarchal sexual politics. We decided to develop through improvisation a dramatization of what we imagined the women who were the models for Richer's figures might have been trying to say. Their images were voiceless, and we wanted to give them words, wishing to fill the gaps we felt in their communications by providing a context that would make their postures intelligible. Taking the postures to their conclusion involved us in performing them in a theatre, not only because of the way the poses have an implied spectator built into them, but because of the way Charcot, at the end of his career, succeeded in theatricalizing madness for medical theory.

As Mary Russo has written of the Salpêtrière photographs, they are hyperbolic and can be read as double representations. They are 'mimicries of the somatizations of the women patients whose historical performances were lost to themselves and recuperated into the medical science and medical discourse which maintain their oppressive hold on women'.[6] This medical mimicry doubles hysteria as simulated illness; and so, recognizing the Salpêtrière photographs as male-authored artistic representations, we decided to treat them as though they were real and at the same time to contextualize them as cultural constructions.

In playing with hysterical mimesis we hoped not to reduce ourselves to it, but to explore and clarify the space in which women were exploited by Charcot's discourse. By deliberately assuming the role of the feminine-as-the-surveyed, we were submitting ourselves to ideas that have been elaborated according to the logic of male domination; but our intention, similar to what Irigaray has said of femininity as masquerade, was to make visible by an effect of playful repetition and contextualization what remains practically invisible in Charcot's theory: a possible operation of female social rebellion.[7]

We decided to animate the figures in the photographs and drawings in a

6 Richer sequence, Row J enlarged

fashion that could comment ironically on Charcot's verbal explanations of hysteria and on his role as a dominating, charismatic figure whose psychiatric authority was fraudulent, yet an advance on the clerical theory of demonic possession. We felt that making a credible drama out of the epidemic of hysteria associated with the Salpêtrière required a central male figure playing the role of a charming prick, a role similar to that played by Jacques Lacan in Jane Gallop's *Feminism and Psychoanalysis: The Daughter's Seduction*.[8]

As a basis for our work, we assumed that Salpêtrière hysteria was a kind of angry, coquettish, self-repressed dance; that this dance was dominated by an attractive paternal figure; that this figure objectified what he saw and reserved for himself the privilege of naming it; and that he took great satisfaction in displaying his hypnotic magnetism, power to dominate, emotional distance, and verbal fluency. Our project was to subvert Charcot's objectifying pose as a lecturer and to show how his involvement with hysteria undermined his position as a medical authority.

Since we saw Charcot as a symbol of male dominance and repressiveness, we thought he should have various male reflectors as part of his drama, so we developed parts for Freud, Dr Breuer, and Charcot's assistant, Dr Babinski. At the same time, we wanted to dramatize Charcot's own hysteria and its connection with his own histrionics, so we paired him with the figure of Sarah Bernhardt, who served as a mediator between Charcot's fame and the melodramatic poses of a group of hysterics with personal histories connected to the history of women's struggles to overcome their position of being dominated and silenced. We wanted the drama to end in collective rebellion spurred by the articulation of rebellious speech spilling into rebellious movement as the result of collective female mutual gaze, culminating in tearing up Salpêtrière photographs and then their ritual burning.

Since we wanted to demonstrate how hysteria is the result of a shared, unconscious structure charged with anxiety, pleasure, and dismay for both the histrionic patient and the observers, we thought the best vehicle for our performance would involve environmental staging. We hoped to undermine Charcot's confident verbal commentaries on his patients by devices such as exaggeration, slides, music and dance, with which we hoped to appeal to the imagination and emotions of our audience. In order to work out a playable scenario for this, Champagne, Dworin, Roth, and I worked with environmental set designer Jerry Rojo and a performance ensemble of students in an undergraduate Theatre and Dance seminar, 'Representing Hysteria', which culminated in a work-in-progress performance of *Dr Charcot's Hysteria Shows* in April 1988.

II

The first part of this production began in the lobby of Trinity's Arts Center, where, after purchasing tickets, the audience could absorb a display of photographs and simulated artifacts conveying historical information about the context of hysteria as used in the performance. The environment of the lobby showcased paraphernalia from contemporary media. A TV camera, lighting instruments, electrical cable and monitors set the stage for a Victorian Ladies interview, which served as the prologue and was the first acted scene of the piece. This environment mixed historical and contemporary images leading the audience back and forth in time, to unite the contexts of past and present. The show business, media-hyped atmosphere was designed to excite the audience to become searching and aggressive in its desire to take in the surroundings. The interview scene was played among the spectators, blurring the line between audience and performers, and set the tone for the production style, which encouraged the spectators to experience and perceive themselves as performers sharing the hysterics' stage space. While three Victorian women characters answered questions on their roles as respectively, Lady of the House, Governess, and Maid, a Wild Woman interjected unruly shouts from a stairwell above them, counterpointing their sedateness with exhibitionist movements and loud laughter; and she twice descended the stairs to break into the scene by attacking the assistant interviewer.

The second part of this production invited the audience to the Arts Center's main proscenium theatre, where a Lecture–Demonstration was presented. Actors appearing as newsmen in the Prologue had been transformed into Dr Charcot and his assistant, Dr Babinski. Now the audience took part in a formal and conventional theatre environment with a single frontal relationship between audience and performers. The presence of a live, compact, attentive, orderly, arranged audience was supposed to emphasize Charcot's charisma. Like the historical model, our Dr Charcot was in an ideal position to demonstrate his ideas and to exercise tactics of mind-control and persuasion on a passive audience.

The third and final section of this production used yet another part of the Arts Center's theatre complex. The audience was invited to a small 'black box' theatre adjacent to the main stage used for the Lecture–Demonstration. The black box theatre had been radically transformed into a very complex environment especially constructed for the section of our performance titled 'The Wards'. The room was completely filled with a variety of playing levels up to six feet high, stairways, aisles, underpasses, runways, and three banks of diagonally facing, tiered audience-seating areas containing ninety fixed seats. Once members of the audience were seated they could not move around in the space. The frontal gaze arranged for the Lecture–Demonstration was now fragmented as performances took place throughout the space in a carnivalesque style in specially designated areas and amidst the audience. The effect was that while this arrangement allowed for good center-focus sightlines, many of the scenes were played in areas where the spectators had a variety of vantage points from which to watch. At times, simultaneous action was played around the room, forcing the spectator to choose what to observe, further fragmenting the audience's gaze. The spatial metaphors established by this set worked to suggest the activity and content of the scenes. For example, a runway leading to a stage was reminiscent of a cabaret situation; and the semi-circular tiered seating suggested the dynamics of a medical theatre.[9] Spectators looked down on much of the action, rendering most poignant the distress of the hysterics in their private worlds on the wards. The function of this part of the piece was to engage the audience in the richness and complexity of the patients' fantasy lives and to open to view a shared, unconscious set of images.

'The Wards' climaxed in an hysterics' ball in honor of Charcot's saint's nameday, during which the patients offered fruit to the audience. In a final ritual the hysterics emerged from their poses in eerie slow motion in a T'ai Chi-like way we hoped would suggest the birth of the cinema out of moving pictures as well as the coming to life of the photographs. Upon stirring from their fixed poses, the hysterics ran through the space in a dance in which the environmental set was used as a percussion instrument. Though the set was sturdy, it did not seem that way as the audience felt their chairs vibrated by the stamping performers at the end of the piece. The last image of this performance was of one lone hysteric performing the poses of row J in a column of light against a background of stomping, accompanied by unearthly synthesized sound – a single middle A-note that ceased before the final pose (figure 7).

III

This first version of our performance proved to be emotionally powerful, yet we felt a greater coherence would be welcome overall and especially in 'The Wards', where some members of our original audience were bewildered by our attempts to dramatize the shared unconscious. While we were determined to have the finale take a nonlinear form, we felt that the emotional intensity we achieved in 1988 depended in large part on the environmental set built for part III, a set impractical to recreate for the short run we planned for the New York performances the following year; so we decided to stick with a visually diffuse and carnivalesque staging for the Wards sequences, and yet at the same time to develop a more coherent

7 Judy Dworin as Isèlle, last scene of *Dr Charcot's Hysteria Shows*, Ohio Theatre, New York City, 1989. Photo: Vivian Selbo

'through line' that would narrate in a more intelligible way what we took to be the significance for us of Charcot's staging of hysteria and the imagery we associated with it, and that would as well plot means of escaping and expelling Charcot's power.

We had arrived at the conclusion that 'grand hysteria' mimes profoundly disorganizing emotions in order to communicate them to a spectator perceived as powerful; that such hysteria displays an anarchy of parts, a contradictory, ambivalent relation to gender, to the body and to authority; and that miming gender anarchy and anatomical anarchy, hysteria goes beyond words in a grotesque display managing to be simultaneously alluring, comedic and disturbing. We wanted to stay with this interpretation of hysteria and keep the disorganizing effect of our first production; but we also wanted to tell a comprehensible story that would put hysterical display into an historical context within which we could ritualize expulsion of paralysis and move toward transcendence of, or flight from, the twisted forms of creative expression we saw in the poses.

To this end, our 1989 production enlarged what had been a small display of artifacts to include photographs of all the female hysterics posed, in costume, with what purported to be case histories. To our more extensive display of still images we added a video tape which included players representing Freud, Cassandra, Charcot's Augustine/Freud's Dora, Herr K., and actresses announcing themselves as the Moser sisters, the daughters of Freud's patient Emmy von N. Simultaneous with the video in the PreShow ran eighty slides projected by a revolving carousel on a 5-second timer. This show included Salpêtrière photographs and drawings, slides of paintings by the Belgian surrealist Paul Delvaux, which we chose for their somnambulism, frozen eroticism, and mordant views of sexual politics; and various images we had drawn on in developing the imaginary world of the piece, including Fuseli's *The Nightmare*, Robert-Fleury's *Pinel Delivering the Madwomen of the Salpêtrière*, the cover photograph of Hélène Cixous's novel *Souffles* (which turns Fuseli's *Nightmare* upside down, into an image of a woman in flight), and various representations of Ophelia, Freud, Lacan and Charcot. This visual barrage was designed to show the iconic inscription of patriarchally-prescribed sex roles, and the relationship between hysteria and the cultural dissemination of powerful images linking female sexuality with madness and with spectacle.[10]

In 1989, in place of the Victorian Ladies prologue, we substituted a dance of three witches interrupted by a witch brought in by a procession of priests and burned at the stake, in a position suggesting the end of Richer's Row J, followed by a dialogue between Florence Nightingale and her mother, who stood as if joined at the back arguing in overlapped speeches about Florence's role as a woman and her vocation as a nurse.

8 Brad Roth as Dr Breuer reaches towards Anna O. (Allison Friday) sitting in her cell with Isèlle (Judy Dworin) and Blanche Wittman/Odette (Leah Garland). Photo: Vivian Selbo

Then followed in quick succession four emblematic scenes leading up to the Lecture–Demonstration: 1) A Dance of the Orange, in which two young girls toss an orange back and forth until a young boy catches their orange and runs away with it, the two girls chasing after him. 2) Rosalie crosses the space singing 'Liese, Lie Down' and carrying a bowl to her father, who lies in bed. As she kneels to feed him, he pulls her down, and after a noisy struggle in which Rosalie gasps for breath, he climbs on top of her and mimes orgasm. 3) Lights come up in a different area of the playing space where Bulimia stands in front of a mirror retching and examining her body. 4) Rosalie's father presents her to Charcot for treatment. Then the audience was herded into the medical theatre for the Lecture–Demonstration, kept largely as it was in 1988. To the Wards section, played within cagelike frames of wood and wire and softer enclosures of tobacco netting, we added a dancing master, played by the male actor from the PreShow Dance of the Orange, who doubled as a male hysteric in the Lecture–Demonstration and as Dr Breuer in a staging of Freud's Irma dream and in emblematic dance sequences on the Wards. In one sequence, for example, from within an enclosed and veiled cell (figure 8) where she sits with Isèlle and Blanche/Odette, Berthe/Anna sings, 'All the king's horses and all the king's men couldn't put Humpty together again.'

Breuer [*at the periphery of the cell*]. Why don't you drink, Anna? Aren't you thirsty?
Anna. Who are you?
Breuer. It's Dr Breuer. Anna, touch me.
Anna. Jamais acht nobody bello mio please lieboehn nuit. Give me some melon, please.
[*Breuer holds up an orange.*]
There's a darkness in my head. I can't think. I'm blind and deaf. I'm evil and real. I'm thirsty, but I can't drink because the dog lapped water from the soupbowl.
Breuer. What's the matter with your arm?
Anna. Snakes! [*Screams incomprehensibly, speaks gibberish, and laughs seductively.*] Welcome to my private theater. Here we perform the talking cure. Chimney sweeping is how we get the dirt out! [*She pants as he approaches her and lies down and imitates giving birth. Isèlle and Odette assist her delivery.*]
Breuer. What's the matter, Anna?
Anna. I'm having a baby! Dr Breuer's baby!
[*Breuer turns round and round in circles, and then falls to the ground.*] Is it a boy or a girl?
Isèlle. It's a girl!
Chorus of Voices. Ah!!

Pas de Deux

[*Isèlle comes out of the cell to the rescue of Breuer.*]

Breuer. Who am I?

Isèlle. You are what I say. [*She shapes his body.*]
[*Music: Pierre, the Dancing Master's theme.*]
Breuer. Who?
Isèlle. What I say.
Breuer. I say.
[*During this next exchange, Breuer shapes Isèlle into Richer's row J, position 3, as she struggles against his domination:*][11]

Isèlle:	*Breuer:*
What . . . who . . . am I say	Who am?
I . . .	Say . . .
I say . . .	You?
Who am?	What I say . . .
Who?	What?
Who . . . am I?	You are what I say.
	Who am I?
Who am I?	You are my pain.

[*The hysterics begin running, hitting the walls and trying to get through 'doors'. They run until they are distorted and their inner anxiety is converted to physical signs/symptoms.*]

This scene was followed by a staging of Freud's dream of 23–24 July, 1895:

[*Slide: Schloss Belle Vue*]
Freud. A large hall – numerous guests were arriving. Among them was Irma. I took her to one side and said to her –
[*Dr Pierre Marie shines a flashlight into Isèlle's mouth.*]
If you still get pains, it's your fault. . .

After a scene with each of his patients Dora and Emmy von N., Freud appeared at Charcot's *bal des folles* in the final section of the piece, which staged a conspiracy by the hysterics, their rebellion, and the escape of the hysteric Augustine disguised as a doctor during festivities ostensibly celebrating Charcot's nameday but which turned out to be his expulsion. Charcot was hissed off the stage and his chair was overturned by Isèlle (figure 9).

The verbal climax of this performance was a monologue spoken in the character of a modern Cassandra by the performer who played Breuer's patient Anna O. in preceding scenes. Here, in twentieth-century costume, she addressed her rage to an image of Jacques Lacan projected over Charcot's upset chair. Cassandra's evoking the power of the female gaze seemed to release in slow motion the hysterics from their poses, and the piece ended as it had in the first version:

Cassandra. Doctor, do you mind if I take more than five minutes? My research hasn't been going very well lately. I keep working in fits and starts. But my mind keeps wandering – to women of the past. I'm caught in a preoccupation with precedents. I find the extremism of Greek tragedy appeals to me – the unselfconscious enacting of emotion, the resort to violence – Medea, for instance. Although I came to her in a roundabout way.

9 Isèlle (Judy Dworin) hisses Dr Charcot (Jaroslav Stremien) from his chair on the wards. Desirée (Debra Walsh) looks on. Photo: Vivian Selbo

10 Jaroslav Stremien as Dr Charcot introduces a case of hysteria during the Lecture–Demonstration in *Dr Charcot's Hysteria Shows*. Dr Babinski (Christos Balis) stands behind him. Projected onto the scrim at the back is a slide of Robert Fleury's *Pinel Delivering the Madwomen of the Salpêtrière* (1878). Photo: Vivian Selbo

11 Debra Walsh as Desirée demonstrates the gesticulations and frightful poses of a 'Demoniac' during the Lecture-Demonstration. Dr Charcot (Jaroslav Stremien) interprets her. Dr Bliss (Norman Bliss) serves as her attendant. Photo: Vivian Selbo

12 Blanche Wittman (Leah Garland) gasps for breath as Dr Charcot (Jaroslav Stremien) explains to his audience at the Lecture–Demonstration the traumatic origin of '*globus hysterectus*, a ball in the throat'. Dr Babinski (Christos Balis) and Dr Bliss (Norman Bliss) assist. Photo: Vivian Selbo

13 Dr Bliss (Norman Bliss) and Dr Babinski (Christos Balis) subdue outpatient Marie-Odile Floque (Dianne Hunter) at the end of Dr Charcot's Lecture–Demonstration. Photo: Vivian Selbo

14 At the *Bal des Folles* celebrating Dr Charcot's nameday, Charcot (Jaroslav Stremien), Showman and Healer, Promenades between Sarah Bernhardt (Lenora Champagne) and Florence Nightingale (Katharine Power). Photo: Vivian Selbo

[*She turns and begins addressing Dr Marie and then moves to Pierre, the Dancing Master.*]
I was searching the stacks under Greek tragedies and I came to Medusa. I must have gotten them confused. I'd read something by Hélène Cixous where she'd talked about sight and power, and how women can't look men straight in the eye, and until they can they will always be submissive.
[*to Albert Londe, the photographer*] Well, if men looked at Medusa, they were turned to stone. She had hair made of snakes and she turned men to stone. I started thinking, hey, this is pretty phallic – I mean, snakes! – we all know about them, and stone, which is hard – see what I mean?
[*The hysterics, catching one another's gaze, slowly get up.*]
Then I came across Freud's piece on Medusa, where he argues that her power to turn men to stone is in fact her power to make them erect and immobilize them in the sphere of public action. [*Weird droning sound.*] Anyway, I started looking for a play that resembled Medusa, and I found it – *Medea*, of course. Medea is expressive in a contorted way, and she's destructive to others as well as her self. She's like Medusa in that she has to be turned away from. Her demands/crimes are unreasonable; and she is incapable of passivity.

I had such a visceral response to it all. One absorbs feelings of powerlessness at abandonment/betrayal, so that one acts out despite the strongest codes of demeanor.
[*Sarah Bernhardt has begun passing photographs to the hysterics. The photographs seem to move in slow motion among the performers. The droning sound becomes more insistent. Once the photographs have made the rounds among them, the hysterics begin to move in slow motion.*]
I feel admiration for Medea's having the abandon to express her rage. Medea/Medusa has the power to frighten, to act, to be vengeful – whether consciously as outraged or unconsciously as victim. I find myself craving revenge . . .[12]
[*Blanche Wittmann gives Cassandra a photo.*
Desirée laughs.
Cassandra tears a photograph. The other hysterics begin tearing theirs. The performers move back and forth in initial confusion and then run through the space, throwing the torn pieces of photographs into the cauldron. Augustine, Rosalie, and Louise (the initial three witches from the PreShow) end up around the cauldron, which Rosalie sets on fire. Music: droning A-note. All the performers coordinate into a stamping rhythm. Isèlle walks out and performs Richer's Row J.]

IV

Within its context of the intellectual vogue hysteria has had within late twentieth-century psychoanalytic feminism,[13] I think our work, work largely on and of iconographic politics, indicates that Charcot and his hysterics became for us vehicles for expressing the mad contradictoriness of what it means to be a woman in a man's world. In describing her response to the Ohio Theatre production, reviewer Mady Schutzman wrote that the men and women in *Dr Charcot's Hysteria Shows*

force the spectator into the murky territory of gender. To observe on the one hand the convulsive contortions, animalistic sexuality, and . . . rage of the hysterics, and on the other hand, . . . the note-taking balletic refinement of the black-tuxedoed, white-aproned, psychic surgeons, is to participate within a painfully self-denigrating reality. That is, watching these primitive female grotesques amidst the civilized male aesthetes incites . . . two antagonistic sensations in the female spectator: first, a disturbing personal/historical recall of hysterical objectification that triggers a re-traumatization filled with inexpressible anger, terror, fear, and depression . . . Second, the internalized stance of the male gazer that accompanies, perhaps propagates, the very despair and rage that hysteria is made of. Women watch themselves through the eyes of the ubiquitous male presence; they are accompanied by an image of themselves which represents a cultural standard, a specular mold. Finally, in this state of renewed and traumatically heightened ambivalence, when the spectator is goaded by the performers' seductive offerings of delectable fruit, one doesn't know if the simple pleasure to be derived in accepting and indulging is worth the humiliation of saying 'yes'.[14]

In sum, in exposing the repression and contradictoriness that the iconography of the Salpêtrière expresses, *Dr Charcot's Hysteria Shows* involved our audience in a ritual designed to undermine the gender hierarchy out of which we believe hysteria is generated and maintained. The medical hierarchy of doctor and patient became for us a metaphor of the dilemma of being split subjects whose femininity belongs to the cultural domain of the surveyed.

NOTES

1 Jan Goldstein, 'The Hysteria Diagnosis and the Politics of Anticlericalism in Late Nineteenth-Century', *Journal of Modern History* 54 (June 1982), 209–39.

2 Sigmund Freud (1893), 'Charcot', *The Standard Edition of the Complete Psychological Works of Sigmund Freud*, trans. and ed. James Strachey (London: Hogarth Press, 1962), vol. iii, pp. 11–23.

3 These journals are stored in the Charcot Library at the Salpêtrière Hospital and at the Bibliothèque Nationale in Paris, as well as in large medical school libraries throughout the world. Good reproductions of some of the plates can be found in Georges Didi-Huberman, *Invention de l'hystérie: Charcot et l'iconographie photographique de la Salpêtrière* (Paris: Macula, 1982), which develops the thesis that Charcot theatricalized hysteria.

4 *Dr Charcot's Hysteria Shows* was created by Lenora Champagne, Judy Dworin, Dianne Hunter and an ensemble of undergraduate students as part of an interdisciplinary seminar in Representing Hysteria taught at Trinity College during the spring of 1988. The following spring Champagne, Hunter and Dworin taught a seminar in 'Words and Movement', in which the performance was developed with a second group of students in preparation for New York production in June 1989. The performances were directed by Champagne and Dworin. The scenery was designed by Jerry Rojo, with assistance from Ed Haines. The music was composed and performed by André Gribou. The lighting was designed by Tracy Eck. The choreography was by Dworin. The

dramaturgy was by Hunter. The costumes were designed by Liz Prince. The text was drawn from the works of Christos Balis, Josef Breuer, Lenora Champagne, Jean-Martin Charcot, Hélène Cixous, Catherine Clément, George Frederick Drinka; Judy Dworin, Henri Ellenberger, Sigmund Freud, Dianne Hunter, Jan Goldstein, Cynthia MacDonald, Fanny Nightingale, Florence Nightingale, A. R. G. Owen, J. B. Pontalis, Elisabeth Roudinesco, Anne Sexton, Elaine Showalter, Christine Spellman, Lytton Strachey, Etienne Trillat and Gerard Wajeman.

In addition to a workshop performance at the New York Theatre Workshop in 1989, *Dr Charcot's Hysteria Shows* was produced at Austin Arts Center, Trinity College, Hartford, 1988, 1989; Oberlin College, 1989, the Ohio Theatre, New York City, 1989; and the Bronson and Hutensky Theater, Hartford, 1989.

It was previewed/reviewed on Massachusetts Public Radio, 14 April 1988; and on National Public Radio, 2 June 1989; and in *The Hartford Courant*, 15 April 1988, 13 October 1989, and 14 October 1989; in *Artforum*, September 1989; in *Women & Performance* 5:1 (1990); and in *Theatre Journal* 42:2 (1990).

The Ohio Theatre performers were

Christos Balis..............Dr Joseph Babiński
Norman Bliss ....Dr Norman Bliss
Camille Carida............Witch, Augustine, Dora
Lenora Champagne.....Sarah Bernhardt
Allison Dubin..............Witch, Rosalie
Judy Dworin ....Witch, Isèlle
Allison Friday ....Fanny Moser, Berthe, Anna O., Cassandra
Leah Garland..............Mentona Moser, Blanche Wittmann
André Gribou..............Sigmund Freud
Dianne Hunter............Priest, Marie-Odile Floque, Dr Pierre Marie
John Marinelli.............Priest, Albert Londe
Toni Oram..................Witch, Bulimia, Geneviève, Louise
Katharine Power.........Florence Nightingale
Brad Roth ....Young Boy, Philippe, Pierre, Dr Josef Breuer
Jaroslav Stremien........Dr Jean-Martin Charcot
Debra Walsh...............Fanny Nightingale, Desirée, Emmy von N.

5 For discussion of transformation of a similar scenario in Freud's early development of psychoanalytic theory, see Martha Noel Evans, 'Hysteria and the
Seduction of Theory', *Seduction and Theory: Readings of Gender, Representation, and
Rhetoric*, ed. Dianne Hunter (Urbana and Chicago: University of Illinois Press,
1989), pp. 73–85.

6 Mary Russo, 'Female Grotesques: Carnival and Theory', *Feminist Studies/Criti-
cal Studies*, ed. Teresa de Lauretis (Bloomington: Indiana University Press,
1986), p. 223.

7 Luce Irigaray, *This Sex Which Is Not One*, trans. Catherine Porter with Carolyn
Burke (Ithaca: Cornell University Press, 1985), p. 76; originally published as
Ce sexe qui n'en est pas un (Paris: Minuit, 1977).

8 Jane Gallop, *Feminism and Psychoanalysis: The Daughter's Seduction* (London: Macmillan, 1982), p. 36.

9 My description of the set for the 1988 work-in-progress draws on unpublished

production notes by the designer Jerry Rojo, '*The Hysteria Project, Post Mortem*, Fall 1989, comments about *Dr. Charcot's Hysteria Shows*, Environmental Settings and the *Mise-en-Scene*.'

10 For a history of iconographic bonds between female sexuality and insanity, see Elaine Showalter, 'Representing Ophelia: Women, Madness, and the Responsibilities of Feminist Criticism', *Shakespeare and The Question of Theory*, ed. Patricia Parker and Geoffrey Hartman (New York and London: Methuen, 1985), pp. 77–94.

11 This scene uses Gerard Wajeman's analysis of hysterical discourse in *Le Maître et l'hystérique* (Paris: Navarin/Seuil, 1982), pp. 11–30.

12 Cassandra's speech was adapted from an unpublished monologue written by Christine Spellman.

13 A sample of recent psychoanalytic-feminist commentary on hysteria includes: Charles Bernheimer and Claire Kahane, eds. *In Dora's Case: Freud–Hysteria–Feminism* (New York: Columbia University Press, 1985). Catherine Clément and Hélène Cixous, *The Newly Born Woman*, trans. Betsy Wing (Minneapolis: University of Minnesota Press, 1986), originally published as *La Jeune Née* (Paris: Union Générale, 1975); Joan Copjec, 'Flavit et Dissipati Sunt', *October* 18 (Fall 1981), 21–40; Mary Ann Doane, 'The Clinical Eye', *Poetics Today* 6:1–2 (1985) 205–27; Martha Noel Evans, *Fits and Starts* (Ithaca: Cornell University Press, 1991); Stephen Heath, *The Sexual Fix* (New York: Schocken Books, 1984); Dianne Hunter, 'Hysteria, Psychoanalysis, and Feminism: The Case of Anna O.', *The (M)other Tongue*, ed. Garner, Sprengnether, and Kahane (Ithaca: Cornell University Press, 1985); Joanna Isaac, 'Mapping the Imaginary', *PsychCritique* I:3 (1985), 187–203; Mary Jacobus, *Reading Woman* (New York: Columbia University Press, 1986); Claire Kahane, 'Hysteria, Feminism, and the Case of *The Bostonians*', *Feminism and Psychoanalysis*, ed. Richard Feldstein and Judith Roof (Ithaca and London: Cornell University Press, 1989); Elaine Showalter, *The Female Malady: Woman, Madness, and English Culture, 1830–1980* (New York: Pantheon, 1986); Carole Smith-Rosenberg, 'The Hysterical Woman: Sex Roles and Role Conflict in Nineteenth-Century America', *Social Research* 39:4 (1972), reprinted in *Disorderly Conduct* (New York and Oxford: Oxford University Press, 1985); Sharon Willis, 'Hélène Cixous's *Portrait de Dora*: The Unseen and the Un-scene', *Theatre Journal* 37:3 (October 1985), 287–301.

14 Mady Schutzman, '*Dr. Charcot's Hysteria Shows*', performance review in *Women and Performance: A Journal of Feminist Theory* 5:1 (1990), 186–7.

Blanche Dubois and Salomé as New Women: old lunatics in modern drama*

KAARINA KAILO

All women become like their mothers. That is their tragedy. No man does, that is his.

(Oscar Wilde)

Tennessee Williams and Oscar Wilde both challenged the stereotypes of sex-appropriate behavior and of 'madness', creating thought-provoking 'New Women' in *A Streetcar Named Desire*[1] and *Salomé*.[2] My purpose in this paper is to compare the two classic lunatic women of modern drama, Blanche Dubois and Salomé, who occupy the opposite ends on the spectrum of 'female' madness. The muteness of Blanche's self and voice contrasts with Salomé's assertive verbal force, her insatiable oral-sadistic desire to kiss and incorporate the source of prophetic power – Jokanaan's mouth.

On one level these 'New Women' are of course mouth-pieces for Williams's naturalism and symbolism, and for Wilde's decadence. However, the increased complexity with which they reanimate the old stereotypes, the damsel in distress and the castrating bitch, provokes us to delve deeper into the dramatized female reality. Critics have touched upon the feminist or matriarchal subtexts of the plays to some extent but the seven veils of Salomé's dance have not all been lifted.[3] The subtle references to pre-Christian mythology, the hypothetical matriarchal roots of modern drama in *A Streetcar Named Desire* have likewise received scanty attention. The tragic fates of Blanche and Salomé can in my view be fruitfully approached through the lens of the Greek myth of Demeter and Kore. This is a myth which women have now reappropriated – and to some extent even reinvented – in their search for an alternative to the Oedipus paradigm with its male-specific model of psychic reality. The matriarchal myth can also be seen as a pre-Oedipal counterpart to the Freudian myth which derives 'normality' from the resolution of the phallic stage, valuing the mode of detachment–separation from the mother over the symbiotic stage with its alternative symbolism.

* A draft of this paper was presented at the *Themes in Drama* International Conference held at the University of California, Riverside, in February 1991.

To the extent that modernist plays diverge from the Aristotelian model with its attributes of 'masculine linearity', great tragic heroes, the Apollonian values of enlightenment and catharsis, they are in relative terms neo-Dionysian and 'feminine' in spirit – or, should we say – body and mind. In the feminine moonlight, the relationship between text and reader, a play and a spectator is no longer governed by detached, or vicariously self-indulging voyeuristic observations, unilinear projections of our own fantasies and fears, but with a momentary fusion with the psyche and world of another. Both plays are bathed in an alluring, lurid moonlight that casts self-revealing shadows behind the characters. Moonlight is the 'master' trope in both plays; the image of a paper-moon is an apt symbol for Blanche's frail selfhood since she fears the glaring exposure, Stanley Kowalski's penetrating male gaze. Salomé's perversion also comes to a head, the climactic demand for male castration, in a gloomy lunar atmosphere. I offer then that we immerse ourselves in the moonlight perspective of the plays, in which they were written, to lend a contrast to the critics who have penetrated them with the alternative, Apollonian paradigms of sight. This mode does not so much substitute the Apollonian for an idealized Dionysian or matriarchal visioning, as it consciously aims to blur the gaze, so we might, paradoxically, see better. I am referring to the 'other' bisexual writing and responses of women and of mother-identified men; responses based on double identification, double vision, a double sense of time.[4] C. G. Jung, whose aesthetic theories express the values of the pre-Oedipal rather than the Oedipal model, is one of the few male theorists to have discussed the relevance of the Demeter/Kore myth to women. He writes:

> It is immediately clear to the psychologist what cathartic and at the same time rejuvenating effects must flow from the Demeter cult into the feminine psyche, and what a lack of psychic hygiene characterizes our culture, which no longer knows the kind of wholesome experience afforded by Eleusinian emotions.[5]

In a nutshell, the Demeter/Kore myth is a dramatization of women's cyclical psychic journey through life from a state of fusion and uninterrupted bonding with the maternal psyche to the pain of separation of self and m/other.[6] Women's matriarchal rites, the Eleusinian ritual, are the prototype of the subsequent Christian myth of death and resurrection, of a symbolic descent into one's inner being, followed by a new awareness of self and other. Patricia C. Fleming, in discussing the ritual significance of the myth, wonders:

> Is not Eleusis the scene of descent into the darkness, and of the solemn acts of intercourse between the hierophant and the priestess, alone together? Are not the torches extinguished, and does not the large, the numberless assembly of

common people believe that their salvation lies in that which is being done by the two in the darkness?[7]

The tragic lunacies portrayed by Williams and Wilde can be seen to result from the unresolved tensions between two enraptured and enraged anti-couples: Blanche and Stanley, Salomé and Jokanaan. In terms of the psychic mysteries, both plays dramatize the hierophant's and the priestess's moonlight encounter. Whether we think of the rape under the paper moon, or of the beheading of Jokanaan in his dark cistern, in both plays we are participating at a ritual release of Dionysian forces.[8] However, why do the 'New Women' fail in their ritual ravishment and why is their search for a voice of their own doomed from the start?[9]

The myth at the basis of the Eleusinian Mysteries (the Homeric 'Hymn to Demeter') details Demeter's response to the abduction of Persephone by Hades, god of the underworld. The pre-Oedipal stage of girls' development is dramatized in the myth by the initial bliss which Kore experiences in the bosom of nature. One day she was gathering flowers when she suddenly noticed a narcissus of striking beauty. She ran to pick it, but as she bent down, the earth gaped open and Hades appeared. He seized her and dragged her with him down into the depths of the earth.[10] Jung notes that 'the Demeter–Kore myth exists on the plane of mother–daughter experience, which is alien to man and shuts him out' and notes that 'the psychology of the Demeter cult bears all the features of a matriarchal order of society, where the man is an indispensable but on the whole disturbing factor'.[11] It is appropriate from a matriarchal perspective that Williams and Wilde should fantasize their 'New Women' as victims of rape or failed ravishment. Whether we interpret Zeus and Hades literally as men or as the principles of patriarchy and the shift of consciousness from rapturous eros to ravishing logos, they break the mother–daughter bond in its most hermetic form and bring the notion of lack into the female consciousness. In the myth, Demeter, the goddess of grain, reacts to this loss by depriving the earth of its fertility; during her mourning for Kore nothing grows and famine spreads. This represents what happens, collectively and individually, when we are cut off from our inner daughter, whether we interpret her as our future potential, our Self, or our sense of continuity, within and through our progeny.

We can also look upon Demeter, Kore and Persephone as the older and younger aspects of the feminine consciousness. As Jung writes: 'The man's role in the Demeter myth is really only that of seducer or conqueror.'[12] According to Jung the source of self-knowledge and creativity is to move psychologically from hermaphroditism to androgyny. When the 'masculine' and 'feminine' as psychosocial behavioral and experiential configurations of the self are undifferentiated, the expression of psychic otherness is unconscious. In contrast, the true androgyne has consciously synthesized and integrated the differentiated 'masculine' and 'feminine' dimensions of psychic reality (the heuristic poles of difference serving as metaphors for the dominant and less developed psychic functions).[13] Kore can be interpreted as the state of female hermaphroditism, while Persephone refers to the more Self-conscious androgynous woman who has eaten of the seed of 'masculinity' or psychic otherness and will experience a rebirth for having confronted the Hades of the unconscious.[14] In the Demeter/Kore myth, Zeus is compelled to respond to Demeter's sanctions. Every Olympian deity comes to her bearing gifts and honors for sterility will prevail until Kore's return from Hades. When Kore finally returns, she tells the horrified Demeter that she has tasted of the fatal pomegranate fruit. She must thus live with her husband for one-third of the year and pass the other two-thirds with her mother. However, Demeter sets aside her anger and fertility is restored on earth. The ties between the Demeter/Kore myth and the two plays become more evident when we consider the failed ravishment between the hierophant and the priestess, the monologue of two split subjectivities. Marion Woodman's definition of rape and ravishment is a good starting point for our interpretation of female lunacy, the dilemma of the 'New Woman', no longer a static stereotype, yet not a fully-embodied New Human Being either:

> The words rape and ravishment come from the same Latin root, *rapere*, meaning 'to seize and carry off'. The connotations of the two words, however, are very different. Rape suggests being seized and carried off by a masculine enemy through brutal sexual assault; ravishment suggests being seized and carried off by a masculine lover through ecstasy and rapture. Rape has to do with power; ravishment has to do with love.[15]

A Streetcar Named Desire begins with Blanche Dubois's arrival in the Elysian Fields, a post-edenic New Orleans neighborhood which contrasts ironically with the mythological allusion. The very name of Blanche Dubois hints at her psychically hermaphroditic state: white, virginal, untouched by the 'crude otherness' of New Orleans, she is still the sleeping beauty or Snow White, waiting for a prince to rescue and ravish her. Blanche resembles the Kore of the Greek legend in her narcissistic desire to cling to the 'Elysian fields' of 'innocence' and psychological virginity. We can see Blanche as a Kore picking a narcissus in the Paradise of her imagination, as she is gradually seized and carried off into her psychic death–marriage.[16] Blanche is of course past virginity and innocence and the Varsouviana leitmotif alludes to the origin and effects of Blanche's initial abduction. Like Salomé, Blanche suffers from the 'hysteric's' classic dis-ease: reminiscences. It is carefully established that the young man to whom Blanche was once married shot himself while the Varsouviana played in the background. As her feelings of entrapment in the past increase, the Varsouviana's role as the sound-track of trauma and abduction becomes more prominent and audible. A distant revolver shot finally coincides with Blanche's own mental disintegration, her final loss of self and voice. Blanche's initial abduction from a pre-Oedipal paradise takes the form of a marriage where her feminine desires are thwarted by her homosexual husband's psychic celibacy. For both Salomé and Blanche the seeds of rape and dissociation lie dormant in their past experiences with men. The suicide of Blanche's husband is more than an expression of the suffering of 'feminine' men. Its traumatic effects on Blanche's pastoral self bespeak the effects of symbolic homosexuality on women.[17] Throughout the play Blanche remains stuck in a state of hermaphroditic femininity; what might have been her reservoir of energy, imaginative potency, creativity, solidity – her fertile unconscious – becomes increasingly a fragile world of make-believe, an escapist haven of theatrical fantasies, of art as mere artificiality. But Blanche is not a promiscuous, artificial faker, sham with her cheap furs and jewels as much as she is a New Woman trying to break away from the fake theatrical roles handed down to her and her sisters by the great theatrical directors of women's lives. All her attributes are perversions of a feminine potential that might have yielded fruit, had the growth not been halted by a projective misogynist environment. Blanche's compulsive bathing and drinking are perverted substitutes of the Eleusinian purification rites where excess intoxication and sexual indulgence are to have a rejuvenating rather than a self-destructive function. Stanley's intrusive reactions not only block Blanche's access to her femininity, but scare, traumatize the living daylight out of her.

Salomé also deals with a 'hysteric', a virgin soon to be psychically deflowered by a corrupt court:

> How good to see the moon! She is like a little piece of money, a little silver flower. The Moon is cold and chaste. I am sure she is a virgin. She has a virgin's beauty. Yes, she is a virgin. She has never defiled herself. She has never abandoned herself to men, like the other goddesses.
>
> (p. 6)

'Silver, chaste, cold, money' are all appropriate attributes for Salomé as the Kore living in a state of innocence, best understood here in a non-moral meaning of 'in-no-sense'. The color silver, a typical symbolist attribute of the feminine moon, underlines Salomé's unadulterated identification, at this stage, with the undifferentiated feminine. But she seems to already have an intuition that as a girl, she is 'money', i.e., an object of exchange between men. From a patriarchal, Freudian perspective, Blanche and Salomé are just what the men of the plays perceive them to be – masochistic, narcissistic, perverted and promiscuous – i.e., lacking in superego and the capacity for sublimation, vain and self-absorbed – i.e., born if not inborn lunatics. From the matriarchal myth's angle, Blanche and Salomé become deviants and lunatics because they have been literally led astray, diverted from their proper path (*se-ducare* does, after all, mean 'lead aside'). They are lured into Self-alienating theatrical roles. However, to idealize women as mere victims is to keep them in the position of helplessness and dependence. To consider the plays from Persephone's rather than Kore's perspective is then not to let the intrusive Kowalskis or Herods off the hook but to discuss why Blanche and Salomé allow themselves to become hooks for male projections.

While searching for Kore, Demeter nurtures the son of Metaneira, trying to make him immortal. The attempt is aborted because of Metaneira's mistrust of the divine nursemaid. To nurture another's son is an apt image for women's need to nurture their 'masculine' potential without the incestuous intensity implied by smothering mother–son relationships. Metaneira stands for all the fears and mistrust that prevent women from nurturing their psychic integrity – androgyny. None of Blanche's 'magic wands' (the Rhinestone tiara, the clothes, the masks) protect her from her internal and external enemies. Past and present collide dramatically in the unconscious associations that bring together Blanche's two abducters – the Polish Varsouviana and the Polish Stanley and which represent the beginning and end of her past and future potential. Blanche projects on Stanley the very attributes she would need in order to protect her 'belle [sic] rêve' – assertiveness, inner conviction and outer confidence. The projection brings out Stanley's need to bully what is his own underdeveloped femininity or otherness. The Dionysian energies, 'feminine' fantasies constellate the outraged anima in the obsessively realistic hierophant. In a way, psychologially Blanche is willing to be sacrificed; Stanley is willing to be the brutal sacrificer. Together they are one. Unconsciously, at opposite ends of the spectrum of lunacy, they constellate the wound and the sword. As long as Stanley is a 'rapist' in Blanche's mind, her unexpressed but subtle violence mirrors his. We might say that Blanche suffers from an unconscious, perverted attraction to her demon lover. Such women have a defensive, compensatory and inflated view of the imaginal feminine, living out fantasies to fill the gap left by the attributes society does not let them articulate consciously. While idealizing the masculine, looking to men for rescue, they are either terrified of the aggressive masculine or challenge it because those qualities echo what has remained hermaphroditic, underdeveloped in them. Blanche's hermaphroditism – her failed 'other bisexuality' to allude to Cixous – is thus bound to meet a Don Juan out to prove his masculinity for both are essentially unrelated to their sexuality. When the anima or the animus are unconscious, they inevitably take over.[18] But to rape Blanche is not only to rape a socially underprivileged, hence more vulnerable being, it is to silence the female viewpoint, the Dionysian dimension and origins of drama. We can interpret the idea that Kore is seduced by Hades and thereby transformed into Persephone as her initiation into mature womanhood.[19] But what chance would a Blanche have of cultivating her own voice in a world of double-morality Kowalskis where her potential is bound to run to seed? Her magic paper moon, her lunar 'part-self' becomes a symbol of mere escapism because the rigid, compulsively masculine Stanley has no appreciation for the art and drama of life.[20] Blanche can also be seen as a representative of all those whose alternative – more Dionysian than Apollonian – mode of creativity has limited chances of being cultivated in patriarchy. As Andrew Samuels has noted:

> The essence of patriarchy is having and needing to have things in their places. It is characterised by order, perhaps rank, certainly discipline . . . Patriarchy does not like 'diffuse awareness' (Claremont de Castillejo, 1973, p. 15); it does not search for 'wisdom in change' (Perera, 1981, p. 85); it disdains a sense of 'elemental being' (E. Jung, 1957, p. 87); 'moonlike reflection' is not approved of (Hillman, 1972, p. 111). This is anima.[21]

As Jungians point out, the western world continues to repress its eros, its body, and to abuse matter. Salomé is another variant of the eros to be crushed by the shields of patriarchy. Sander Gilman sees her as the prototype of degeneracy, madness and pathology – the classic attributes of women, homosexuals and Jews.[22] As Gilman notes, Herod's stepdaughter is a hysteric because her stepfather wishes to seduce her.[23] Herod's lusty gaze, his desire to see Salomé dance and unveil her erotic mysteries are the corrupting traumas that make the uninitiated Kore eat of the seed of Hades.

A symbolic rape, rape on the level of the symbolic order and language, is represented by Jokanaan, who does not consider the female desire even worthy of his truly homosexual, self-serving gaze:

> Who is this woman who is looking at me? I will not have her look at me. Wherefore doth she look at me with her golden eyes, under her gilded eyelids. I know not who she is. I do not desire to know who she is. Bid her begone. It is not to her that I would speak . . . Back, daughter of Babylon! . . .
>
> (pp. 10–12)

Robert Johnston likens Psyche's desire to look upon Eros to a woman's challenge of the authority of her inner male:

> A woman usually lives some time during her life under domination of the man within her . . . the animus. Her own Inner Eros keeps her, quite without her conscious awareness, in paradise. She may not question, she may not have a real relationship with him, she is completely subject to his hidden domination. It is one of the great dramas in the interior life of a woman when she challenges the animus's supremacy and says, 'I will look at you.'[24]

This is what Blanche feared and what Salomé was only too brave to do. To look. Throughout the play, Jokanaan's rhetorical, biblical pathos contrasts with Salomé's haunting, monotonous, repetitive, trance-inducing litanies – her Dionysian aesthetics. The tension of the play resides in the electric attraction between the disembodied male mind with its inflated language – and the excess embodiment of the erotic body, divorced from spirituality, lacking in mental maturity – Jokanaan and Salomé. This is the dialogue of the hierophant and the priestess. Just as Jokanaan reacts to Salomé with all the repressed power and lust of a psyche out of touch with its body, Salomé falls head over heels in love with this paradoxical embodiment of male spiritual potency; the thundering voice of prophetic power: oral power. It is the power of the male analysts, whom Mary Daly (known for her furious stabs at patriarchy) calls the-rapists, women's 'spirit-erasers', the 'Great Sponge Society';[25] the power of the male priest, whose sacred words have traditionally silenced women by legislating on their behalf. Jokanaan rapes Salomé's innocent capacity for love and by denying her the life of the soul he condemns her to fulfill patriarchy's self-fulfilling prophecy. From the beginning, Salomé is a walking dead; she is predestined by patriarchy to die to anything but the role that also kills her. Salomé literally becomes Jokanaan and now turns on mankind the intrusive gaze with which she has herself been seduced. Jokanaan reacts with increasing passion as Salomé comes closer to the source of his prophecies, also the source of his lack. Salomé wants to partake of the power of speech all the more so that she realizes the exclusion of women implied by Jokanaan's abuse of power. Prophets are the mouth of God on earth, God is supreme, he is everything, he is all power. In kissing Jokanaan's lips, Salomé will incorporate the god himself, partake of the divinity that dismisses her and her other so single-mindedly.

Just as the Eleusinian rites are a ritual of overkill, excess and ecstasy, *Salomé* as a play thrives on polymorphously perverted similes that form bizarre hybrids. The celebration of body parts is heightened by Salomé's use of incongruous imagery. Salomé becomes the ivory knife cutting the pomegranate, the scarlet band on a tower of ivory; she is the negative eros penetrating the negative logos: 'I will kiss thy mouth' (p. 14). Salomé reveals her initiation to the ways of destructive patriarchy by learning the distancing mechanisms of anatomical scattering, the Petrarchan standard by means of which male poets portrayed female beauty.[26] From occupying the Oedipal role of the one who looks, names and controls, Salomé moves to the ultimate blasphemy of appropriating the prophet's biblical style – his oral style.[27] Salomé dances not only on behalf of women in the name of the repressed Dionysian energies of patriarchy but wears a mask under which we find a man; Oscar Wilde, the homosexual, the 'feminized man'.[28] The play is not simplistically perverse; the real decadence is in the gaze of those who fail to analyze Jokanaan's and Herod's fears of the evil (female) eye. Jokanaan as John the Baptist and Herod fear retribution,

15 The eyes of Herod: Aubrey Beardsley drawing to illustrate Wilde's *Salomé*

'the beating of the wings of death', the ominous prophetic stirrings rising up from the masculine unconscious or cavern for denying the other half of the kingdom. Herod's efforts to buy Salomé off through the objects of vanity fail, for only masochistic 'old style' women settle for the power of being seductive ornaments at the King's court. Even this point echoes the Demeter/Kore myth for when Demeter refused to restore growth and fertility on earth, the gods came to her bearing gifts and honors. So, too, does Herod try to appeal to Salome's vanity by offering objects ranging from traditional jewels to the radical 'sacred veil' of the temple. Having access to the ultimate bastion of mystery is not enough for a psychic nymphomaniac like Salomé: no peaceful dove, as her attributes and name (shalom) might misleadingly suggest, she wants nothing less than the power to be herself the giver of gifts.[29] Is she not offering the head of Jokanaan to Herodias, her mother, the queen of sterility so that women might in the future experience a social rebirth? Decay and corruption are seen in the Greek myth as a stage through which it is necessary for women to pass in their evolution, a stage beyond rape and rage, the natural decay and naturalism. Salomé's gift is a re-venge in the name of mother and daughter. Demeter is also power, the unleased godly power of vengeance and death. What Mary Daly writes about feminists as 'harpies' and 'hags' expressing collectively women's anger at their exclusion from oral power could be applied to Salomé's fury of revenge: 'Hags are workers of vengeance – not merely in the sense of re-venge, which is only reactionary – but as asserting the primal energy of our be-ing. The Furies were believed by the Greeks and Romans to be avenging deities. As Harpies and Furies Feminists are agents for the Goddess Nemesis.'[30] For Daly the primordial mutilation of women is the ontological separation of mother from daughter and of women from one another. However, by having Jokanaan beheaded, Salomé is not just acting out her enamored revenge, becoming the voice of death, but she is also trying to remove her own Medusa's head: 'We have to find our own inner Perseus and arm him with the right weapons . . . Once the head is off, Pegasus, winged horse of creativity, is released . . .'[31] The ending of the play is not hopeful, though, for New Women. Herod asks the moon to be hidden, proposing a reveiling of Salomé, the feminine, the Dionysian, the unconscious:

> Surely some terrible thing will befall. Manasseh, Issadar, Zias, put out the torches. I will not look at things, I will not suffer things to look at me. Put out the torches! Hide the Moon! Hide the Stars!
>
> (36)

If the Demeter/Kore myth was one of descent and arising, the recovery of Kore as our lost daughter, the fates of Blanche and Salomé can hardly be seen as reassuring rebirths of the feminine. However, the old myth does

16 The dancer's reward: Aubrey Beardsley drawing to illustrate Wilde's *Salomé*

remind us that renewal cannot be separated from decay, that it is death that makes life fertile. The reversals and ironies of Williams's and Wilde's plays together with their veils masking both men and women as onesided hermaphroditic narcissists allow us to reconsider the results of the suppression or negative portrayal of the feminine and Dionysian in drama. Not just a 'New Woman' but a 'New Human Being' has a better chance of emerging from the ashes of worn-out stereotypes if the focus shifts from confused hermaphrodites to the humanized, fullbodied androgynes. The meaning of androgyny for Jungians is the ability to shift perspectives by undoing the fake dichotomies of gender, by undoing all limiting false boundaries. Thanks to the withdrawal of contrasexual projections, psychological breakdown might then become a breakthrough. As Woodman puts it:

> Without psychological rape mankind would have remained in a state of unconscious identification with the Great Mother – at one with nature. We would still be picking flowers with Persephone, blissfully unaware. Where this state of unconsciousness – life in the oceanic world of the womb – remains the ideal to which we yearn to return, the intimate connection between rape and ravishment does not exist.[32]

Victims of rape, such as Blanche, long to return to the unadulterated visions of their beautiful 'rêves'.[33] The strong regressive pull unconsciously frustrates their efforts to wake up. They may not wish to stay in the world that has castrated their potential; they may prefer to re-enter the womb. In Woodman's words: 'They are traumatized by rape because they cannot find its connection to ravishment . . .'[34] Jokanaan, too, is locked up in his spiritual womb/tomb and needs female ravishment in order to be born as an androgyne – a full human being, a full artist, a Self-knowing patriarch.

In this paper, I have discussed two varieties of female lunacy; one deriving from excess fantasizing, another from excess 'self-assertion', both expressing perversions of the Self. Neither Blanche nor Salomé succeeds in becoming a Persephone, the reborn, conscious woman. Blanche's fantasies are a sign only of the absence of meaning, not of true female identity. Receptive, passive or active and assertive are not modes that the New Women adopt as the need arises; both remain stuck in polarities. Blanche becomes mere Self-effacing passivity, Salomé mere Self-beheading aggressivity. Their lives and 'deaths' dramatize the tension between the loss of Self through 'capitulation' and 'decapitation', something that concerns both sexes but which the Oedipal myth couches in terms that are more castrating for women. The Jungian and feminist countermyths are not perfect either. The very terms anima/animus, masculine/feminine reinforce sexual polarities among those who don't perceive them as analytical models. The plays discussed thrive on stereotypes while calling attention to them. Yet, critics, readers, are themselves often hermaphrodites, willing to merely replace the old stereotypes. Jungians are labelled as promoters of 'saccharine transcendental spinach', their theories of Dionysian–spiritual numinosity are seen as escapist 'Songs of Sirens', 'tutti frutti for effeminate androgynes' and Freudians are dismissed by the Jungians themselves as incest-obsessed male bullies.[35] Like women, Jungians continue to be the mad lunatics in the male body politic. Jungian theory is not, after all, based on stiff, hard, respectable (father-identified) facts but thrives on creative speculation around the self–ego axis. And us feminists are too quick to stereotype all male critics as potential seducers or rapists.[36] There are many varieties of literal, symbolic, academic rape.

But why should we dig up old matriarchal myths to replace the Oedipus model? Reader-response theories and studies on spectator response are poorly designed to account for women's and mother-identified viewers' aesthetic reactions and experience. More than that, women need their own mythologies to live by, their own symbolic discourses to rebel against, their own narratives to play with. If even the Dionysian model is still male-defined, we realize the extent to which we have been conditioned by the dearth of symbolic discourses touching women as women rather than as male projections. As my analysis reveals, the moonlight perspective in the plays is present only as a faint background shadow; we are so far removed from woman-centred matriarchal narratives that women, like Salomé and Blanche, can only be experienced by female readers or spectators as male projections, as perversions and spinners of fantasies – not as directors of their own scripts.

As we have seen, rape can be seen as the brutal severance from a previous state of being, while ravishment refers to restoration of that previous state on a higher plane of consciousness. This would mean having a voice, not just rhetorical, oral power but experiencing the empowerment that resounds through the voice of hearing, and of being also heard. This applies not only to the daughters of matriarchy, but also to the closet or self-declared homosexuals – Williams and Wilde – forced to express their feminine self through their female characters, Blanche and Salomé.

NOTES

1 Tennessee Williams, *A Streetcar Named Desire* (New York: Meridian, 1974); all references to the play, followed by page numbers in brackets, are to this edition.
2 Oscar Wilde, *Salomé* (Boston: Branden Publishing Co., 1989); all quotations from this play, followed by page numbers in brackets, refer to this edition.
3 For Salomé's self-destructive usurpation of male prerogatives see, for example, Gail Finney, *Women in Modern Drama: Freud, Feminism and European Theater at the*

Turn of the Century (Ithaca: Cornell University Press, 1989); Kate Millet, *Sexual Politics* (New York: Ballantine, 1969); Elaine Showalter, 'Women's Time, Women's Space: Writing the History of Feminist Criticism', *Feminist Issues in Literary Scholarship*, ed. Shari Benstock (Bloomington: Indiana, Indiana University Press), pp. 30–41. Katharine Worth touches on goddess imagery in *Oscar Wilde* (New York: Grove, 1983), p. 60. The theme of 'new women' is explored by Elliot L. Gilbert in '"Tumult of Images": Wilde, Beardsley, and Salomé', *Victorian Studies* 26 (1983), 133–59; Jane Marcus, 'Salomé: The Jewish Princess Was a New Woman', *Bulletin of the New York Public Library* 78 (1974), 95–113, and Linda Dowling in 'The Decadent and the New Woman in the 1890s', *Nineteenth-Century Fiction* 33 (1979), 434–53. Nicholas Joos and Franklin E. Court, 'Salomé, the Moon and Oscar Wilde's Aesthetics', *Papers on Language and Literature* 8 (1972), 96–111, allude in their analysis of moon-imagery to Astarte (p. 98), Circe (p. 100) and other general mythological images.

4 I am referring to the theories on female subjectivity by Hélène Cixous, 'The Laugh of the Medusa', *New French Feminisms*, ed. Elaine Marks and Isabelle de Cortivron (Brighton: Harvester, 1980), pp. 245–64; Teresa De Lauretis, *Alice Doesn't: Feminism, Semiotics, Cinema* (Bloomington: Indiana University Press, 1984) and Showalter, 'Women's Time'.

5 C. G. Jung and C. Kerényi, *Essays on a Science of Mythology* (Princeton: Bollingen, 1973), pp. 149–50.

6 According to Patricia Fleming, 'Persephone's Search for Her Mother', *Psychological Perspectives* 15.2 (Fall 1984), 127–47: 'Early Christians were much against the worship of Demeter and Elysinian rites, well established in the 13th century BC at Mycenae, because of their overt sexuality, even though their goal was regeneration and forgiveness of sins' (p. 143).

7 Ibid., pp. 144–7.

8 Of course, to refer to women's mysteries through a feminized male deity – Dionysus – is in itself highly problematic. He may be seen as the beginning of women's continued alienation from their own spiritual powerbase, but that is in itself the topic of yet another paper.

9 As Gilbert remarks ('Tumult of Images'): 'the late-nineteenth century was concerned with what it perceived to be a serious decline of authority on a number of fronts – social, political, economic, and metaphysical – and to this decline can be linked the growing interest we have already noted in the figure of the *femme fatale*. Authority in the West has traditionally been associated with patriarchal culture and what that implies: an historical record, a controlling genealogy, a sense of the world as possessing an objective reality independent of, and more absolute than, any individual. The forces – natural, cyclical, ahistorical, subjective – commonly arrayed against such authority have long been connected with women and with female values, and never more so than during the *fin-de-siècle* period when patriarchal culture was felt to be particularly under attack, and, simultaneously, a growing female self-assertion as an historical fact was becoming more and more difficult to ignore. "The New Woman," one critic writes, "was perceived to have ranged herself perversely with the forces of cultural anarchism and decay"' (p. 148). Blanche and Salomé are 'New Women' by virtue of the fact that they seem to embody

anarchism by being 'promiscuous', 'perverse' and for having stepped out of the realm of 'true femininity' – the idealized motherhood as a sense of female identity. Thanks to the modernist subtleties of Williams and Wilde, we are, of course, made to participate in the deconstruction of preconceived ideas and are made to become more conscious of our subjective, selective interpretative strategies. For all that, the New Women present possibilities of interpretation that have helped free women from the worst stereotypical fates.

10 I have based my summary of the myth on the *New Larousse Encyclopaedia of Mythology*, ed. Robert Graves (London: Hamlyn, 1968), pp. 152–5. I have recently come across an 'updated', more feminist version of the myth by Charlene Spretnak, 'The Myth of Demeter and Persephone', in *Weaving the Visions: New Patterns in Feminist Spirituality*, ed. Judith Plaskow and Carol P. Christ (San Francisco: Harper, 1989), pp. 72–7. Spretnak offers us a version with no male figures, just the anecdotal severence of a mother from her daughter. She points out that the version with a male god as the rapist/intruder is already itself a 'later', and more 'patriarchal' version.

11 *Aspects of the Feminine*, trans. R. F. C. Hull (London: Ark Paperback, 1982), p. 164.

12 Ibid., p. 145.

13 I would like to anticipate possible reactions to Jungian binary opposites such as 'anima' and 'animus' and the masculine and feminine because the dominant critical practice, at least in North America, has stereotyped Jungian psychology and set it up as the 'other' of the dominant psychoanalytic revisionary theories. I am aware of the problems inherent in using such binary couples as 'masculine' and 'feminine' as paradigms or metaphors of 'otherness'; as feminists and deconstructionists have often noted, in western culture the pair implies a hierarchy or a questionable complementarity which only serves to mask that the masculine is on top, that the feminine and women are the inferior or subjugated 'other' deviating from male norms. Even when Jungians do not imply that masculinity and femininity are biological, universal opposites (and unknown to most of their critics, many Jungians, particularly post-Jungians, use the 'opposites' merely as differential metaphors), the very terms serve to reinforce the ideology of compulsory heterosexuality. I am using the opposites here heuristically as the stereotypical, cultural codes for self and whatever its unexpressed 'other' may be. The dichotomy refers to areas of the psyche that we are *less* rather than *more* aware of. Often the deconstructionist critique of binary thinking – projected practically on all but itself – is itself guilty of dichotomies; in assuming that Jungians, for example, are necessarily binary thinkers, they are paradoxically themselves always already assuming a rigidness that is not characteristic of Jung's feminine, circular and anti-western writing but of their own assumptions of his philosophy and writing. On this point, see Andrew Samuels, *Jung and the Post-Jungians* (London: Routledge, 1985), p. 207.

14 The term 'androgyne' has been under much criticism from female theorists; See Demaris Wehr in *Jung and Feminism: Liberating Archetypes* (Boston: Beacon Press, 1989) and Mary Daly, *Gyn/Ecology: The Metaethics of Radical Feminism* (Boston: Beacon Press, 1978), p. xi, pp. 387–8. They and others argue that the word is

itself androcentric and reinforces attitudes where man is the norm and woman the deviation (the Adam-then-Eve-order of presenting things). While I agree with this view, I argue that many of the women criticizing Jung's writing on androgyny have not given credit to or have failed to grasp the complexity of its existential interpretation in analytical psychology. Androgyny refers to intrapsychic, ontological issues, not simply to the interpsychic dynamics between the sexes. On that issue see June Singer's classic *Androgyny: Toward a New Theory of Sexuality* (New York: Norton, 1964; 1982). For Jungians androgyny is often a metaphor for a sense of vital energy when it feels as if we were flowing between polarities, a 'still point' beyond gender and mere physical sexuality.

15 *Addiction to Perfection: The Still Unravished Bride* (Toronto: Inner City Books, 1982), p. 134.

16 For an interesting analysis of the Old South as the cultural, American 'belle rêve' or national 'paradise' see Thomas E. Porter in 'The Passing of the Old South: A Streetcar Named Desire', *Myth and Modern American Drama* (Detroit: University of Detroit Press, 1969).

17 To quote Eugene C. Bianchi in 'Psychic Celibacy and the Quest for Mutuality', *From Machismo to Mutuality: Essays on Sexism and Woman–Man Liberation*, ed. Eugene C. Bianchi and Rosemary R. Ruether (New York: Paulist Press, 1974), pp. 87–101: 'When men turn to women for sexual relief from the tensions of the job grind it is often done as an act with a subordinate rather than as a relationship with a cherished equal. Cheerleaders, bunnies and broads of all varieties are strictly sideline diversions to help the boys return refreshed to the all-male playing field. Physical sex in our culture is performed in an atmosphere of psychic celibacy. Sex needs to be compartmentalized and controlled in the male mentality lest its offshoots of tenderness and warm concern distract them from making it in the competitive arena of peers. A growing number of women are giving up on men as partners for loving relationships beyond the sex act' (p. 89).

18 I am referring to Marion Woodman's analysis of demon lovers, *Addiction to Perfection*, pp. 135–55.

19 We could, of course, replace Hades by the mother and use the earlier version of the myth, if we wanted to focus on the myth's specifically matriarchal rather than Dionysian roots. As that further complicates matters, I will tackle that in a later study.

20 Classic psychoanalytic theory in the 'masculine tradition' tended to dismiss the 'feminine' aspects of the unconscious, which is why fantasies were seen as mere hallucinations, illusions to be outgrown. However, a clear rapprochement between Jungians and post-Freudians is in my opinion taking place now, for D. Winnicott's notion of a transitional space between reality and fantasy (a space where he locates the basis of health) comes close to Jung's view of the positive aspects of fantasy. See Winnicott's *Playing and Reality* (New York: Basic Books, 1971). Blanche is, of course, weaving unproductive, escapist fantasies, but in different circumstances somebody like her might have had a rich inner life, something that Stanley instinctively knows and envies.

21 *Jung and the Post-Jungians*, pp. 228–9.

22 To quote Sander Gilman, *Disease and Representation: Images of Illness from Madness*

to Aids (Ithaca: Cornell University Press, 1988): 'If the "degenerate", the greater category into which the nosologies of the nineteenth century placed the "pervert", was according to Max Norday, the "morbid deviation from an original type", the difference between the original type – the middle-class heterosexual, Protestant male – and the outside was a morbid one – the outsider was diseased. There is a general parallel drawn between the feminization of the Jew and the homosexual in the writings of assimilated Jews, Jews who did not seek to validate their difference from the majority during the late nineteenth century but who saw themselves as potentially at risk as such a morbid deviation from the norm' (p. 175).

23 Ibid., pp. 168–9.

24 *She: Understanding Feminine Psychology* (San Francisco: Harper & Row, 1977), p. 23. Even though aspects of these kinds of male theories of femininity can be useful, Johnston is an example of the projective essentialist Jungians who have given all Jungians a bad name. He treats femininity as an essentialist transcultural given and mixes his own desires of ideal femininity with cultural prescriptions. The notion of animus can be translated into feminist language as 'the internalized, woman-belittling patriarchal voice' – with the significant addition that there is nothing necessarily universal or inborn about it.

25 *Gyn/Ecology*, pp. 280.

26 For John Berger in *Theatre: Ways of Seeing*, 'the ideal spectator is always assumed to be male' (quoted in Finney, *Women in Modern Drama*, p. 62).

27 'By depicting the woman not as a totality but as a series of dissociated parts, the male poet could overcome any threat her femaleness might pose him. This obsessive insistence on particular body parts produced during the Renaissance the genre of the blazon . . . which praised individual fragments of the female body in a highly ornamental fashion; the new genre even provided an occasion for contests of rhetorical skill in which, for example, one poet pitted his description of a breast vs. another's celebration of an eyebrow. The blazon functioned as a power strategy, since to describe is in some senses . . . to control, to possess, and ultimately, to use to one's own ends' (Finney, *Women in Modern Drama*, p. 63).

28 In Euripides' *Bacchantes* and in Maureen Duffy's 'Rites', *Plays By and About Women*, ed. Victoria Sullivan and James Hatch (New York: Vintage Books, 1974), women in ecstasy end up murdering, in the former, their own son, in the latter, another woman; similarly, Wilde's Herod crushes under the shields not just a lustful woman but all those 'feminine' men who hide under the seven veils. By crushing Salomé, patriarchy is crushing its own men as the veiled other.

29 It is not meaningless for women to remember the matriarchal background meaning of 'dove', which is a reference to the cosmic mother, not to tamed, 'pure' maidens. As Mary Daly notes: 'When we see the Triple Goddess in the Background of the various trinities of gods which foreshadowed the christian trinity, other christian symbols fall into perspective as dim derivatives. Thus, in the Pelasgian creation myth, Eurynome, the Goddess of All Things, assumed the form of a dove and laid the Universal Egg. Her Sumerian name was Iahu meaning "exalted dove". This title later passed on to Yahweh as creator. When

we see the traditional symbol of the holy ghost as a dove in the light of this Background, its absurdity becomes obvious. One is tempted to speculate about how "he" could lay an egg . . .' (*Gyn/Ecology*, p. 77). Daly's comments lend support to the view that Salomé's love–hate relationship with Jokanaan also derives its intensity and passion from the primal competition that it animates: that of matriarchal versus patriarchal power.

30 Ibid., pp. 40–1.

31 Woodman, *Addiction to Perfection*, p. 7.

32 Ibid., p. 182. It is important to note here that rape and ravishment as intrapsychic symbolic concepts serve not to conceal and avoid the realities of the many women who have been raped and abused. It is clear that in psychotherapy actual cases of abuse must be dealt with without blaming the victim, which unfortunately continues to be done and which further increases a woman's sense of internalized oppression and self-blaming guilt. However, we must not either go to the other feminist extreme of treating every female problem and fantasy as an effect of patriarchal rape – we need to be discriminating and consider each individual case in its own context.

33 The somewhat irritating 'belle rêve' in Williams's play may be just his French mistake and should properly be termed 'beau rêve' – unless the masculine-/feminine hybrid is an intentional device to call attention to Blanche's mixing of gender categories – in itself a transgression within the Symbolic.

34 Woodman, *Addiction to Perfection*, p. 182.

35 See in particular Frederick Crews's *Out of My System: Psychology, Ideology and Critical Method* (New York: Oxford University Press, 1976) in which he mocks the opponents of Freudian theory as 'humanistic sewing circles', exposing his sexist view that androgynous men (or men that do not correspond to the hard-line, linear mode of reasoning) are effeminate, i.e., that femininity is to be avoided (p. 17). Morton Kaplan's and Robert Kloss's *The Unspoken Motive: A Guide to Psychoanalytic Literary Criticism* (New York: Free Press, 1973) also contains disparaging references to the 'Jungian Peril' (a 'jellied logic' that resides, apparently, in the feared feminization of psychoanalysis). When Kaplan writes that Freud 'determined the significance of the father to each of us and the father in each of us' (p. 163), we see the extent to which the feminine and a mother-identified response to aesthetic experience has been neglected and despised.

36 Practically all feminist critiques against Jung are based on the monolithic stereotypes of misogynist patriarchs and many of them are totally uninformed (see Daly, *Gyn/Ecology*, for example). They ignore the fact that Jung not only preferred maternal rather than phallic imagery, that he criticized patriarchy's neglect of the material, bodily, 'feminine' dimension, that he was a staunch phenomenologist anticipating the postmodern realization that there is no objective or value-free point outside of the psyche but that we are all prisoners of our subjectivity. The reality of Jung's sexism and contradictions has been amply recorded; I am now in the process of reworking my doctoral thesis, 'The Short Fiction of Gérard de Nerval and Nathaniel Hawthorne – A Study in Post-Jungian Aesthetics' (University of Toronto, 1990) to expose the numerous affinities that exist between analytical psychology and feminist approaches – not in terms of Jung himself but the philosophical premises of his less known post-archetypal theories.

Mad Messiah: censorship and salvation in Bulgakov's *Flight*

ROB K. BAUM

Good men . . . sensuall men thought mad, because they would not be partakers, or practisers of their madnesse. But they, placed high on the top of all vertue, look'd downe on the Stage of the world, and contemned the Play of Fortune. For though the most be players, some must be Spectators.

(Ben Jonson)

When 'Lizzie Borden took an axe and gave her mother forty whacks', she walked out of a small town and onto the world's stage. What madness it must have seemed, to neglect her quiet role for disquieting fame, to thus cut down the fourth wall of propriety.

No longer a medical designation, madness has more to do with pro-scription than prescription, with prisons and asylums interchangeably protecting actor from spectator. Morality[1] constitutes one of the earliest and complex lessons imparted, and for the social majority, a behavioural governor or censor is unconsciously internalized to uphold encoded norms. Without them, 'when the job was neatly done', we might all give our fathers forty-one. Madness grants license, a method of acting without regard to audience expectation.

Censorship pervades mental activity, as Freud explored through dreams:

The dream work is not simply more careless, more irrational, more forgetful and more incomplete than waking thought; it is completely different from it qualitatively and for that reason not immediately comparable . . . Little attention is paid to the logical relations between the thoughts . . . [they] have to be reproduced exclusively or predominantly in the material of visual and acoustic memory traces, and this necessity imposes upon the dream work considerations of representability . . . *the dream has above all to evade censorship.*[2]

SEEKING FLIGHT

Poetry is the dream of man waking, and dreams the poetry of man sleeping.

(Mazzoni)

Mikhail Afanasievich Bulgakov was painfully awake to the ramifications of dream, difference and censorship. His stories of Russian enchantments, politics filigreed with fantasy, voiced sentiments inappropriate to the building of a Marxist nation. The government censorship which plagued his writing was to become its ironic focus, his dream of free expression a nightmare. *Flight (Beg)*,[3] Bulgakov's dream play about the impossibility of escape from Mother Russia, captures the ambience of dream in a vertiginous fast-forward of dissolving frames. The playwright creates a performable experience of reality, dramatizing Gasset's *idea del teatro*: illusion and anti-illusion converge, 'the stage and the actor [are] the universal metaphor incarnate', and the theatre 'visible metaphor'.[4]

Compressing absurdity, fantasy, verbal and imagistic poetry, Bulgakov punctuates with reflexive commentary, signing the correspondence between theatre and dream. The Russian allegory teems with figures self-consciously trapped behind the curtain. Golubkov states: 'How strange it all is, really! Do you know, at times, it seems to me I'm dreaming! . . . and the farther we go, the more incomprehensible it all becomes . . .'[5] Serafima cries, 'We are running from Petersburg, running and running . . . Where? To safety under Khludov's [another character] wing! All you hear is Khludov and Khludov . . . You even dream about Khludov!' (p. 30), while Khludov muses, 'Nobody loves us, nobody. All our tragedies come from that, just like in the theatre' (p. 21). In the tantalizingly brief introductory scene, Archbishop Afrikanus – disguised as the chemist Makhrov – says of General Charnota – disguised as the pregnant Barabanchikova: 'Mysterious, a most mysterious character!' (p. 7). As Khludov asks, 'What sort of comedy is this?' (p. 50).[6]

What sort *is* it? A tragic sort, in which the audience unwillingly, nauseatingly, identifies with a man called 'vermin', 'insect' and 'hyena'. One in which an extended childhood memory of cockroaches becomes metaphor and metonymy for exodus and desertion, repeated throughout the play and its Russian title.[7] One where buyers exist for every body and survival is paramount. Where bestiality thrives, the general populace resembles 'civilian lice' and a latterday 'Noah's Ark' reveals humanity's destiny to infest the new world.

Categorical single-mindedness marks better-known dream plays: one narrator frames the journey, standing between the intelligence of writer and audience. In *Flight*, a complex machinery hums, spiral gears of discrete minds. The audience must assemble conflicting images delivered at dark and violent speed. Help is unavailable. No caustic doorman hovers, eager to slam the gate. On the contrary, evil can crash the gate – and does.

MAD MESSIAH

Men's bodies tired with the business of the day betaking themselves to their best repose, their never-sleeping souls laboured in uncouth dreams and visions, [and] suddenly appeared to me the tragic muse.

(Thomas Heywood)

Flight's central motif resides in Roman Valerianovich Khludov's sins against his countrymen at the Crimean. It is the time of the White Terror (1920–21), when Russian soldiers, peasants and workers fought over the interests of Entente capital. Fleeing before the ravages of the advancing Bolsheviks (Reds), a group of 'former people'[8] bands, sharing only the dubious bond of White sympathizing.

His superiors escape, but General Khludov persists at the Front, a White devil of principle ordering the hangings of alleged Bolsheviks from lampposts. His mission to secure Russia from revolutionaries becomes a horror of commission: victims dangle like game in dark bags.

In Bulgakov's earlier *feuilleton Red Crown (Historia morbi)*,[9] the narrator is haunted by the images of his dead brother Kolya and a man hanged by Kolya's superior, a White general. Responsibility for the barbarism lies with both general and narrator, a guilty connection:

> Who knows, perhaps that dirty begrimed man from the lamppost in Berdyansk comes to you. If so, we suffer justly. I sent Kolya to help you hang others, and you did the hanging.

Under the intolerable burden of murder, the narrator goes mad.

In the general madness of *Flight*, General Khludov's acts evade censorship. The small light which the orderly Krapilin is commanded to shed upon the First Dream becomes fatal illumination in the dream following, when he denounces his superior:

> . . . you can't win the war with rope alone! Why did you butcher the soldiers at Perekop, beast? But one human being [Serafima] did come your way, a woman. She took pity on the strangled ones, that's all. But nobody can get past you, nobody! Right away you grab him, and into a bag! Do you feed on carrion?

Finding a 'glimmering of sound sense about the war in his words', Khludov urges him to continue, asking his name. Krapilin raves,

> A name, what's the difference? It's a name nobody knows – Krapilin, an orderly![10] But you will perish, jackal, you'll perish, wild beast, in a ditch! . . . You're only brave to hang women and locksmiths! . . . All the provinces spit on your music!

Khludov listens with respect. Krapilin does not condemn himself until the moment he drops fearfully to his knees and recants. Khludov cries,

> No! You're a poor soldier! You began well, but the end was rotten. Groveling at my feet! Hang him! I can't bear the sight of him!

At which, according to the stage directions, 'The counter-intelligence men instantly throw a black bag over Krapilin's head and drag him outside' (pp. 32–3).

Thereafter, Khludov is haunted by the silent, invisible Krapilin, to

17 and 18 A. Bosulayev's designs for Bulgakov's *Flight*, Pushkin Theatre, 1958

whom he defers: 'Come, ease my soul, nod to me. Nod at least once, eloquent orderly Krapilin!' (p. 89). In one of many arresting images, Khludov nervously opens the door beyond his office to confront a 'series of dark, abandoned rooms with chandeliers wrapped in dark muslin bags', mute witness. Surely this is the artist dreaming himself, waking at the end of each scene to fearful darkness.[11] Khludov 'murders sleep'.

Soviet audiences would have recognized the character of Khludov as the real and sensational General Slashchov, a brilliant 34-year-old strategist awarded the honorific 'Krymsky' for his defense of the Crimea in 1920. He was often unreliable, a drug addict and alcoholic noted for brutality; he himself 'admits that there was a general feeling [I] was suffering from upset nerves if not actual madness'.[12] Following 'summary execution of a Colonel Protopopov' (upon whom Krapilin is probably based), Slashchov complained of attempts at discrediting his distinguished career.

Khludov surfaces in the Second and only three successive Dreams. But he is always present beyond the curtain, a grotesque mirror in the dressing room. The dislocation and impotence of the schizoid is revealed through a postmodern world of fragmentation and alienation, amid a carnival of lurid sights, sounds, smells, diseases and foul temptations. This is Khludov's dream, and we in darkness dream with danger: 'tripping' through derangement's hyper-space we may be caught. As Serafima tells her torturer,

> Now I'm like you, I cannot sleep . . . The Cossacks were allowed to go home. I'll ask to go, too, I'll go back with them, to Petersburg. It was madness. Why did I ever leave? . . There is one thing . . . that keeps me here – what will become of you?
>
> (pp. 90–1)

For many, Khludov *is* the curtain.

With military jurisdiction over the 'glorious army of Christ' as well as power to dole out misery, redemption, charity and murder, Khludov is one with Russia, the 'kingdom divided against itself'[13] to which Archbishop Africanus obliquely refers. His messianism is corrupt, the charge to lay his body between the Reds and his nation's leadership a patriotic but futile sacrifice. The gods have fled.

Khludov's crazy dream to evade censorship (Freud's injunction) can only lead to trial and execution – and simultaneous rebirth in the Motherland. The matrix of the future is Russia's spiritual revolution, a condition without need for censorship *or* madness.

> Neurosis . . . is presented as a literary analogue of a sociopolitical malaise afflicting a given society in general and certain segments of that society in particular . . . The 'madness' of a certain social order or ideology . . . is transformed into the psychological disorder of a literary protagonist who,

through his own words and example, then shows that order or that ideology to be flawed or 'mad' in some degree . . .[14]

As in Strindberg's chamber play *To Damascus*, the struggle for *Flight* remains internal and solitary, hidden in an iconographic landscape. The flight of the Whites wings them from the monastery to the Crimean, from Constantinople to a Parisian flat, and back to Rome. These are Stations of the Cross which Khludov shoulders, reflected in Sevastopol lampposts strung with the black bags of his victims. They are also the spirit's obscene body: 'crimes', printed on signboards, form the crosses' arms; the full, hanging bags testify to the barrenness of Mother Russia.[15]

For Khludov's odyssey is a spiritual violation. In the madness of war Russian Orthodoxy has gone underground: having 'tied up the bells' tongues' in the beleaguered monastery, the monks' choir sings by candle-light in the recesses below. Like any conqueror the Bolsheviks buried Russia's ancient divinity. The new, unholy god unearthed a deep spiritual hunger.[16]

FORMER PEOPLE

Decidedly this tree will not have been the slightest use to us. (*Waiting for Godot*)

Khludov can neither escape nor embrace his action: by the Fourth Dream he is waking. Reproaching the Commander in Chief for pending deser-tion, Khludov shares an agonizing moment of self-recognition:

Do you have any idea of the hate a man must feel when he knows that nothing will come of his actions, and yet must act? It is because of you that I am sick! However, this is not the time, we are both passing into nonbeing.

(p. 46)

Nothing, Descartes told us, can be more false than dreams. Internal concepts of good and evil survive externally; like the individual, truth exists independent of discourse.

If you want to keep a secret you must also hide it from yourself. You must know all the while that it is there, but until it is needed you must never let it emerge into your consciousness in any shape that could be given a name. From now onwards [you] must not only think right; [you] must feel right, dream right.[17]

Khludov personifies the primary life-and-death struggle of humanity, but flounders at Hegel's initial level of self-consciousness. As his actions accelerate they become more exclusive, driving Khludov to the critical matchpoint of self-negation without essential differentiation.

The 'dialectic' is one of a blocked contradiction – an irresolvable conflict between unrelated opposites – and a resulting rise of consciousness to break the deadlock and smash the object-state in which the subject has been confined.[18]

To Soviet censors, Bulgakov's dream universe was all too Russian and Khludov a dangerously unfunny joke – the hygienically deconstructing man, a concatenation of falsehoods. The actor playing Khludov – a dreamed murderer, hence, unmade-man – becomes a truly monstrous Platonic mimesis: an abstraction of an abstraction of an abstraction. In short, the perfectly Marxist 'modern man'.

In the dehistoricizing movement spawned by the Counter-Revolution, class segregation gives way to group oppression and Russian proletarians take the place of Sartre's 'natives'. As a result, 'the humanity of the native is alienated into a state of quasi-animality. Since animality and humanity are antimonies, the contradiction will inevitably explode, and the native will regain his humanity. He must first smash the state of inhumanity in which he has been imprisoned.'[19] This 'new man', writes Sartre, begins his life at the end of it.

> What matter the victims, if thereby the individual affirms himself? . . . What matter the death of vague human beings, provided the gesture is beautiful?[20]

Sartre's theories on violence recognize Marxism as a new form of Russian colonialism, a collective human philosophy which collectively dehumanizes. (Note that the Reds and Whites use like measures.[21]) Bolsheviks will overthrow the feudal system to enforce a modern utopian homogeneity. Khludov resists not because of the ideals the Bolsheviks espouse – not even because he is an aristocrat – but because he is a soldier. It is his duty.

SOILED SUIT

> The making of one's life into art is after all the first duty and privilege of every man.
>
> (Arthur Symons)

Bulgakov wrote *Flight* without the restrictions imposed upon his previous play *Days of the Turbins* (*Dni Turbinykh*), then playing at the Moscow Art Theatre (MKhAT). (*Turbins* deals with the events of the Counter-Revolution, 1916–18.)[22] Under Stanislavski's direction, revisions for the more conventional, realistic *Turbins* were formal and reductive: a dream sequence was cut, geography limited, scenes reduced, and an un-Bulgakovian ending imposed (in which actors listen quietly to a parade band playing the 'International').[23]

The dream-within-a-dream motif fully exemplifies Bulgakov's intensive grasp of dramatic structure, his ability to nest ideas like Russian eggs –[24]

> Lovers and madmen have such seething brains
> Such shaping fantasies, that apprehend
> More than cool reason ever comprehends.
>
> (Shakespeare)[25]

– while the tendency to introduce or 'disrupt' his fictions and plays with autobiographical detail[26] is typical of a previous era.

Employing epigrammatic techniques, sandwiching social comment between sides of verse, poets such as Ben Jonson impaled the contemporary world – author, audience, friends and critics – in a politically acceptable manner. But blatant politicizing of the present became foolhardy under Stalin's regime. Banning the play before its premiere, Stalin wrote:

> *Flight* is a manifestation of an attempt to elicit pity, if not liking, for certain levels of anti-Soviet émigré society – therefore an attempt to justify or half-justify the White Guard movement. *Flight*, as it stands, is an anti-Soviet phenomenon.[27]

Despite the play's February 1929 banning, MKhAT avidly pursued the staging of *Flight*; not until 1934 was Stanislavski convinced that it would not receive official permission for production.[28] After Stalin's letter, three other Bulgakovian plays were promptly dropped from repertory throughout the country, including *Days of the Turbins* which had already had 250 performances since its opening in 1926. Virtually every work written by Bulgakov after 1929 met with hostility if not rejection.

The playwright was unofficially branded with the title 'satirist', an 'unthinkable' genre in the Soviet Union. He took to wearing slippers and pajamas, adopting this old-fashioned – madman's – appearance as a protest: 'There, you wanted to see me like this . . . so there, here you are . . . that's how I am.'[29] It was Hamlet's mischosen stab, by an artist sinking into inaction, destructive self-obsession and censorship. Critic R. Pikel exulted:

> His talent is as obvious as is the socially reactionary nature of his works . . .
> The withdrawal of Bulgakov's plays signifies a thematic sanitary cleansing of the repertory.[30]

As his plays disappeared from libraries, Bulgakov developed insomnia and a nervous tick. Yermolinsky writes of his friend: 'He was convinced of the necessity of pitilessly satirical depictions of life. This was not just the play of a mocking mind, but the author's civic stance.'[31] Bulgakov wrote to Stalin several times asking to be allowed to emigrate, identifying his desire to be a 'modern writer' with Gogol's inability to remain in Russia for any length of time.[32] Fortunately for Bulgakov, Stalin merely ignored the request.

He climbed still further out the limb in 1929, beginning work on *The Cabal of Hypocrites Molière* (*Kabala svyatosh Mol'yer*), a play which exposes bureaucratic censorship of the writer Molière.[33] The same theme, stripped of biographical metaphor, appears in *The Master and Margarita* (*Master i Margarita*), written secretly from 1928–40. But there is a more insidious censor than government, as Bulgakov knew. Ashamed by the quality of his new play, the barely fictionalized playwright Master discovers:

> People are right when they say you can't destroy something once you've written it. You can tear it up or burn it . . . or conceal it from people. But from yourself, never! That's it! It's irrevocable![34]

To the artist, censorship is akin to murder.[35]

At the heart of Bulgakov's genius beats an ability to dematerialize theatre. He implies dreamy fantasy but implements nightmarish reality, expounded with grim economy. His protagonists live in shadow while he shines forth a fatal light.

Khludov's bagged victims signify his own hood-winking. With his maker Bulgakov, he is the naïve soul of Russia, her madness and salvation, a kingdom divided. He – and She – have lost spiritual compass; dream and life are indissolubly fused, a treacherous coastline uncensored even by darkness. Unable to pilot Russia, to plot the Promised Land, Khludov is a false messiah. The spirit, too, can be censored. This is Bulgakov's concluding statement, the truth which must not be named.

At dream's end, the White sympathizers, with Khludov, are returning to their country. Russia may be wrong, but she is Mother. The lights at last blink out; dreamers awake; the audience, too, is going home. Perhaps the street lamps have been lit. The theatre, which is only illusion, evaporates. But madness hangs in the air.

NOTES

1 Michel Foucault gives an exhaustive discussion on what is meant by 'morality' in volume 2 (*The Use of Pleasure*) of his extensive treatise on human relationships, *The History of Sexuality*, trans. Robert Hurley (New York: Vintage Books, 1986). I use the more ordinary (yet inclusive) definition here.

2 Sigmund Freud, *The Interpretation of Dreams*, trans. James Strachey (New York: Science Editions, 1961), p. 507.

3 While the English title *Flight* speaks to the questions of emigration and return, the Russian title *Beg* is not directly translatable. It might also be 'running' or 'race'. Bulgakov had considered calling the play the Russian equivalent of 'Cockroach Race', recalling the events of the Fifth Dream (Act).

4 See Jackson I. Cope, *The Theater and the Dream. From Metaphor to Form in Renaissance Drama* (Baltimore: Johns Hopkins University Press, 1973), p. 218.

5 Mikhail Bulgakov, *Flight & Bliss*, trans. Mirra Ginsburg (New York: New Directions Publishing Corporation, 1969), p. 6. All quotations from *Flight* are

drawn from this source. Ensuing parenthetical citations refer to pages in the Ginsburg text.

6 In this initial comic assembly, as in the figures of General de Brizar and even Charnota (who takes up de Brizar's curious litany in his physical absence), Bulgakov demonstrates a keenly informed economy and the manifold substrata of text and symbology.

7 Khludov remembers having seen cockroaches falling into a pail of water; thus he calls the Commander in Chief's abandonment of the Front 'sinking into a pail of water'.

8 The type of people common to the pre-NEP – Lenin's New Economic Policy, an experiment in 'free enterprise' established by *ukase* in March 1921. NEP, a result of agricultural disasters and labour standstill, created a veritable epidemic of Khlestakovianism, during which a host of so-called 'NEP men' ranged Russia, fleecing people for all they were worth, feverishly amassing large fortunes before disappearing abroad.

9 Published in 1922.

10 The name 'Krapilin' is quite as arch as Gogol or Beckett would have intended.

11 Diverse translations insist upon 'darkness' rather than the theatrical 'blackout'. Only two of the dreams give any subsequent direction: 'silence' in the Fifth Dream and 'fades out forever' in the Eighth and final Dream.

12 See A. Colin Wright, *Mikhail Bulgakov: Life and Interpretations* (Toronto: University of Toronto Press, 1978), pp. 124–5. Later Slashchov was to return to Russia, 'where incredibly he was pardoned and served in the Red Army until 1928'.

13 Cf. Matthew 12:25.

14 From William Riggan, *Pícaros, Madmen, Naïfs and Clowns: The Unreliable First Person Narrator* (Norman: University of Oklahoma Press, 1981), p. 128. Consider also this observation from Eric Newman: 'Neurosis is a sacred disease.'

15 At the risk of donning the Freudian duncecap, one could call them Khludov's testes.

16 Displacing the physical hunger prevalent in Russian and Soviet drama. This is the essence of the Khlestakovian figure, itself drawn from Gogol – always hungry.

17 In George Orwell's *1984* (New York: New American Library, 1961), p. 231.

18 See James Lawler, *The Existentialist Marxism of Jean-Paul Sartre* (Amsterdam: B. R. Grüner Publishing Co., 1976), p. 197.

19 Ibid., p. 220.

20 Attributed to Laurent Tailhade.

21 Kautsky differentiates Red and White terrorism thus: 'They do not renounce their principles when they sacrifice human life in order to retain their power, but the Bolsheviks can only do this when they become untrue to the principle of the sacredness of human life which they themselves have exalted and vindicated' (Karl Radek, *Proletarian Dictatorship and Terrorism*, trans. P. Lavin (Detroit: The Marxian Educational Society, 1921), p. 49).

22 Bulgakov hastily adapted the play from his novel *White Guard* (*Belaya gvardiya*) in 1925. Despite its success, he was highly dissatisfied. There is much scholarly speculation that *Flight* is a 'sequel' to *The Days of the Turbins*. Though concerned

with a different military heirarchy, both plays treat the White Guard sympathetically. It is easy to find similarities in plot and character between the two plays (even the metaphor of the rats deserting a ship in *The Days of the Turbins* has its parallel in the cockroaches of *Flight*). To this end, scholars suggest that Khludov's character stems from the figure of Alexei Turbin, the White General who, like Khludov, commands at the Front.

23 This ending was used in other plays of the period, as one might guess, for political rather than artistic reasons.

24 Carl and Ellendea Proffer call this the most unorthodox of Bulgakov's plays. *Flight* is also considered 'the more Bulgakovian in form' (*The Early Plays of Mikhail Bulgakov* (Bloomington: Indiana University Press, 1972), p. 162). Although Bulgakov himself made a number of alterations in the script at Stanislavski's suggestion, *Flight* retains the basic lyricism and techniques the playwright originally intended. His economical use of characters; well-constructed, cinematic plots; non-moralizing, instructive yet interesting tone and lack of superfluous detail are unique among dramas of the NEP period, which typically call for theatrically impossible geographical panoramas dominated by a single, Khlestakovian character.

25 *Midsummer Night's Dream*, v, i, 4–6.

26 As when *The Days of the Turbins* is referred to in Bulgakov's 1927 farce *The Crimson Island* (*Bagrovy ostrov*).

27 Joseph Stalin in a letter to playwright Bill-Belotserkovsky, 2 February 1929. See Proffer, *Early Plays*, p. 162.

28 Following Bulgakov's death by hereditary disease in 1940, *Glavrepertkom* gave permission for *Flight*'s publication, but it remained unpublished. In 1955, N. P. Akimov proposed production at Theatre of the Lensoviet (honouring writer V. Kaverin, who initiated Bulgakov's rehabilitation); R. Simonov and A. Abrikosov of the Vakhtangov proposed again in 1957. But neither production occurred. *Flight* first opened at the Gorky Dramatic Theatre in Volgograd (Stalingrad) in March 1957.

29 Cited in Proffer, *Early Plays*, p. 129.

30 Ibid., p. 142. Pikel later became a 'somewhat unwilling employee' of the NKVD (acronym of the Secret Police).

31 See Sergey Yermolinsky's biography of the playwright (Moscow, 1982).

32 'The present is too animated, too mercurial, it irritates the senses; and the writer's pen shifts imperceptibly into satire . . . It has always seemed to me that in my life some great self-sacrifice awaits me, and that precisely in order to serve my native country I shall be obliged to go and develop somewhere far away from it . . . "I knew only that I was going away not at all in order to delight in foreign lands, but rather in order to endure, just as though I had had a presentiment that I would recognize the worth of Russia only outside Russia, and that I would attain love for her far away from her."' Cited in J. A. E. Curtis, *Bulgakov's Last Decade: The Writer as Hero* (Cambridge: Cambridge University Press, 1987), p. 125.

33 Stanislavski proposed major alterations for this work as well, feeling that Bulgakov was going off the rails. A record of the dialogue between the two

artists appears in Nikolai Gorchakov, *Stanislavski Directs*, trans. Miriam Goldina (New York: Limelight Editions, 1985).

34 Mikhail Bulgakov, *The Master and Margarita*, a bizarre and surrealist fiction.

35 Cf. Bulgakov's early 'motto', submitted with a play to a writing contest: 'To the free god of art!'

Madness and magic in Eduardo De Filippo

MIMI GISOLFI D'APONTE

His madness is a case of lucid madness, a madness which is kinder than sanity; a madness to which one goes for shelter when life becomes crushing and unbearable.[1]

Luigi Pirandello is well known in both literary and theatrical circles for having created this lucid quality of madness besetting his character Enrico IV (*Henry IV*, 1922). The lucid, collective madness of his even more widely acclaimed *Sei personaggi in cerca d'autore* (*Six Characters in Search of an Author*, 1921) has become in and of itself a metaphor for 'acting out', since it requires a vehicle in which to complete incomplete lives. Pirandello's presentation of a consistently tragic form of madness is notable in his lesser known works as well. In *Cosi e' se vi pare* (*It Is So If You Think So*, 1917), for example, Signora Frola lives an essentially schizophrenic life, appearing to fill two contradictory relationships in order to maintain what she considers the fragile sanities of her daughter and her son-in-law. In *Trovarsi* (*To Find Oneself*, 1932) actress Donata Gensi barely avoids being rent into psychological halves by the tremendous conflict she experiences between work and love. In *Quando si è qualcuno* (*When One Is Somebody*, 1933) protagonist ***, who is a highly successful writer (and clearly in many ways a Pirandellian self-portrait), struggles against, but ultimately succumbs to the suffocation of his psychic vitality by the demands of success. Indeed, it might be said that the individual Pirandellian protagonist, surrounded by unrelenting victimizers, hangers-on, and busybodies, treads a line between psychosis and sanity in what is usually a vain attempt to establish identity and/or stabilize selfhood.

After Pirandello there has been a continuing tradition of theatrical madness employed by Italian playwrights. Particularly notable in this regard, as well as in their general brilliance, are the works of Eduardo De Filippo and Dario Fo. In the dramaturgy of Dario Fo tragedy is supplanted by a sort of giddy, madcap comedy in which the protagonist finds himself victimized by ominously anonymous social institutions. *Gli arcangeli non giocano al flipper* (*Arcangels Don't Play Pinball*, 1959) *Morte accidentale di un anarchico* (*Accidental Death of an Anarchist*, 1970) and *Clacson,*

trombette e pernacchi (*About Face*, 1980): each of these plays features a
Chaplinesque little man who gets into trouble with the powers that be and
escapes by the skin of his teeth, all the while dealing almost inadvertent
blows to those powers. In Fo's works generally and in these three plays
specifically there reigns a healthy sense of magic which complements the
movement of hilarious madness. In *Arcangels Don't Play Pinball* a simple
citizen attempts to claim his disability pension only to learn that he is
registered by the government as a hunting dog and must spend a night in
the local pound to straighten out his status. *Accidental Death* is based upon
an actual case of 'defenestration' in which anarchist Giuseppe Pinelli 'fell'
to his death from the window of a Milanese police station in 1969. In the
play the character of the Fool (representing Pinelli) 'falls' from the
window of the police stage set, only to reappear very much alive in
another costume at the same 'police office' before the final curtain. *About
Face* also features a real-life personality. In it Italian Fiat magnate Gianni
Agnelli spends a fair amount of time – thanks to a car accident, amnesia
and plastic surgery matched to a mistaken identity – as a worker in his
own factory. The magic created by these mad situations derives from a
delicious sense of implausibility which each plot engenders, and the consequent sense of make-believe which lowers audience resistance to Fo's
potent social and political messages.

The work of Eduardo De Filippo lodges both chronologically and
generically between that of Pirandello and that of Fo. It is fair to contrast
Pirandello's use of tragic madness in his drama with the comic madness
perfected by Fo in his. And it is equally fair to suggest that the term comi-
tragedy might be coined to describe Eduardo's position in this measuring
of madness quotients in Italian twentieth-century drama.

> In my theatre, the audience is not in the theatre, but where the play takes
> place. When the play is over, the audience should wake up in the theatre, as if
> it has been dreaming.[2]

Such a premise concerning the whereabouts of his audience was symptomatic of Eduardo's fascination with magic. During this and other conversations with the author during 1970–71, it became clear that Eduardo's
theatrical vision demanded the precise, almost scientific creation of a
magical aura; appearance, disappearance and simultaneity were essential
tools of his trade. The other equally essential component of his work was
that it speak to social issues, a goal that he repeated publicly in 1973:

> At the basis of my theatre is always the conflict between man and society . . .
> This conflict is based upon a reaction to injustice, anger over hypocrisy,
> solidarity and sympathy with a person or group, rebellion against anachron-
> isms of the world today.[3]

Madness generally erupts in De Filippo's plays when this conflict between the individual and his societal situation reaches the point of no return. *Questi fantasmi!* (*Oh, These Ghosts!*, 1946), *La Grande Magia* (*Grand Magic*, 1948) and *Le voci di dentro* (*Inner Voices*, 1948) are particularly notable for their fusion of magic, both structurally and thematically, with such erupting madness. All three were written at the height of the post-World War II depression/renewal, when the Italian nation in general and the city of Naples in particular were attempting to remedy agonizing combinations of disfunction and unemployment, and when so many citizens, especially those of lower-class origins, were attempting to escape war-time patterns of unremitting poverty and hunger. As Mario Mignone suggests in his excellent study, Eduardo's use of neo-realistic themes in his plays clearly preceded their use by great Italian film makers such as De Sica, Rossellini and Visconti.[4]

Oh, These Ghosts! is a strange play in which tight psychological portraits of desparate characters are drawn against a backdrop of gigantic proportions. The setting is a sixteenth-century palace purported to have 366 rooms and to be inhabited by numerous ghosts. The protagonist is a man of insufficient means who has tried unsuccessfully to provide well for a youngish wife who does not return his love. Pasquale Lojacono's current solution has been to move into an eighteen-room apartment of the palace, provided rent-free by its owner on condition that he, Pasquale, prove it ghost-free. To this end the new tenant has agreed to appear morning and night upon each of the apartment's seventy balconies and beat rugs while whistling a happy tune. His private plan is to fix up and sub-let as many of these spacious rooms as possible as soon as their reputation for being haunted has been laid to rest.

The minor characters are, for the most part, as desparate as Lojacono. His wife Maria is pursued relentlessly by her lover Alfredo, who becomes the apartment's 'ghost' in order to see her, and who is pursued with equal relentlessness by *his* wife. Only the off-stage character, Professor Santanna, whose role is to 'listen' from an unseen, adjacent balcony as the other characters confess their concerns to him, would seem to possess sufficient equilibrium to survive in the world of poverty, debt and jealous love which they describe.

'Comi-tragedy' lies, not only in the absurdity of the situation, but in the fact that the 'ghost' is generous, placing one thousand lire notes in the pockets of Pasquale's jacket with astounding regularity. While his wife is disgusted with his ability to accept the gifts of this 'ghost' without question, Pasquale admonishes her not to discuss these matters.

> *Maria.* What kind of man am I living with? . . . One beautiful morning, as if by magic, you find a completely furnished aluminum kitchen and the only reaction from you is a sort of idiotic smile, and you let the kitchen stay! Furniture for five bedrooms – was it put there by an elf?[5]
>
> . . .

> *Pasquale.* You're a woman of quality and you must live well; you're not
> satisfied easily. Let's leave all this discussion, this foolishness of yours that
> doesn't get us anywhere. I've got to go down now.[6]

Belief in a generous ghost is the 'answer' for Pasquale, a magic solution to
the woes of unemployment and poverty, and he calls openly upon this
benefactor for greater support and a way out of debt. The jealous love of
the ardent Alfredo, however, is no match for Pasquale's psychosis coupled
with Maria's passivity and his own wife's determination that he return to
his family. The audience imagines the pitiful epilogue of Pasquale Lojacono's total collapse as the final curtain falls on Alfredo's last financial
contribution to this magical household.

In *Grand Magic* a variation of the 'magic as remedy for jealous love'
theme is played out through the victim–victimizer relationship of two
anti-heroes – one a magician by trade and very poor, the other an overbearing, possessive husband and very rich. 'Comi-tragedy' is again an
appropriate term, as Calogero Di Spelta becomes psychotic before the
drama ends.

The play opens at an Italian seaside resort where guests are discussing
the magic show to take place in the evening, and we hear of the talented
Professor Otto Marvuglia, 'Master of Occult Sciences and Celebrated
Illusionist' for the first time. Eventually it becomes clear that these
plaudits, as well as the engagement itself, have been rigged. Also rigged is
the evening's vanishing act during which Marta, Di Spelta's wife, enters
the magician's sarcophagus and disappears. The trick has been arranged
and paid for by her lover with whom she had expected to spend a stolen
fifteen minutes, but by whom she is literally abducted in the rendezvous
motor boat to Venice. When Di Spelta asks that his wife be returned from
the magic sarcophagus, the troubled magician has already heard the
motor boat recede into the distance, and covers his tracks by introducing
the question of jealousy and by assuring Di Spelta that what he is
experiencing is pure illusion: 'I'm afraid that if your wife has vanished at
all, you yourself made her vanish. It's now up to you to make her
reappear.'[7] And Otto then proceeds to give the anguished husband a
small Japanese box measuring seven by sixteen inches.

> *Otto.* Your wife is in that box. Open it. One moment. Are you in good faith?
> *Di Spelta.* In what way?
> *Otto.* Are you sure that your wife is in that box? Now look, unless you believe
> it, and very firmly at that, you will not see her. Do you understand? Unless
> you're certain she's there, please do not open it.[8]

The second act reveals the wretched poverty in which Otto and his
wife/assistant Zaira live, as well as the extent of his charlatan activities.
As the third act opens four years later, we learn that Di Spelta, terribly

aged and still entertaining the illusion of his wife Marta's fidelity, has never opened the magic box which 'contains' her. Tragic resolution ensues when she returns, much sadder and wiser after her Venetian adventure, but not wise enough to follow Otto's admonition that she robe her reappearance in his box formula. When she enters seconds *before* Di Spelta opens his coveted little box and proclaims her actual whereabouts during the past four years, her poor husband crosses completely into the world of illusion, dismisses wife and conjurer, and is left with only his servants and the reality of his good faith inside a Japanese box seven by sixteen inches.

In *Inner Voices*, Eduardo utilizes a dream as the magic means of causing his characters both to scrutinize their feelings about one another and to reveal their own motivations for action. Through the strange encounter of two neighboring families, the psychosis of an entire war-sick society is revealed, and condemned. The Saporito brothers, Alberto and Carlo, live in a Neapolitan apartment building across the landing from the Cimmaruta family. While Carlo sponges a complete meal at the Cimmaruta table on the pretext of having felt weak from hunger while climbing the stairs, his brother Alberto has gone to bring the police to arrest the entire family as suspects in the murder of their common neighbor, Aniello Amitrano. But the murder, it turns out, has only taken place in Alberto's head; that is to say, although Aniello has really disappeared, the family's role in this disappearance has simply been dreamed by Alberto. Although the Cimmarutas return from the police station free agents, each is now convinced of the reality of Alberto's dream, and each secretly approaches him with the name of the murderer – aunt accuses nephew, nephew accuses aunt, wife points to her husband and husband to his wife, sister accuses brother. The dreamer is shocked, not only by the terrible suspicions which his dream has unleashed in this family, but also by his brother's demand that he sign over his share of their common property in case he, Alberto, should be jailed. When the missing Aniello Amitrano returns safely from an overnight stay (inspired by a marital spat) with a relative in the next town, one aspect of post-war psychosis becomes abundantly clear: suspicion and jealousy have completely dislodged the former trust and loyalty upon which this community had once based their daily lives. No one has been murdered, and yet now each knows the murder capable of being entertained in his own mind and in the minds of those with whom he lives.

It is interesting to note the role in aiding and abetting the madness–magic mix which cameo parts play in each 'comi-tragedy'. The off-stage Professor Santanna who is the chief 'listener' in *Oh! These Ghosts* has already been mentioned. His existence in the mind's eye of players and audience alike creates a magical sense of life beyond the set, and his silent absorption of the small madnesses related to him creates a sense of all-knowing presence. In contrast to such calm is the sense of frenzy generated by the sister of the apartment's porter. Carmela is a forty-five-year-old woman who looks seventy. Her semi-madness and sudden white hair have been brought on by some mysterious contact with former 'ghosts' inhabiting Pasquale's apartment, and her inability to explain coherently what she saw on the fateful night of her mishap creates an unsettling emblem of actual madness which permeates *Oh, These Ghosts!*.

Another all-knowing presence, although of a different order from the off-stage Professor, is Zi' Nicola in *Inner Voices*. While physically present in his crude but private loft (from which he often spits) located above the living room of the brothers Alberto and Carlo, Zi' Nicola's is another non-speaking role. As Carlo explains to a visitor, Zi' Nicola gave up speaking years ago when he decided it was a waste of time: 'Humanity's deaf. So why bother talking to it.'⁹ He does, however, communicate on occasion with Alberto – by setting off fireworks. 'Give him a thunder flash, and two or three catherine wheels and he can be surprisingly eloquent.'¹⁰ So unusual a character offers both amazement and a sense of magic, so it is more than a slight blow to the audience when Zi' Nicola dies at the end of act II after setting off a wonderful green roman candle from his loft.

Death is also present in *Grand Magic*. Amanda, the daughter of Otto's side kick, Arturo, has a heart condition identified early in the play. Some-how, however, we are not allowed to take this foreshadowing too seriously, for in act I she turns her nose up at the fresh egg her concerned father has bought her, and in act II scolds her off-stage boyfriend because he hasn't yet asked the name of her favorite flower. Amanda seems, in short, all too young and human to die, but die she does, as if the playwright were determined to have us experience awe and anger (magic and madness perhaps?) in response to death's injustices.

In these plays each protagonist, originally acted by Eduardo, is a *commedia dell'arte* figure, a Pulcinella who is down and out financially, is low on self-esteem and has little to look forward to. Yet each is capable of great attachment and concern – Pasquale Lojacono for his wife, Otto Marvuglia for his magic, Alberto Saporito for his brother and for humanity-at-large. Each is a survivor, physically and psychologically, despite the worst the war has had to offer. And each has used some form of illusion as a means to that survival. Pasquale's willingness to entertain belief in a good ghost, Otto's clinging to his art of magic when all else fails, Alberto's vivid dreaming all suggest Eduardo's affinity for the magic of theatre which, it would seem, was his method of dealing with an insane world. Despite each persona's potent powers of survival, however, a hope has been extinguished by each final curtain: Pasquale's wife will never love and respect him, Calogero will never return to normalcy, members of the

Cimmaruta and Saporito families will never really trust one another again. The tragedy of the 'comi-tragedy' has left its mark on the increasingly fragile psyches of Eduardo's characters.

While *Oh, These Ghosts!*, *Grand Magic* and *Inner Voices* are particularly appealing in their mating of magic and madness, there is no De Filippo drama which does not touch upon some psychological weakness – in Ben Jonson's day we might have called them humors – and upon its specific connection with some terrible social injustice. In his two greatest portraits of war-riddled Naples, *Napoli Milionaria* (*Millionaires' Naples!*, 1945) and *Filumena Marturano* (1946), Eduardo makes a case for the potential psychosis of the soldier returning home to an uncaring family and society, and a case for the potential psychosis of the single mother and her illegitimate sons. Illegitimacy was a social/psychological concern close to Eduardo's heart since he and his siblings were themselves 'figli d'arte', and the subject is explored even more thoroughly in *De pretore Vincenzo* (1957).

The fear of death is explored in *Il contratto* (*The Contract*, 1967) as another magician protagonist promises resurrection contracts with surprising terms, and the fear of life without patriotic ideals is dissected in *Il monumento* (*The Monument*, 1970) through an anti-hero who prefers to remain in the past. It is fair to say that in his last play, *Gli esami non finiscono mai* (*Exams Are Never Over*, 1973), Eduardo forthrightly identifies the neuroses available to each individual at each succeeding stage of human development. At once enormously amusing and most heart-rending – indeed a fitting emblem of Eduardo's creation of comi-tragedy – is the image of the dead protagonist whose living travail we have followed for three acts, as he cavorts freely and gleefully among the pall-bearers at his own funeral. Guglielmo Speranza's grin overcomes his face, for he is free at last of unfaithful friends, greedy relatives and ungrateful offspring. Here is Eduardo's comic response to Hamlet's tragic soliloquy – not to be is better.

Eduardo's plays are difficult to translate into English. Historically speaking, they have fared far worse before American than British audiences. Neapolitan humor, while not perfectly replicated in British translation, is understood perhaps for its continental quality in a manner which to date, at any rate, has eluded Broadway and off-Broadway producers of *Filumena Marturano*.

Perhaps the best place to look for a sense of this comi-tragic humor is in the plays of one of our greatest regional playwrights, Thornton Wilder. Indeed during his mature years Wilder spoke often of Eduardo as his 'favorite living playwright'.[11] A careful look at the character of Sabina in *The Skin of Our Teeth* reveals a *commedia* character, female to be sure, who possesses as effective physical and psychological survival techniques as any of Eduardo's personae, but who is equally savy about the possible advantages of death over life. Congratulating herself on her own ability to philosophize, she declares during the play's opening monologue: 'In the midst of life we are in the midst of death. A truer word was never said!'[12]

A final barometer perhaps of Eduardo's taste for madness, for magic and for the comi-tragic was his response to an invitation by Einaudi in 1984 to publish his translation of a Shakespearean play of his own choosing. Eduardo chose to render *The Tempest* in 'a slightly modified version of 17th-century Neapolitan', with the rationale that he was impressed by the 'protective love' of Prospero for Miranda, and that he saw Ariel as a 'Neapolitan urchin, cunning and prankish'.[13] Might Eduardo's choice not also have been motivated by Prospero's magicianship, by Caliban's madness, and by the comi-tragedy of representative humankind adrift on a special island? Eduardo was surely the Prospero of Neapolitan post-war theatre. His theatre magic helped to tame the anger and anxiety of his contemporaries, and has helped posterity to understand to some degree the madness of war and its aftermath. Eduardo did confess to another reason for translating *The Tempest*: 'It teaches tolerance and benevolence and what better lesson can an artist give us today?'[14]

NOTES

1 Domenico Vittorini, *The Drama of Luigi Pirandello* (New York: Russell & Russell, 1969), p. 159.

2 Mimi D'Aponte, 'Encounters with Eduardo De Filippo', *Modern Drama* 16: 3 and 4 (December 1973), 349–50.

3 Eduardo De Filippo, 'Eduardo De Filippo', *Théâtre en Europe* (April 1985), 5.

4 Mario Mignone, *Eduardo De Filippo* (Boston: Twayne Publishers, 1984), p. 68.

5 Eduardo De Filippo, *Neapolitan Ghosts*, trans. Marguerita Carra and Louise H. Warner for the Yale Repertory Theatre/Yale School of Drama, II–17.

6 Ibid., II–20.

7 Eduardo De Filippo, *Grand Magic, Three Plays* (Northumberland Press, 1976), p. 126.

8 Ibid., p. 127.

9 Eduardo De Filippo, *Inner Voices*, English version by N. F. Simpson (London: Amber Lane Press, 1983), p. 39.

10 Ibid.

11 Mignone, 'Preface', *Eduardo De Filippo*, unpaged.

12 Thornton Wilder, *The Skin of Our Teeth, Three Plays* (New York: Bantam, 1961), p. 71.

13 George Romney, 'O beato munno nuovo', *The Economist*, 9 June 1984, p. 111.

14 Ibid.

A dramaturgy of madness: Suzuki and the *Oresteia*

JOHN J. FLYNN

Tabi ni yamite yume wa kare-no wo kake-meguru

On a journey, ill,
and over fields all withered, Dreams
go wandering still.

(Bashō, Haiku Master, c. 1690)[1]

Much has been written about the performance theory of the noted Japanese director Tadashi Suzuki, but little has been written in Europe or America that addresses his playwriting. This seems natural in light of the fact that the results of his performance theory can be found everywhere; he has trained many American and European actors, and his more advanced students are inspiring still more practioners of the 'Suzuki Method', a unique performance style which combines elements of Nō, Kabuki, and the Japanese avant-garde. Although his three 'Greek' plays (*Toroiya no onna* or *Trojan Women*, *Bakkosu no shinjo* or *The Believers of Bacchus*, and *Ōhi Kuryotaimesutora* or *Queen Clytemnestra*) have served as the main showpieces for his technique and have been seen in Europe and America, only *Ōhi Kuryotaimesutora* has been published in English.

All three texts engage the critic in two discussions which are vital in contemporary theatre: the notion of 'updating' or transplanting a play from the classical repertory into a more recent time period, and the notion of 'fusion' or 'interculturalism', the combination of European or Euro-American and Asian (or Latin, or African, etc.) content and form. By examining them we can find reflections and elaborations of similar work in Europe and America, and a fascinating set of tools with which to consider European and American revivals of the classical canon.

In this paper I will examine Suzuki's efforts in this regard, focusing on his *Ōhi Kuryotaimesutora* (hereafter, *Queen Clytemnestra*). I shall examine his dramaturgy, and explore the connection of his text to the Greek originals. I shall argue that the resultant text is the product of a dramaturgy of madness – a dramaturgy which in content mirrors, and in effect recreates, insanity. By pushing traditional Japanese dramaturgical conventions and Greek plays to their limits, madness is achieved. I shall conclude with some general comments on Suzuki as both an interculturalist and as a 'renovator' of classical works.

In a recent article Professor Yukihiro Goto, a renowned expert on Suzuki's work, attempted to delineate two underpinnings of Suzuki's dramaturgy: *honkadori* and *sekai*. In *honkadori* (the technique of 'taking a foundation poem'), 'new poems are composed drawing on elements or images in existing well-known poems'.[2] The Nō theatre exemplifies this technique, for often a playwright will make use of ideas and imagery to compose and deepen the meaning of a play. *Honkadori* provides a context or springboard for the new work. However, in Suzuki's playwriting, bringing the new into existence creates tensions between the old work and the new, adding to the depth and experience of the play. In Suzuki's words: 'By using some familiar materials, I aim to destroy their known values and at the same time create totally original ones.'[3]

It is important to note that the use of the term is not precise. Suzuki claims that he is 'not using the term *honkadori* in an authentic sense',[4] for part of his stated purpose is 'to destroy [the various texts'] known values'. Suzuki goes farther than earlier practioners of this technique in three important ways: the older play assumes far greater importance than in other Japanese works employing *honkadori*; the work suggested by *honkadori* is brought into conflict with *sekai* (literally, 'world', although we might translate it as 'milieu'); and a violent confrontation with the sensibilities of the older play transpires.

Suzuki's radicalization of the technique is clear when compared to a classical example. In Zeami's *Kayoi Komachi* one finds the lines, 'In Yamashiro, In the town of Kowata, There were horses to hire.'[5] This is authentic *honkadori*: a brief but unmistakable reference to a love poem by a poet named Hitomaro. It opens the way for a further sentiment (though there were horses, the man showed his devotion by walking, in this case), it establishes certain ideas about locale and the season, and it creates a series of emotional and aesthetic echoes between Zeami's play (which concerns a lover whose devotion passes even the boundary of death) and Hitomaro's poem. In many cases such a reference is the very first line of a play. From this simple allusion Zeami constructs his plot, for now he has a foundation (*hon* – the Japanese character is a tree with a slash at the bottom, directing the reader to the 'root' or 'foundation').

Suzuki uses much more than just the 'root'. In his *Queen Clytemnestra*, instead of starting with the Greek myth of Orestes as a foundation, Suzuki uses it as a near-complete entity. Whole passages of Aeschylus are left virtually intact. Compare, for example these passages from the ancient and the modern texts.

> Wait, son, wait. My baby, soften
> towards this bosom where so many times

> you went to sleep, with little gums
> fumbling at the milk which sweetly made you grow.[6]

and

> Wait! Please wait! Orestes, be scrupulous, tremble at what you may do.
> Remember who I am. My own child! You, who clung to these breasts! You
> nibbled on them in your sleep as I held you, drinking your fill of my delicious
> milk![7]

This is not the only example of a direct use of Aeschylus; there are many of
them, and Aeschylus is not alone on Suzuki's list of citations. Suzuki uses
not only the *Oresteia* of Aeschylus (though it is the most obvious inspiration), but also the *Electra* of both Sophocles and Euripides, and most
particularly the *Orestes* of Euripides. I could go on to cite similar passages
from the other five plays which serve as the central structure of *Queen
Clytemnestra*, but I will leave their intrusion/collision for my discussion of
meaning below. Suzuki uses a sum (not *the* sum) of various aspects of the
legend of Orestes in his invocation of *honkadori*.

If the story of Orestes is the frame of the play, then two other elements
will complete its construction. The first is Suzuki's own rewriting and
additions which connect the other texts, elaborate on them, and unify
them in terms of style. These are many and obvious, and for the moment
we need not concern ourselves with them; their major function is to create
continuity in what might otherwise be a confusing collage. The other
element, *sekai*, is more germane to our examination of Suzuki as a
playwright. As Professor Goto explains, 'Suzuki's adaptation technique is
similar to [Japanese] traditional drama's regular system of plotting and
drawing upon known "worlds" (*sekai*) . . . A *sekai* is a historically known
situation . . .'[8] The key word here is 'known', not 'historically', for the
worlds that Japanese dramatists draw upon are sometimes more fictional
than factual. Examples of *sekai* in Europe and America might include
Camelot, Agincourt, the Alamo, and Rick's Café in Casablanca; each of
these suggest a milieu, a set of characters and relationships, and a specific
set of emotions. In traditional Japanese theatre, *sekai* and *honkadori* comp-
lement each other, for they both come from or refer to a distant past. In
Suzuki's work they are usually the distant past and the near past brought
into direct conflict. Thus in *Queen Clytemnestra*, 'by quoting and
reconstructing the dialogue of six plays written by the three writers of this
tragedy', Suzuki tries to 'present an internal view of contemporary man
who is becoming more and more isolated because he cannot help but live
in a spiritually chaotic state'.[9] *Sekai* is the shell which rests on the structure
of the ancient story and Suzuki's own patches and revisions. In the case of
Queen Clytemnestra we see not only the story of Orestes, but also the story of
modern intra-family violence – a modern *sekai* which is of much concern to

19 and 20 *Queen Clytemnestra*, directed by Tadashi Suzuki

Suzuki. On one level, the play shows a modern Japanese family playing out the story of the House of Atreus. The play's modernity is heightened by the inclusion of 'River of Fate', a well-known Japanese pop song of the 1980s. On another level, the characters speak in the formal tones of the Greek original and with the precision and elaboration of a Nō or Kabuki actor. Design, too, feeds this dialectic: some costumes and motifs are modern, and some are traditional.

Thus, within *Queen Clytemnestra* three elements rage against each other: the legend of Orestes, intra-family violence, and the sensibilities of the author combining and commenting on these two. It is the particularly Japanese sense of time, of dream/memory and of 'flashforward/back' which brings the various elements of the texts into relief and creates meaning in Suzuki's work. Here again we confront a basic technique in Japanese dramaturgy, expanded and played out in a startling way.

That technique is the fluidity of time which occurs in many Nō plays. In the Nō there are often two phases of action: the main one (which brackets the second) usually involves a traveler or a priest on a journey to some destination (he is the *waki*, or side-character, and is usually the one responsible for delivering the *honkadori* at the opening). This person happens upon a being, usually a ghost or a magical spirit of some sort, who is the *shite* (or 'do-er', the principal character). The *shite* tells his or her story, and in so doing transports the play in time and space to the incident of which he or she speaks. The time shift is understood to be complete and true, for Nō assumes a fluidity of time. Usually at the end we are returned to the *waki*, and often the *waki* is able to offer some assistance or absolution for the troubled spirit. It is crucial to note that while technically this is similar to the 'flashback' that has become a stock dramatic convention, in actuality it relies wholly on the performance of the *shite*, and stands somewhere between storytelling and 'flashback'. In *Queen Clytemnestra* time is more than fluid – at certain points it almost holds no meaning. The following is the basic scenario for the action of the play.

Prologue: Beginning of *The Libation Bearers* and both of the *Electra* plays. Chorus & Electra bemoan their fate, Clytemnestra argues with Electra.

Scene 1: Orestes in the *Orestes* of Euripides: plagued by the as yet unseen Furies, he is being driven mad. Statues of Apollo and Athena watch unmoved in what has now become the interior of a temple. We are led to understand that Clytemnestra is *dead* at this point. Orestes threatens unseen furies.

Scene 2: An extension of Aeschylus' *Eumenides* invades Euripides' *Orestes*: Apollo and the Furies debate (inside of Orestes' mind?).

Scene 3: Electra brings the body of Aegisthus to an amazed Orestes, who realizes that it is he who has done the deed. At this point we find Clytemnestra *alive* again.

Scene 4: A memory intrudes, from *Agamemnon*. It is Clytemnestra's victory
    speech after killing Agamemnon and Cassandra (whose bodies she
    drags on).
Scene 5: The play moves forward to the closing moments of *The Libation
    Bearers*, including Clytemnestra's pleas and her murder.
Scene 6: Athena and the Furies debate (*Eumenides*), Orestes speaks on his
    own behalf at the end of the scene.
Scene 7: Agamemnon and Clytemnestra reappear in the famous tapestry
    scene from *Agamemnon*.
Scene 8: Orestes repeats his speech from the end of scene 6 *in toto*, and he
    and Apollo debate with the Furies (*Eumenides*).
Scene 9: Tyndareos from *Orestes* enters the debate and Apollo and Athena
    lapse into silence, becoming statues once more. The Furies also drop
    out of the action. 'The scene returns to reality, as in Scenes One and
    Three.' Tyndareos apparently gains the upper hand by appealing to a
    socially composed justice – there is no rejoinder to his arguments, for
    the Gods are all silent.
Scene 10: Electra and Orestes, in the depths of guilt and despair, consider
    suicide, and are slain by the ghost of Clytemnestra.

I shall try to create a 'rational' overlay for the action, and to
demonstrate the complexity and elusiveness of Suzuki's sense of time and
reality. If the stage direction for scene 9 cited above is to be believed,
reality exists in scenes 1, 3, 9, and 10, and all of the other scenes occur
outside physical reality: they are memory, madness, clairvoyance, and/or
internal debate. The story belongs primarily to Orestes, and secondarily,
to his sister Electra: it is the story of the overwhelming guilt that they have
incurred by murdering their mother. Orestes, who is both the Orestes of
Greek legend and the Orestes of modern Japan, is our way into the play,
for it is his madness that we see for the most part. We witness his delibera-
tions about his fate and responsibility from *Orestes* and from *Eumenides*, and
see his memories from *The Libation Bearers*. If there is a reality, then it is
one with Orestes at its core, and the intrusions of the other scenes are
clearly the projections of his mind.
    But what of the scenes to which only Electra would be privy, particu-
larly those from the *Agamemnon*? They would seem to indicate a *combination*
of Orestes and Electra as the 'core' of the play. If the play is dominated by
scenes of memory and madness brought onstage, then whose memory and
whose madness are we watching? The text is purposely vague on this
point, and a traditional European or Euro-American critique is frustrated
by an inability to divine a consciousness at the core of the piece. One
could make a strong argument that this play has a perspective similar to
Strindberg's *Dream Play*, but even there we can view the whole of the play
as the experiences of a single sensibility (Indra's Daughter). In *Queen*

Clytemnestra that role would seem to belong to Orestes, Electra, and Suzuki himself, all in combination. Ultimately, the play frustrates any attempt to order its elements. It exists to frustrate expectations, and to contradict itself.

Furthermore, what are we to make of the appearance of a *living* Clytemnestra at the end of scene 3? The play contains several hallucinatory shifts (underlined by Suzuki's smooth but oblique staging style) such as the one that connects scenes 3 and 4. Scene 3 is already on unsteady ground, since Electra drags the dead body of Aegisthus on the stage and throws it in front of Orestes. At first he is 'amazed' (p. 137) but soon states that he has in fact done this deed. We are led to believe that Clytemnestra is dead also, but at the close of the scene Clytemnestra appears.

> *Electra.* . . . Somehow her chariot and clothes seem to be glittering with light. She has brought her entourage along. *Electra and Orestes drag the mutilated body out of sight.*
>
> SCENE FOUR
>
>   . . . *the Furies and the Citizens appear, waiting for Clytemnestra . . . she comes in, dragging the bodies of the just-murdered Agamemnon and Cassandra. This scene is from the memories of Orestes and Electra.*
>
>   (p. 139)

There is no clear shift between memory (*Agamemnon*, the approach of the Queen) and current reality (*The Libation Bearers*), just as there is no clear shift between the consciousness of Electra (the Prologue) and Orestes (later scenes). Furthermore, just as memory (scene 4) intrudes on reality (scene 3), the distinction between reality and the supernatural is confused. If we read 1, 3, 9, and 10 as 'reality' scenes, we may neatly dispose of the supernatural elements of the play in *almost* all instances. In other scenes the statues of Apollo and Athena are only brought to life by Orestes' feverish guilt, and the glowering Furies are merely the personification of that guilt.

As the scenario above indicates, the pace and complexity of these shifts intensifies as the play goes on. The vortex of the text is finally resolved by a truly horrific *coup de théâtre.*

> *The ghost of Clytemnestra appears and slashes at the two with her knife as they embrace . . . The dead bodies of Electra and Orestes now lie stretched out in a corner of the temple . . .*
>
>   (p. 158)

In the final analysis, logic (that is, linear, Aristotelian, plot-oriented logic) collapses in on itself. Form here equals content, and the content is madness. The structures that I have described above are useful in the sense that they allow one to discuss the elements of the plot in relation to each other, but they are useless in constructing meaning in the sense that a traditional European or Euro-American critic would: the structures are almost, but not quite, completely logically integrated. My structures would also be lost on an audience watching the play, because for them the experience is even more irrational since they are unable to backtrack, compare, and reread. For the audience, *Queen Clytemnestra* becomes a relentless flood of worlds, times, and realities. *Queen Clytemnestra* takes place with the speed and illogic of emotionally charged thought. It happens as a story, and it happens in the minds of the murderous siblings. It is here that Suzuki proves himself the master of a more overarching concern in Asian literature and thought: the sustainable paradox. At the risk of overgeneralizing, the sorts of closure which obsess a Judeo-Christian culture have little appeal for one steeped in Buddhism and Taoism. Thus, in the Nō the world of the *waki* and the story of the *shite* are *both* 'real' events in the play, and (as Brecht observed of the Chinese) the actors are at once themselves and the characters that they play – a fact which is wholly unremarkable to audiences who are unaffected by Aristotle or Realism. In Japanese art (heavily influenced as it is by Buddhism and Taoism) different realities, identities, and times need not be reconciled with each other. As the Chinese Taoist philosopher Chuang-Tzu said (upon waking from dreaming he was a butterfly), 'Do I dream of being a butterfly, or is the butterfly dreaming of me?'

Answering such a question is unimportant. Perceiving it and sustaining the paradox is – that is the final truth of Suzuki's dramaturgy. Due to the specific subject that *Queen Clytemnestra* addresses (matricide), the irreconcilable tensions between worlds, times, and realities are necessary, for they dramaturgically express the plight of the protagonists. What can one reasonably do when one has killed the first object and giver of life and love? Shattering that primary connection shatters all else. This ultimate betrayal of filial piety (a paramount concern throughout Asia) guarantees that the family as a whole is doomed to come to a quick and unahppy end. The fact that the murder of Agamemnon is somehow less of a crime is also explicable under filial piety: vertical aggression is always more despicable than horizontal aggression.

In contrast with the Greeks, Suzuki has sifted the same events and uncovered vastly different materials. Suzuki has professed a great respect for Greek texts and for Japanese literary techniques and performance traditions, and yet he is quite free in his use of the materials of both cultures. The main deviations from the traditional versions of the Orestes tale are that no new social structure presents itself to solve the seemingly insoluble problem of matricide, and the fact that Orestes and Electra do not find absolution at the end of the play.

These deviations directly oppose the traditions associated with the story, traditions which most of us encounter first in the *Oresteia*. That trilogy is, to many, the quintessential portrayal of the development of

European notions of justice and government, for during its course we see the blood feud replaced with trial by jury. An impartial agent of 'truth' is elected to end the vendetta and convert the Furies into the Eumenides. Gender is also part of Aeschylus' agenda, for the balanced patriarchy manages to assert itself over the unbalanced matriarchy, in terms of action and of imagery.

Madness and bloodthirst, in Suzuki, are not gender-specific: there is no recognition of a patriarchy, nor is there a condemnation of a tribal matriarchy. Furthermore, the play does not offer any rational way out of the problem it poses for its leading figures. The action of the *Oresteia* is all pointed towards the moment where Athena declares, 'This man stands acquitted on a charge of blood.'[10] In *Queen Clytemnestra*, neither acquittal nor condemnation comes from the debates in the play. Instead, Orestes proclaims

> Apollo, even if your self-proclaiming justice is only the most ordinary, the fulfillment of all this suffering will here and now be all too clear . . . Will any of the devout and pious of other lands look me, a murderer, in the face? . . . This cannot be endured. For I took the hair of her head . . . grasped the robes above me, took my sword, and made her the object of my sacrifice.
>
> (p. 158)

Orestes himself sees no exoneration; from the moment he committed the murder he was doomed. Even if he and his sister are found innocent, or merely banished, their crimes will not be expiated; the situation is unendurable.

The fact that the Gods are powerless in this play brings it into sharp opposition with the Euripides plays. In *Electra*, the Dioscuri (Castor and Polydeuces) appear to right things, and in *Orestes*, Apollo himself appears. In *Queen Clytemnestra*, the Gods have fallen silent well before the final fate of the characters is decided. Although they have wrestled with the problem throughout, delineating the various positions as they do in the Greek plays, they have no existence in the 'real' world.

In tone and style, there is much similarity between Aeschylus, Euripides, and Suzuki. Kitto, in his analysis of Euripides, points to a factor which has repeatedly drawn Suzuki to Euripides' texts, 'He is drawing a certain extreme type of character (reminiscent of Medea) and therefore wishes to place her in circumstances which push her to the extreme.'[11] Extremes, physiological and psychological, are the hallmarks of the Suzuki style, and it is for that reason that characters such as Orestes, Electra, Cassandra, and Pentheus have all been brought to life on his stage.

I mention Aeschylus in this context, because in the *Oresteia* his technique is what one might call pre-Sophoclean. It is linear, but it does not feature the sort of tight, relentless plotting that characterizes Sophocles and much of Euripides. Instead, Aeschylus displays a meditative, etiological style – a style which, as we have seen in the analysis above, is akin to the flow and structure of *Queen Clytemnestra*. Samuel Beckett, another dramatist who influenced Suzuki, belongs in this 'non-Sophoclean' grouping, and is often compared to the Nō, a tradition which influences Suzuki in the extreme.

Finally, in comparing Suzuki and his sources, mention should be made of the tradition in Euro-American drama of 'updating' the classics (for Suzuki is certainly engaged in that activity), and of his 'interculturalism'. Suzuki brings something new to the discussion of 'updating', and it is the conflict between those two entities in the play: his particular use of *sekai* and *honkadori*. Suzuki's attitude is much like those directors who seek to 'update' the play, for he uses modern Japan because that 'society strongly resembles the earlier situation'.[12] Many directors cast about for similarities, for milieu or situations which are conducive to the text. The difference in Suzuki is that he is quite clear about the distinction between the past and the present, and he encourages tensions between the two. For most the objective is a happy marriage between past/text and present/setting. For Suzuki the tension between them is never forgotten, for it is built into his structural conception of the piece and the acting and design elements of the piece. The tension is the point where art is created, and it is this disjuncture which places him squarely in the ranks of directors such as Peter Sellars (particularly in his recent Mozart operas) and Anne Bogart (in her *South Pacific*, which is set in an insane asylum). He says that with *Queen Clytemnestra* he is, after his more traditional version of *Trojan Women* and the more modern style of his version of *Bacchae*, trying to 'break through those other styles and create a play that shows the relationship between them'.[13]

In the case of interculturalism, it is possible to fault him as critics have faulted Peter Brook for his production of *The Mahabharata*. In that production Brook attempted to cram as much of the actual story of the *Mahabharata* into his performance as possible, and the critics cried foul. What Brook essentially did was to pluck out the elements that a European or Euro-American audience might expect from its drama (i.e., plot) at the expense of what are considered more ephemeral elements of the performance by that audience (performance, dance, music, etc.). It was a *Mahabharata* made safe for European and American consumption. So too with Suzuki, for he has cut away European and Euro-American concerns (the development of justice, the suppression of the blood feud, etc.), and substituted Japanese ones (filial piety, the family, etc.). The crime is somewhat less heinous in Suzuki's case, though, for he does not claim to be presenting *The* Orestes story.

If one can accept his conventions and his vision of the irredeemability of the crime, the drama becomes a dark and frightening experience indeed. The slips of time and reality create a tension in the play, and they lead us into the madness that Electra and Orestes suffer – madness that is only heightened by the visceral acting style of which Tadashi Suzuki is the master.

NOTES

1 Bashō (Matsuo Manefusa), from *Masterpieces of the Orient*, expanded edition, ed. G. L. Anderson (New York: W. W. Norton, 1977), p. 749.

2 Yukihiro Goto, 'The Theatrical Fusion of Suzuki Tadashi', *Asian Theatre Journal* 6: 2 (Fall 1989), 109.

3 Tadashi Suzuki, *Naikaku no wa* (*The Sum of Interior Angles*) (Tokyo: Jiritsu Shobō, 1973), p. 231, trans. in Goto, 'Theatrical Fusion', p. 109.

4 Ibid., trans. in Goto, 'Theatrical Fusion', p. 109.

5 Zeami, *Kayoi Komachi*, trans. Eileen Kato in *Twenty Plays of the Nō Theater*, ed. Donald Keene (New York: Columbia University Press, 1970), p. 60.

6 Aeschylus, *The Libation Bearers* in *The Orestes Plays of Aeschylus*, trans. Paul Roche (New York: Mentor, 1962), p. 144.

7 Tadashi Suzuki, *Ōhi Kuryotaimesutora*, trans. J. Thomas Rimer in *The Way of Acting* (New York: Theater Communications Group, 1986), p. 142. All references in the text are to this edition.

8 Goto, 'Theatrical Fusion', p. 111.

9 Ibid., p. 112.

10 Aeschylus, *The Libation Bearers*, p. 191.

11 H. D. F. Kitto, *Greek Tragedy* (New York: Methuen, 1973), p. 331.

12 Suzuki, *The Way of Acting*, p. 122.

13 Ibid., p. 123.

'Mad with love': Medea in Euripides and Heiner Müller

CHRISTIAN ROGOWSKI

In Greek mythology, Medea embodies 'otherness' in multiple ways: as a representative of barbarism versus civilization, the supernatural versus the natural, the magical versus the commonsensical, and madness versus reason. She represents what is alien to Greek society, a society that provides the basis of our western tradition. The myth surrounding the princess from Asia Minor had existed in multiple permutations before Euripides' time. Yet it is in the tragedy of Euripides that it finds the form which ensured its place in the western tradition. The myth of Medea runs through our tradition in various guises, and continues to occupy the European mind in literature and the fine arts, most notably in dramatic treatments from Seneca to Corneille and to Heiner Müller.

While it is highly significant that the various forms of 'otherness' are represented in a woman, I do not wish to focus primarily on the anthropological and psychosexual implications of the myth. Instead, I shall examine the dramatic presentation of the myth in Euripides and Heiner Müller by tracing the association between the figure of Medea and the concept most charged with cultural value, that of 'madness'.

Heiner Müller is widely recognized as one of the most important playwrights of our time.[1] He has treated the Medea myth no less than three times in the most diverse manners. In a number of ways, his versions mark the end of the tradition initiated by Euripides. Broadly speaking, in Euripides the myth can be seen as part of the self-definition of a civilization. Heiner Müller appropriates the Medea myth into a comprehensive critique of civilization.[2]

The question of Medea's sanity is of central importance to the tragedy of Euripides. The motif of madness associated with Medea runs through the text in leitmotivic fashion. It is introduced right at the beginning in the opening speech of the Nurse. The Nurse laments in Medea the sad fate of a woman who gave up everything for the love of a man:

> If only they had never gone! If the Argo's hull
> Never had winged out through the grey-blue jaws of rock
> And on towards Colchis! [. . .]

> Then neither would Medea,
> My mistress, ever have set sail for the walled town
> Of Iolcus, mad with love for Jason;[3]

Medea is not presented as a ruthless, blood-thirsty savage. She is endowed with a personal history that makes her present predicament understandable. Her fate is clearly embedded in a larger frame, that of the unholy mission of the Argonauts. On the one hand, Euripides changes the traditional myth by psychologizing the figure of Medea.[4] On the other hand, Medea as woman and as foreigner is placed in the context of a male power structure. Traditionally, Medea had been viewed as a demi-goddess with magical powers. As the descendent of the sun god Helios, the daughter of the union of a king and a sorceress, Medea embodies a tension between the divine and the animal aspects of human nature, a tension between the civilized and the barbaric.[5] Euripides, however, emphasizes the human qualities of the figure by endowing Medea with complex psychological motivations. Her mythic status as demi-goddess is downplayed in the text until the end when the miraculous and the supernatural invade the scene as Medea is carried off in a chariot drawn by dragons. The deus-ex-machina effect seems to suggest that archaic forces prevail despite the attempts to impose cultural restraints. Medea literally gets away with murder. The woman 'mad with love' escapes persecution at Corinth, taking refuge in the safe haven of Athens.

Throughout the text, the lines that divide civilization from barbarism are not as clear as the mythic tradition would have suggested. The Nurse evokes the atrocities committed by Medea ascribing them to madness, an excess of passion. The significance of Medea's guilt is downplayed as the Nurse focuses on the wrong done to Medea herself:

> But now her world has turned to enmity, and wounds her
> Where her affection's deepest. Jason has betrayed
> His own sons, and my mistress, for a royal bed,
> For alliance with the king of Corinth.
>
> (pp. 17–18)

Jason has betrayed Medea, the Nurse maintains, both for sexual and for political reasons. Now that Medea finds herself abandoned, she is lost in the 'agony' of her rage. Medea, the Nurse maintains, is ruled by a single affect. This implies that there is an inherent danger in her character: if the dominating affect cannot be controlled the result will be destructive. Greek civilization is marked by an endeavor to avoid extremes of emotionality, to go the 'middle way', as the Nurse puts it (p. 21). Emotional balance is a cultural ideal. The lack of control over the dominating affect is viewed as madness. In the context of the Greek cultural value system it would appear that Medea is indeed 'mad'.

The motif is picked up by the Chorus of Corinthian women who chide

Medea's obsession with Jason as 'madness' (p. 22). Medea's alleged lack of control is associated with metaphors of wild animals, for instance the 'mad bull' and 'lioness' (p. 23) or the 'tiger' (p. 58). Yet the motif of madness is ironically undercut in various ways. Jason likens Medea to a 'fool' for not accepting his pragmatic decisions to secure his position in Corinth (p. 30). Medea herself concedes at one point that in becoming an accomplice of Jason she showed 'much love and little wisdom' (p. 31). In her second encounter with Jason, Medea appears to have accepted Jason's view that she is 'mad' (p. 43). When Jason sees Medea's gifts for his new wife he again chides her excessiveness as that of a 'foolish woman' (p. 46).

In fact, the overall dramatic presentation of the character of Medea constantly belies the epithet 'mad'. It is clear that there is a certain logic in her behavior. Medea's 'madness' does not at all seem to rule out what appears to be perfectly rational behavior. She shows a great deal of self-awareness about her situation as a woman in exile, pleading her cause so eloquently with the Chorus that the Corinthian women agree that her revenge on Jason is justified (p. 25). The dramatic irony is stressed repeatedly as the audience is informed of Medea's cruel plans before observing her in interaction with other characters. When she is with others, Medea displays considerable shrewdness. For instance, she feigns weakness and repentance in her encounter with King Creon, and manages to win him over by appealing to his paternal instincts. Medea does not appear to be acting on impulse governed by her affect. Rather, she carries out her scheme of revenge with great circumspection, for instance when she seizes the opportunity to secure for herself a refuge in Athens. Medea's first words in the drama expressed her desire to die. Yet she is eager to escape punishment and to live on in the triumphant knowledge of having destroyed Jason. Several times Medea indicates that she is aware of the extent of the atrocity she is planning to commit by murdering her children:

> I understand
> The Horror of what I am going to do; but anger,
> The spring of all life's horrors, masters my resolve.

> (p. 50)

Paradoxically, Medea appears to remain subject to the affect which governs her behavior despite being able to identify it.

Moreover, the sympathy of characters and audience alike is with Medea almost throughout the entire drama: over and over, the Chorus laments her fate as that of a woman wronged. It is only upon her decision to kill her own children in the pursuit of revenge against Jason that the Chorus recoils in horror.[6] Medea has overstepped a limit, her obsession with revenge has become a perversion of justice. Her passion appears to call into question the values of cultural restraint and self-control upon which Greek society is based. In the western tradition Medea is therefore often seen as an emblem of atavistic madness, the embodiment of an unruly passion which threatens civilization.[7]

Yet to view Medea as a woman gone mad with passion is essentially to accept the views expressed by the characters of the drama. The opinions of the various characters, however, at best represent limited perspectives, which themselves are called into question. The Nurse's self-restraint, for instance, is coupled with misogyny, just as Jason's human pragmatism is counterbalanced by his political opportunism. The characters cannot be accepted as simple voices of Reason; their pronouncements are entangled in contexts of complex ambivalence. This complexity has led Albrecht Dihle to reinterpret the figure of Medea altogether.[8] Dihle dismisses the notion central to the western tradition that Medea's murder of her children represents madness, an instance of Passion overruling Reason. Throughout the drama, Medea is characterized by an intellect superior to that of any other person in her environment. This leads Dihle to reinterpret the soliloquy quoted above, in which she seems to announce her decision to kill her children.

In Dihle's reading, to summarize his complex argument briefly, Medea expresses her 'Horror' over her own inability to kill her children.[9] Her identity as a woman is based on an honour code traditionally restricted to the male warrior. It is this male value system which she has accepted for herself which forces her to overcome her womanly feelings of motherly love for her children. Medea is thus not ruled by an overpowering affect but rather by an internalized male value system that ultimately destroys her identity. Rather than marking the defeat of Reason by Emotion, the murder of the children represents just the reverse: the core of Medea's tragedy lies in her inability to assert her emotionality over socially imposed norms of rationality. In a way, this renders the question of Medea's 'madness' obsolete. I am inclined to follow Dihle in his reinterpretation of Euripides' tragedy, since his approach addresses the crucial ambiguities of the drama: on the one hand, Euripides' text demonizes woman as the 'other'; on the other hand, it allows this 'other' to articulate and to maintain its otherness. It is this dual stance which allows us to draw parallels between Euripides' model and Heiner Müller's reworking of the Medea myth.

Heiner Müller has treated the myth of Medea three times. In his play *Cement* of 1971, set in Soviet Russia during the chaos of the civil war that followed the October Revolution, Dasha, a female revolutionary, loses her daughter. Her political activism makes it impossible for her to look after her child. The daughter is sent to a nursery where she starves in the hunger winter of 1921. A bourgeois intellectual interprets the death of the child as a heroic sacrifice and compares Dasha to the mythic figure of

Medea in a segment entitled 'Medea Commentary'. The skewed perspective of the would-be radical ironically undermines this ascription, which is at best based on a vague analogy.[10] Three years later, Müller returned to the Medea motif in a short text entitled *Medeaplay* (1974). It is a one-page scenario without words, a fragmentary visualization of certain aspects of the myth. Two nameless figures are led to a bed, where they ritualistically enact the episodes of courtship, sexual intercourse, birth and murder of the children. Here, the Medea myth is radically reduced to a bleak vision of love as a battle between the sexes. Infanticide, the fragment seems to suggest, is a logical outcome of the oppression of both women and men. There is no perspective of breaking the vicious circle that entraps both. In a destructive structure, offspring cannot survive.

Müller's third adaptation of the Medea complex is found in a text entitled *Despoiled Shore Medeamaterial Landscape with Argonauts* of 1982.[11] It is on this, Müller's most extensive treatment of the Medea myth, that I wish to focus in this paper. As the cumulative title suggests, it is a collage of disjointed dramatic texts centered on the myth of the Argonauts.[12] It is divided into three parts, which – as the author states in a note – are supposed to take place simultaneously. Parts one and three feature only fragments of disembodied discourse, the lines are not attributed to any identifiable speaker. Part two, *Medeamaterial*, mainly consists of an extremely condensed version of the *agon*, the confrontation between Medea and Jason.[13]

To a certain extent Müller follows the Euripidean model. In Heiner Müller's text, too, Medea's frenzy is a function of the violation of her identity. She has been victimized by a foreign civilization that made her become an accomplice in the destruction of her own civilization. Yet Müller does not focus so much on the conflict between an individual and a society or on the juxtaposition of barbarism and civilization. Rather, Müller's postmodern collage of three short dramatic fragments places the figure of Medea in the context of a comprehensive critique of western civilization. In an interview with the German news magazine *Der Spiegel*, Müller emphasized the association between the Medea myth and colonialism. Commenting on the point that Jason should be killed by a piece of timber from his own ship, the Argo, Müller remarked:

> European history, the way it's been going so far, begins with colonialization. That the vehicle of colonialism should slay the colonizer points to the end of colonialization. This is the threat of closure with which we are confronted. The 'End to Growth'.[14]

Müller's allusion to *The Limits to Growth* of 1971, the report by the Club of Rome expressing concern over the global destruction of the environment by industrialized nations, puts the figure of Medea in the context of what Müller broadly defines as colonialism.

Müller gives ironic suggestions for the staging of the texts. *Despoiled Shore* (*Verkommenes Ufer*), for instance, he writes, could be performed in a peep show during its regular operations.[15] In alluding to the voyeurism implied in the theatre and the dual exploitation of the female body and of male desire in pornographic establishments, Müller collapses the distinction between drama and social reality. Both the theatre and the pornographic industry are implicated in a system of oppression. The collage of textual fragments of extraordinarily stark and provocative metaphors creates a complex system of references on multiple levels. The 'despoiled shore' of the title is the mythical shore of Colchis where the Argonauts landed on their colonial mission. The perennial Argonauts have left their traces on the landscape. Dead fish drift on this 'despoiled shore' as well as the debris of 'civilization': cookie boxes, cigarette butts, menstrual napkins, and condoms. Splinters of discourse associated with depersonalized sex suggest the connection between sexuality and violence.

Images of modern alienated life flash up: commuters on trains and their unfulfilled longings, wives engaged in mindless housework 'Ejecting babies in batches against the advance of the maggots' (*HM*, p. 127; 'Kinder ausstoßend in Schüben gegen den Anmarsch der Würmer', T7, p. 91). This life is based on violence; those killed by the oppressive system turn into 'Earth shat upon by survivors' (*HM*, p. 128; 'Erde von den Überlebenden beschissen', T7, p. 92). At the end of the collage of disturbing images the figure of Medea appears in an ambivalent gesture of violence and tenderness:

> Yet on the ground Medea cradling
> The brother hacked up to pieces She expert
> In poisons   (*HM*, p. 128)

> Auf dem Grund aber Medea den zerstückten
> Bruder im Arm Die Kennerin
> Der Gifte   (T7, p. 92)

Medea is introduced in a kind of *pietà*, apparently mourning the loss of her brother, the victim of her complicity with the male system of oppression.[16] She seems to want to undo the crime she has committed. In Euripides' *Medea*, the focus had been on the murder of her children as the measure of Medea's sanity. In Müller's version, the focus shifts to the murder of her brother. In fact, the infanticide motif, central to virtually all adaptations of the myth, including Müller's own previous treatments, is no longer the crucial issue in Müller's latest version. One reason may be that in a universe of atrocities the murder of one's own children might be regarded as merely one violent excess amongst others. Yet more important, it seems to me, is the fact that Müller focuses on the murder of Medea's brother as her first transgression.

The conflict between Medea and Jason in the second part of Müller's text, entitled *Medeamaterial*, concentrates on this first act of transgression. In this segment, characters and 'drama' in the conventional sense seem to be restored, inasmuch as we have dialogues with clearly identified speakers. The language is terse and, with its iambic pentameter, highly stylized. The piece begins with a brief exchange between Medea and the Nurse that evokes the basic situation in Euripides' play, stressing Medea's anxiety over Jason's new allegiance. The dialogue culminates in Medea questioning her own identity: 'Bring me a mirror This is not Medea' (*HM*, p. 128; 'Bring einen Spiegel Das ist nicht Medea', T7, p. 93). The ensuing confrontation between Medea and Jason indeed centers on the notion of Medea's feminine identity. When Jason challenges her with the question 'What were you before I came woman' (*HM*, p. 129; 'Was warst du vor mir Weib', T7, p. 93), she responds with her name:

Medea.	Medea	
	You owe me a brother Jason	
Jason.	Two sons I gave you for one brother	(*HM*, p. 129)

Medea.	Medea	
	Du bist mir einen Bruder schuldig Jason	
Jason.	Zwei Söhne gab ich dir für einen Bruder	(T7, p. 94)

Jason turns the conflict over the dead brother into a strange question of exchange of property. This affords Medea the opportunity to articulate her grievances in an extended speech that takes up about a third of the entire text.

Initially, Medea's speech seems to reformulate the traditional notions of sexual jealousy and obsessive emotions. Yet these notions are explicitly placed in a more political context, for instance when Medea exclaims:

> Oh could I bite her out of you your whore
> To whom you have betrayed me and my treason
> That once was your lust   (*HM*, p. 130)

> Könnt ich sie aus dir beißen deine Hure
> An die du mich verraten hast und meinen
> Verrat der deine Lust war   (T7, p. 94)

Throughout his work, Müller is preoccupied with the notion of 'Verrat', the betrayal of values, treason instigated by an oppressive system.[17] His vision of Medea is not that of a woman driven to madness, to 'unnatural' excesses of violence. Rather, the emphasis is on the conflict caused by the betrayal of her cultural identity. In becoming Jason's lover and wife, Medea has become the accomplice of colonialism in the widest sense. As such, she is emblematic of general historical and political constellations. Her violence is seen as a response to the violence of colonialism.

The motif of infanticide is only obliquely invoked when Medea associates her sons with the treason she committed against her own culture and family:

> Take Jason what you gave to me
> The fruits of treason that grew from your seed
> And stuff it into your whore's eager womb
> My bridal present for your and her wedding   (*HM*, pp. 130–1)

> Nimm Jason was du mir gegeben hast
> Die Früchte des Verrats aus deinem Samen
> Und stopf es deiner Hure in den Schoß
> Mein Brautgeschenk für dein und ihre Hochzeit   (T7, p. 95)

The dense metaphoric texture of Medea's speech does not allow us to read any of her statements as expressions of Medea's state of mind.[18] There are no stage directions to clarify the dramatic situation. Euripidean motifs are evoked and reinterpreted, yet there is no effort made to motivate actions or words in terms of individual psychology. Medea's violent fantasies cannot be read as symptoms of her alleged madness. Instead, they assume a self-referential quality that applies to the dramatic text itself:

> The bride is young Her hide is smoothly stretched
> Not wasted yet by age or any breeding
> It's on her body that I write my play   (*HM*, p. 131)

> Die Braut ist jung wie Glatt spannt sich das Fell
> Vom Alter nicht von keiner Brut verwüstet
> Auf ihren Leib jetzt schreibe ich mein Schauspiel   (T7, p. 96)

As Medea's speech reaches a pitch of frenzy, the self-referential irony of her remarks becomes more and more poignant. 'My play it is a farce Why don't you laugh' she asks her children (*HM*, p. 132); 'Mein Schauspiel ist eine Komödie Lacht ihr', T7, p. 97). Her murder of her children is clearly associated with the question of her female identity. Medea's words:

> I want to break mankind apart in two
> and live within the empty middle I
> no woman and no man What do you scream   (*HM*, p. 132)

> Will ich die Menschheit in zwei Stücke brechen
> Und wohnen in der leeren Mitte Ich
> Kein Weib kein Mann Was schreit ihr   (T7, p. 97)

are apparently spoken as she kills her sons either on stage or in her imagination. Medea's act of violence is not presented as an instance of madness, but rather as contingent upon a quest for identity outside the confines created by definitions of gender. Müller's Medea thus intensifies the critique of male power structures implicit in Dihle's reading of Euripides' tragedy. Medea's infanticide in this context emerges as an ambivalent mixture of male violence both internalized and externalized. Medea is not mad in the traditional sense. Rather, she becomes the instrument of an act of counter-violence provoked by the destructive nature of the male power structure.[19] In Müller's treatment, Medea represents the 'return of the repressed' in multiple ways: on the political, historical, and psychological level male dominated society is confronted with the crimes upon which it is based and which come back to haunt it. Medea can stand for a multitude of aspects of western history such as gender conflicts, class conflicts, racism or the conflict between the countries of the Third World and their former colonizers.

The motif of Medea's madness survives in the *Medeamaterial* segment in the final exchange between Medea and Jason. Stooped over her dead children, Medea appears to have achieved a firm identity:

Medea.   O I am wise now I am Medea I
           Don't you have blood left Now it is all quiet
           The screams of Colchis silenced too And nothing left
Jason.   Medea
Medea.   Nurse Do you know this man   (*HM*, p. 133)

Medea.   O ich bin klug ich bin Medea Ich
           Habt ihr kein Blut mehr Jetzt ist alles still
           Die Schreie von Kolchis auch verstummt Und nichts mehr
Jason.   Medea
Medea.   Amme Kennst du diesen Mann   (T7, p. 98)

Is Medea mad for not recognizing the very man upon whom she had been fixated in her passion? Or is she deliberately rejecting Jason by refusing to acknowledge who he is? Medea's final question can be interpreted either as a symptom of madness or as a gesture of defiance.

The fundamental ambivalence cannot be resolved, but it is clear that Müller rejects the tradition that portrays Medea as madwoman. *Medeamaterial*, the author suggests in his note, could be set at a lake near Straußberg, a Beverly Hills swimming pool, or in the baths of a psychiatric clinic (T7, p. 101). Müller exempts no aspect of the dominant tradition from his critique. Straußberg used to be the seat of the head-quarters of the East German Army as well as a major site for Soviet nuclear missiles in the former GDR. Beverly Hills evokes what Horkheimer and Adorno have branded Hollywood's imperialist 'culture industry'. The psychiatric clinic recalls Foucault's theses concerning the criminalization and institutionalization of the allegedly insane. To Müller, the military (including the supposed stalwarts of socialism), the entertainment industry, and psychiatry are all implicated in the perennial structures of oppression.

Despoiled Shore Medeamaterial Landscape with Argonauts presents us with the results of the intrinsically irrational power structures by evoking both the omnipresence of colonialist violence and the aftermath of a nuclear holocaust. Müller's text suggests that the patriarchal power structures of western society, the unholy alliance of politics and economics, of military and industry, of environmental abuse and imperialist exploitation, have turned the entire planet into a 'Landscape with Argonauts'. In Müller's universe there is no such thing as sanity, just as there is no culture untainted by imperialistic interests, no love free from violence, and no political order that does not participate in global destruction. The simultaneity of the three textual fragments suggests that destructiveness and war permeate all levels of reality from the supposedly private world of personal relationships to the global politics of colonial exploitation and nuclear warfare. In Euripides' tragedy, the psychology of an overpowering affect was called into question. Medea was not 'mad with love' in the sense suggested by the Nurse. Heiner Müller radicalizes the critique of civilization implicit in Euripides' tragedy. In Müller's dramatic world, there is only the pervasive irrationality of universal violence, a madness without love.

NOTES

1 In an interview with the West German weekly *Die Zeit*, Müller ironically endorsed the view: 'Ich bin der beste lebende Dramatiker, keine Frage', *Die Zeit* 34 (17 August 1987), 29.

2 On Müller's use of myth in this context cf. Wolfgang Emmerich, 'Der vernünftige, der schreckliche Mythos. Heiner Müllers Umgang mit der griechischen Mythologie', in *Heiner Müller Material. Texte und Kommentare*, ed. Frank Hörnigk (Göttingen: Steidl, 1989), pp. 138–60.

3 All quotations from Euripides are from the Penguin edition of Euripides, *Medea and Other Plays*, translated and with an Introduction by Philip Vellacott (Harmondsworth: Penguin, 1979), here p. 17. Other page references will be given in brackets in the main text.

4 Cf. Konrad Kenkel, *Medea-Dramen. Entmythisierung und Remythisierung* (Bonn: Bouvier, 1979), pp. 17ff.

5 Cf. Karl Kerény's introduction to Joachim Schondorff (ed.), *Medea* (Munich, Vienna: Albert Langen, Georg Müller, 1963), pp. 9–28.

6 On the cultural significance of the infanticide motif cf. Emily McDermott, *Euripides' 'Medea': The Incarnation of Disorder* (University Park and London: Pennsylvania State University Press, 1989), pp. 9ff.

7 Cf. the description of the tradition that views Medea as a 'stock example of the conflict between reason and passion' in E. R. Dodds, *The Greeks and the Irrational* [1951] (Berkeley, Los Angeles, London: University of California Press, 1973), p. 200.

8 Albrecht Dihle, *Euripides' 'Medea'* (Heidelberg: Winter, 1977) (=Sitzungsberichte der Heidelberger Akademie der Wissenschaften, Philosophisch–Historische Klasse; Jg. 1977, Abh. 5).

9 Cf. Ibid., p. 13.

10 Cf. Genia Schulz, 'Medea. Zu einem Motiv im Werk Heiner Müllers', in

Weiblichkeit und Tod in der Literatur, ed. Renate Berger and Inge Stephan (Cologne: Böhlau, 1987), p. 248.

11 *Verkommenes Ufer Medeamaterial Landschaft mit Argonauten.* Heiner Müller, *Herzstück*, Texte 7 (Berlin: Rotbuch Verlag, 1983), pp. 91–101. German references are to this edition (abbreviated as T7), followed by the page number.

12 On the significance of the fragmentary structure cf. Johannes Birringer, 'Brecht and Medea: Heiner Müller's Synthetic Fragments', *The Theatre Annual* (1987), pp. 1–15.

13 Cf. the thesis of Medea as the 'prosecutor' and Jason as the 'defendant' in Pietro Pucco, *The Violence of Pity in Euripides' 'Medea'* (Ithaca and London: Cornell University Press, 1980), p. 104.

14 'Deutschland spielt immer noch die Nibelungen', *Der Spiegel*, 19 (1983), 196 (my translation).

15 Cf. T7, p. 101. English quotations are from the English version of Müller's text in *Hamletmachine and Other Texts for the Stage*, ed. and trans. Carl Weber (New York: Performing Arts Journal Publications, 1984), abbreviated as *HM*, followed by the page number, here: *HM*, p. 126.

16 Cf. Schulz, *Medea*, p. 251.

17 Cf. Georg Wieghaus, *Zwischen Auftrag und Verrat. Werk und Ästhetik Heiner Müllers* (Frankfurt am Main, Bern, New York, Nancy: Peter Lang, 1984).

18 The extraordinary complexity of Müller's text is documented in the program book of its first production at Bochum in 1982: the book comprises nearly 500 pages of notes and other material which help to 'decipher' the eleven pages of Müller's scenario.

19 Cf. Klaus Teichmann, *Der verwundete Körper. Zu Texten Heiner Müllers* (Freiburg: Burg-Verlag, 1986), pp. 197–211.

Ionesco and textual madness

ELIZABETH KLAVER

Consider these scenarios. An old couple invite friends to hear the story of their lives; instead, an audience of proliferating empty chairs slowly fills up the room. A man moves into a new apartment; endless quantities of furniture soon take up all the space, eventually burying him under mounds of household goods. A man goes on a trip only to find his luggage undergoing a kind of maniacal cell division. A woman frenetically piles a sideboard with countless cups of coffee. A corpse grows exponentially. Townsfolk experience an unstoppable transformation into rhinoceroses.

Of course, these scenarios are not the nightmares of a mad person; they are the plays of Ionesco – *The Chairs*, *The New Tenant*, *The Man With the Luggage*, *Victims of Duty*, *Amedee*, and *Rhinoceros*. Several critics have made insightful analyses of the plays' thematic implications, seeing an Einsteinian explosiveness at work in the universe, a reflection of our increasing preoccupation with the world of human-created matter, or a pre-Big Bang universe in which things accumulate ever more quickly.[1] I would suggest, however, that a kind of compulsive behavior operates deep within these texts, an obsessive semiotic effect at the ontological level which exposes the firing of dramatic signifiers as uncontrollable permutation. A textual madness is encoded within the written fabric of the plays themselves. This condition helps explain why Ionesco's drama is so absurd.

Victims of Duty, performed in 1953, is a case in point. In this play, a detective is looking through the images of Choubert's memory for a man named Mallot 'with a t at the end'.[2] The insistence on the 't at the end' suggests a search for a transcendental signifier which could locate Mallot. Unfortunately for the detective, the search is ineffectual. 'A letter', as Jacques Derrida has noted, 'does not always arrive at its destination.'[3] Rather than finding Mallot, the text produces digressive chains of signifiers, generating in Choubert's mind images of his family, wife and childhood. Concurrently, an explosive proliferation of dramatic signifiers occurs in other areas: Madelaine, Coubert's wife, piles the sideboard with endless cups of coffee, while the detective himself rams food into

Choubert's mouth again and again in order to plug the gaps in his memory.

The effect of madness in this splurge of dramatic semiosis springs from the kind of lack endemic to sign structures that Lacan identifies as desire. In the case of *Victims of Duty*, though, desire turns into obsession not only as a search for the absent Mallot but also for textual signification. The gaps in the images or signs of Mallot 'with a t' within Choubert's unconscious mind indicate a compulsive movement of deferral within semiotic structure, a movement that leaves sites of absence in the textual apparatus which must be filled with images of some kind, even food or coffee cups. The desire on the part of the text to complete signification is frustrated, which in turn effects a transference of linguistic proliferation onto various semiotic systems, replicating itself as unmanageable desire in the detective as well as in the play.

Therefore, in opening gaps in the discourse of Choubert's memory, incomplete signification ends up creating sites of silence within the linguistic machinery. Interestingly, these gaps are not only necessary for textual generation, but also formulate in Ionesco's plays a hidden discourse of the Other, a discourse of silence which, according to Shoshana Felman's definition in *Writing and Madness*, can be recognized as madness: it is a lack of language, the silence of a stifled, repressed discourse.[4] Of course, the silence of madness cannot be said, as Derrida points out, in a logos.[5] Rather, in a play such as *Victims of Duty*, an *effect* of madness is rendered as a by-product of silence, an uncontrollable barrage of signifiers. The play becomes a semiotic machine run amok.

The semiotic madness encoded in *Victims of Duty* arises because of problematics which extend to all of its dramatic signs, permeating the gestural and scenic codes as well as the linguistic. On stage, the dramatic sign does not indicate a referent; it refers to categories of possible signifiers which may be ostended on the stage as provisional referents.[6] Signifiers may be substituted for each other, allowing both interpretation and performance to proceed. This condition is necessary, for without a range of possibility within sign structures only one production, one time only, could occur. Since the dramatic sign encodes an endless process of silence and deferral within its production of possible signifiers, representation can never be completed. If a play focuses on this problematic, on textual generation out of its sites of semiotic absence, fantastic, surreal theatre can occur. The detective asks for a cup of coffee, he gets a million.

This compulsive production of signifiers occurs in many of Ionesco's plays. In *The Chairs*, for instance, the chairs are signs used to mark the sites of absence within the discourse of the old couple. When the invisible lady arrives, the old couple escort her downstage:

Old Man.	You've had good weather.
Old Woman.	You're not too tired? . . .
Old Man.	At the edge of the water . . .
Old Woman.	It's kind of you to say so.
Old Man.	Let me get you a chair.[7]

As the sites of absence grow the need for more chairs as markers grows, so that a proliferation of chairs is not only set in motion, but is generated as necessity by the dictates of semiosis. As well, the invasion of a lack within the sign is problematizing the play in other areas. The old couple would like to tell their history, a story which, it turns out, is never completed. At the end of the play they commit suicide, leaving to a tongue-tied orator the task of delivering their final message to 'interpretants', the empty chairs. The orator can produce nothing but linguistic non-sense, so that the story remains silent and forever deferred.[8]

In *Amedee*, performed in 1954, the holes within language actually appear as a thorough-going discourse of silence, a repressed text which nevertheless writes itself as silence and reappears in a transformed state as the exponential growth of a very tangible corpse. Amedee, the main character, has been trying to write a play for fifteen years and has gotten no further than two lines.[9] His inability to write is closely linked with the arrival of a corpse that has been growing uncontrollably in the apartment. Critics often see the corpse as symbolizing the death of love between Amedee and his wife, Madelaine, (see Kyle, Donnard, and Lamont) or the death of Amedee's creative powers (see Kyle).[10] It seems possible, though, that the silent play, the always deferred text, is even more intimately connected with the corpse – that the body of the text, the corpus, is displaced onto the body of the corpse.

Evidence for this transference can be seen in numerous places in the text. Often, when Amedee's plays are mentioned, the corpse undergoes growth:

> *Amedee. [gazing at the dead man as he mops his brow, he says to himself]* What about my plays? I shan't be able to write any now . . . [*The feet advance another twelve inches.*][11]

As well, Madelaine accuses Amedee of morbid writing, claiming that 'it's [the body's] world, not ours' (p. 53), as if Amedee, in being responsible for a corpse instead of a play, has produced a text which, in turn, is generating a world of its own. In fact, the corpse is disseminating mushrooms all over the apartment.

The textuality of the corpse thus encodes a language which springs from and points to a language of absence, the writing of a silent discourse as Amedee's repressed play. Curiously, though, the corpse also inscribes the problematics of semiotic silence within its own textual structure, within its own dramatic signs which reveal the fleshy body itself as a signifier undergoing morbid multiplication. In other words, the corpse is not only the effect of textual madness derived from the 'presence' of a silent discourse, but also inscribes textual madness as the growth of its own internal vacuity. The corpse is, paradoxically, both substantial and vacuous, a hollow text – as Ionesco says about the word itself, a 'sounding shell devoid of meaning'.[12]

The plays, then, are plagued by an emptiness situated within the sign that Ionesco himself recognizes as language. And since this endemic silence cannot be written or staged, a noisy proliferation of 'sounding shells' occurs instead which, in turn, produces Felman's notion of madness as the active incompletion of meaning.[13] Certainly, in *Amedee* the silent text of Amedee's play can never hope to complete meaning, and as for the corpse, the play forecloses on a determination of meaning by inscribing unreadability.

Amedee and Madelaine, for instance, are thoroughly puzzled by the corpse. They really don't know why it is there, how it got there, or what it means. Amedee is not sure if he even killed the man at all. He says to Madelaine: 'Why shouldn't he have died a natural death anyway? Why do you insist I killed him?' (p. 39). They don't remember if it is the body of a young man, Madelaine's lover, or the nextdoor neighbor's baby. Although they try to read it as a text, the corpse remains impenetrable. In fact, this incompletion of meaning is a condition the play develops in the process of its rewriting from Ionesco's short story, 'Oriflamme'. In the earlier work, Amedee clearly killed Madelaine's lover. Indeterminacy, on the other hand, is stressed in the play.

The image of the text as a nightmare of unreadability, an effect of madness in illegibility, carries into *The Man with the Luggage*, written in 1975. In this play, the First Man is experiencing a disturbing world of irrationality, so that textual madness erupts in a kind of insane logic. Recording the First Man's vital statistics, the authorities enter a question mark for his father's name and the name 'Joan', randomly chosen from a list, for his mother's. Since the First Man doesn't know how old he is, they enter 'indeterminate age', and since he has grown during the course of his life, they enter 'height variable'.[14] The entire play is saturated with such instances of indeterminacy, producing anxiety and frustration for both the main character and the viewer. In a subversion of the quest motif, the First Man never does discover or reach the end of his destination and the final image of the play is a parade of proliferating luggage, carried by people in a hurry to get who knows where. Like the corpse in *Amedee*, *The Man with the Luggage* effects a mad text. And like Amedee and Madelaine, the First Man also encodes the viewer's bewilderment when confronted by such a phenomenon.

Illegibility, endless growth, unreadability, incompletion. As in so many of Ionesco's plays, *The Man with the Luggage* never ends and never achieves closure. The proliferating luggage in the last scene suggests a permutation that does not recognize a final curtain, and is perhaps the result of an obsessive desire for completion in a system which only generates deferral. *The Chairs* and *The New Tenant* also sound this note of endless permutation and open-endedness. *The Chairs* has no real sense of finality, since the textual machinery works against the completion of the old couple's story, thereby interrupting the closure of the play itself. Furthermore, the growth of empty chairs continues as the theatre audience leaves, spreading vacuity into the seats long after the play is 'over'. Similarly, *The New Tenant* suggests that the proliferating furniture could extend forever, since it has already jammed the staircase, the yard and the street, backed up traffic and the tube, dammed up the Thames and cluttered the whole country.[15] Even *Rhinoceros* implies that rhinoceritis, as Ionesco terms that 'wild collective madness' of conformity, is already spreading across the land as the curtain comes down.[16]

Other plays encode deferral as an obsessive circularity, an endless semiotic loop in which incompletion ceaselessly transforms itself into more incompletion. Two of Ionesco's early works, *The Bald Soprano* and *The Lesson*, have endings which only revolve the characters back to the beginning. In *The Bald Soprano* the Martins start to repeat the opening lines of the play, lines which the Smiths had originally delivered. At the end of *The Lesson* the professor prepares to act out, for the fortieth time that day, the same violent scenario we have just witnessed. The play, *Macbett*, indicates entrapment within a textual loop by developing the idea implicit in Shakespeare's text that at the crowning of Malcolm as the new king a tyrant is waiting to emerge. *Macbett* ends with a long, verbatim quotation from Malcolm's speech to Macduff (*Macbeth* IV, iii, 50–99) in which he describes his own tyrannical nature:

> *Macol.* In me I know
>   All the particulars of vice so grafted
>   That, when they shall be opened, black
>   Macbett will seem as pure as snow . . .[17]

Unlike Shakespeare's play, there is nothing in *Macbett* to indicate that Macol is kidding and everything to suggest that a text like *Macbett* is about to begin over again. Similarly, after killing the detective in *Victims of Duty*, the adversarial Nicholas turns into him and takes up the task of force-feeding Choubert and searching for Mallot 'with a t'. Trapped in the madness of its own textual machinery, the mystery story begins over and can never be completed.

In fact, the unsolvable mystery story at work in the fundamental structure of *Victims of Duty* poses an irrational theatre, a theatre of the Other, against rational, Aristotolian logic. Critics such as Donald Watson consider this play as revealing aspects of Ionesco's own approach to drama in which the logical and the illogical coexist within the same dramatic setting.[18] During a discussion of the theatre, Nicholas claims that he would

> introduce contradiction where there is no contradiction, and no contradiction where there is what common-sense usually calls contradiction.
>
> (p. 158)

The detective, on the other hand, claims that 'everything hangs together, everything can be comprehended in time' (p. 159) even while he is cramming Choubert with food. In a classic Ionesco tactic, the stage action plays against the text;[19] the effect of madness encoded in the text's compulsive search for Mallot 'with a t' works against the rational discourse. As a result, the play subverts the possibility of making good sense.

The clash between the two discourses, the irrational and the rational, reveals the kind of disruption madness poses to sanity. As Foucault points out in *Madness and Civilization*, the danger of madness lies in the fact that its images denote nothingness.[20] In the case of *Victims of Duty*, or other instances of irrational theatre, the mad text threatens any form which pretends to closure, completion, and understanding. The kind of Aristotelian theatre the detective holds dear promotes successful illusion, whereas the kind of irrational theatre Nicholas describes exposes the empty space. The theatre, built on semiotics, is built on the nothingness at work in semiotics. Lacking in referentiality, the theatre can only sustain itself out of a web of signs and out of the silence which they involve. When Nicholas turns into the detective at the end of the play, it is a sure indication that the threat implicit in textual madness is coming to the foreground. Irrational discourse murders rational; nothingness perforates illusion; an effect of madness permeates the text.

Ionesco's plays are riddled wtih grotesque images, bizarre plots, contradictions, compulsive behavior. And at the bottom of it all lies a fascination with language and semiosis which writes silence into the textual web and allows the signifiers to fire into outrageous patterns. As the audience we experience an absurd dramatic world pervaded not so much with existential angst as with textual madness. When an Ionesco play 'ends', its inability to end continues to drive the structure. Chairs? Luggage? Furniture? Coffee cups? It's a mad, mad, mad, mad text.

NOTES

1 Kenneth S. White, 'The Explosiveness of the Planet: Ionesco and Einstein', in *Alogical Modern Drama*, ed. Kenneth S. White (Amsterdam: Editions Rodopi B.V., 1982), p. 62. Rosette C. Lamont, 'The Proliferation of Matter in Ionesco's Plays', *L'Esprit Createur* 2 (1962), 197. J. P. Little, 'Form and the Void: Beckett's *Fin de partie* and Ionesco's *Les Chaises*', *French Studies* 32 (1978), 53.

2 Eugene Ionesco, *Victims of Duty* in *Three Plays by Eugene Ionesco*, trans. Donald Watson (New York: Grove Press, 1958). See, for example, p. 123. The phrase 'with a t at the end' occurs throughout the play. All further references to this work will be given in the text.

3 Jacques Derrida, 'The Purveyor of Truth', trans. Alan Bass in *The Purloined Poe: Lacan, Derrida and Psychoanalytic Reading*, ed. John P. Miller and William J. Richardson (Baltimore and London: Johns Hopkins University Press, 1988), p. 201.

4 Shoshana Felman, *Writing and Madness*, trans. Martha Noel Evans and Shoshana Felman (New York: Cornell University Press 1985), p. 14.

5 Jacques Derrida, *Writing and Difference*, trans. Alan Bass (Chicago: University of Chicago Press, 1978), p. 37.

6 See Umberto Eco, 'Semiotics of Theatrical Performance', *Drama Review* 21 (1977), 110.

7 Eugene Ionesco, *The Chairs* in *Classics of the Modern Theater: Realism and After*, trans. Donald M. Allen, ed. Alvin B. Kernan (New York: Harcourt, 1965), pp. 486–7. All further references to this work will be given in the text.

8 See Elizabeth Klaver, 'The Play of Language in Ionesco's Play of Chairs', *Modern Drama* 32 (1989), 521–31.

9 Jean-Herve Donnard suggests that Amedee may be trying to write *The Chairs*. See Jean-Herve Donnard, '*Amedee*: A Caricatural Ionesco' in *Ionesco: A Collection of Critical Essays*, ed. Rosette C. Lamont (Englewood Cliffs: Prentice-Hall, 1973).

10 Linda D. Kyle, 'The Grotesque in *Amedee, Or How To Get Rid Of It*', *Modern Drama* 19 (1976), 285. Donnard, '*Amedee*', p. 40. Lamont, 'Proliferation of Matter', p. 191. Kyle, 'The Grotesque', p. 284.

11 Eugene Ionesco, *Amedee, Or How to Get Rid of It* in *Three Plays by Eugene Ionesco*, trans. Donald Watson (New York: Grove Press, 1958), p. 29. All further references to this work will appear in the text.

12 Eugene Ionesco, *Notes and Counter Notes*, trans. Donald Watson (New York: Grove Press, 1964), p. 179.

13 Felman, *Writing and Madness*, p. 54.

14 Eugene Ionesco, *The Man With the Luggage* in *Plays: Eugene Ionesco*, trans. Donald Watson and Clifford Williams (London: Calder, 1979), p. 64.

15 Eugene Ionesco, *The New Tenant* in *Three Plays by Eugene Ionesco*, trans. Donald Watson (New York: Grove Press, 1958), p. 114.

16 Ionesco, *Notes*, p. 151.

17 Eugene Ionesco, *Macbett*, trans. Charles Marowitz (New York: Grove Press, 1979), p. 104.

18 Donald Watson, 'Retrospect' in *Three Plays by Eugene Ionesco* (New York: Grove Press, 1958), p. i.

19 Ionesco, *Notes*, p. 26.

20 Michel Foucault, *Madness and Civilization: A History of Insanity in the Age of Reason*, trans. Richard Howard (New York: Vintage, 1965), p. 107.

Black madness in August Wilson's 'Down the Line' cycle

MARK WILLIAM ROCHA

In all jazz, and especially in the blues, there is something tart and ironic, authoritative and double-edged . . . Only people who have been 'down the line', as the song puts it, know what this music is about.[1]

(James Baldwin, *The Fire Next Time*)

In the short time since *Ma Rainey's Black Bottom* premiered at the Yale Repertory Theater in 1984, August Wilson has himself become a historical phenomenon in the American theatre by completing five plays in his grand historical project, which to date have garnered for Wilson two Pulitzer Prizes (for *Fences* in 1987 and *The Piano Lesson* in 1990), two Tony's, four New York Drama Critics Circle awards, and countless other accolades in the United States and Great Britain. Wilson's first five plays have reached Broadway (in order: *Ma Rainey's Black Bottom* (1984), *Fences* (1987), *Joe Turner's Come and Gone* (1988), *The Piano Lesson* (1990), and *Two Trains Running* (1992)). Such a record confirms Wilson as America's preeminent playwright. I draw upon Baldwin above to refer to Wilson's five major plays as the 'Down the Line' cycle because Wilson's historical project provides everyone with a ticket 'down the line' whose destination is the culture of what Amiri Baraka calls America's 'blues people'.[2]

Prior to Wilson, only Eugene O'Neill, Arthur Miller, and Tennessee Williams had staked such a swift and convincing claim upon the American consciousness. Today, with Wilson's five plays before us, it is becoming increasingly clear that Wilson is indeed supplying something exceptional to the American theatre that it has never had: an American history that is the product of an African rather than a European sensibility. Accordingly, one is not surprised to find in Wilson's plays a consistent and explicit rejection of an Anglo-European consciousness that perceives human beings as commodities. Such a rejection extends to the issue before us, that of the concept of madness, and I shall argue that Wilson shows black madness to mean something different than the term 'madness' means in western culture. My concern here is not so much to define 'black madness', as though such a definition were even possible, but to describe what we may mean when we use the term 'madness' in a black context. That is, I want to describe what members of Wilson's black communities *do* when a madman is within their midst, and I hope it will become clear that what blacks do is often different from what whites do.

Such a description would do well to begin with Wilson's first Pulitzer Prize winning play, *Fences*. Early in the play Troy Maxson is approached by his younger brother Gabriel:

> *Gabriel.* You ain't mad at me, is you?
> *Troy.* Naw . . . I ain't mad at you Gabe. If I was mad at you I'd tell you about it.
> (i, ii, 126)[3]

What could Troy Maxson, the prideful family patriarch, possibly be mad at his younger brother Gabriel for? After all, Gabriel is certifiably insane according to standard western medical practice. Wounded in World War ii, Gabriel has a metal plate in his head, and long after the war in 1957, 'he carried an old trumpet tied around his waist and believes with every fiber of his being that he is the Archangel Gabriel' (i, ii, 125). Everyone in the black Hill District of Pittsburgh knows and acknowledges Gabriel as he peddles his discarded fruits and flowers to earn enough to 'buy me a new horn so St. Peter can hear me when it's time to open the gates' (i, ii, 127). For his part, Troy Maxson has done right by Gabriel, for he used Gabriel's war disability compensation to buy a house where Gabriel enjoyed a proper home and care. So it is unlikely that Troy could be mad at his brother Gabriel simply for being what he cannot help – for being mad – even on the day Gabriel announces he is going to move out to have his own place. Yet Gabriel persists in thinking Troy may be mad at him. Again, what is it in Gabriel's moving out that could be making Troy Maxson mad?

To answer directly, Troy is not mad because Gabriel's departure unwisely places the war veteran in the greater jeopardy of the outside world, but because Gabriel's departure represents an irreparable loss to the House of Maxson. Gabriel himself might concur, since one who truly believes he is the Archangel would obviously understand how any community would be the poorer for his absence. It therefore may be Gabriel's very self-confidence in his value to his community that causes him to question whether Troy is mad. This revised, reversed relationship of the madman to his community brings us to the start of a consideration of what we may mean by the term 'black madness'.

First, I draw upon the House of Maxson (read as: 'Maximum-Son') as a metaphor for America itself and I do so to emphasize the reversibility of the relationship between madness and civilization that is implied by black madness. For the House of Maxson suffers not when the madman Gabriel is present but when he is absent, and this is precisely the opposite relation that Foucault exposes in modern western society in *Madness and Civilization* in which he notes that in seventeenth-century Europe, 'A sensibility was born which had drawn a line and laid a cornerstone, and which chose – only to banish' (p. 64).[4] August Wilson's conception of madness is born of an avowedly African sensibility that perceives banishment itself as *the* act of madness. Why? Because banishment of the madman denies the community a dialogue with madness which is vital. Foucault notes:

> In the middle ages and until the Renaissance, man's dispute with madness was a dramatic debate in which he confronted the secret powers of the world; the experience of madness was clouded by images of the Fall and the Will of God, of the Beast and the Metamorphosis, and of all the marvelous secrets of knowledge. In our era, the experience of madness remains silent in the composure of a knowledge which, knowing too much about madness, forgets it.
>
> (p. xii)

August Wilson clearly does not wish us to forget about madness and in his plays he restores the dramatic debate with madness that, as Foucault puts it, 'deals not so much with the truth and the world, as with man and whatever truth about himself he is able to perceive. [Madness] thus gives access to a completely moral universe' (p. 27). Thus in *Fences* as long as Gabriel is present in the House of Maxson, Troy and others have access to Gabriel's moral universe which is ordered upon the importance of the Judgment Day – a truth one might do well to consider.

It is crucial to bear in mind that Wilson's representation of black madness is deeply imbedded in what I term a 'vernacular telling community'. Identity for any American character in Wilson's plays, black or white, depends upon inclusion in a black vernacular telling community whose 'field of manners and rituals of intercourse',[5] to borrow a Baldwin phrase Wilson often cites, enable one to tell a story – a personal creation myth – that realizes a *self-in-performance*. Membership in such a telling community implies a mutual responsibility both to tell one's story and interpret the stories of all the other members. Thus the telling community's inclusion of Gabriel in *Fences* is hardly a matter of paternalistic charity. Instead, Gabriel is included because he is valued as a teller, even if his story seems as inexplicable as the one a tribal African might receive from the god Esu.[6] To the African-Americans in Wilson's telling communities, inexplicability is an interpretive problem for the listener, not a sign of the teller's disfunction. There is a *quid pro quo* at work in the African-American telling community in which the medium of exchange is discourse itself. Each member hears and interprets the madman Gabriel so that they will in turn be heard and interpreted and therefore quite literally 'told' into existence.[7]

Troy Maxson is therefore disturbed not at Gabriel, but at the forces that conspire to separate Gabriel from the community and would turn the

House of Maxson from African-style dialogue to the kind of western-style monologue Foucault describes. Troy is 'mad' because he anticipates how white American culture will impose itself by ultimately institutionalizing Gabriel, which of course is precisely what ends up happening to Gabriel.

In linguistic terms it may then be said that absence – the inability to render presence – is what incites black madness. When Gabriel is present in the House of Maxson, he is an essential communicant in a process of signification, the very enactment of which signifies to all in the House of Maxson the values of community, family, inclusion. Such values are especially cherished if one considers how the history of the House of Maxson has been informed by the economics of slavery which demands the break-up of black families and thus imposes absence as the fundamental condition of African-American experience. When Gabriel is absent, the very process of signification is shut down and any effort to render Gabriel present in language must itself be the signification of a cruel absence.

One now wishes to import the blues into this discussion of what black madness means in August Wilson's plays. Wilson himself is explicit. The following comment from a 1987 interview with Dinah Livingston of *Minnesota Monthly* is but one of many on record:

> I think that what's contained in the blues is the African-American cultural response to the world . . .

> The thing with the blues is that there's an entire philosophical system at work. And I've found that whatever you want to know about the black experience in America is contained in the blues . . .

> They couldn't stop 'em singing and passing along all their information in songs. This is what I've found the blues to be. So it is the Book. It is our sacred book, so I claim it as that. Anything I want to know, I go there and find it out.[8]

The evidence of Wilson's own plays demonstrates conclusively that 'Blues is the bedrock of everything I do.'[9] A blues song by W. C. Handy supplies the title of *Joe Turner's Come and Gone*, the very subject of *Ma Rainey's Black Bottom* is the real-life Mother of the Blues, Gertrude 'Ma' Rainey, and blues songs suffuse the texts of the other three plays in the 'Down the Line' cycle. Wilson's plays therefore seem ideally suited for the kind of analysis Houston Baker proposes in *Blues, Ideology, and Afro-American Literature*:

> the analytical project that may serve as a paradigm for the future study of Afro-American literature and expressive culture is a vernacular model, one that finds apt figuration in the blues.[10]

The playwright Wilson and the critic Baker are in clear agreement that to learn about black madness (or black *anything*) one must become what

Baker calls a 'blues detective' who has the 'ability to break away from traditional concepts and to supply new and creative possibilities' (p. 135). A blues detective might consult Michael Taft's anthology, *Blues Lyric Poetry* (1983), which contains the lyrics of over 2,000 blues songs commercially recorded between 1920 and 1942. Of the sixty-five blues songs in which the words 'mad' or 'insane' appear, every single one is an articulation of absence, invariably that of a lover. In these songs, 'madness' is the rage brought on by the suffering of absence, as is articulated for one example in 'Mad Dog Blues' (1928) sung by Rosie Mae Moore:

> Read my search warrant lady I'm just looking for my man
> I got my razor in my bosom and my pistol in my hand
> I'm just like a mad dog I snaps at everything I meet
> But if I find my man he sure is going to be my meat
> I'm going to cut him with my razor I'm going to use my pistol too
> Now they can call the undertaker to put your last clean shirt on you
> I'm going to kill my man then I'm going to kill myself
> I'd rather we both to be dead than to see him with someone else.[11]

The extreme violence expressed in this lyric is typical and serves to underscore how the black response to absence is powerfully 'mad' given the cultural memory of the loss of loved ones and one's status in America as the 'other'. The blues constitute an ontology that is the very idea of America itself: the sign 'America' signifies the broken promise of presence. All blues songs begin from an ontological awareness of the American condition as the sign of an absence, a broken promise – usually the specific premise is, as above, 'my lover's gone' – and this absence is mediated and filled up by the blues. As Ma Rainey puts it, 'You don't sing to feel better. You sing cause that's a way of understanding life . . . This be an empty world without the blues. I take that emptiness and try to fill it up with something' (II, 67). To put it another way, the blues is the way African-Americans *do* community.

Gabriel in *Fences* is but one embodiment of the Wilsonian madman who is obsessed, due either to physical impairment or personal choice, and whose obsession brings the risk of exclusion from the community. In *Joe Turner's Come and Gone* it's Herald Loomis who is obsessed after his release from a prison chain-gang with his quest to find his wife and regain his place in the world; in *Ma Rainey* it's the trumpet player Levee who is obsessed with getting his own band; in *The Piano Lesson* it's Boy Willie who is obsessed with selling the family piano to raise money to buy a farm; in *Two Trains Running* it's Hambone, a retarded character who is obsessed with getting his due from the store owner who never paid him properly for painting a fence. The presence of the madman serves to illuminate the fundamental principle of inclusion that guides the ethical practice of Wilson's vernacular telling community.

Understanding this principle of inclusion of the madman as the major premise of the 'Down the Line' cycle helps also to reveal the basic structure of Wilson's plays. *Joe Turner's Come and Gone*, the play Wilson cites as his favorite,[12] is paradigmatic. With some minor variations, each of Wilson's plays could be accommodated to this recitation of the dramatic action of *Joe Turner*: into the settled black vernacular telling community of Seth and Bertha Holly's boarding house in Pittsburgh in 1911 comes the archetypal Wilsonian madman, Herald Loomis, whose commitment to self-realization is of classically tragic proportions. Herald Loomis's quest imposes a *crisis of inclusion* on the telling community whose very existence is imperiled by its attempts to keep the madman among them. As some in the community start to call for the exclusion of the madman Loomis, the rituals of intercourse that enable every member to tell his or her story begin to have their effect. The idea of separation itself becomes the antagonist and the community eventually works its way toward the identification of each member and the preservation of the community that includes the madman. Once the madman is 'identified', that is, once he has been *meant* by the community as an individual, the madman is then and *only* then free to leave for the very reason that he remains a permanent member of the community as a performed self, a story, an oral text.

By seeing how the very form of *Joe Turner* is determined by the operation of the black vernacular telling community, one then emulates the critical posture recommended by the African playwright and Nobel Prize winner, Wole Soyinka. Soyinka's ideal critic 'embraces the apprehension of a culture whose reference points are taken from within the culture itself'.[13] Such an embrace might have deterred critics who have worried about the issue of Wilson's 'clumsy construction',[14] which is less worrisome if one remembers that Wilson's 'Down the Line' cycle is the product of an African rather than a European sensibility.

A brief survey of the plays that comprise the 'Down the Line' cycle raises our awareness of the African sensibility that informs Wilson's treatment of madness, a treatment that depicts a 'hermetic universe of forces' in which there is a 'conjunction of the circumcentric worlds of man, social community, and Nature in the minds of each character, regardless of role'.[15] In *Joe Turner's Come and Gone* Wilson introduces his protagonist Herald Loomis: 'He is at times possessed. A man driven not by the hellhounds that seemingly lay at his heels, but by his search for a world that speaks to something about himself' (1, i, 216). Loomis has been driven to his mad quest by the absence imposed on him by Joe Turner, the infamous brother of the Governor of Tennessee sung of by black women in the blues song: 'He came with forty links of chain/ He's got my man and gone.' Without charges or trial, Loomis was taken from his wife and daughter and put to work on a chain gang for seven years. Now Loomis has come north to look for his wife because, 'That's the only thing I know how to do. I just wanna see her face so I can get me a starting place in the world . . . I've been wandering a long time in somebody else's world. When I find my wife that be the making of my own' (II, ii, 269).

Loomis is so driven that he can rage, 'Why God got to be so big? Why he got to be bigger than me' (I, iv, 150)? His presence in the boarding-house is unsettling and there are those who would be glad to have him go, but the crucial point is that Loomis is permitted to stay and is even aided in his quest by another important member of the community, the conjure man Bynum Walker who proclaims the power of his Binding Song. It need hardly be pointed out that the conjure man is himself an archetypal madman, a 'witch doctor' traditionally banished by western culture, but one whose salutary role has been deemed essential in black communities. Thus in the persons of Herald Loomis and Bynum Walker, madness permeates this community; rather than relegate madness to the margin, the community in *Joe Turner's Come and Gone* insists upon including madness as a central aspect of daily experience. At the end of the play, Herald Loomis does find his wife and in an appropriately mad gesture intended to symbolize that he is his own savior, slashes himself across the chest with a knife and departs the boardinghouse. The accommodation of the madman has resulted in a community transformed by serving as witness to what Wilson calls Loomis's 'song of self-sufficiency', a song, it is clearly implied, difficult for a man of African descent to hear in western culture.

This status of the African-American's song of self-sufficiency in white American culture is at the heart of *Ma Rainey's Black Bottom* in which the blues is merely a commodity to be sold by the white producers who own the record companies. Against this appropriation of black blues by the white commodity culture, the legendary singer Ma Rainey describes the blues as the 'always already' of black culture, saying, 'The blues always been here' (II, 68).

The black madman in this community is a trumpet player named Levee who is tired of playing 'Ma's music' and wants to form a band of his own. Throughout the recording session he tries to subvert Ma's authority by substituting his own musical arrangements. The other band members recognize Levee as a madman in two respects. First, Levee's madness is motivated out of his personal history of absence, for his daddy was murdered by white men when he sought revenge for the rape of his wife. Second, in the words of one band member, Levee is 'spooked up with the white man' because he tries to curry favor with the white record producer who has promised to look at the songs Levee wrote. Levee displays a constant churlishness and a maniacal obsession with himself that prompts such outbursts as, 'That's who I am. I'm the devil. I ain't nothing but the devil' (I, 34). Notwithstanding all of this, the other band members not only accommodate and accept Levee, rebellion and all, they defend him to Ma Rainey who is so cranky with Levee she threatens to fire him. Yet even Ma abides Levee's musical improvisations, going so far as to permit them on the final cut of the record.

But ultimately Levee banishes himself and the result clearly shows the madness born of absence. Levee goaded Ma into firing him, mistakenly believing that banishment from his black community will be compensated for by acceptance in a white community that will buy his songs and grant him power and fame. But Levee has yet to learn what Ma knows all along:

> They don't care nothing about me, All they want is my voice . . . As soon as they get my voice down on them recording machines, then it's just like if I'd be some whore and they roll over and put their pants on.
>
> (1, 64)

Levee literally goes crazy when he makes this discovery. After the white record producer offers him a paltry five dollars apiece for his songs, 'All the weight of the world suddenly falls on Levee and he rushes at Toledo with his knife in his hand' (II, 92). Levee has murdered his fellow band member for the transgression of stepping on his new shoes. Here the madman has been accommodated long past any normal criteria for exclusion, which indicates the tenacity with which the values of presence and inclusion are held in the black community. In addition, the catastrophic effects of banishment, in this case self-inflicted, underline how absence – being without community – is the root of black madness.

Madness is the very premise of *The Piano Lesson*, a play which rises out of W. C. Handy's, 'Yellow Dog Blues' (1914). It is 1936 and Boy Willie, a southern sharecropper, has come north to Pittsburgh to try to persuade his sister Berniece to sell the family's piano whose carvings bear the family's personal history. Boy Willie wants to return to the south to buy his own farm. Berniece refuses to sell, partly because she is haunted by the ghost of Sutter, the white man who murdered her husband for taking some firewood. The play then becomes a contest of madnesses, a competition between beliefs in different ghosts. Berniece's is the ghost of a white man named Sutter who had once owned her family in slavery and thus owned the piano her grandfather had made. Boy Willie's is the ghost of a black man – his and Berniece's father, Boy Charles. In 1911, Boy Charles stole back from Sutter the piano his father had made. Although Sutter never regained the piano, Boy Charles was hunted down to a railroad boxcar which was set afire, cremating Boy Charles and three unlucky hobos. These four men become the Ghosts of the Yellow Dog, hallowed in a revenge myth that identifies 'the Ghosts of the Yellow Dog as the hand of God' (II, ii, 69).[16] When a number of white men fell to their deaths down wells under mysterious circumstances, the responsibility was assigned to the Ghosts of the Yellow Dog. The struggle between brother and sister, between a black man's ghosts and a white man's ghost, is again enacted within a context of a community that withholds judgment and acknowledges both ghosts.

The exorcism of the white man's ghost in the emotional final scene of *The Piano Lesson* serves as testimony to the healing power of presence. In this the antidote to Berniece's madness is the presence of her past in the form of her father's ghost. The intimidating ghost of Sutter – one might term it the power of an absence – is dispelled the moment Berniece can once more play the piano she has left untouched since the day her mama died. Wilson describes the moment:

> She begins to play. The song is found piece by piece. It is an old urge to song that is both a commandment and a plea. With each repetition it gains in strength. It is intended as an exorcism and a dressing for battle. A rustle of wind blowing across two continents.
>
> (II, v, 106)

When Berniece invokes the spirit of her dead father by singing, 'I want you to help me/ Papa Boy Charles' (II, v, 107), she offers a way to read the ghosts within the absence/presence matrix I am proposing as the site of black madness. If one takes the ghosts as a traditional literary sign of absence/madness, then one debilitative kind of madness – i.e. 'white madness' – is being exchanged for another therapeutic kind of madness – 'black madness'. That is, in exorcising the ghost of the white man Sutter, this black community has rendered absent a powerful intimidating presence. And by invoking the ghost of the black man Papa Boy Charles, this black community has rendered present a previously invisible historical absence. Papa Boy Charles is now quite present through the mediation of the blues song. Black madness, in other words, is the willingness and ability to (re)create a world inhabited by the ghosts of one's ancestors.

Wilson's most recent play *Two Trains Running*, set in a Pittsburgh diner in the epoch-marking year of 1969, can be read as a crowning statement on madness. While much of the action of this play concerns the struggle of the black proprietor of the diner against the city that wants to buy his property cheaply for the sake of 'urban renewal', the heart and soul of this play is a retarded character named Hambone and his tragic quest to get his due. Ten years earlier, Hambone painted the fence of the neighborhood grocery store owned by a white man who promised him a fresh ham in payment. But when Hambone finished the job, the white man broke his promise and offered Hambone a chicken instead. This Hambone refused. Consequently, Hambone comes into the diner each day with but one thing to say, 'He gonna give me my ham' (I, i, 47).[17] This becomes a mantra that occasions a running conflict between those who want Hambone to take his chicken and shut up, and those who support Hambone. An elder among the diner's regulars states Hambone's case: 'he might have more sense than me and you. Cause he ain't willing to accept whatever the white man throw at him' (1, ii, 50). The entire community ultimately adopts this position, and when Hambone is killed in his quest to get his ham, another diner regular steals a ham from Lutz's Grocery so that Hambone can be buried with it. In a pungent irony, Hambone has been described throughout the play as an 'idiot', when of course the value of this madman to his community is beyond measure.

This review of Wilson's 'Down the Line' cycle of plays may suggest how Wilson rejects the western (mis)conception of madness that has usually resulted from the economic necessity to exclude those who cannot produce. Wilson substitutes his African conception of madness that results from the emotional need to include *especially* those whom American society deems useless. The African principle of inclusion that dictates acceptance of the madman is rooted in the instinct for physical and spiritual survival. Such a principle of inclusion preserves the tribe as well as to confirm to its members the distinctiveness and superiority of the African sensibility. More to the point of the issue of race in the United States of America, Wilson's presentation of black madness exposes and corrects the dominant culture's notion of black Americans as a commodity.

The relationship of the black madman to his community therefore reverses the long-standing western ethics of exclusion and confinement. This reversal may suggest a parallel reversal that is implied by Wilson's larger historical project. Just as the black madman is not only included by his community, but judged to be of such value that the community effectively joins *him*; so the Anglo/European-American must not only include the black American, but, as James Baldwin puts it, 'consent, in effect, to become black himself, to become part of that suffering and dancing country that he now watches wistfully from the heights of his lonely power and, armed with spiritual travellers's checks, visits, surreptitiously after dark' (p. 129). Baldwin might point out that when you enter August Wilson's theatre 'after dark', you will participate in the cure for the madness of western culture, and learn that the site of rehabilitation is Africa.

NOTES

1 James Baldwin, *The Fire Next Time* (New York: Dell, 1962), pp. 60–1.
2 'Blues people' is Amiri Baraka's appellation for his book, *Blues People* (New York: William Morrow, 1961).
3 Citations from *Fences, Joe Turner's Come and Gone*, and *Ma Rainey's Black Bottom* are from August Wilson, *Three Plays* (Pittsburgh: University of Pittsburgh, 1991). Each of Wilson's five major plays debuted at the Yale Repertory

Theater in the following order: *Ma Rainey*, 6 April 1984; *Fences*, 30 April 1985; *Joe Turner*, 29 April 1986; *The Piano Lesson*, 16 November 1987; *Two Trains*, 27 March 1990. There is one other unpublished play that could be considered part of the 'Down the Line' cycle: *Jitney*, set in the 1970s, was written in 1979 and performed in St Paul, Minnesota, and Pittsburgh in 1982. Wilson is currently at work writing Moon Going Down, set in the 1940s. (A previous play, *Fullerton Street*, was also set in the 1940s but never published or formally produced.)

4 Michel Foucault, *Madness and Civilization: A History of Insanity in the Age of Reason*, 1961 as *Histoire de la folie*, trans. Richard Howard (New York: Vintage, 1973). Subsequent references are to this text.

5 See Dinah Livingston's interview with Wilson for one instance of such a citation in 'Cool August: Mr. Wilson's Red-Hot Blues', *Minnesota Monthly* (October 1987), p. 30.

6 For more on the worship of the African deity Esu-Elegbara and its relevance to African-American literature, see Henry Louis Gates, Jr, *The Signifying Monkey* (Oxford: Oxford University Press, 1988).

7 Robert Stepto elaborates the storytelling paradigm in African-American literature in 'Distrust of the Reader in Afro-American Narratives', *Reconstructing American Literary History*, ed. Sacvan Bercovitch (Cambridge, Mass.: Harvard University Press, 1986), pp. 300–22. Stepto shows how black texts demonstrate for the reader 'the *responsibilities* of listenership as they are defined in purely performative contexts' (p. 306).

8 'Cool August', p. 32.

9 April Austin, 'August Wilson: Running on Two Tracks', *Los Angeles Times*, 1 January 1991, p. F-16.

10 (Chicago: University of Chicago, 1984), p. 112.

11 Michael Taft, *Blues Lyric Poetry: An Anthology* (New York: Garland, 1983), p. 206.

12 Wilson does so in an article written for *The New York Times*, 'How To Write a Play Like August Wilson', 10 March 1991, Section 2, pp. 5, 17.

13 Wole Soyinka, *Myth, Literature, and the African World* (Cambridge: Cambridge University Press, 1976), p. vii.

14 One application of this phrase to Wilson is in a review of *Ma Rainey* by Stanley Kauffman, 'Bottoms Up', *Saturday Review* (Jan/Feb 1985), pp. 83, 90.

15 Soyinka, *Myth, Literature and the African World*, p. 52.

16 Citations are from August Wilson, *The Piano Lesson* (New York: Plume, 1990).

17 Citations are from August Wilson, *Two Trains Running* in *Theater* 12 (Fall/Winter: 1990–1), 42–72. *Theater* is the magazine of the Yale Repertory Theater at which all of Wilson's five major plays debuted and it has published the first edition of each play. *Two Trains* has undergone a number of changes in its pre-Broadway tour and a subsequent published edition is likely to reflect these changes.

Madness and political change in the plays of Caryl Churchill

AMELIA HOWE KRITZER

'The unitary self', as Toril Moi observes, is 'the central concept of Western male humanism.' Moi argues that this concept is 'in effect part of patriarchal ideology', because it constructs the ideal self as 'a phallic self . . . gloriously autonomous, [which] banishes from itself all conflict, contradiction and ambiguity'.[1] This patriarchal ideal of unitary identity, of course, provides the foundation for the concept of sanity in western societies, as is emphasized in the common description of one major form of insanity as split personality. Thus, definitions of madness and normality function within a system governed by patriarchal assumptions and attitudes.

Caryl Churchill has been acutely critical of the assumptions and attitudes at the basis of patriarchy. In her dissections of traditional relations of power – not only between the sexes but also among different social groups – Churchill uses the multi-dimensionality of theatre to explore both the surface of social structures and the mental territory beneath that surface. Analyzing traditional assumptions and attitudes, Churchill returns again and again to the states of mind that underlie behavior. To Churchill, political change always begins with personal change. The profound change of mind that results in a new consciousness of one's social and political environment often involves a departure from traditional rationality. Though her works testify to a belief in the capacity for change on both personal and societal levels, Churchill also acknowledges the difficulties and potential painfulness of such change. Thus, a number of her plays present attitude change as a mental revolution defined by society and often experienced by the individual as madness.

From her beginnings in radio drama to recent experimental work for the stage, Churchill's view of madness, consistently reflecting a tension between the individual and society, suggests that the change of mind identified as madness be seen as the necessary breakdown of a whole that has been formed through patriarchal coercion. Madness is a powerful, if anarchic, source of energy with the capacity to disrupt, fragment, and overthrow the tyranny of phallic unity – and, by extension, those social structures that have been created to preserve it. Four of the plays examined here are dominated by the tragic voices of doomed patriarchs who cannot maintain their integrity against the assault of fragmenting forces. The final play discussed, *A Mouthful of Birds*, focuses on those at the margins of patriarchy who reject or fail to conform to its norms, and celebrates the liberatory potential of multiple personae and non-rational states.

In *Lovesick* (1967), one of her first radio plays, Churchill gives an ironic twist to the familiar dilemma of a character who loves someone but is not loved in return. In this case, the unrequited lover is Hodge, a psychiatrist who specializes in behavior modification. Through aversion therapy, Hodge 'cures' people of behavior, ranging from serial murder to homosexuality, which is deemed by society to be 'sick'. Typical of the middle-class characters created by Churchill during her radio period, Hodge occupies a middle ground of power, serving as the agent and protector of an oppressive power structure and controlling those less powerful than himself while accepting without question the dictates of the system he serves. Hodge experiences a change of mind when he finds himself consumed with desire for Ellen, a young woman who lives on the margins of social acceptance.

Having served as a model as well as an agent of social control, Hodge suddenly finds himself unable to maintain command of his own mental life. In his opening monologue, he half-admits to the similarity between his own use of power and that which society identifies as criminally violent:

> When Smith raped he didn't find what he was looking for, so then he dissected wth a chopper and was left with a face and meat to stuff in a sack. I cured Smith. But I could dissect Ellen, not so crudely, not even surgically, applying every known stimulus to that organism and getting all her reactions by analysis, by hypnosis, by abreactive drugs, by shaving her red hair and laying bare her brain, yes, surgery perhaps or a chopper.[2]

Falling back on the only pattern he knows to re-establish control, Hodge dictates clinical case notes on the progress of his obsession with Ellen.

Ellen fascinates Hodge, as his monologues strongly suggest, because she defies unitary identity. Fusing the polar opposites of beauty and ugliness, as Hodge perceives them, Ellen presents a compelling mystery. Hodge does not know how to define, and therefore does not understand how to control her. The socially marginal people with whom Hodge associates as he seeks to spend more time with Ellen display an anarchic disregard for social norms: one young man casually dismisses Hodge's concern about Oedipal tendencies with the comment, 'I do sleep with her' (p. 17), while Ellen herself, who is attracted to Kevin, is not at all disturbed by his homosexuality. Hodge experiences this social world as a disturbing threat and cannot even imagine enjoying the freedom it represents. The product of conditioning no less rigid, if less visible, than that to which he subjects his patients, Hodge can only see Ellen and her friends as a special challenge to his methods of behavioral control.

A request from Kevin's mother to make him 'normal' gives Hodge justification for taking on the entire group, to reconstruct these individuals who have situated themselves outside the accepted boundaries of the sane and proper while also placing Ellen in a satisfactory relationship to himself. He hospitalizes Kevin for a routine 'cure' of homosexuality through aversive techniques and gets Ellen into the hospital on a pretext, so that he will be able to use the same techniques to first 'cure her of Kevin', then 'addict her' to himself (p. 16). He explains the process to Kevin's brother Robert, offering to extinguish Robert's sexual desire for his mother. Robert, however, not only refuses to participate, but later, in Hodge's absence, interferes with the process. What was to have been Hodge's most satisfying triumph turns into his total defeat: he returns to find Kevin obsessively attracted to him, and Ellen delighted wtih her new sexual identity as a lesbian and in love with a nurse she has met at the hospital.

As the brief play ends, Hodge, with photographs of Ellen and supplies of a nausea-producing drug, prepares to 'cure' himself of Ellen. He wonders if life will be bearable without her, but then reminds himself, 'By next week, if I don't turn back, I could be free to concentrate on my work, with no thought of Ellen, whose beauty is great' (p. 19). Hodge's tragedy is not that he loses Ellen, but that he proves unable to experience his intense attraction to her – and to the anarchic disregard for proper wholeness that she represents – as a liberating change of mind. He cannot respond to Ellen and her friends other than as an agent of social control. That for him the social is the personal means only that he inhabits a world where power dictates meaning. The most powerful segment of society defines as mad that which threatens its position and uses middle-level agents such as Hodge to enforce its standards. Resistance, however, lives on: not only does the previously depressed Ellen find happiness as a lesbian, but also Robert and his mother find in each other a realm of 'wonder', and the lover who loses out to Robert finds satisfaction when he returns to his wife and exchanges roles with her. The play, finally, points to a precarious stalemate between the repressive power structure and the socially stigmatized but irrepressible force of forbidden desire which constantly threatens to disrupt the status quo.

In a later radio play, *Schreber's Nervous Illness* (1972), Churchill explicitly links the issue of madness with societal gender expectations. Based upon the memoirs of a turn-of-the-century figure, Daniel Paul Schreber, the play focuses intensely on this high court judge who suffered a mental breakdown and was confined to an asylum for ten years. Schreber's vividly descriptive monologues – passages from the memoirs – dominate the play, alternating with occasional clinical reports read by his doctor and by the presiding judge at his eventual appeal for release from confinement. The often arbitrary division between the sane and the mad was suggested in the original stage production by having one actor perform all the parts.

This play uses the unfamiliar territory of madness as reported primarily by the person suffering from it to explore familiar dichotomies that form the basis of traditional assumptions. The most fundamental dichotomy in patriarchal societies, as feminist theorist Hélène Cixous has pointed out, is the binary, hierarchized opposition between masculine and feminine.[3] This division so permeates traditional western thought that it separates all oppositions – for example, nature and culture – into masculine-identified and feminine-identified categories. The perceived opposition between rationality and irrationality, too, correlates with the fundamental division between masculine and feminine. Churchill, writing *Schreber's Nervous Illness* several years before the publication of Cixous's ground-breaking essay, displays an intuitive grasp of the way in which the masculine /feminine opposition structures perceptions and attitudes.

As high court judge, Schreber served as a model of rationality, eschewing even religious faith in his determination to reject all but scientific evidence. He states:

> It seems psychologically impossible that I suffer from hallucinations. The hallucination of being in contact with God can only develop in someone who already has faith in God. But I was never a believer. My gift lay in cool intellectual criticism rather than an unbounded imagination. I had occupied myself too much with the doctrine of evolution to believe Christian teaching.[4]

In his change of mind, however, Schreber becomes obsessed by the passionate conviction that he has become irresistibly attactive to the 'nerves' of God:

> God is all nerve and his nerves turn into whatever he wishes to create. But although he enjoys what he has created he has to leave it to its own devices, and only rarely make contact with human nerves because they have such an attraction for God's nerves that he might not be able to get free and would endanger his own existence . . . Nerve contact was made with the Schreber family regardless of the danger . . .
>
> (p. 61)

Thus Schreber understands God as a supremely powerful but totally irrational force. For Schreber, this perception fuses oppositions and violates the boundaries of the modes of thought in which he has been so thoroughly schooled. Thus, from that point on, Schreber's thought system becomes inconsistent with any external definition of sanity.

Schreber's change of mind propels him from one side of the masculine

/feminine opposition to the other. Having committed himself to the feminine-identified mental spheres of faith and imagination, Schreber feels himself to be penetrated by God's nerves. Thus he becomes convinced that he is turning into a woman. While viewing everything through the distorted lens of his madness, he brings his considerable powers of logic to bear on his own experiences – not to question the validity of what he has experienced, but rather to organize it into a system which is, in its own terms, consistent and coherent. Therefore, he concludes that the world has ended, that those he sees around him are only 'fleeting-improvised men' (p. 67), and that the 'Order of the World' requires that he be 'unmanned so that he could bear children and repopulate the world' (p. 65). Schreber goes on to observe, 'Twice the male genitals have withdrawn into my body and I have felt a quickening like the first sign of life of an embryo' (p. 65). According to the complex and logically impressive, if unquestionably mad, system of beliefs through which Schreber seeks to explain his experiences, the only 'unsolved riddle' (p. 71) is a visit from his wife, whom he knows to have perished when the world ended and left him as the only remaining human.

Schreber, like Hodge conditioned to play a controlling role in society, loses his powerful position as soon as he reveals the breakdown in his unitary identity. In fact, it is Schreber's social position, once he has succumbed to madness, that strongly reinforces the connection between madness and femininity. He is kept in close confinement under strict supervision; he interprets his change in status as evidence that God intends to humiliate him by using him as a whore. Though he complains bitterly of his sufferings, Schreber consistently identifies his feminized state, as well as that of God, with a continual physical pleasure he terms 'voluptuousness'.

When, after several years in the asylum, Schreber begins to accept his status and to comply with the desires of those around him, he gains a measure of freedom and is allowed to write letters and diary entries. It is not until he finds ways to trivialize his femininity, however, manifesting it only in episodes of posing in front of a mirror wearing ribbons and cheap jewelry, that he succeeds in obtaining release from the asylum. This dressing-up ritual, the writing of diaries and letters, and a wordless crying out – all activities associated with the feminine – form Schreber's only means of expression by the end of the play. Schreber continues to perceive these activities as part of the unique relationship he maintains with God, but acknowledges that anyone who observed him would 'hardly understand what I was doing and might really think he was seeing a madman' (p. 93).

Though possibilities for actual political change lie only outside this play, *Schreber's Nervous Illness* questions patriarchy through its analysis of the link between femininity and madness, both in terms of perceived irrationality and actual powerlessness. It examines what Elaine Showalter has called 'the female malady' in her 1985 monograph of that title, by exposing the connected oppositions of masculine/feminine and rational/irrational that underlie common assumptions about order in human minds and human societies. The play shows us that not only does patriarchal society, of which Schreber's turn-of-the-century Germany provides a particularly acute example, construct femininity as an irrational state, but also that it forces an individual defined as mad to accept a status and role similar to that assigned to women.

The Hospital at the Time of the Revolution, written by Churchill in the early 1970s, but not performed and only recently published, approaches madness from the perspective of political activism. Crediting the works of Frantz Fanon and R. D. Laing in the introduction, Churchill presents madness in this play as a natural reaction of humans to an inhumanly brutal society. The action of the play takes place in the psychiatric ward of the Blida-Joinville Hospital in Algeria during the Algerian struggle for independence. Fanon, the central character, directs the hospital's attempts to heal the casualties of a society in which an oppressive ruling minority is being challenged and is fighting back with all the violent tactics at its displosal. Though a constant presence on stage, Fanon speaks little; instead he elicits from other characters the brilliantly self-parodying monologues for which Churchill is well known and through which she illustrates clear connections between societal ills and individual illnesses.

In the first scene of the play, a European civil servant and his wife – known only as Madame and Monsieur – bring their teenage daughter Françoise in for treatment. They complain of her behavior to Fanon in a long, self-focused diatribe, the details of which present a compressed picture of the world of wealth and privilege they inhabit, and the form of which demonstrates their pattern of dominating what they see as alien to themselves. The methods of repression and denial by which Monsieur and Madame deal with their daughter's illness mirror those by which they have attempted to put down the growing rebellion: monopolizing the conversation in this and subsequent scenes, they deny that anything is going on, while using force and intimidation to eradicate any sign that something is, indeed, going on. Having forbidden her to see a certain young man, they refuse to accept Françoise's statement, 'I think of [him] when I touch myself at night,' insisting:

> No you don't . . . That couldn't possibly happen. You wouldn't want to do that. You can't tell me of a single occasion when it's happened. Can you? No, you see, it obviously never happens at all.[5]

Similarly, in regard to the revolution in progress, they maintain that 'except for isolated incidents the whole thing is completely under control', and 'the majority of the natives look to us to protect them and restore order' (p. 110). Monsieur and Madame represent the standard of sanity in their society. Clearly that standard is warped by the determination of the ruling elite to maintain their position.

When Françoise is permitted, briefly, to speak for herself, she asserts that the food her mother prepares for her is poisoned: 'All my life she's been trying to poison me. It started in the milk when I was a baby . . . think how much poison there is in me now' (p. 112). As the conversation progresses, she accuses her father of killing people and claims that she 'hears the screams all night'. The father admits, 'Yes I bring my work home with me'; his work, as it happens, includes interrogating 'subversive elements' and 'misguided sympathisers' in 'the empty wing of our house' (p. 114). Both parents reveal attitudes that have been, without doubt, poisoning their daughter since she was born; for example, they matter-of-factly state that 'the Algerian naturally has criminal tendencies' (p. 110). In this play, as in the later and better-known *Cloud Nine* (1979), Churchill makes the connections between patriarchy and colonialism unmistakably clear. Monsieur rules both the family and the nation; to do so, he defines both the family and the nation. If those definitions directly contradict the felt experience and identity of the ruled, it means only that the patriarch /colonizer must work harder to suppress any expression of that experience and identity.

The patients with whom Fanon interacts all present illnesses that relate to the conditions in which they are forced to live. A light-skinned Algerian who has tried to ignore politics and pursue a career in engineering obsessively believes that he is viewed as a coward and traitor and fears that he will be subjected to reprisals. A young revolutionary has attempted suicide because he cannot get the consequences of his bombing raid out of his mind – even though he says he would do it again. Another man has become psychotically withdrawn after enduring interrogation under torture. A police inspector who comes to see Fanon as an outpatient, complaining of night terrors and uncontrollable outbursts of violence against his family, speaks of the pride he takes in his 'flair' for the 'specialist work' of torturing suspected revolutionaries. Fanon recommends that he leave the police force, but the man emphatically rejects that suggestion:

> You can't say that. It's not a possibility at all. You'll have to find some other solution. What am I then if I'm not a policeman? I've always been a policeman. You're asking something out of the question.

> (p. 144)

On one of his visits, the police inspector encounters the withdrawn man; each recognizes the other. The man who had been tortured attempts to hang himself, believing that the police inspector has come to take him back to the police station, and that dying is the only way to avoid further torture.

The play's evidence of societally induced illness pervades those who have the responsibility of healing as well as those who come to the clinic as patients. In a scene with a young doctor, Fanon confers about a young Algerian brought in for examination after committing a triple murder. Fanon's junior colleague has a simple explanation for the patient's violence:

> Since the African doesn't use his frontal lobes it is just as if they had been removed so that the African is like a lobotomised European. It accounts for the impulsive aggression, the laziness, the shallowness of emotional effect, the inability to grasp a whole concept – the African character.
>
> (p. 119)

Later the same young doctor makes it clear that he identifies with and supports the ruling elite. He justifies his decision to report a nurse who was stealing supplies for the revolutionaries with, 'it's better to keep out of politics' (p. 131). At the same time, he reacts favorably to the police request that he assist at interrogations, reasoning that 'it's a very good thing to have a doctor standing by to look after the patient between sessions because otherwise they might kill him' (p. 131). As for the police superintendent's suggestion that he inject prisoners with a 'truth drug', he hardly hesitates:

> It's an opportunity to learn more about how successful these drugs are in liberating the patient from the conflict that prevents him speaking, because a prisoner of course is very highly motivated not to speak.
>
> (p. 132)

He argues that by helping the police he would 'lessen the suffering of this war and bring it to a conclusion as quickly as possible', then returns to his previous theme of the inferiority of the African. Finally, he voices his suspicion that Fanon sympathizes with the revolution and says to him, 'I just hope very much that I never meet you as one of the superintendent's patients' (p. 133).

The final scene takes place between Fanon and Françoise. She has been brought to the hospital again because of an episode in which she destroyed a special dress her mother had given her as a birthday gift. Françoise says: 'The dress looked very pretty, but underneath I was rotting away. Bit by bit I was disappearing . . . that was a poison dress' (p. 146). Thus Churchill ends the play with a renewed emphasis on the link between colonialism and patriarchy. Not only has Françoise been filled with poisonous racist attitudes, she has also been denied any real sense of self by the feminine role the dress symbolizes.

Fanon does not respond verbally to the anguish that surrounds him. At the same time, his later role in the Algerian revolution is well known and is documented in a brief introduction to the text of the play. *The Hospital at the Time of the Revolution* presents Fanon, not in a moment of action, but rather in a period of observation during which he gains full awareness of the sickness of the society he inhabits. The view thus afforded of colonialism and patriarchy explains why Fanon the healer of minds must inevitably divide himself and become, in addition, Fanon the revolutionary.

In the stage play *Softcops*, written in 1978, but revised and first produced in 1983, Churchill begins to move from analyzing the myth of unitary selfhood and identifying the cracks in that myth produced by various changes of mind, to focus on the potential for actively challenging patriarchal power. Beneath its critique of modern methods of state control, *Softcops* celebrates the power of irrationality. The very form of the play defies rationality in its ironic fusion of seeming opposites: the well-known academic treatise, *Discipline and Punish* by Michel Foucault (1977), and the music-hall revue, consisting of comic skits, songs, dancing, and acrobatics.

Softcops identifies the rational mind with the structure of the state. Madness is a socially marginal position separate from and opposed to the power of state authority. Madness disrupts the smooth functioning of the state through its fusion of oppositions. While agents of the power structure attempt to control the populace through the rational means of inducing fear or promising pleasure, the mad condition is one in which fear and pleasure cannot be separated. Thus, madness resists appeals or threats to ordinary self-interest and constitutes a zone of freedom from rational restraint.

The first scene sets the tone for the entire play. It begins with eager preparations for a public event: workmen construct a scaffold and drape it with black cloth, while musicians rehearse, and waiting schoolchildren read explanatory placards. Pierre, the dedicated but comically ineffectual advocate of rationality, who proclaims 'Reason is my goddess',[6] supervises all this activity. The event, as it happens, is a public execution. Two men are brought forward, the first to have his hand cut off for stealing and the second to be hanged for strangling his employer. The execution takes place after the condemned man has given, with considerable prompting, the required speech of repentance. The second man, however, balks at giving his rehearsed speech and instead shouts defiance: 'Want to know what I did? Killed my boss . . . I'm not sorry, I'm glad. It wasn't easy but I did it' (p. 12). The crowd riots, part of them rescuing the prisoner and attacking the executioner while others beat up the prisoner. Thus the event intended to promote rational behavior in accordance with society's demands instead dissolves into anarchy.

The power of irrationality, emphasized continually in *Softcops*, lies in its defiance of patriarchy's carefully constructed categories. Like the crowd at the execution which breaks up and battles over the prisoner, each group of people subjected to the power of the state shows a capacity to enact its own contradictions in a way that disrupts the effective exercise of that power. In what is perhaps its most dramatic example, the play demonstrates the paradoxically freeing aspect of imprisonment when Pierre observes a boy being held down and clamped into the iron collar of a chain gang. Impressed by the boy's desperate struggle and frantic screams, and by the warder's explanation that 'you can't get no lower than the chain gang', Pierre thinks exhibition of the chain gang might prove a most effective deterrent of crime:

> Who wouldn't weep to see them pass? The man will put back his master's hen, the child will put back the biscuit. The crowd gazes in silent awe. They turn back thankful to their honest toil.
>
> (pp. 33–4)

As soon as the boy is chained, however, he becomes loudly defiant, cursing and bragging about the crimes he has committed. He joins with the other chained prisoners in ecstatic dancing and a song that incites rebellion. As Pierre is forced to acknowledge, the men on the chain gang, who have nothing left to lose, have gained a degree of freedom unavailable to the ordinary citizen.

Pierre, the indefatigable but bumbling bureaucrat whose quest for the perfect method of control connects the play's episodes, undergoes a change of mind in the course of his search. He begins with the naive belief that the power of the state over the individual is perfectly reasonable. Therefore, he feels that law is best served through the establishment of internal control within the average citizen – an end best served by education rather than by brutality. Pierre envisions a 'garden of laws' that will make the legitimacy of state power understandable to the masses.

Pierre, in the course of the play, receives an education that exposes contradictions inherent in his original position. When the arch-criminal Vidocq becomes chief of police and proves the effectiveness of criminal tactics in fighting 'crimes against property' (p. 19), Pierre learns that the only real difference between being a lawbreaker and a defender of the law may be who profits from your work. When Vidocq encourages the public to make a romantic hero of the petty criminal Lacenaire, he shows Pierre that trivialization of crime may be a more successful means of reducing crime than moralizing about it. Despite all this, Pierre clings to his ideal of some form of moral education until he encounters Jeremy Bentham. Bentham demonstrates his invention, the panopticon, and proves the effectiveness of direct and continual surveillance. Seeing this external control in operation, Pierre agrees that it is 'like a machine. It's a form of power like the steam engine. I just have to apply it' (p. 40). By the final episode, all that is left of Pierre's original convictions is the system by which he categorizes different groups under his control. However, as he attempts to compose a speech rationalizing the control of these groups, he becomes confused, and this system, too, breaks down:

> I shall just explain quite simply how the criminals are punished, the sick are cured, the workers are supervised, the ignorant are educated, the unemployed are registered, the insane are normalised, the criminals – No, wait a minute. The criminals are supervised. The insane are cured. The sick are normalised. The workers are registered. The unemployed are educated. The ignorant are punished. No. I'll need to rehearse this a little. The ignorant are normalised. Right. The sick are punished. The insane are educated. The workers are cured. The criminals are cured. The unemployed are punished. The criminals are normalised. Something along those lines.
>
> (p. 49)

The play, then, shows us the process through which the power structure rejects indirect methods of control, from spectacles of execution to categorization, in favor of direct application of power. If such application is made feasible through use of Bentham's panopticon, it is no less significant that indirect methods do not suffice to keep the populace under control. Order cannot be maintained through rationality, if order is to be established through state power. Power cannot be rationalized without being diminished. The state cannot maintain power without giving up wholeness. The only reality that remains at the end of the play is the difference between the powerful and the powerless.

Churchill uses the difference between the powerful and the powerless as the starting point of the 1986 *A Mouthful of Birds*, co-written with David Lan as part of a Joint Stock workshop production. The seven characters around which the play is constructed represent a cross-section of society's powerless – the economically marginal, non-white, unemployed, and sexually or socially nonconformist. These characters prove susceptible to possession – an experience necessarily identified with fragmentation of the self. This play explores the personal disintegration commonly associated with madness and finds in it the capacity not only to disrupt the patriarchal system but also to generate new, non-patriarchal forms of selfhood.

A Mouthful of Birds exposes the artificiality of the unified self. The first image it presents to the audience is one of regeneration through disintegration: a ramshackle house, open to the audience on two levels, is invaded by a live sapling. Dionysos, who initiates the action and links the play with the ancient myth of *The Bacchae*, shows a striking combination of gender-identified characteristics: played by a bare-chested man, he wears his hair in long braids and is dressed in a ruffled petticoat. The form of the play frustrates audience expectations for a unified and coherent narrative; it unfolds in layers composed of the stories of seven contemporary characters, the primary action of *The Bacchae*, and wordless sections expressive of common experience. The performance involves the audience in a disconnected sequence of scenes and images associated with dream and madness.

Change of mind for the seven contemporary characters is initiated by the 'undefended day' – a concept explored in the workshop. After the section titled 'Excuses', in which the characters offer increasingly strange and unlikely excuses ('I've hurt my hand . . . the dog's gone missing . . . my sister's been kidnapped . . . the army's closed off the street'[7]), they break from their 'usual routines' and experience a period of time in which 'there is nothing to protect you from forces inside and outside yourself'.[8] In the course of this day, they abandon conscious choice and self-control. They split and re-form repeatedly as each becomes possessed by a spirit or passion and then takes part in a violent ritual of dismemberment as the spirit of *The Bacchae* possesses *A Mouthful of Birds*.

The non-rational experience of possession frees each of the characters from her or his artificially constructed self and allows for the possibility of creating new selves and a new community. The clearest example of the way in which this happens can be seen in Derek. At the beginning of the play, Derek, an unemployed laborer working out in a gym, voices this memory of his father: 'He thought he wasn't a man without a job' (p. 20). Derek becomes possessed by the spirit of Herculine Barbin, a nineteenth-century hermaphrodite. Herculine tells Derek the story of her life: reared as a girl and allowed to develop highly pleasurable intimate relationships with girls, she was later forced to live as a man, found this role unbearable, and committed suicide. As she talks, she takes from a suitcase objects and bits of clothing associated with events in her life and gives them to Derek. Accepting the objects and dressing himself in the clothing, Derek becomes Herculine; he then repeats Herculine's narrative as his own and hands the things back to her one by one. As Herculine, Derek experiences the pleasure of non-unitary selfhood and the pain caused by imposition of a unitary, gendered identity upon his naturally multiple self. In the violent climax of *The Bacchae*'s action, Derek, as Pentheus, undergoes dismemberment by the crazed Bacchantes. At the end, when each of the seven characters briefly describes the aftermath of possession, Derek speaks of the happiness he has attained by undergoing sex-change surgery:

> My breasts aren't big but I like them. My waist isn't small but it makes me smile. My shoulders are still strong. And my new shape is the least of it. I

smell light and sweet. I come into a room, who has been here? Me. My skin used to wrap me up, now it lets the world in.

(p. 71)

Derek's surgery allows him to elude unitary, gendered definitions of the self and, for the first time, to feel comfortable in his body.

While all the characters experience significant change, not all find happiness through their episode of self-abandonment. Paul, a meat exporter who becomes possessed by passion for a pig, ends up depressed and alcoholic; he says, in his final monologue, 'When you stop being in love the day is very empty. It's not just the one you loved who isn't exciting any more, nothing is exciting. Nothing is even bearable' (p. 71). Doreen, who starts out with physical pain, inflicts pain during her episode of possession and finishes her narrative with anguished images. It is Doreen's final speech that is echoed in the title of the play:

I can find no rest. My head is filled with horrible images. I can't say I actually see them, it's more that I feel them. It seems my mouth is full of birds which I crunch between my teeth.

(p. 71)

The opportunity to see the self for the artificial construct that it is inevitably brings pain to some, as well as the risk that this pain may be its only legacy.

The most significant outcome of the experience of possession, however, goes beyond the individual stories and involves the possibility of a non-patriarchal society. The play uses the ancient myth transmitted through *The Bacchae* of Euripides, but also revises it in one important way. In the original, after Agave has led the Bacchantes in their orgy of violence and only too late has realized that the victim is her own son Pentheus, she submits to patriarchal authority and follows the corpse back to the city. In the Churchill and Lan play, Agave arrests the movement of the Bacchantes back toward their everyday responsibilities, stating, 'There's nothing for me there. There never was. I'm staying here' (p. 70). Their ecstasy has disrupted the stasis of their personal and political behavior and attitude patterns. Having moved outside their ordinary reality and having tried power, even if the results have been tragic, the women decide to stay on the mountain. Their change of mind has led to rejection of existing society and holds out the possibility of an alternative one. The play thus reverses the meaning of powerlessness. Powerlessness gives the seven characters the capacity to relinquish their old selves, and in the process to change themselves and society.

Churchill's plays give us the opportunity to rethink madness. They allow us to see temporary insanity as the healthy breakup of an artificially

constructed self that has served to defend against an inherently fragmented and often self-contradictory reality. Madness is shown as a means
through which one may throw off the oppressive blinders kept in place by
patriarchal social structures and for once experience a new way of seeing
not controlled by social conditioning. Through altered states of consciousness one may find the possibility of alternative political states.

NOTES

1 Toril Moi, *Sexual/Textual Politics* (London: Methuen, 1985), pp. 7–8.
2 Caryl Churchill, 'Lovesick', *Churchill: Shorts* (London: Nick Hern Books, 1990),
  p. 3. Page numbers in parentheses refer to this edition.
3 Hélène Cixous, *La Jeune Née* (1975). For English translations and interpretations of this essay, see Elaine Marks and Isabelle de Courtivron, eds., *New
  French Feminisms* (New York: Schocken Books, 1981) and Toril Moi, *Sexual/Tex-
  tual Politics* (London: Methuen, 1985).
4 Caryl Churchill, *Schreber's Nervous Illness* in *Churchill: Shorts* (London: Nick Hern
  Books, 1990), pp. 68–9. Page numbers in parentheses refer to this edition.
5 Caryl Churchill, *The Hospital at the Time of the Revolution* in *Churchill: Shorts*
  (London: Nick Hern Books, 1990), p. 108. Page numbers in parentheses refer
  to this edition.
6 Caryl Churchill, *Softcops* in *Plays: Two* (London: Methuen, 1990), p. 6. Page
  numbers in parentheses refer to this edition.
7 Caryl Churchill and David Lan, *A Mouthful of Birds* (London: Methuen, 1986),
  p. 23. Page numbers in parentheses refer to this edition.
8 Caryl Churchill, 'The Workshop and the Play', preface to *A Mouthful of Birds*
  (London: Methuen, 1986), p. 5.

Three recent versions of *The Bacchae*

ELIZABETH HALE WINKLER

Even a simple dictionary definition of madness indicates a wide variety of possible meanings: 'insanity', 'great folly', 'fury', 'rage', 'enthusiasm', 'excitement' are just some of the equivalents mentioned in the *American Heritage Dictionary*. Most of us will probably think of madness initially in terms of a state of mental illness in which human beings cannot function in society, are unable to feed, clothe or house themselves, and are so unaware of the consequences of their actions that they cannot be held legally responsible.

But any definition of madness is linked to the issues of power and control. Who decides what is legal, proper, or sane action, and how is a human being who does not, or does not wish to, conform to accepted and codified standards to be treated? Unconventional or dissident behavior can easily be lumped together with mental illness. The definition of madness is always contingent on what society considers normal and who influences or determines society's codification of acceptable behavior. From the perspective of the dissident, however, unacceptable behavior may represent a form of protest, a refusal to conform, or a rejection of society's norms. Such behavior is not irrational; the persons labelled 'mad' are in possession of reason, and have reasons, know what they are doing and why. For example, women who do not conform to the proper womanly role in their society may be labelled abnormal from a man's point of view. Examples abound in the political sphere as well.

A somewhat different aspect of 'madness' is presented in human beings who feel themselves under the control of supernatural powers, whether divine or evil; they are possessed, completely filled by another spirit, another voice, to the point where they have no control over their actions and often no conscious awareness of their behavior. The sense of identity disintegrates, evaporates, and the rational will is submerged or displaced. In contrast to the subversive, rational form of 'madness', which can continue over extended periods of time, the state of possession is usually a temporary or sporadic one, and the human being will return to his or her 'normal' self periodically, or develop a divided or multiple personality structure.

Yet another form of divine (or devilish) madness is present in the experience of collective possession and of communal ritual. Group ritual leads people into a phase of altered consciousness where they feel the power of a supernatural force and are encouraged in their behavior through the participation of others. Choral dance, music, traditional religious rites, or mass political rallies can all bring on states of mind in which the individual is beside him/herself, and malleable in ways he or she would not normally be. Mass possession may lead to mass psychosis or even to acts of collective violence which no one individual would have perpetrated alone.

All of these questions about definitions of madness, codification of acceptable norms, the issues of control and treatment of nonconformity, as well as the proper roles of men and women in society, gender role reversals, the nature of possession and collective psychosis are raised in *The Bacchae*, Euripides' last, posthumously produced drama of 406 BC. The central character is of course Dionysus, god of wine, sensual ecstasy and animal instinct. On the one hand the play treats various forms of divine madness or possession in his followers and depicts their collective orgiastic rites of worship. On the other hand, the work also clashes the world view of Dionysus with that of ancient Greek patriarchy, represented through Pentheus. Through this collision of world views, the problems of definition, power and control of madness are explored.

Although conceptions of what constitutes madness have changed throughout the centuries, with the potentially divine aspect of possession being emphasized at some times, and the subversive aspect of derangement at other times coming into the forefront, it should be recognized that in *The Bacchae* both of these facets are already present. The range of issues raised by this drama, especially its exploration of gender roles, appropriate gender behavior and the implied criticism of the entire patriarchal and western political system, all make the play interesting as a starting point for modern feminist and post-colonial dramatists. Charles Segal claims that *The Bacchae* is 'one of the most contemporary of ancient Greek texts'.[1] Indeed, as Philip Vellacott suggests, many of the ideas in Euripides' work were not only alien to the audiences of his day but also to viewers and critics of the intervening centuries, so that it is only today that we can begin to appreciate the radicalism and the profound ironies of his dramatic questioning.[2]

One of the major undertakings of feminist and post-colonial literatures is the critical reexamination of western traditions, the reconsideration of sexual and imperial politics. The two feminist reworkings of *The Bacchae* that I shall analyze here are Maureen Duffy's *Rites* (1969) and Caryl

Churchill and David Lan's collaboration *A Mouthful of Birds* (1986). I then wish to end with a view of a Bacchic rewrite which appeared between these two, a version written not from a feminist but from a post-colonial viewpoint, Wole Soyinka's *The Bacchae of Euripides: A Communion Rite* (1973). I have chosen these variants as offering the most significant and interesting reinterpretations, but they are by no means the only ones. The interested reader is referred to the extensive list compiled by Susan Harris Smith of modern dramas using classical mythical themes.[3]

Duffy in *Rites* emphasizes Bacchic madness as a reaction against patriarchal standards, a reaction which culminates in a sudden eruption of collective violence and frenzy. She shows her all-female cast as trapped within the patriarchal framework, returning at the end to their routines, never entirely conscious of their own positions, and never articulating any vision of a different social organization. Churchill and Lan, in contrast, concentrate on Bacchic madness as irrational behavior, as self-erasing possession which may lead to change. These forces, too, result in outbursts of violence and destruction, both individual and collective, but the drama ends with the characters trying to free themselves from their traditional roles and tentatively attempting to articulate what a new gender freedom might bring them. Both plays parallel the climax of *The Bacchae*, the frenzied killing of Pentheus by the demented Maenads under the leadership of Pentheus' mother Agave, without attempting any elaborate correspondences in the story line. Soyinka's *The Bacchae*, which follows the original much more closely than the feminist rewrites, is the only one of these modern versions which places emphasis squarely on the aspects of subversion and rebellion.

I would like to remind the reader of some of the major conflicts and issues raised in Euripides' drama before I turn to the modern plays. Central is the definition of insanity and the connections between this definition and power or authority. We are presented with two sharply distinct conceptions of madness. The foreign, strangely dressed and oddly feminine Dionysus appears mad to the representative of Greek civilization, masculinity and patriarchal authority. To Pentheus, the Bacchic rites of the wild female followers of Dionysus seem like 'crazy folly'.[4] But from the point of view of the god and his chorus of Maenads, Pentheus is the insane one; his madness is revealed in his pride, self-worship and defiance of divinity (p. 223). *The Bacchae* also illustrates the clash between patriarchal repression and sensual freedom. Pentheus is characterized through his misogyny, his fear of women, his bent towards authoritarianism, and his tendency to exercise control through violent means. (His first move is to clap everyone involved with Dionysus into jail.) The god Dionysus symbolizes the joy of sensuality, the power of the subconscious emotions, and freedom from patriarchal restriction. The god defeats the mortal king at the end, driving him insane, subverting his sexual identity by making him dress in women's clothes, and causing his physical destruction.

The idea of madness as possession is also present in Euripides' play, especially in the chorus of Maenads. The drama distinguishes between these Maenads, oriental women and true believers, and the group of Theban women led by Agave, whom Dionysus has 'sent raving from their homes' (p. 192) as a form of punishment for doubting the god and denying his divinity. The oriental Maenads engage in secretive and exotic practices, but are normally delirious with joy rather than violently destructive. Their predominant mood is rapture and ecstasy, and they are not even present on the mountainside when Pentheus is killed.

It is Agave who is literally 'not in her right mind' (p. 232), and becomes an animal or demon, leading her band in random pillage and finally to the murder of her own son. It is the terrible wrath of the spurned god which rouses and incites her to the point of murder. The Maenads utter a special prayer to reinforce their god's vengeance:

> Hounds of Madness, fly to the mountain, fly
> Where Cadmus' daughters are dancing in ecstasy!
> Madden them like a frenzied herd stampeding,
> Against the madman hiding in woman's clothes
> To spy on the Maenads' rapture!
>
> (p. 227)

The idea seems to be that possession, if experienced willingly as a divine overpowering, represents an apotheosis of ecstasy, but if resisted and forced it can turn into self-destructive violence. The historical cult of the Maenads in ancient Greece probably did not involve random pillage and murder and was more like the peaceful practice described in the earlier parts of the play. Dionysus' worshippers were drawn mainly from suppressed social groups, especially slaves and women. Participation in Bacchic rites was one of the few outlets through which respectable Athenian wives could free themselves for a time from patriarchal constrictions.[5]

Since the conception of gender identity is inextricably bound up with the issues of power and control, critics have tended to disagree about the overall message of the play, with their judgment often based on their own ideological position. One of Euripides' translators, G. S. Kirk, for example, is unwilling even to attempt a judgment, to assert whether the Greek playwright intended the tragedy to convey any moral at all. Charles Segal, however, insists that *The Bacchae* implies radical criticism of the 'great Athenian experiment' of the polis; the god Dionysus embodies both a public, civic threat and a private, psychological one.[6] Arthur Evans argues that in social terms the cult of Dionysus represented a subversive counter-culture, a different way of looking at nature, sexuality, religion and gender roles. According to this view, Euripides' ending strongly implies criticism of patriarchal restrictions and of Athenian misogyny.[7]

Modern feminist scholars take a cautious and sceptical approach. Pointing out that a society which creates a mythology and a literature also tends to use these to support the status quo, these scholars attempt to place the individual tragedy within a broader framework. Thus Froma Zeitlin demonstrates that the god Dionysus in particular and the whole institution of Greek tragedy in general were clearly identified with female experience, but she cautions that the ultimate function of these tragedies must be seen as 'masculine initiations . . . designed as an education for . . . male citizens in the democratic city'[8] – thus reinforcing the patriarchal system. Sarah Pomeroy similarly views tragedy's mythology of terrible women as a 'nightmare of the victors',[9] caused by an uneasy fear of rebellion among the subordinated. Ruth Padel interprets Bacchic madness as ultimately controlled and manipulated by the male society of its day: 'It is men who create and use the myths depicting women "out of their mind", whose mental and physical displacement from the norm destroys society'.[10]

If madness in *The Bacchae* is connected to the restrictions of patriarchy in its emergent stages, Maureen Duffy's *Rites*[11] shows us a different kind of madness in which patriarchy has landed us more than two thousand years later. Her overall conclusions are decidedly negative. This drama was written in the very early stages of the feminist movement in Britain, partly out of an urging by actress Joan Plowright for better roles for actresses. It reflects a feminist consciousness at the most in its critique of the status quo, its criticism of gender role stereotyping, but not in any vision of a better future or in the creation of positive role models. As in *The Bacchae*, it contains a climax of insane violence, but most of its emphasis is placed on the repression and frustration which lead to such irrationality. Significantly, the god Dionysus has lost all his power in Duffy's version; he is represented by a lifesize boy doll. *Rites* turns out to be a perversion of the original. When the women in their climactic fury destroy an intruder it is not a male disguised as a woman but a woman disguised as a man. It is not the wrath of the god which possesses these modern-day Maenads and drives them insane, but rather the pent-up anger and frustration of their everyday lives. Their action is a violent reaction against their situation as women.

The location of the action is symbolic of the degraded position of the protagonists. It takes place in a women's public lavatory with all the paraphernalia of toilets, sanitary towel machines and perfume vendors; I like to think of the lavatory as being situated underground, although Duffy does not specify this. This set embodies the isolation, claustrophobia, emptiness, and triviality of the characters' lives. The lavatory, set up by workmen in white overalls at the beginning, is framed and controlled by the male world. Although the drama features an all-female cast, the reality of the women's lives is powerlessness and depersonalization.

In Duffy's view, gender role stereotyping in the mid-twentieth century has led to an impasse of sterility and lack of communication between the sexes. Her main character Ada, the lavatory matron, is a rough parallel to Agave. Duffy writes, '*The Bacchae* is Pentheus' story; *Rites* is Agave's' (p. 27). If the ancient Agave denies life, in her madness killing her own son, Duffy's modern parallel Ada denies life by 'translating sex and love into money and revenge' (p. 27). The view we get of all the characters is that of a dehumanization of personal relationships and a denial of true emotion. Instead of possession we see total emptiness. Ada treats sex as a mercantile product to be sold at her advantage to the highest bidder. The young office girls feel like 'cattle in the market' (p. 23) in their relations with their young men. The mothers with their boy doll Dionysus wish that 'Mummy's little prince' (p. 21) would never grow up, preferring instead to worship an image. And the elderly matrons deny the spirit of Dionysus by acquiescing in their roles as virtual slaves to their husbands in joyless marriages.

The destructive effects of gender stereotyping are vividly illustrated in the women's rituals. Instead of the ecstatic night-time dances on the mountains and joyous chants of the Maenads, we find only women engaging in empty, trivial secular rituals such as putting on their make-up in the morning, gossiping about unsatisfying sex with their boy friends and singing snatches of banal popular love songs. Duffy's implication is that this modern sterility is a form of madness, the total perversion of the Maenads' divine possession. Much of the action throughout the play consists of such empty, trivial and disjointed conversation.

At the climactic moment, however, something wells up in this emptiness and draws each of the characters out of her individual isolation into a collective moment of violent irrationality. As a collective the women first turn menacingly on one of their own, a helpless old woman, and then, even more insanely, murder a supposedly male intruder and Pentheus surrogate. But the victim turns out to be another one of their own, a woman in men's clothing. The playwright comments, 'In the very moment when the women have got their own back on men for their type-casting in an orgasm of violence they find they have destroyed themselves' (p. 27). Duffy's conclusion is a clear-cut rejection of all stereotyping, whether on the part of men or of women: 'All reductions of people to objects, all imposition of labels and patterns to which they must conform, all segregation can lead only to destruction' (p. 27). At the end, the women snap out of this collective frenzy and, without a hitch, go back to their daily rites. On them, the event has had neither traumatic nor cathartic effect. The characters, mindless in the first place, have no emotions to be purged and no social conscience through which they can experience catharsis.

But we the audience may be being asked to think, feel and act in their stead. If the characters in their empty-mindedness do not look for change of the conditions which caused their insanity, surely Duffy is asking that we do. A few elements in the drama reinforce my interpretation and hint at the possibility for change. At the very beginning of the phase of collective action, before it turns violent and murderous, the women join in a communal dance, swaying and moving together. The only one *not* to join in is the bitter and vengeful Ada, and it is she who subsequently directs the women's attention away from themselves and on to a victim. Ada's perversion is visible in the fact that her first victim is an old woman, personification of old age; Ada, because her female attractiveness is her weapon of revenge against men, is terrified of ageing. Perhaps Duffy wishes us to recognize Ada's negativity here and to suggest a more sane alternative in comfort and solidarity.

The most important element which to me suggests the possibility of change is Duffy's use of fantasy and comedy in what is basically a sordid and sombre play. She calls her drama a 'black farce' and continues, 'Purposely it is pitched between fantasy and naturalism . . . My ladies' public lavatory is as real as in a vivid dream and it need be no more real than that' (p. 27). Duffy's stylistic disruptions serve to snap us out of too much involvement and keep us aware of rational alternatives to such insane behavior. Especially the final scene, in which the women make a suave, smooth transition from mad violence back to their ordinary lives after incinerating the body of their victim, is one such disruptive moment of black farce where the audience cannot possibly follow the characters emotionally. The audience will be shaken, and will leave the theatre contemplating the depths of irrational violence which lie hidden just beneath the surface of everyday gender relations in such a society.

While Duffy examines madness and violence as a negative reaction against the restrictions of women's roles, Churchill and Lan look at both this negative aspect of insanity and violence as well as at the more positive possibilities of solidarity, possessive madness, pleasure, and even ecstasy suggested by *The Bacchae*. *A Mouthful of Birds* is a collaboration between one of Britain's leading feminist playwrights and South African writer David Lan, who brings the perspective of colonial oppression to bear on that of gender restriction. Churchill has long been working on issues such as sexual politics, role playing and gender stereotyping. Lan, a playwright who also holds a Ph.D. in Social Anthropology from the London School of Economics, has a long-standing interest in such phenomena as ritual, magic, possession, and spirit mediums. Lan's Ph.D. thesis was published under the title *Guns and Rain: Guerrillas and Spirit Mediums in Zimbabwe* (London: James Currey, 1985).

A Mouthful of Birds[12] is considerably more ambitious than Duffy's *Rites*, but also less coherent and less easily accessible. While Duffy's play is really a perversion of the original Greek drama which leaves out the divine power and the pleasure of the Bacchic rites, Churchill and Lan's modern rewrite follows the spirit of the original more closely, making the god Dionysus again a central figure and giving his powerful spirit an all-important function. It is, however, a symptom of patriarchy in its late stages that the androgynous god in *A Mouthful of Birds* is still fragmented and without a voice: he is incorporated by two dancers and sometimes possesses one of the characters, and he expresses himself only physically, through the medium of dance.

The episodic and disjointed form of the drama mirrors the playwrights' exploration of the various disoriented, fragmented, or demented psyches of their characters. At first reading, the play appears as a jumble of disconnected scenes, thoughts, and feelings. On closer examination, many of the pieces fall together, but the authors never do attempt to present a single, coherent story line. In Part One, a series of seven brief character and situation sketches hint at the frustrating entrapment of gender roles which may (and later do) lead to irrational and violent outbursts. Many of these relationships resemble those in Duffy's *Rites*. Throughout the drama, this negative, reactive form of irrationality and madness is one of the major lines of thought uniting the various actions.

Beginning in Part Two, as each of the seven characters experiences some form of psychic emergency, a second major line of thought becomes equally important: this is the idea of possession or obsession as pleasure, ecstasy, collective frenzy and solidarity. Although the element of religion, of divinity, is not stressed, this aspect of pleasurable possession is obviously more positive. It derives from the ecstatic rites of the original divinely possessed Bacchants, and in this late twentieth-century drama such possession at least allows hope for some way out of the destructive restrictions of gender role stereotyping. In Part Three the very brief monologues of the seven characters in their post-possessive phase mix both lines of thought and leave us with some positive and some negative visions. This ambivalence, together with the constant experimentation with cross-dressing, role-playing, gender ambiguity and gender switching, leads to a much more fluid sense of gender identity and of personal identity, and this fluidity suggests the possibility of transformation. As Churchill phrases the idea in her 'Author's Note', Agave and the Bacchants in this modern version of *The Bacchae* 'stay on the mountain, accepting that they can't go back to their previous lives and welcoming further change' (p. 5).

All of the characters in Part Two experience states in which they feel crazy, out of their minds, out of control, or possessed. (Churchill reminds us of how often we use phrases such as 'I don't know what got into me', or 'I was beside myself.') Churchill calls these states 'undefended days' (p. 5) in which the characters are not protected by the routines of their everyday lives. Some of them engage in acts of destructive or self-destructive violence. Lena apparently kills her baby. Yvonne becomes an alcoholic. David Lan, in his author's note entitled 'The Politics of Ecstasy' emphasizes possession as a form of resistance, as 'a means of challenging the state' (p. 6). The example shown in the play, however, illustrates the exact opposite process, the domination of the Trinidadian medium Marcia by a white, middle-class spirit. As her psyche is colonized Marcia can only writhe in speechless agony.

Others experience their possession with mixed feelings of pain and pleasure. Dan, possessed by Dionysus, dances to the innermost desires and needs of other figures who die at the moment of ecstasy: 'This dance is precisely the dance that the woman in the chair longs for. Watching it, she dies of pleasure' (p. 37). Paul, the businessman obsessed with profit, presents the most striking image of the pleasure, power and irrational obsession of love. ('I'm crazy about you', we often say.) A dealer in meats, he falls in love with a pig. 'Paul and the Pig dance, tenderly, dangerously, joyfully' (p. 46). Derek becomes the counterpart of the nineteenth-century French hermaphrodite Herculine Barbin who experienced his/her sexual ambiguity with pain and anguish; Derek, however, quietly repeating the story and becoming Barbin, seems to achieve an attitude of peace and acceptance.

Doreen is the character who most clearly illustrates the transition from destructive madness to a more positive power of possession. Significantly, hers is the last episode shown in Part Two. At first she erupts in a reactive way, responding to minor irritations with irrational violence. However, as her friends persist in helping her she subsides, and together they begin to realize the positive powers of the psyche, making objects fly about the room at their will. Churchill insists that it is important for women to recognize their capacity for violence and their ability to 'choose not to use it' (p. 5). The dramatist in her author's notes resists gender stereotyping of women as peaceful and men as violent, and she strives to make us aware of the dangerous pleasures of power and violence.

The most important medium the playwrights use to illustrate the linking of violence and pleasure is that of dance. Throughout the drama the dance episodes express both the ecstasy and the violence of possession. The Fruit Ballet combines the 'sensuous pleasures of eating and the terrors of being torn up' (p. 28). The dances of Dan/Dionysus link extreme elation with death. And Doreen's moment of exhilaration at the end of Part Two is followed immediately by the danced Death of Pentheus: 'Pentheus is brought by Dionysos [sic] into a dance of the whole company in which moments of Extreme Happiness and of violence from earlier parts of the play are repeated' (p. 66). In Part Three, Doreen's final monologue (from which the title is derived) is one of the most despairing: 'My head is filled with horrible images . . . It seems that my mouth is full of birds which I crunch between my teeth. Their feathers, their blood and broken bones are choking me' (p. 71). But these final spoken words are followed by one more sensuous dance by Dionysus.

Elin Diamond interprets this ending as a reassertion of 'the structure of disciplinary control . . . Possessed bodies attempt to represent the release from representation and in the futility of that endeavor a feminist politics is made visible'.[13] Dionysus, however, represents not just violence but also, in Lan's words, 'abandonment of control' (*Mouthful*, p. 6), and surely the playwrights intended this ending to represent the hope, for some, of resistance and change. Lan writes 'For our Agave this is a moment not to abandon herself to the bureaucratic powers of the state, but to fight to take back control' (p. 6). Janelle Reinelt praises the Churchill and Lan collaboration as a work which attempts to explore an alternative to traditional gender polarization, 'a diffused, multivalenced sexuality which escapes and exceeds the current representations of defined sexuality'.[14] Although the ending is ambiguous, the entire play in its profound questioning of power, gender roles and gender identity is intended to be subversive of patriarchy.

These two feminist rewrites show above all frustration and fragmentation; there is only a hint of the process of healing, a vague hope for the future. While David Lan does emphasize Bacchic madness as a form of political opposition and subversion in his preface, the drama itself singularly fails to show this aspect of the myth. Lan's personal political consciousness may be close to that of post-colonial writers such as Soyinka, but this does not come across in the drama. *A Mouthful of Birds* is of course a collaborative venture, and it would appear that the experience of fragmentation took precedence over the idea of political subversion. The post-colonial male alone is perhaps further along the path of change than the women still caught up in western patriarchal structures. In any case, Nigerian dramatist Wole Soyinka's rewrite of *The Bacchae* is significantly more emphatic in equating Dionysiac possession with political rebellion.

The setting and action of Soyinka's *The Bacchae of Euripides: A Communion Rite*[15] are closer to the original, but the alterations Soyinka introduces make the theme of revolt against authoritarianism and colonial oppression more central than in the feminist versions. Classical Greek democracy, as we all know, was based not only on the oppression of women but also on an extensive slave economy. The power and authority of a Pentheus was a direct corollary of the exploitation of an economic underclass. In his introduction to the play Soyinka discusses the connections between the rise of the urban slave culture in Greece, the mine workers, and the spread of the Dionysiac cult.

In his dramatic rewrite Soyinka adds to the chorus of Bacchantes a chorus of slaves with a revolutionary slave leader. Throughout, Pentheus feels threatened by the possibility of slave rebellion. As Soyinka's version draws to an end, most members of the slave chorus make the decision to join the Bacchantes in anticipation of a new world order of justice, restitution and equity. The pity for Agave's fate is offset by the slave leader's pity for years of suffering and death among the slaves. By means of echoes from African and oriental rituals and anachronistic features, Soyinka expands his vision to other slave cultures in other centuries.

Rather than having the god Dionysus reappear at the end to proclaim his judgment of banishment and exile on the remaining family, Soyinka creates a new ending which extends the communal ecstasy and the ritual from the mountainside and establishes a new fertility rite, 'a tumultuous celebration of life . . . a Nature feast' ('Production Note', p. xiii). The presence of the deity is felt in a divine miracle in which blood is turned into wine flowing from the head of the dead Pentheus. All present are joined in a mystic 'communion rite': 'Slowly, dreamlike, they all move towards the fountain, cup their hands and drink. Agave raises herself at last to observe them, then tilts her head backwards to let a jet flush full in her face and flush her mouth' (p. 97).

Soyinka's version of *The Bacchae* thus combines the features of political rebellion with the healing of Agave's madness, and a final celebration of continuing life. As Soyinka comments in his introduction:

I have . . . sought a new resolution in the symbolic extension of ritual powers . . . Agave's final understanding is . . . fundamentally a recognition and acceptance of those cosmic forces for which the chorus (the communal totality) is custodian and vessel in the potency of ritual enactment . . . The ritual . . . is both social therapy and reaffirmation of group solidarity . . . Man re-affirms his indebtedness to earth . . Re-absorbed within the communal psyche he provokes the resource of Nature; he is in turn replenished . . .

(pp. xi–xii)

Euripides' original ending in which the god meted out the punishment was, in Soyinka's view, clearly a myth of wish fulfillment. The dramatist implies that we have now reached a stage in which the downtrodden can 'cast themselves in the role of protagonists of vengeance' (p. ix) and can create their own solution of rebellion, healing, and renewal.

So the strange, androgynous god who causes madness and tests others' conception of sanity and identity remains a powerful symbol of both subversive and possessive behavior. In the fifth century BC Euripides used him to question the limits of state control, to investigate gender standards and to illustrate the pervasive power of the irrational. In the twentieth century AD the spirit of Dionysus is still alive and remains a warning to those who claim that law, order and sanity are based on the control of passion and the suppression of the subconscious – or of supremacy over any other sectors of humanity.

NOTES

1 Charles Segal, *Dionysiac Poetics and Euripides' Bacchae* (Princeton, NJ: Princeton University Press, 1982), p. 3.

2 Philip Vellacott, trans., *Euripides: Alcestis, Hippolytus, Iphigenia in Tauris* (Harmondsworth: Penguin, revised 1974), pp. 9–15.

3 Susan Harris Smith, 'Twentieth-Century Plays Using Classical Mythic Themes: A Checklist', *Modern Drama* 29 (March 1986), 110–34.

4 Euripides, *The Bacchae and other Plays*, trans. Philip Vellacott (Harmondsworth: Penguin, revised 1973), p. 203.

5 See Arthur Evans, *The God of Ecstasy* (New York: St Martin's Press, 1988), pp. 17–18; Charles Segal, 'The Menace of Dionysus' in *Women in the Ancient World*, ed. John Peradotto and J. P. Sullivan (Albany: State University of New York, 1984), p. 209; E. R. Dodds, *The Greeks and the Irrational* (Berkeley: University of California Press, 1959), pp. 76–7. But compare Ruth Padel, 'Women: Model for Possession by Greek Daemons' in *Images of Women in Antiquity*, ed. Averil Cameron and Amélie Kuhrt (Detroit: Wayne State University Press, 1983), pp. 6–8.

6 'The Menace of Dionysus', pp. 197–9. In *Dionysiac Poetics*, p. 20, Segal is more cautious: 'Euripides dramatizes the fundamental ambiguity of Dionysus' nature and that therefore the problem . . . is meant to have no resolution.'

7 *The God of Ecstasy*, p. 19.

8 'Playing the Other', *Representations* 11 (Summer 1985), 66.

9 *Goddesses, Whores, Wives and Slaves: Women in Classical Antiquity* (New York: Schocken, 1975), p. 97.

10 'Women: Model for Possession', p. 8.

11 In *Plays by Women*, 2, ed. Michelene Wandor (London: Methuen, 1983).

12 (London: Methuen in association with Joint Stock Theatre Group, 1986).

13 '(In)Visible Bodies in Churchill's Theatre', *Theatre Journal* 40:2 (May 1988), 188–204, p. 204.

14 Janelle Reinelt, 'Feminist Theory and the Problem of Performance', *Modern Drama* 32.1 (March 1989), 48–57, p. 53.

15 (London: Eyre Methuen, 1973).

Madmen or specialists? Uses of insanity by Soyinka

IPSHITA CHANDA

Wole Soyinka's play *Madmen and Specialists* opens with the rattle of dice: four 'mendicants', as Soyinka terms them, are playing a game of chance. Written in the aftermath of the Biafran war, the play expresses Soyinka's reaction to the madness that engulfed Nigeria; an episode in the nation's history in which Soyinka's personal role was to be a turning point in his life. He was imprisoned by the Federal government for his efforts to create a 'third force' that was meant to bring the violence and suffering to an end through the personal efforts of a group of like-minded intellectuals. The failure of this programme, for whatever reasons, seems to pervade this play and the cruel game of political power played between the military governments of Gowon and Ojukwu is symbolized by the opening sequence. As we watch, the battered war-cripples stake parts of their bodies with each throw, and fight over which limb belongs to whom. This is Soyinka's dramatic metaphor for the madness of the powerlust that the rulers of each region exhibited as they gained or lost territory, the pawns in their game being human lives. But it is not only military violence that is at issue in this play; it also takes a close look at those men who professed to be leaders of the people and in that guise tinkered with human minds to discern how the majority's unquestioning allegiance to certain ideologies could be consolidated. I will attempt to trace all the various nuances of insanity that are contained in the play. I contend that the structure of the play is circumscribed by these interactions and that they also determine the direction the playwright wishes to take as a cultural producer in contemporary Nigeria.

The work of Michel Foucault is an obvious area where strategies to read the text for a hierarchy of discourses that serve to maintain the hegemonic social order may be sought. But in this case, such an attempt is not without its problems. For a start, madness here is not only a strategy of containment; it is also a structural element. For a playtext especially, analysis of the content would exclude 'authorial discourse' and remain an analysis of the verbal level only. It is necessary to relate this to the way in which this level is dramatically realized. For this purpose, I shall borrow a lead from the oratures of African tradition. This is an idea that Soyinka himself has focused on in *Season of Anomy*.[1] The hero is Ofeyi, an urban poet who goes to live in a rural community. Here, he is talking to an elder of this community. He asks him:

> '. . . why do you make such a fuss about a little tonal deflection?'
>
> 'Ah,' the old man wagged his head, 'it tells a lot you see. It isn't only that you change the meaning to what it isn't, to the opposite of what it is, but it tells a lot of your state of mind. You've been defeated by life and it shows in your tone.'[2]

Ruth Finnegan[3] tells us that difference in tone, not content, is the basis of genre differentiation in the oratures of Africa. This means that the response a narrative elicits depends on the tone in which it is spoken. Though both Soyinka and Finnegan refer to the narratorial voice, I will use it to designate the pervading mood of the play, to serve as the concretized version of the absent 'authorial' voice. Finally, the play will be read as situated within a context built at the interstices of several overlapping discourses. This I deem to be necessary as the play was written within a situation which its creator characterized thus:

> The war no longer united people in stoicism so they are trying to unite them in bestiality and guilt by the titillation of the power cravings of the meanest citizen.[4]

The stance that he took also is not unknown:

> Do not cover up the scars
> In the quick distillery of blood
> I have smelt
> Seepage from familiar opiates
> Do not cover up the scars[5]

The play needs to be read in this context, and we have Soyinka's authority to proceed along these lines:

> Any theory of what theatre can do, what it can achieve must be anchored in the sociology of what is written, done and experienced.[6]

This play is invaded by several kinds of madness; at least two of these are obvious in the title, one explicitly and one implicitly.[7] The madmen, the crippled mendicants are at one end of the scale. They have been made insane by necessity. At the other end is Dr Bero and the Old Man, whose madness is the lust for power, the desire to control other human beings. The 'mad' mendicants are strung between the madness of Bero and the obsessive specialism in the person of the Old Man. Both are revealed to be hankering after power over the handful of crushed human leftovers that cavort around the stage. The play stretches between the opening of visual and verbal insanity and the more subtle but ominous kind of mental tinkering that is a result of obsessive powerlust.

The play is divided into two parts, but within these larger divisions it progresses in the form of sequences each built around a nuance of madness that functions simultaneously as an element of the structure contributing to the 'tone'. Broadly, the first part establishes the absurd character of the playworld wherein war cripples are engaged in a grotesque game with their mutilated bodies. This is not all, of course, for it is in their horseplay and mockery that the true nature of the situation emerges: it is an ambience of insanity. An example of this is the 'Fair Trial' sequence (p. 220), during which the tone of farce in the presentation suggests that the dramatist's purpose is to criticize the nature of justice in war-torn Nigeria. This inverted justice, or the justice of insanity, is represented by a trial. It consists of a single line of dialogue: 'You are accused'; then there is a mimed pistol shot: 'Bang'. It is to be noted that the 'trial' is taken as a compulsory phenomenon. When the 'accused' falls down 'dead' *before* the trial, he is woken up by, 'Resurrect you fool. Nobody tried you yet.' This does not end the insanity, however. For there is still a review of the trial left. The tribunal pat each other on the back:

> *Blind man.* Fair trial, no?
> *Aafaa.* Decidedly, yes
> *Blind man.* What does he say himself?
> *Goyi.* Very fair gentlemen. I have no complaints.
> *Blind man.* In that case, we permit you to be buried.

> (p. 220)

This lunatic attention to matters of form devoid of content characterizes the first few sequences, where the tone is that of farcical enjoyment with a touch of the grotesque. The 'Creatures of AS in the timeless parade' (p. 218), at this stage, seem akin to an Elizabethan freak show. The philosophy of AS has a more ominous connotation for the core of the play, but at this point, the serious tone is nowhere in evidence. The first movement presents the dark humour in a situation of insanity. This tone is progressively developed throughout the first part to set the scene for the more serious consequences of madness as obsession with power.

Not that each of the sequences is self-contained and complete. Various nuances of the structuring theme, insanity, link them to one another, and the action builds up around these overlaps. For instance there is a smart shift from the trial to the logic of a megalomaniac who likes to think that he has a popular power base (applicable to many postcolonial states at all times and certainly to Nigeria during the war). None of this is begun in a serious tone; the salient feature of the first part is that most of the time, the officially designated 'madmen' are horsing around. But in the process, the thin line between the absurd situation they create in play and the insane

'reality' of the playworld often disappears, exposing the madness that
underlies a generated crisis. When Aafaa acts as the dictator, both he and
the audience are aware that he begins in jest.

> *Aafaa.* (*posing*) In a way you may call us vultures. We clean up the mess made
> by others. The populace should be grateful for our presence. (*He turns
> slowly around*) If there is anyone here who does not approve us, just say
> so and we quit. (*His hand makes the motion of half-drawing a gun*) I mean
> we are not here because we like it. We stay at immense sacrifice to
> ourselves, our desires, vocation, specialisation, et cetera, et cetera. The
> moment you say so, we . . . (*He gives another inspection all around, smiles
> broadly, and turns to the others*) They insist we stay.
>
> (pp. 220–1)

This recalls not only the innumerable staged 'elections' and
'referendums', it also echoes the logic of the colonizers who were in the
colonies for the good of the colonized. There is also a telling symptom
which could easily be labelled 'madness' in the acts of this sequence: the
spoken words contradict the action completely. But the condition of
divergence between word and action is more 'normal' than its opposite of
complete convergence. The playworld is thus built up in such a fashion as
to confuse the boundaries between sanity and insanity. The text functions
in this condition of ambiguity, and the creation of this ambiguity is the
task of the middle sequences of the first part.

Here, we learn that the mad mendicants are there for a secret purpose.
They are assigned to keep an eye on Si Bero, a woman who is learning the
secrets of medicinal herbs from two old women (the reverse of Macbeth's
weird sisters?). Si is the only positive, 'sane' and humane character in the
play, a fact that we can be sure of because, following the inverted logic
established in the play, she is described by one of the mendicants as 'mad'
(p. 221). The function of this part is an intermediate one. Soyinka uses it
to shift the focus from the mocking play of insanity to the ugliness that
pervades the insanity of powerlust. Beginning with a bit of sexual horseplay where one of the mendicants, Goyi, is the victim, the sequence
climaxes thus:

> *Aafaa.* Believe me, this hurts you more than it hurts me. Or, vice versa. Truth
> hurts. I am a lover of truth. Do you find you also love truth? Then let's
> have the truth.
>
> (p. 223)

The action accompanying these words is that Aafaa 'holds a "needle" low
at Goyi'. Every time he finishes speaking, he jabs the needle into Goyi,
who screams. Aafaa continues:

> *Aafaa.* Think not that I hurt you but that truth hurts. We are all seekers after
> truth. I am a specialist in truth. Now shall we push it up all the way,

all the way? Or shall we have all the truth, all the truth? (*Another push. Goyi screams, then his head slumps*) Hm, the poor man has fainted.

(p. 223)

This is reminiscent of the interrogations that Soyinka experienced during his prison term, which he describes in his prison memoirs *The Man Died*.[8] But its importance for the play lies in the fact that this is our first encounter with the methods of Specialists. The core of the play in fact revolves around the madness of specialism. On the level of content, too, this sequence introduces us to the intentions of a Specialist whose name we do not know. Yet it is obvious that he is the person on whom Aafaa's act as the interrogator is modelled. There is also a hint that the presence of the mendicants involves a deep secret. Aafaa thinks it is an Official Secret, while Goyi holds that it is 'Simple family vendetta'. From their speculating banter, we learn that the Specialist's father is also involved here. The suspense that forms the dynamics of the plot is indicated clearly for the first time. In order to guard Si and the Specialist's father, the mendicants are forced to live close to the two old women who are presented (in a bit of a fancy manner) as 'earth mothers'. Be that as it may, they are the forces of balance. As Iya Mate, one of them, tells Si, 'You don't learn good unless you learn evil' (p. 225). But the paradox is that in an insane world, it is not the insane who must be guarded or confined. Here, the madmen keep watch on Si, whose sanity and goodness threaten their mad world. And as a result of this proximity, often the two worlds mingle, as when the old women sing to the spirits for their aid and the madmen join in, in a raucous, cynical tone. Their intervention contaminates the *tone* of the song, defeats its purpose and offends the old women. The power of these madmen to subvert all Si Bero's efforts at preparing healing medicine is also evident in the sequence when they are helping her to sort the herbs. The beneficial task is transformed into a menacing act of swift, painful amputation.

Goyi.	First the roots.
Cripple.	Then peel the barks.
Aafaa.	Slice the stalks.
Cripple.	Squeeze the pulps.
Goyi.	Pick the seeds.
Aafaa.	Break the pods. Crack the plaster.
Cripple.	Probe the wound or it will never heal.
Blindman.	Cut off one root to save another.
Cripple.	Cauterize.
Aafaa.	Quick, quick, quick, quick, quick, amputate.
	(*Blindman lets out a loud groan*)
Aafaa.	What do you mean Sir. How dare you lie there and whine?
Goyi.	Cut his vocal chords.

(p. 228)

The task, begun as one of healing, thus becomes one of chopping up the world and its inhabitants to suit the whims of insane powerseekers. Irony is rife in Si Bero's query, 'Have you gone mad?' (p. 229). This sequence is distinctive in its faster pace with a swiftness needed to negotiate the fine line between sanity and insanity. And this leads to the final movement of the first part, graduating from the element of play and of doubt to a darker and more dangerous tone of calculated obsession.

The final movement introduces Dr Bero, the 'Specialist'. Soyinka uses the dramatic device of distraction to create the maximum effect upon Bero's entry. While our attention is occupied by a fight raging among the mendicants, Bero enters. We do not actually notice this act of entry, and so it seems as if he has 'emerged' propelled by a superior force whose workings are not visible to human eyes. This is the effect required, too, for Bero brings with him a menacing sense of power. The sudden 'presence' of Bero is less of a theatrical shock tactic than a deliberate signal of an ominous malevolence. This 'presence' is also established as overpowering by the actions of the others present on stage. The servile fear that the mendicants display as they flock around the Specialist is further heightened by the complete disappearance of the play and the banter that had characterized their earlier exchanges. Bero's speciality is a refined violence. It is paradoxical that he, a doctor by 'vocation', has made sickness his field of operation, while his sister Si, a lay person, is trying to unlock the secrets of medicinal herbs. The contrast between them is stark and smacks of an unquestioned privileging of tradition. Perhaps Soyinka can be defended on the grounds that his harrowing experiences in a modern 'specialist' prison may well have led him to valorize some kind of organic innocence. The dramatic effect of the contrast, however, is not to privilege goodness so much as to further intensify the aura of calculated evil around Bero. Rather, another contrast, between Bero's apparent sanity and his father's professed insanity, is more striking and important for the play. Bero tells his sister that their father has 'mind sickness' (p. 236). As witness, he calls the mendicants:

Bero.   You! Come here! Tell her. Would you call yourself sane?
         (*The mendicants have approached, Aafaa in the lead*)
Aafaa.   Certainly not, sir
Bero.   You got off lightly. Why?
Aafaa.   I pleaded insanity.
Bero.   Who made you insane?
Aafaa.   (*By rote, raising his eyes to heaven*) The Old Man, sir. He said things, he
         said things. My mind . . . I beg your pardon, sir, the thing I call my
         mind, well, was no longer there. He took advantage of me, sir, in that
         convalescent home. I was unconscious long stretches at a time.
         Whatever I saw when I came to was real. Whatever voice I heard
         was the truth. It was always him. Bending over my bed. I asked him,

> Who are you? He answered, the one and only truth . . . Always at me
> he was, sir. I pleaded insanity.
>
> (p. 242)

This happened not only to Aafaa but to all of the other 'madmen'. In words reminiscent of the Christian miracle, the Blindman describes his experience:

> You can see me he said, you can see me. Look at me with your mind. I swear,
> I began to see him. Then I knew I was insane.
>
> (p. 243)

The Old Man was playing a game more dangerous than the power-play of his son; as Bero says:

> . . . he began to teach them to think, think, THINK! Can you picture a more
> treacherous deed than to place a working mind in a mangled body?
>
> (p. 242)

It is treacherous indeed from the point of view of the ruling powers. But as is revealed in the second part of the play, the Old Man creates the philosophy of AS to form the basis of another oppositional group which demands complete obedience, not to the state power anymore, but to himself as founder. Imprisoned in Bero's surgery, his 'crime' is trying to create solidarity among the commoners, here represented by the cripples. The Old Man may be a sort of Soyinka-figure himself. Like the writer, he too decides to get involved in the war. As the old garrulous priest says, Bero's father one day suddenly decided he wanted to see what was going on. According to the priest, the Old Man's words were, 'We've got to legalize cannibalism' (p. 239). Paradoxically, this is precisely what happened at the front, according to Bero. His father was instrumental in getting him to develop a taste for human flesh. Bero's reaction is suggestive:

> It was the first step to power, you understand. Power in its purest sense. The
> end of inhibitions. The conquest of the weakness of your too too human flesh
> with all its sentiment.
>
> (p. 241)

In fact, this was the founding of the philosophy of AS, a brainchild of the Old Man. The course taken by this philosophy in the play is rather uneven. It begins with the taste of human flesh, partaken by the powers-that-be. But in the latter half of the play, we see the mendicants chanting the mantra of AS. It would seem that when its popularity spread, the rulers, true to form, became wary of its effect and imprisoned its founder. One could draw a parallel between the Old Man and the imprisoned artist, but one is a little hesitant about the nature of the Old Man's philosophy. Is Soyinka trying to suggest that the ideology prevalent in a time of war is necessarily destructive and pessimistic? Be that as it may, this creation prevents us from imagining any neat binary opposition between Bero as 'bad' and his father as 'good'. And this also hints at the ending, which shows the Old Man as no less power hungry than his son, except that his desire is apparently more innocuous. He wishes to 'understand' the human organism, to teach men how to think. This is evident in the final parts of the play. When all the cripples are chanting the mantra of AS, the blindman suddenly says, 'I have a question'. The Old Man's response is: 'Shut that gaping hole or we fall through it' (p. 275). At this, the other cripples attack the Blindman. Here, the Old Man shows his true colours. His quest is 'pure' knowledge. To find out 'what makes a heretic tick' (p. 276), he is ready to cut him open with a scalpel to study the internal machinery. He wants the doubter's soul laid bare to find out the secret of dissent.

The second part of the play is a gloomy horror-filled working out of forces amassed in the first. It acts against the background of the insanity created earlier. The function of this part is to represent the history of the Old Man's time in the army, his so-called 'dangerous' activity involving the mendicants and his final imprisonment by his son, who wants to learn the secret of AS. The cold, suave menace that is in the Specialist's manner becomes more and more obvious in the second part of the play. His relation with the mendicants is contrasted with the Old Man's relation with them. As the second part develops, it is clear that though the Specialist induces fear in the cripples, the Old Man places upon them some kind of spell which makes them develop a relationship different from that between the master and the slave. Perhaps it is this which makes the rulers wary of the Old Man and leads to his imprisonment. Or perhaps it is Bero who, wanting to learn this secret for his own use, imprisons him. Whatever that may be, neither of them is free of the lust for power that leads them to use humans as pawns. The second part is built upon this powerlust, which is represented as insanity. That the Old Man is certified as insane and confined to keep him from 'harming' others certainly indicates the strategic use of insanity as a means of containment. Paradoxically, those whom he is supposed to have rendered insane are the ones designated as his guards. The uses of insanity are innumerable and each of its facets takes the play one step further.

But of course, the final question we must ask is where all this leads. In the end, Bero kills his father who is about to cut open the Blindman, to see what bodily function is responsible for making a man dare to raise questions. The old women, earth mothers who have so far not deserted the Bero neighbourhood because of their love for Si, now lock horns with Dr Bero. The end comes when these women set fire to their herb store and leave the Beros, father and son, engulfed in a pall of smoke. This abandonment by the forces of good is followed by the madmen singing the hymn to AS. The desertion of the positive forces and the 'smoking-out' of the negative ones leaves the stage clear for those who have so far been at the mercy of others. Is this to be interpreted as the passing of responsibility for their own fate to those who have hitherto suffered? The song they sing raises no very great hopes. The hymn to AS is

> Even as it was
> So shall it be
> Even as it was
> So shall it be
> Even as it was at the beginning of the act . . .
>
> (p. 276)

This is hardly revolutionary. For all his talk of humbling oneself before the masses, Soyinka doesn't present a very positive picture of them. Neither does he offer them any great opportunity. Technically, the play does not conform to Soyinka's idea of a tragedy. His theory is:

> The concept of tragedy can be open-ended . . . the circumstance constitutes the end of the tragic act. Man overreaches himself, displays a flaw, he is destroyed and that is the end, that is the whole tragic story. On the other hand, I spoke earlier of the human experience of disintegration and re-assemblage of the human personality for the sake of, for the benefit of, the community. Now that does not itself cancel this process, this epilogue of reassemblage does not nullify the tragic experience . . . the community in fact absorbs the experience of tragedy . . . this is part of the gain that this particular approach to the tragic experience holds for the community.[9]

None of this is in evidence in this play; in fact if the tone is to be considered, it is pessimism that emerges as a structuring tone. Given Soyinka's role in the period of the war, given also his sense of responsibility as a cultural producer, this ending is a little strange. He is reported to have told an interviewer: 'Whatever it was I believed in before I was locked up, I came out a fanatic in those things.' This can't be mapped from this play. One does not ask for a completely close-ended propaganda play. But the fragmented, episodic nature of the structure does not make it an absurd play as has been claimed by some critics. The organizing principle in both content and form is the motif of insanity, which explains the action of the play perfectly. The playworld is one of absurdity, no doubt, but that is not the criterion of an absurd play. The abrupt silencing of the voices of the singers and the sudden final blackout seems to have been used more because the dramatist had no other way to end, rather than to create an open ending. There is no indication that anything further may happen within this context, be it positive or negative. It seems to be more of an unrealistically presented 'slice of life', in itself a contradiction in terms. For all the complicated wordplay, intricate structure and masterful switching from one level to another, the play remains curiously slight. The depths of pessimism to which it descends do not evoke any strong emotion – not even of extreme disgust. This is what leaves us in doubt about Soyinka's claim that he has a special responsibility because he can 'smell the reactionary sperm' years ahead. In fact, that seems to be just the odour that emanates from Soyinka's own effort. Either that, or it is, as he has said elsewhere, an effort at exorcism. In that case, it is a personal document, in the strictly biographical sense. One can speculate on Soyinka's self-imposed retirement into exile which could well be seen to follow such pessimism. The insanity of the world he represents cannot be denied; one's only complaint is that representation of this insanity completely negates the dramatist's own professed demands from his art. Elsewhere, he has said:

> Liberation is one of the functions of theatre, and liberation involves strategies of reducing the status and stature of the power-weilding class in public consciousness, exposing and demystifying its machinery and oppression.[10]

The form of this play does nothing towards the realization of this ideal; the 'emergence' of Bero on stage, apparently a supernatural feat, is only one of the many ways in which the form of the play undermines any radical intent of the theme. The lust for power, not a very fresh theme by any means, is dramatized with Soyinka's usual spectacular brilliance, but it seems a hollow spectacle.

The idea of a marginal man, not 'normal' in any sense, is one that can be traced in many of Soyinka's works. Indeed, his idea of the tragic hero, modelled after Ogun, the Yoruba god, is also one which works within the space of marginality. Ogun, initially, is not a part of any community; to become a part of a collective existence, he has to undergo conflicts and trials. Also, he often loses sanity under the influence of palm-wine; but on the other hand, it is he who dares to forge a path for his community to follow.[11] The Soyinkan tragic hero who destroys himself for the good of his community is an Ogun-like figure, by no means conforming to the balanced 'normal' view of man. The 'carriers' of the evil that exists in society have appeared as central characters in two of Soyinka's plays. In *The Strong Breed*,[12] Eman takes upon himself the role of the carrier to spare the helpless half-wit chosen for the purpose by the elders. Here, Eman's commitment is to the eradication of the inhuman custom of killing the carrier for the sins of the community. So obsessed is he with this idea that *he* is willing to die for it. In *Death and the King's Horseman*,[13] the necessity of the carrier to the community is emphasized; for a man to be willing to die for the expiation of the sins of his group also requires an obsessive belief in the mores that form the basis of the group's common culture. It is not the 'normal' man, therefore, who is at the centre of Soyinka's texts. He always seems to have been fascinated by the limits of normality, both physical and spiritual. In *Madmen and Specialists*, too, it is not the conventional sense in which insanity occurs. But the difference is that in the other works, abnormality is used as part of the structure, a means to an end, as it were. But here, insanity is an end in itself, the purpose being to unveil its ominous presence in the lust for power. In a situation of war, one does not really expect anything else. The metaphor of madness has been used time and again in conjunction with the situation of war. In fact, in keeping with Soyinka's satiric vision, the condition of 'normality' could have been more profitably explored under the sign of insanity. This seems especially pertinent because Soyinka wishes to demystify the aura around power. Also, the pretence at 'sanity' that characterizes much of the political strategies, which in turn build up reputations of power, are more likely to yield to the weapon of satire in times of 'normality'. Because of the context within which the play demands to be read, this critique is possible, but this certainly does not mean that the play is a futile exercise. The charge of pessimism or despair is not new in Soyinka criticism, and the writer has forged a defence for himself:

> I cannot sentimentalise revolution. I recognise the fact that it often represents loss. But at the same time, I affirm that it is necessary to accept the confrontations which society creates, to anticipate them and try to play a progressive part in advance before them. The realism which pervades some of my work and which has been branded pessimistic is nothing but a very square sharp look.[14]

In itself this is perhaps nothing to quarrel with, though the critique of the realistic 'look' may bring to mind, in this day and age, Williams,[15] McCabe[16] and other British media theorists.[17] Also, the individualistic orientation of the realist genre does not readily offer support to a dramatist with revolutionary preoccupations, unless it is the revolt of a single individual that is at issue. Even if these considerations are somehow laid aside, the nature of reality as perceived by Soyinka remains open to question. To introduce the problem of power and violence, not confined merely to the physical plane, is certainly a necessary and timely intervention. But to represent this within an abyss of despair can be called anti-negative at best. The dramatist admitted in an interview in 1984[18] that he felt an investigation of power, without 'obfuscation' by ideology, to be a pressing need. *Madmen and Specialists*, written more than ten years earlier, seems to have fulfilled Soyinka's own programme in advance. The concentration on power for its own sake is the obsession raised to insanity in this play. Soyinka's obsession seems to be also to emphasize this negative aspect, rejecting all else. It needs to be pointed out that in doing so, Soyinka does not put himself in the clear, so to speak. For the single-minded obsession with a sole element, however necessary in context, is likely to render the work two-dimensional. As Adorno, another exile from another holocaust put it:

> Even in the most sublimated work of art there is a hidden 'it should be otherwise'. When a work is merely itself and no other thing, as in a pseudo-scientific construction, it becomes bad art – literally pre-artistic.[19]

The tone that Soyinka takes up with respect to the insanity of power is, rather, 'it *cannot* be otherwise', which I would view as a dangerous obsession in itself.

NOTES

1 Wole Soyinka, *Season of Anomy* (London: Rex Collings, 1980).
2 Ibid.
3 Ruth Finnegan, *Oral Literature in Africa* (Nairobi, Oxford).
4 Quoted by Albert Hunt, 'Amateurs in Horror' in *Critical Perspectives on Wole Soyinka*, ed. J. Gibbs (Washington, DC: Three Continents, 1980), p. 113.
5 Wole Soyinka, 'Après la Guerre', Transition no. 39.
6 Wole Soyinka, 'On Barthes and Other Mythologies' in *Black Literature and Literary Theory*, ed. H. L. Gates (London: Methuen, 1984), p. 39.
7 Wole Soyinka, *Madmen and Specialists* (hereafter cited as *MS*) in *Collected Plays*, vol. II (London: Oxford University Press, 1976). All references are to this edition.
8 Wole Soyinka, *The Man Died* (Harmondsworth: Penguin, 1979).
9 Interview, at Los Angeles African Studies Centre, 1979, quoted in K. Katrak, *Wole Soyinka and Modern Tragedy* (New York: Greenwood Press, 1986), p. 19.
10 'On Barthes and Other Mythologies', p. 40.
11 E. Bolaji Edowu, *Oludmare – God in Yoruba Belief* (London: Longman's Green, 1962).
12 Wole Soyinka, *The Strong Breed* in *Collected Plays*, vol. I (London: Oxford University Press, 1973).
13 Wole Soyinka, *Death and The King's Horseman* (London: Eyre Methuen, 1975).
14 Interview, cited in John Agueta, ed., *When the Man Died* (Benin City, Nigeria, 1975).
15 Raymond Williams, *Drama from Ibsen to Brecht* (Harmondsworth: Penguin, 1981).
16 Cited in Anthony Easthope, *British Post-structuralism* (London: Routledge, 1988), pp. 43–8.
17 Catherine Belsey, *Critical Practice* (London: Methuen, 1980).
18 Interview, *New Haven Advocate*, 28 November 1984.
19 Theodor Adorno, 'Commitment' in *Aesthetics and Politics*, ed. Ronald Taylor (London: Verso 1990), p. 194.

Fragmentation and psychosis: Fugard's *My Children! My Africa!**

MARCIA BLUMBERG

Madness through the centuries connotes a range of conditions that varies from a gift of the gods to punishment for sin. In *Phaedrus*, Socrates distinguishes between two kinds of madness, 'one brought on by mortal maladies, the other arising from supernatural release from the conventions of life',[1] but constructions of madness can also be analyzed as the site of the conflicting discourses of psychoanalysis, history, politics, and literature. In the post-war era, where mushroom clouds and gas ovens have forever altered the parameters of madness and sanity, the deleterious effects of forty years of apartheid in South Africa have blurred the boundaries between reality and illusion or delusion. For Hélène Cixous, 'apartheid will not stop shamelessly uttering its real name "apart-hate"', with its putrid breath'[2] as injustice and oppression engender hatred and psychosis on a vast scale. From this milieu, the plays of the South African dramatist, Athol Fugard, foreground dissenting voices of personal despair, disintegration, and, sometimes, dogged survival, which reverberate against a wall of political insanity.

My Children! My Africa! is a typical Fugardian three-hander exemplifying intense personal confrontation amidst political strife yet it also marks departures: his first play set in a post-Sowetan context and an emphasis on black-on-black rather than black-on-white conflict. While the drama portrays the inflammatory period prior to the 1985 State of Emergency, the June 1989 premiere in South Africa and other international productions[3] occur amidst increased turbulence and challenge the audience to heed Derrida:

> there is nothing 'beyond the text.' That is why South Africa and *apartheid* are, like you and me, part of this general text . . . [which] is always a field of forces.[4]

Rereading *My Children! My Africa!* exposes a field of forces, which

* A draft of this paper was presented at the *Themes in Drama* International Conference held at the University of California, Riverside, in February 1991. The author is grateful for the support of the Social Sciences and Humanities Research Council of Canada.

emphasizes the psychopathology of apartheid in the construction of three characters in search of autonomy – a seeming political impossibility for blacks under the repressive regime of 1984. Van der Spuy's contention that 'the official, legally enforced racial discrimination is just as harmful [psychologically] to those who discriminate as those who are discriminated against'[5] is evident in the characters, whose three contrasting journeys of political initiation epitomize national psychosis and personal fragmentation.

My Children! My Africa! partially fits Rosen's categorization of the major mode of contemporary drama, 'plays of impasse':

> serious plays relentlessly depicting characters at the edge of despair; characters lost in a situation of pain, anguish, and powerlessness; characters cornered, subjugated to the will of an overwhelming social setting.[6]

Yet, Fugard's drama differs in that characters, while entrapped in the overwhelming structures of the apartheid system, nevertheless voice dissension in anguish and in madness to rail against their psychic and social confinement. *My Children! My Africa!* also depicts the collapse of political, social, and moral values and a concomitant shipwreck of characters who steer between the Scylla of compliance and repression and the Charybdis of dissent and self-authenticity. As vast political changes presently sweep South Africa, Nadine Gordimer's epigraph for her novel, *July's People*, quoted from Gramsci, is pertinent to the Fugardian context: 'The old is dying, and the new cannot be born; in this interregnum there arises a great diversity of morbid symptoms.'[7] The interregnum proffers urgency, resolve, and hope, accompanied by cataclysmic violence that epitomizes the bursting of the dam wall of repression in an irreversible process. The morbid symptoms stress the effects of a political system that has arbitrarily but legally fragmented society according to race. Moreover, the apartheid dictum, 'divide and rule', has split many blacks into tribal factions, whose bid for dominant political voice and acts of violence and revenge, often goaded by right-wing white vigilantes and supported by more reactionary elements in the government, have erupted in the madness of internecine war and the subversion of black freedom.

A comparison of the constructions of madness in *My Children! My Africa!* and Fugard's 1978 drama, *A Lesson from Aloes*, reveals analogies such as the learning of lessons in a pattern of linked triangles where two men and a woman endure crisis to emerge in three distinct states: exile, determination to survive, and descent into madness. In the earlier play the characters are contemporaries divided by race classification and a suspected act of informing by Piet, a white Afrikaner, who, with his English wife Gladys, awaits their coloured friend, Steve, after his release from jail; in the later play, however, the generation gap between black characters, the old schoolteacher Mr M, and his brilliant pupil Thami, is the chief locus of tension, while the white schoolgirl, Isabel, is an agent of communication, albeit defective and limited. Although other parallels exist, the dichotomies between the two plays, which are set in 1984 and 1963 respectively, characterize the deepening national psychosis that has emerged over two decades. Whereas both plays reveal madness as an effect of politics and violence, whether physical, verbal, or psychological, *A Lesson from Aloes* posits the present in terms of the past, in particular a raid by security police and the removal of Gladys's diaries; recollection of the physical intrusion and psychic violation, which signify rape for Gladys, precipitates another descent into madness and her desperation in the final tableau to re-enter a mental institution is indicative of escape from a violent political milieu.

The construction of madness in *My Children! My Africa!* is inextricably linked to the present political process as it impacts on three journeys of initiation into what is illusory and real for the Other. Multiple significa-tion addresses Felman's notion that:

> the French word 'folie' is both more inclusive and more common than the English word 'madness': 'folie' covers a vast range of meaning going from slight eccentricity to clinical insanity, including thus the connotations of both 'madness' and 'folly', and in addition, appearing as an indication of excess.[8]

Thami characterizes his friend's spirited support as mad/foolish and admits anger at Mr M: 'he makes me so mad sometimes',[9] yet the teacher forms the central representation of madness. His unbending belief in words and dialogue rather than violent deeds is realized in the deliberate act of informing on his pupils to avert a school boycott; ironically, words constitute weapons of violence against a movement that initially thwarted hegemonic structures with dialogue and non-violent means. Moreover, Mr M's impotence to reverse the tide of political action and 'stop the madness' (p. 54) engenders personal disintegration and signifies the lack of will to escape the brutality synonymous with certain death. Albeit that 'necklacing' (the ringing of a victim with a gasoline-filled tyre, which is then ignited) is abhorrent on any terms, the audience is denied a simpl-istic verdict of barbarism. Van der Spuy argues:

> we may be horrified by the consequences of guerilla warfare and acts of terrorism, but we must remember that most Black nationalist movements initially asked for relatively small concessions from the ruling Whites and used mild methods. It is only in the accumulative frustration of continuous rejection of their demands that resentment and hatred have grown ever stronger . . . resulting in actions of ever-increasing extremism.[10]

Hence, in a context drained of moral values and warped by political privilege the psychosis associated with support of the apartheid regime, especially those complicit within the Black community, marks betrayal of a long and bitter campaign for freedom.

Another dichotomy between the two plays is structural and speaks directly to the constructions of madness; while both plays constitute two acts, the earlier drama builds in a progression of unease positing an intense dialogue between husband and wife in act 1 and altered dynamics in act 2 with the catalytic intrusion of a third party and triadic interaction until an explosive climax. Gladys's bombshell confirms distrust: 'Piet is an informer',[11] but she retreats from the verbal shrapnel with a disclaimer:

> Of course he didn't do it! What's happened to you Steven? He isn't an informer . . . you are not the only one who has been hurt. Politics and black skins don't make the only victims in the country . . . They've burned my brain as brown as yours.

> (pp. 74, 76)

The play ends as it began with the dyadic relationship; Gladys's closing lines prior to being institutionalized, 'You're a good man, Peter, and that has become a terrible provocation. I want to destroy that goodness' (p. 78), indicate her psychosis, yet the opening tableau implies survival in Piet's self-categorization like his hardy aloes. Madness is thus thematized but is also contained within a circular structure that conforms to some Fugardian drama.

The structure of *My Children! My Africa!*, however, while a two-act play, is atypical and exemplifies political psychosis and personal disintegration. Hayden White's *caveat* is applicable:

> narrative is not merely a neutral discursive form . . . but rather entails ontological and epistemic choices with distinct ideological and even specifically political implications.[12]

Thus, what White terms the 'content of the form' is integral to the construction of madness. Unlike some Fugard plays whose circular structure, I have argued,[13] also reflects a claustrophobic containment of violence and by extension political psychosis, this two-act play is fragmented into eleven scenes. Moreover, lengthy monologues render problematic the dynamics of the drama. For Gray:

> Fugard scarily declares his own 'state of emergency' in dramatic terms, suspending the rules of theatrical law and order, as it were, just as in the outside world this occurs in the history we live.[14]

Fugard characterizes the play's structure as 'fascinating':[15]

> When I started off writing the play there were five characters . . . In getting rid of [Isabel's father and Thami's grandmother] I lost certain scenes . . . Part of the reason for those monologues comes out of the need to give exposition. What I also realized, which was in a sense more important, is that there are

three very different journeys involved . . . no one of those journeys is more
important than the other and I wanted them to be treated with equal value.

(Interview)

While the structure of the slowly-building expository first act and the fast,
viscerally-powerful shorter second act is 'a bit of old Fugard' (Interview),
the wordy monologues, especially the three of equal weight, protract a
lengthy first act and fragment the play into a static/dynamic oscillation.
Nightingale's review of the London production reacts to the verbosity:
'Many in the audience must have wished that [Fugard's] creative kit
contained secateurs, for trimming his earnest outpourings.'[16] In contrast
with other international productions, the La Jolla Playhouse performance
in Los Angeles offered a faster, more animated rendition by Isabel and
Thami, which enlivened act 1. Nevertheless, since words comprise the
action of the play, deconstruction of the 'content of the form' of the
monologues foregrounds an aporia; they are modes of connection with the
audience and concomitantly underscore the crisis of repression in the
dyadic and triadic exchanges.

The structuring of monologues contrasts with another South African
play, *Born in the RSA*, which dramatizes a 1986 State of Emergency context. Almost entirely a montage of monologues, this play ironically stresses linkage since all actors remain on stage throughout and, although
individuals are isolated in spotlight during monologues, the rapid cross-
cutting emphasizes nexus.[17] In addition, the 'living newspaper' mode of
Born in the RSA offers succinct titbits in the first act in contrast with the
weighty 'public speech as testimony'[18] mode of the Fugardian confessions.

In *My Children! My Africa!* each monologue epitomizes a pivotal moment
for the characters. Fugard's directorial note is revealing:

'Trust the audience, they are your friends. You can tell them intimacies . . .
things you can't even tell your mother and your father. You are safe with the
audience.' That way I hope to involve the audience into all three of those
separate journeys.

(Interview)

While the monologues emphasize differing tensions, they all display the
psychopathology of apartheid. Although Fugard considers that communication 'is what will break down walls between black and white, and save
South Africa',[19] the structure of the play exemplifies the limited capacity
of characters to communicate across racial and more importantly generational gaps. In addition to long monologues, the often formal and repressed flow of dialogue or, by contrast, the heightened escape into the world
of literature foregrounds the silent subtextual screams of anguish enunci-
ated in violent actions at the climax of the play. Even in the Los Angeles
production, where a thrust stage increased the intimacy between actors
and audience and all the actors stayed on stage, the long monologues

heightened the scopic interaction but concomitantly emphasized each character's isolation. Furthermore, direct communication between character and audience indicates more than a release of pent-up frustration; the audience is 'entrapped' in the schoolroom, where involvement in the debate and encounter with the national psychosis are imperative. The monologues thus teach the audience and reinforce the didacticism of the play, which is evoked by the visual signification of the stage.

The setting and sound effects enrich the texture of the discourses employed in the construction of madness. The stark schoolroom harks back to Fugard's esteem for Grotowski's 'theatre of poverty' but the few items nevertheless imply a symmetry that displays order, while the positioning emphasizes authority as Mr M stands in front of a blackboard at the centre of the desk between the two seated pupils. The formal attire also underscores a sense of order: the grey-haired Mr M attired in suit and waistcoat lends an air of distinction, while Isabel and Thami's neat school uniforms connote compliance with authority; moreover, Isabel's blazer bedecked with sport and merit pins reveals a high achiever, but the badge motto, 'wees trou' [be faithful], anticipates the inner fragmentation associated with the dilemma of her imminent political initiation.

Although the set visually indicates order, aural effects shatter the equilibrium and the audience finds itself in the middle of a noisy debate. The loud clanging schoolbell and Mr M's opening shout, 'Order please' (p. 1), briefly halt the verbal battle but stability is only restored with another violent clanging. Bell ringing, both on stage and in memory, forms a chain of signification throughout the play that ranges from apparent order to actual cataclysm and is also inextricably linked to the construction of madness. Mr M's desire for order and unfailing belief in the efficacy of words to liberate his people obstructs his comprehension of the young adults' motives and *modus vivendi*.

The debate format of the opening prefigures in microcosm the structure of the play, which dramatizes intensely argued personal ideas and political positions by all three characters in various forms. The initial debate formally pits a White schoolgirl and a Black schoolboy in a vigorous contestation of gender politics. The Black schoolboys vote Isabel the winner of a debate proposal that both sexes merit equal education while the apartheid hierarchy ironically places Black women on the lowest rung; yet the burning issue of the play is racial equality and self-determination. More significant than the debate topic is the 'content of the form' of the first scene, for Mr M's paternalistic attitude to the class of school leavers, and by extension to the audience whose 'vote' is counted, mark inability to bridge the generational chasm causing a misjudgment of their political will. Audience reactions vary with the production; Gray notes at the South African premiere:

The audience is forced to take sides, too, for Fugard uses the Market Theatre ushers – strapping youths . . . as unruly hecklers, Thami's classmates . . . What is this but every South African's nightmare? Being caught in the cross-fire of your own most basic choices?[20]

As an audience member at two preview performances in New York, I was struck by the silence of the audience, some of whom complained about the protracted first act and preachy tone, while many members of the Toronto and Los Angeles audience clapped and accepted their role as participants. However, regardless of audience reaction, effects of control increase and precipitate personal and political disintegration, which is intensified by Mr M's descent to madness.

Isabel's post-debate euphoria stems from a hard-fought victory but more importantly connotes initiation into a world on the edge of the town, the Black location, which she confesses overturns the known centre/margin dichotomy of her previously insulated domain. The quickly deflated illusions, her outsidership, and a recognition of privileged status are juxtaposed with verbal communication on an equal footing for the first time with Black contemporaries, which comprise 'one of the most real experiences [she has] ever had' (p. 14). Isabel's monologue dramatizes Lelyveld's observation that 'apartheid is no longer a concept . . . it is the screen that hides the vast reality of black South Africa from the vision of most whites'.[21] Correction of Isabel's impaired vision and cementing the fragile links with Thami mark enthusiasm for a combined debate but Mr M's dictatorial approach to Thami signifies an ominous unreality: 'I haven't asked him . . . I will *tell* him . . . I teach, Thami learns. He understands and accepts that that is the way it should be' (p. 20). This philosophy succinctly dramatizes what Paulo Freire terms the

'banking' concept of education, in which the scope of action allowed to the students extends only as far as receiving, filing and storing the deposits . . . [and consequently] mirrors the oppressive society.[22]

Mr M's authoritarian discourse epitomizes Van der Spuy's study that links rigidity, high ethical values, internal insecurity, and a lack of empathy with other groups; although mainly an analysis of White Afrikaners, the traits signify many attributes of the educated conservative Mr M, whose unacknowledged appropriation of paternalistic discourse effects a disavowal of Thami's radical ideas and ignites conflict in a doomed attempt to quell rebellion.

Mr M is constructed at the intersection of several discourses; as a 'black Confucian' (p. 22), he espouses his teacher's 'wonderful words' (p. 22), but confesses anguish in applying them to his reality:

(*thumping his chest with a clenched fist*) I've got a whole zoo in here, a mad zoo of hungry animals . . . Hope, has broken loose . . . it is a dangerous animal for a

black man to have prowling around in his heart . . . I feed young people to my
Hope. Every young body behind a school desk keeps it alive.

(p. 23)

As Anela Myalatya he is relegated to the discourse of marginality and
dramatically demarcates his domain utilizing two matchboxes to signify
his back room in the rectory and his classroom at the High School.
Rushing around the stage he shakes the matchboxes in an ironic prefigur-
ation of his madness and demise:

> What I call my life rattles around in these two matchboxes . . . The people
> tease me. 'Faster Mr M . . . You'll be late' . . . They don't know how close
> they are to a terrible truth . . . Yes the clocks are ticking my friends. History
> has got a strict timetable. If we're not careful we might be remembered as the
> country where everybody arrived too late.

(p. 24)

Mr M 's repeated concern with time and this curtain line of his first
monologue provide an intertextual nexus with the White Rabbit. The
blurring of reality and illusion in the apartheid world that constructs these
characters forms a discourse of madness reminiscent of *Alice in Wonderland*:

> 'But I don't want to go among mad people,' Alice remarked.
> 'Oh, you can't help that,' said the Cat: 'we're all mad here. I'm mad,
> You're mad.'
> 'How do you know I'm mad?' said Alice.
> 'You must be,' said the Cat, 'or you wouldn't have come here.'[23]

Like the logical illogicality of the Carrollian text, the political discourse of
South African hegemony implies inversion of norms but also foregrounds
the perversion of power and denigration of Other.

The flight into literature by the triad in a practice match for the new
debate forms a Foucauldian 'node within the [apartheid] network'.[24] For
Isabel this intellectual joint venture signifies the performance of her newly
learned discourse of interracial cooperation while Mr M regards the team
participation as a progressive step that will assure Thami of a fully-paid
university admission. At first a willing participant in the discourse of the
English Romantic poets, Thami ultimately finds his incongruous position
untenable and puts his ideology and political reality above the 'business
as usual' programme of the competition.

The poetry recitation exemplifies a field of disruption as conflicting
discourses intersect and offers the *caveat* that politics must be confronted.
The first line of Coleridge's 'Kubla Khan' resonates intertextually with *A
Lesson from Aloes*; the home of Piet and Gladys is 'Xanadu', which is hardly
a pleasure dome but rather a site of political violation and the inception of
Gladys's madness. Durbach's view that in the earlier play 'the liberal
hopes are cruelly countermanded by the negative corollaries inherent in

the Coleridgean idea itself[25] applies equally to *My Children! My Africa!*, where two decades later time has run out and radical changes are demanded. In addition, Isabel and Thami's shared recitation of Shelley's 'Ozymandias' and analysis of the intertext point to thematic congruences and stress the 'content of the form'. Fragments constitute the medium and message and interrogate Fugard's fragmented structure and the disintegration synonymous with tyranny. However, the Eurocentric discourse embedded in the canonical poetry and the total exclusion of African voices again ironically mark Mr M's unwitting absorption into the discourse of colonialism. His negation of the urgency and militancy of the Black cause leaves Thami dejected and apparently subservient, 'yes teacher' (p. 34), but the widening chasm between surrogate father and son is signified in Thami's anger at control. Mr M's refusal to empathize with the radicals and the disintegration of dialogue is redressed by Thami's intense monologue, which concludes act 1.

While Frank Rich considers this scene 'by far the play's most ambitious piece of writing',[26] his contention that it 'would have nearly the same impact if placed anywhere else . . . or performed on its own' negates the structural montage of the play. Thami's Xhosa school song-lines, 'the bell is ringing . . . the bell is calling' (p. 39), are further links in the chain of signifiers that open the play and underscore the antithetical nature of the joyful childhood experience and the present antagonism. A newly politicized Thami charges that his classrooms and separate education are

> traps . . . to catch our minds, our souls . . . We have found another school . . . the streets . . . anywhere the people meet and whisper names we have been told to forget, the dates of those events they try to tell us never happened . . . Those are the lessons we are eager and proud to learn . . . But the time for whispering them is past. Tomorrow we start shouting.
>
> (pp. 42, 43)

Childhood memories build into a powerful polemic, all the more intense by virtue of its position. This moment fragments the apparently submissive mould, and the call to action, 'Amandla [freedom]', shouted as he jumps on a bench (in the New York production), increases his physical and political stature.

Act 2 renders concrete the subtextual disintegration of act 1, which is voiced in the final monologue, and also emphasizes the two main sound effects, the bell and the shaking matchboxes, in the construction of madness. Thami's sacrificing of the competition for the current political agenda disappoints Isabel, who still empathizes, but Mr M implores, 'if the struggle needs weapons give it words, Thami' (p. 51), and then lapses into an authoritarian mode:

> I will ask all the questions I like . . . I am a man and you are a boy . . . You are

a silly boy now and without an education you will grow up to be a stupid
man.

(p. 52)

Thami's acknowledgement of Mr M's suspected collaboration and his
own commitment to the boycott mark an overt shattering of bonds, which
is expressed in this last triadic interaction in Isabel's expletive: 'This
fucking country' (p. 53). The amplified sounds of matchboxes accompany
Mr M's monologue, which, in the New York production occurs in front of
a curtain on which the projection of dark bars augments the foreboding of
entrapment. Another resonance with *Alice in Wonderland* is Mr M's admission of fear and disbelief:

> It was like being in a nightmare . . . if I didn't hurry I knew that I was going
> to be late so I *had to get to the school* . . . but every road I took was blocked . . . I
> gave up and just wandered around aimlessly, helplessly, watching my world
> go mad and set itself on fire . . . I knew that I wasn't dreaming . . . I was
> coughing and choking . . . in the real world.

(pp. 53, 54)

Unlike Alice, Mr M cannot awaken from the dream and return to the
banal for this nightmare substantiates his worst fear that South Africans
have arrived too late. In a third-person objectification he implores: 'Do
something Anela . . . Stop the madness!' (p. 54).

The act of informing intersects Mr M's philosophical certainty of words
over violence and the admitted jealousy and loneliness of losing Thami.
This rational act is the final catalyst for Mr M's descent into madness;
after sitting in an empty classroom for two weeks ringing a bell, we see
him wildly summoning his pupils in a roll call that asks 'living or dead' (p.
54). The sounds of breaking glass and the pelting stones together with his
lament, 'Oh my children! I have no lessons that will be of any use to you
now' (p. 54), are reminiscent of King Lear on the heath. Grave confusions
about the authority invested in the public as opposed to private role
precipitate the breakdown. Thami visits one last time to implore cessation
of the taunting bell to which Mr M responds in a powerful visual tableau
as he balances his dictionary and a stone: 'This . . . (*Of the stone*) . . . is just
one word in that language . . . Twenty-six letters, sixty thousand words . .
. Aren't you tempted? I was' (pp. 55, 56). Mr M's confession and self-
justification include a Faustian desire: 'I'll sell my soul to have you all
back behind your desks for one last lesson . . . This was my home, my life'
(p. 58). His recollection of the event that prompted his vocation and the
pitiful television image of the destruction wrought by famine in Ethiopia
frame his life from childhood to the present in a paroxysm of psychic pain:
'What is wrong with this world that it wants to waste you all like that . . .
my children . . . my Africa!' (p. 60). This interrogative demands audience
involvement but neither it nor Mr M's poignant exit can deny his mis-

guided act of betrayal. The alteration of his exit from page to stage is significant. In the text, 'Ringing the bell furiously he . . . confronts the mob. They kill him' (p. 60), dramatizes his violent death off stage and frames the bell-ringing in a cycle of disorder and order to death; on stage, however, the loudly rattling matchboxes, which connote necklacing, are juxtaposed with Mr M's startling act, the ignition of his name on the front page of his cherished dictionary, and thus his immolation is located in the words he advocates as weapons.

Mr M's demise reunites the debaters in uneasy dialogue yet the gap between political viewpoints places Isabel closer to Mr M: 'What madness drove those people to kill a man who had devoted his whole life to helping them?' (p. 62); Thami's angry revelation of the dichotomy between murder and self-defence, 'It is your laws that have made simple, decent black people so desperate that they turn into "mad mobs"' (p. 65), exposes language as a field of contestation: '[Mr M] calls our struggle vandalism and lawless behaviour (p. 36) . . . We don't call it [the dreaded "unrest"]. Our word for it is *"Isiqalo"* – the beginning' (p. 47). The differing political and linguistic signification is mediated by their mutual admission of love for Mr M but Thami's regret at truncated dialogue exemplifies the decay of the channels of exchange in an apartheid world where political psychosis distorts communication and clouds vision. Thami's imminent exile permits a leave-taking that is verbally warm but physically distant and, like the aborted physicality of Isabel and Mr M in early scenes, marks another disintegration of normal relations in an apartheid society.[27]

The play ends with Isabel's monologue signifying a linkage of absent Black characters through the White schoolgirl. Affirming Mr M's values as she stands on his revered ground and repeats his words in a final curtain line, 'the future is still ours' (p. 68), accentuates fragmentation in the play. While open-ended and perhaps even hopeful in her certainty of renewal 'You'll have enough flowers around here when the spring comes . . . which it will' (p. 68), the coda also harks back to political conservatism in her reverence for Mr M and his well-meaning outmoded ideology. This parroting of his discourse is no Irigarayan 'mimicry', that 'converts a form of subordination into affirmation',[28] but rather appears to propagate Mr M's vision of what Fugard calls 'civilized dialogue'[29] as a solution for the future. The absence of Thami effectively silences the radical voice and leaves the audience with Isabel's recuperation of Mr M's discourse in an apparent containment of the political psychosis. The audience is, thus, compelled to address the interregnum and ask 'where now?'

NOTES

1 Plato, *Phaedrus*, trans. W. C. Helmbold and W. G. Rabinowitz (Indianapolis: Bobbs-Merrill, 1956), p. 56.

2 Hélène Cixous, 'The Parting of the Cake', *For Nelson Mandela*, trans. Franklin Philip, eds. Jacques Derrida and Mustapha Tlili (New York: Seaver Books, 1987), p. 203.

3 New York – December 1989 (South African and American cast)

Toronto – June 1990 (all South African cast)

London – September 1990 (all South African cast)

La Jolla, California – August 1990 and remounted in Los Angeles – February 1991 (all American cast)

All the above productions were directed by Athol Fugard.

Nelson Mandela's release from prison in February 1990 marks a pivotal stage in the struggle for black rights and signifies the acme of hope for a new future. However the apparent black-on-black violence fuelled by the apartheid system has decimated thousands over the decade and the subversive instability indicates a nadir for the black cause. The play depicts with terrible immediacy an example of one type of brutality often meted out to suspected collaborators.

4 Jacques Derrida, 'But beyond . . . (Open Letter to Ann McClintock and Rob Nixon)', *Race, Writing and Difference*, trans. Peggy Kamuf, ed. Henry Louis Gates, Jr (Chicago: University of Chicago Press, 1986), pp. 367, 367.

5 H. I. J. Van der Spuy, *The Psychology of Apartheid: A Psychosocial Perspective on South Africa* (Washington, DC: University Press of America, 1978), p. 3.

6 Carol Rosen, *Plays of Impasse* (Princeton: Princeton University Press, 1983), p. 6.

7 Nadine Gordimer, 'Living in the Interregnum' (1982), *The Essential Gesture*, ed. Stephen Clingman (New York: Knopf, 1988), p. 263.

8 Shoshana Felman, *Writing and Madness*, trans. Martha Noel Evans (Ithaca: Cornell University Press, 1985), p. 52, n. 15.

9 Athol Fugard, *My Children! My Africa!* (London: Faber & Faber, 1990), p. 11. All further quotations are taken from this edition and appear in the text.

10 Van der Spuy, *Psychology of Apartheid*, p. 40.

11 Athol Fugard, *A Lesson from Aloes* (New York: Random House, 1981), p. 70. All further quotations are taken from this edition and appear in the text.

12 Hayden White, *The Content of the Form* (Baltimore: The Johns Hopkins University Press, 1987), p. ix.

13 Marcia Blumberg, 'Languages of Violence: Fugard's *Boesman and Lena*', *Themes in Drama 13: Violence in Drama*, ed. James Redmond (Cambridge: Cambridge University Press, 1991), p. 239.

14 Stephen Gray, '"Between Me and My Country": Fugard's *My Children! My Africa!* at the Market Theatre, Johannesburg', *New Theatre Quarterly* 6:21 (February 1990), 28.

15 My interview with Athol Fugard in New York on 15 December 1989 at the Perry Street Theatre. Further quotations appear in the text as Interview.

16 Benedict Nightingale, 'Glum Diagnosis of Racial Ills', *The Times*, 7 September 1990.

17 *Born in the RSA*, written by Barney Simon and the original cast at the Market Theatre, Johannesburg, directed by Barney Simon, at A Contemporary Theatre, Seattle in September 1990.

18 Gray, '"Between Me and My Country"', p. 29.

19 Julia Nunes, 'Playwright Sees Apartheid in Past Tense', *The Globe and Mail*, 2 June 1990, p. C6.

20 Gray, '"Between Me and My Country"', p. 28.

21 Joseph Lelyveld, *Move Your Shadow* (New York: Times Books, 1985), p. 28.

22 Paulo Friere, *Pedagogy of the Oppressed* (New York: Continuum, 1989), pp. 58, 59. My gratitude to Susan Harris Smith for drawing my attention to this text.

23 Lewis Carroll, *Alice in Wonderland*, ed. Donald Gray (New York: Norton, 1971), p. 51.

24 Michel Foucault, *The Archaeology of Knowledge*, trans. A. M. Sheridan Smith (New York: Pantheon Books, 1972), p. 23.

25 Errol Durbach, 'Surviving in Xanadu: Athol Fugard's *Lesson From Aloes*', *Ariel* 20:1 (January 1989), 6.

26 Frank Rich, 'A Generation Gap in South Africa', *The New York Times*, 19 December 1989, p. 19.

27 The Los Angeles production maintained the initial awkwardness of Isabel and Thami but portrayed the pain of loss and their final parting in a warm hand clasp of farewell. This physical warmth underscores the limited interracial communication amongst many South Africans.

28 Luce Irigaray, *This Sex Which Is Not One*, trans. Catherine Porter and Carolyn Burke (Ithaca: Cornell University Press, 1985), p. 76.

29 Susan Harris Smith, '*My Children! My Africa!*: A Different Swipe at Apartheid', *The Pittsburgh Press*, 17 February 1991, p. J1.

Some African leaders on stage

OLUREMI OMODELE

Madness does not feature in traditional African dramatic forms, because of the attitudes to mental derangement in traditional cultures. Unlike their twentieth-century descendants who have devised quite complex paradigms for identifying insanity, ancient Africans had quite straightforward and readily perceived standards for determining or defining mental disability. Thus, in many ancient African societies – Egypt, Nubia, Yoruba, Ibo, Urhobo, Edo, Akan, Hausa, Fulani, Luo, Giguyu, to mention just a few – there was a high degree of consensus regarding what constitutes morals, ethics, and laws (commonly labelled as taboos). Consequently, any blatantly deviant or unexplainable behaviour was readily conceived as an indication of a malfunctioning of the 'head', that is, a manifestation of lunacy. In the traditional African world view, madness was considered to be a disease of the head. Also, according to this view, madness did not necessarily involve a violent attack. Very often, its manifestations are quite subtle rather than obvious or functionally incapacitating. For instance, some of the first African products of western education who displayed traits of westernization in blatant ways were either admired or reviled as insane by unwesternized Africans. So also were the early Christian converts, especially those who displayed excessive fanaticism or enthusiasm. People who are familiar with any African society will readily recognize the commonplace reprimand: *O nsi were ni?* or *Se ori e pe?* (Yoruba); *Isi odi kwa gi?* (Ibo); *Ki ura guruka* (Gikuyu); and in Pidgin English *Abi you de craze?*. These are typical ways of questioning or chastising deviant behaviour.

Root causes of madness are various as well as numerous but they are always determinable. It is not uncommon, for instance, for a devotee of a God to be stricken temporarily with madness as a punishment for violating a covenant or failing to perform a prescribed ritual. Similarly, a powerful elder or superior may use a curse to deprive a rude person of sanity. The sanity of the people thus afflicted will return soon after necessary rituals of atonement have been performed. For those permanently afflicted however, there is a high degree of care and tolerance as certain adages and proverbs illustrate. For instance, *Asinwin ile eni lojo. Ti asinwin ita ba nbo, tile a duro de e* ('The insane person in one's household has his place; on the day that an insane person from without attacks, the insane from within will strike back') indicates acknowledgement of the usefulness of the mad person in a given household. This assertion underscores the notion that an insane person still retains some ability to function rationally. This notion is illustrated more directly by yet another ancient Yoruba proverb which suggests that, unlike a drunk, a mentally disturbed person knows his limits: 'Take a drunk and a mad person to a ditch and see who willingly jumps in.'

Not everything about the insane however, is positive. For instance, Yoruba people, who, like most Africans thrive on moderation and reality, harbour no illusions regarding the pains and sorrow which befall the family of the afflicted. They admit for instance that *Were dun un wo, sugbon ko see bi lomo* ('Entertaining as the antics of the mentally deranged may sometimes be, no one prays that his or her child be stricken with madness'). Africans also hold a realistic view regarding medical efficacy in reference to the curability of mental illness: *Ki i tan ko ma ku pe pe pe* – 'Madness is never completely cured' – is a Yoruba expression. Like most Africans, the Yoruba dread *aisan ti o gbo oogun* – that is, an illness which does not respond to herbs.

Thus, although the afflicted is not treated as an outcast, his fate is considered to be sad. Indeed, madness is regarded as one of the most serious of all afflictions known to traditional Africans. After all, it attacks the head, the spiritual as well as the secular governor of the body. Like most serious subjects or situations, madness is thus generally excluded from traditional African entertainment.

Contemporary researchers have suggested several theories to explain the traditional African tendency to exclude tragic and even serious elements from their dramatic forms. Superstition is one of the more frequently offered explanations. Proponents of this maintain that Africans believe that, by performing a role, the actor is inadvertently inviting the content or implications of the role upon himself. There is, after all, the often-repeated ancient warning: 'beware of what you ask for, for you might get it'. Plausible as this standpoint is, however, 'superstition' does not explain the entire reason for the exclusion of grave events or phenomena from African entertainment forms. After all, Africans traditionally realize that not every wish comes to pass. As Yoruba people put it, *A o ki nperi iku ko wa pa'ni* ('One does not die by simply saying "death"').

The main reason for the exclusion is their unwillingness to subject afflicted people to ridicule. Again, as a Yoruba saying goes, *A a ki i toju onika mesan ka a* ('It is bad taste to allude to nine in the presence of a nine-fingered person'). Since madness is considered a tragic and serious affliction, it is not a suitable subject for entertainment.[1]

A remarkable break with this sensitivity becomes discernible with the influence of colonialism. It is needless to enumerate the various ways in which the world order and the sensibility of the average African came to be impacted by colonialism. For our purpose, it suffices to mention that the new religions, education and social order which colonialism delivered all proved quite effective in turning Africans against their old customs and traditions.

The drama of the colonial period was inevitably affected, not only formally, but particularly in terms of content. For instance, for the dramatists of the period, compliance with the principle of verisimilitude, the urge to compare Africa and Europe, and the need to inject morals into every theatrical production all made it necessary to contextualize their plays by infusing *real-life* occurrences into them. These factors affected not only the productions mounted by westernized dramatists but also those by the advocates of traditionalism and absorptionism.[2] In order to make their points as advocates, the dramatists were forced to reproduce on stage instances which are similar to those found in real life. Thus, in his bid to portray traditional Africa in a 'positive light', a traditionalist dramatist would mount a play in which traditional herbalists cure a number of overwhelming and deep-seated afflictions. Conversely, advocates of the new ways would feature plays in which a 'wicked witch' used his or her power to strike an innocent person dead or mad. This after all was the era of the 'gagools', the anti-satan campaigns and the hunger to preach the power and superiority of Christianity. This genre of plays was particularly typical of mission schools.

The impact of colonialism went beyond the generation of new thematic dimensions in the plays of African dramatists. It penetrated the entire psyche of the African. One may say that the emergence of the new themes is an indication of the emergence of a new state of mind, and in and out of the theatre, the African's new state of mind is often characterized by uncertainty as to what is morally correct. Having been deprived of the ability to base their judgement on culturally informed instincts, there is an observable lack of self-confidence, or self-worth which psychiatrists now recognize as a form of psychopathology. This has long been recognized by the insightful element of the lay public as 'colo mentality', that is, a state of mental delusion which causes the afflicted to abandon realistic and meaningful ways of life in search of the romantic.

As Africans move (or should we say crawl?) into the 1990s, it has finally become quite clear that wholesale importation of western values to wipe out and replace the traditional African psyche has not served Africa well. As Ad'Obe Obe opines, after noting the gulf left by the eradication of

African traditions and culture, 'with their culture thus beating to a rhythm of psychopathology, one cannot help wondering if there exists a single African ego that is healthy'.[3] This unhealthy state is often explained in terms of the contemporary African condition, namely its 'harsh and unfavourable social and physical environment'.[4] Many African psychiatrists have observed that due to such an unfit physical environment, 'intensely experienced emotions, revelling in fantasy and reduced reality testing, impairment of judgement and concentration'[5] are prevalent among contemporary Africans.

An in-depth study of most contemporary plays which address African leadership would confirm these observations. Indeed, most African plays with political themes could readily serve as a guide to our perception of the various manifestations of mental disorders which are widespread in much of post-colonial African leadership. (The leadership of the factions fighting currently in Somalia and Liberia, for example, is a typical example of colonial bequest.) Indeed L. Bloom – an expert on psychiatry in Africa – identifies the root cause of these contemporary mental disorders:

> In Africa, the attempt to share the meretricious success of the capitalistic economic activity has not been accompanied by appreciation of the technological, social and political methods devised and developed to organise that activity. [There is, as a result] a collective collision in accepting fantasy as real.[6]

'Accepting fantasy as real' is indeed an apt description of much of African leadership – a fact which is not lost on African dramatists, who have found, in various manifestations of insanity in African leaders, fertile subject matter for their plays. Contemporary African leaders or aspiring leaders continue to constitute the targets of sardonic satire in plays such as Ola Rotimi's *Our Husband Has Gone Mad Again*, Wole Soyinka's *Madmen and Specialists* and *A Play of Giants*, Ugugi's *I Will Marry When I Want* and *The Trial of Dedan Kimathi*.

Ugugi's *The Trial of Dedan Kimathi* is based on aspects of Dedan Kimathi's life with emphasis on his abhorrence of colonialism and his determination to engage in a bloody struggle against it. Kimathi's mother ironically becomes one of the first casualties of his decision. Worry over her son drives her literally out of her mind:

> Poor mother . . . don't cry
> I was right to choose the path of struggle.
> How else would I have looked you in the eyes?
> Forgive me . . .
> That your love for me has turned your head
> To wild imaginings
> Victory will be ours . . .

(p. 32)

Like most heroes, Kimathi bears his mother's plight courageously. What is not so easily overcome, however, is his own appearance as an insane person, an appearance which is corroborated by his audacity and fearlessness in spear-heading an attack on a militarily superior superstructure.

It is perhaps more accurate, however, that Kimathi finally snaps, having exhausted his tolerance for an abusive and imposed system of government. He has been driven 'mad' by his keen and superior awareness of the ills of colonialism. This awareness finally leads him to a realization that he can only impact the colonial system from without, and he consequently declares himself officially an outcast.

Dedan Kimathi is consumed by justified anger against the British. He is convinced about the need to struggle against the colonial system, which was comparable to apartheid. Consequent upon the overwhelming force of his conviction, he consantly succeeds in galvanizing the support and loyalty of a surprisingly large number of Kenya people before whom he always argues his case persuasively:

> With the British, we have been losers all the way . . . but this is a new era. This is a new war. We have bled for you. We have fought your wars for you, against the Germans, Japanese, Italians. This time we shall bleed for our soil, for our freedom, until you let go.
>
> (p. 34)i

Or as he says to the judge at his trial:

> I despise your laws and your courts. What have they done for our people? What? Protected the oppressor. Licensed the murderers of the people: Our people, whipped when they did not pick your tea leaves/ your coffee beans/ Imprisoned when they refused to 'ayah' your babies/ and 'boy' your houses and gardens/ Murdered when they didn't rickshaw your ladies and your gentlemen. I recognize only one law, one court:/ the court and the law of those who fight against exploitation, The toilers armed to say/ We demand our freedom . . .
>
> (p. 27)

To the people in whose interest he fights, Kimathi is not mad. On the contrary, he paints a picture of the imperialist as not only being outside of the African world order but also insane. He extends the same judgement to those Africans who have chosen to collaborate with the colonialist. If Kimathi starts out striking the audience as insane, by the end of the play, he indeed assumes a near-supernatural status.

Ugugi also returns to this strategy in *I Will Marry When I Want*. Again, the colonialist and his African collaborator are portrayed as suffering from impaired judgement.

> That group is now ready to sell the country to foreigners . . .
> Go to any business premise
> Even if you find an African . . .

Know that he is an only overseer, a well-fed watchdog
Ensuring the smooth passage of people's wealth
To Europe and other foreign countries . . .
Exploiters/Oppressors . . .

Another device whereby these 'well-fed watchdogs' are derided and their sanity questioned is via the use of exaggeration, one of the most effective of dramatic techniques. By deliberately blowing their imitative nature and their appetite for foreign goods out of proportion, Ugugi invites his audience to doubt the mental stability of the characters without absolving them. The scene of Wangeci and Kiguunda preparing for a church wedding after fifty years of marriage in (traditional African style) is certainly designed to strike us as a loss of sanity on the part of this couple. First, they have to become Christians, a ritual which commands them to denounce their past. This denunciation is symbolized by the couple's rejection of their African names. Thus, the man becomes Winston Smith and the woman, Rosemary Magdalane (pp. 92–6). In the end, Wangeci and Kiguunda regain their sanity but they pay for the temporary loss of it. Ugugi does not let his characters off, even when they have been misled by sinister characters.

It is perhaps clear that in these plays, mental derangement is not as obvious or blatant as in some Jacobean plays. There are no scenes involving insane characters on a rampage. What is readily discernible, however, are behavioural patterns which do not lend themselves to logical or rational explanations. Sometimes, these patterns are so subtle that the audience is left to judge the degree to which a given character can be assumed to be 'mad'. While this might be regarded as purely a matter of artistic choice, it might also reflect the difficulty in defining madness in contemporary society. After all, behavioural patterns which would have passed for utter madness in traditional societies are now easily explained away or labelled as 'eccentric', 'crass', or simply excessive. These days, eccentricity is indeed a mark of the wealthy, the politician or the politically significant. (All of these people are the same and so the labels are interchangeable.) The definition of madness in contemporary African society is further problematized by the fact that according to some psychiatrists, more than one-fifth of the population suffers from one form of mental illness or another. Thus, madness has become nearly totally subject to individual perception.

Nevertheless, assessing the depiction of madness in African plays is rendered less complicated by the fact that dramatists often focus on the more conspicuous African leaders, whose excessive or eccentric behaviour readily attracts our attention. It is the functional disorder or, to borrow Professor Ebie's phrase, the 'impairment of judgement' of the political leaders that the dramatists often choose to deride.

In Ola Rotimi's adaptation of Sophocles' *Oedipus the King*, appropriately entitled *The Gods Are not to Blame*, it is Odewale's inability to refrain from killing 'the old man' who 'provoked' him which brings him the resulting pain and suffering. Having been forewarned that he will 'kill his father and marry his mother', Ifa, the traditional Yoruba belief system, commands Odewale to desist from killing any man, particularly anyone who might be his father's age. Nor should he have married an older woman. After all, a common Yoruba proverb warns that *Eni ti a ba ni aje ma pa je ki n fi epo para* ('The individual who has been labelled as food for the witches must not use palm oil as body lotion'). Witches are known to love palm oil.

In *Our Husband Has Gone Mad Again*, Major Rahman Lejoka-Brown's madness is equally a function of impaired judgement and concentration. Although it is possible, pathologically speaking, that his senses have been adversely affected by his war-front experiences, it is his post-war judgements which Ola Rotimi chooses to dwell upon.

First of all, his decision to go into politics necessitates his adoption of the antics which inform the neurotic and grotesque aspect of the play. To succeed in politics, Lejoka-Brown must secure the support of four distinct and ever-contending factions – the Ibo, the Hausa, the Yoruba, and women. As a Moslem, he is likely to appeal to the Hausa who often emphasize religion over ethnicity. In order to win the women's votes, he affiliates himself with the President of the Market Women's Association, Mrs Ajanaku, an Igbo woman, by marrying her daughter, Sikira. In the mean time, he has, in deference to his religious dictate, married his brother's widow, Iya Rashida. Lejoka-Brown is also married to Liza, a Kenya girl who he met while fighting in the Congo. Liza has since acquired a medical degree from an American university and has decided to journey to Lagos to join Lejoka-Brown, who, as we can see, has overextended himself. By the time she arrives in Lagos, he has become intertwined with the rather picturesque Lagos, a place charged with crazy personalities and deeds which typify electioneering campaigns in Nigeria. Lejoka-Brown has acquired an obsessed, fragmented personality, unable to discern fantasies from realities. Sikira describes one of his antics:

> Ah politics . . . Not only is the master in love . . . madly in love with Politics, he breathes Politics, he washes his mouth every morning with Politics, he sleeps with Politics and dreams of . . . At night, deep in his sleep . . . holds it high above his head like a flag . . . and sings . . . You wait; you'll see him tonight. You don't even have to keep awake . . . the master's voice will wake you up!

Part of the manifestation of Lejoka-Brown's mental impairment is his belief that he can adequately rise to the challenges which both he and political circumstances have created for him. First, he exhibits impaired judgement in thinking that after six years of separation, he can lure Liza away to Rome or Paris until the elections are over, after which he will

> give Sikira lump sum capital to go and trade and look for another man or something like that; Mama Rashida remains right in this house of my fathers; and I move into Minister's quarters on Victoria Island. Liza joins me there: everybody is happy . . .

In striving to achieve these ends simultaneously, Lejoka-Brown loses the presence of mind necessary for his political life.

Lejoka-Brown's inability to accept women as his equals is yet another indication of his mental imbalance. After all, in Yoruba ontology (and also in Chinese *ying* and *yang*), a healthy existence is maintained by acceptance of all opposites – the positive and the negative, the good and the bad, the warm and the cold, the male and the female. Indeed in a lay person's language, by so blatantly and completely misunderstanding the male–female relationship as one of master and servant, Lejoka-Brown fails to grasp the fine intricacies which make it work. He is shocked when confronted with the notion that matrimony should be a partnership (with the implication of equality). '. . . you are still my wife, and I will remain head . . . You can't set . . . rules . . . Two bulls can't drink from the same bucket at the same time: they will lock horns!'

With his judgement and concentration thus impaired, little wonder that Lejoka-Brown can achieve neither domestic nor political success. Unable to work out conflicts in rational ways, he soon begins to use violence, to which Sikira frequently reacts by alerting the household in the words which form the title of the play: 'Our husband has gone mad again.'

It is of some consolation that Lejoka-Brown remains alone in his impaired perception of realities, particularly of women, for, as the play closes, Sikira, his former door-mat has abandoned him and emerged as an acceptable candidate, strong and competent enough to displace him. 'Vote for me', she declares to a cheering and jubilant crowd. 'It is true that I am a woman but that does not matter . . . Because . . . MEN AND WOMEN ARE CREATED EQUAL!': to which he characteristically responds: 'The world has come to an end.' It is truer to say, however, that what has really come to an end is the world of inequality which his warped mind has laboriously constructed. By Lejoka-Brown's failure in politics, Africa is spared another, although relatively speaking a minute, rascal.

Africa is not thus spared in either Soyinka's *Madmen and Specialists* or in his *A Play of Giants*, where we witness a group of African leaders whose actions and behaviour profoundly underscore their mental disability. *Madmen and Specialists* raises a profound question about the mental state of those specialists, and the play is unrelenting in its argument that the specialists and the madmen are intricately linked. As is typical of

Soyinka's works, we are not informed about the events which led to the chaos being exhibited before us. There are, however, allusions to war and we see its outcome particularly in the Mendicants' grotesque physical deformities, references to military activities and the overall macabre tone of the play. Not only have the Mendicants been deformed physically, but their minds have been distorted as well. Their grotesque physical displays also match or illustrate quite vividly the grotesque state of Bero's mind. Dr Bero, who supposedly 'joined' the war as an idealistic medical doctor has since changed professions and is now a specialist in the intelligence/secret service. In addition to his own admissions, his ill-treatment of his father, the Old Man (who he eventually kills), his disrespect toward Iya Mate and Iya Agba, and his ingratitude to his sister, Si Bero, must all be viewed as Soyinka's masterly and economical way of dramatizing Specialist Bero's other monstrous and dastardly deeds. Another achievement of Soyinka's craftsmanship is his succinctness in referring to the activities of the President in the middle of what is evidently a bloody war. The Mendicants chant the Old Man's song which describes the gleeful, sumptious, all-head-and-no-heart manner in which the President and his wife tour the camps of the disabled:

> He came smelling of wine and roses.
> On his arm his wife was gushpillating . . .

> (p. 84)

Soyinka's coinage of the word 'gushpillating' is also a mark of his creativity, especially his ability to reach beyond regular usage in order to achieve a piercingly precise impression of what he seeks to convey. In this case, we can rely on the sound of the word 'gushpillating' to get a sense of it. The first syllable conveys a sense of excess, over-effusiveness, copious emission of liquid. When coupled with 'pillating' and spat out, a rather offensive image of this couple's actions is achieved and a bad taste is left in the mouth.[7]

Madmen and Specialists is a very sardonic and pessimistic play. The system or cult of AS, whose meaning Bero seeks to have the Old Man divulge, is an adequate metaphor for the entrapment in which contemporary Africans find themselves. As the old man says, AS always is:

> though it wear a hundred masks and a thousand outward forms. And because you are within the System . . . and are part of the material for reformulating the mind of a man into the necessity of the moment's political AS, the moment's scientific AS, metaphysic AS, economic AS, sociological AS, re-creative ethical AS, you-cannot-es-cape! There is one constant in the life of the System and that constant is AS. And what can you pit against the priesthood of that constant deity?

> (p. 110)

Soyinka spells out the fate of those who dare to 'pit [anything] against the

. . . deity [AS]', that is, those who dare to be critical or to confront AS 'priests' with the ugliness of their past and their limitation as human beings:

> Then shall they say unto you, I am chosen, restored, redesignated and redestined and further further shall they say unto you, you heresiarchs of the System arguing questioning querying weighing puzzling insisting rejecting upon you all shall we practice, without passion.
>
> (p. 110)

The depraved nature of that 'practice' is the subject matter of *A Play of Giants*. Characteristically, Soyinka makes no effort to hide the true identity of the 'priests' who are 'at bay in an embassy in New York,'[8] a symbolic linking of them with America and the other powers which not only install but also labour hard to sustain them in power. The play is simply 'a savage portrait of' the late Macias Nguema of Equatorial Guinea, deposed Jean-Baptiste Bokassa of Central African Republic, Mobutu Sese Seko of Zaire, and the deposed Idi Amin, Uganda's nightmare of the 1970s. Although all of these characters (except Mobutu) are now history, their excesses and eccentricities are too well known to require detailed description.

Soyinka's device whereby these men are assembled in one room to confront some of the international personalities, intrigues and politics – in other words, to confront the ultimate source and sustainance of their power – is a superb dramatic achievement. As we witness the obeisance paid to these men by foreign signatories, ambassadors, journalists (Godrum) and artists (the sculptor), it is obvious that for various reasons the foreigners delight in stroking the feathers of the atrocious quartet.

It is a question of time, however, before the relationship between these two groups – that is, the African leaders and their foreign supporters – sour and the foreigners come under fire. The World Bank has refused to grant Kamini's Bugara a loan and Kamini decides to spite the World Bank by printing new currencies. The Chairman of Bugara National Bank, a foreigner, decides to explain the futility of Kamini's decision:

> *Kamini.* . . . go back and get cracking with government mint. When I return, I want to see brand-new currency . . .
> *Chairman.* But Your Excellency, that's why we came to seek this loan in the first place. Now that we haven't got it, there is nothing to back new currency with.
> *Kamani.* What the man talking about? You short of good currency paper at government mint?
> *Chairman.* I'm trying to explain, Your Excellency. Even now, at this moment, our national currency is not worth its size in toilet paper . . .
> *Kamini.* You say Bugara currency only worth shit paper? . . .
>
> (pp. 6–8)

The fate of the Chairman is sealed. From now until the end of the play, he will be made to 'eat good old Bugara shit'.

> *Kamini.* Take this coat-and-tie kondo inside that toilet room there and put his head inside bowl . . . Each time the tank full, you flush it again over his head.
>
> (p. 8)

His fellow Presidents agree with this action. Says Gunema 'Discipline must be imposed.'

By the end of the play, Kamini has managed to find an opportunity to torture and threaten not only the United Nations Representatives of the Super Powers but the Chairman of the United Nations himself. He holds them responsible for the coup d'etat which has been announced in Bugara. Consequently, he holds them ransome until a UN force has been sent to foil the coup and restore Kamini to power. That failing, Kamini indeed carries out his threat to launch bombs and grenades at the UN building and the protesters in the streets. As the lights fade slowly, we see Kamini with 'his gun aimed at the hostages . . . [and] their horror-stricken faces in various postures – freeze' (p. 69).

No appreciation of this topic will be complete without a comment on plays from South Africa – plays whose focus is the prevailing South Africa lunacy of apartheid. As is commonly known, apartheid as a system of government seeks to 'blacken' the African population or pretend that that population consists of ostriches, who, with their heads buried in the inhuman sand of apartheid laws, remain utterly invisible. Various minority leaders – some of whom are finally beginning to recognize the futility of apartheid – pretended for over one century that South Africans on their own native land could be ignored politically. This self-delusion is itself a manifestation of madness.

One of the first well-known plays to dramatize the plight of Africans in South Africa is *Sizwe Bansi is Dead*, a play devised by John Kani, Winston Ntshona and Athol Fugard. In order for them to collaborate, Fugard had to register Kani and Ntshona as his 'boys'! – a reality which is dramatized in *Sizwe Bansi is Dead*. Sizwe Bansi is not allowed to live and work in the city unless he has a Native Identity card. In order to obtain this, he has to prove that he has a job, an apartheid euphemism for 'I an African, belong to Master/Boss X, a European.' For an African to live in any South African city, he has to be a servant to a European, even in instances where the 'baas' is not a South African citizen.

The Bantustans to which Africans are restricted are areas typically known for their aridity or over-crowdedness or both. With little governmental intervention to mitigate the types of hardship which typify Bantustans, most Africans seek to escape to more economically viable

environments. These environments are usually European settlements
where the pass laws and other racially motivated laws await them.

King William's town from which Bansi seeks to escape is a typical
Bantustan – an arid parcel of land where even subsistence farming is
impossible. Sizwe (a name which signifies 'human beings' or 'people')
thus finds himself between the proverbial devil and the deep blue sea.

> The place is fifteen miles from town. There is only one shop there . . . King
> William's town is a dry place . . . very small and too many people. That's why
> I don't want to go back.
>
> (p. 27)

The denouement of the play is familiar, but because its fairy-tale and
rather simplistic nature is often left uncriticized, it is necessary to recall it.

The 'solution' to Bansi's plight comes accidentally one evening when
Buntu and Bansi happen upon the corpse of Robert Zwelinzima. Buntu
quickly realizes that Robert's passbook can be altered to serve Bansi's
need. Bansi will lose his name and assume Robert's name as well as his
job and weekly pay.

To describe this resolution as improbable is an understatement. Buntu's advice that Sizwe become a ghost signifies at the social level a profound sense of frustration, bitterness and hopelessness; and at the
pathological level, an impaired mind. In accepting that suggestion, Sizwe
also assumes a fragmented persona. (I would like to see him at the factory
posing as Robert Zwelinzima whose bearing and personality he has no
notion of!) At best, *Sizwe Bansi is Dead* offers an accurate account of life in
South Africa but not a solution. If indeed the solution works out for Sizwe,
how is it applicable to the millions of desenfranchised and economically
disadvantaged Africans in that region? Unless Buntu is correct in hoping
that they can all become a formidable collective ghost and 'spook [the
regime] to death', the ghost solution is simply as impaired as apartheid
itself. Perhaps that indeed is the whole point of the play – that everything
under any system such as the apartheid regime can only be a manifestation of one impairment or another!

It is interesting that approximately ten years after *Sizwe Bansi is Dead*
premiered, *Woza Albert!* was devised in a similar manner. As Ntshona and
Kani were 'directed' by Fugard, a European South African, Mbongeni
and Percy Mtwa were 'directed' by Barney Simon, a South African of
European descent. Born essentially out of improvisation, the play benefits
from the various elements of improvisation. Most of all, its episodic nature
makes it possible for the play to cover a myriad of situations while still
retaining a sense of unity. The various episodes are either graphic or
subtle dramatizations of the typical injustices and brutalization of Africans under the system of apartheid.

In the opening of the play, Mbongeni is caught playing music at the 'Market Theatre in Johannesburg'. The arresting police officer tells us his offence:

> You work here? If you work here your passbook would be written 'Market Theatre . . .' But look, it is written 'Kentucky Southern Fried'. Is this Kentucky Southern Fried? . . . This is vagrancy . . . Ja, this is what I call 'loafer-skap!'
> . . . You should be in prison.
> . . . I've got a nice little place waiting for him in Modder-B Prison . . .

The next scene indeed shows Mbongeni in Modder-B prison.

The core of the play is a fantasy based on the supposed second coming of Jesus on a visit to South Africa. The irony of the claim that the South African policies are based on Afrikers' Christian (National) principles is not lost on Percy Mtwa and Mbongeni Ngema. How would Jesus (called Morena in the play) feel if he came to South Africa? Mbongeni suggests that he would be moved to tears and forced to speak out against apartheid:

> . . . what place is this? This place where old people weep over the graves of children? I've passed people with burning mouths. People buying water in a rusty piece of tin, and beside them I see people swimming in a lake . . .
> I pass people who sit in dust and beg for work that will buy them bread. And on the other side, I see people living in gold and glass and whose rubbish bins are loaded with food for a thousand mouths . . .
> I see families torn apart, I see mothers without sons, children without fathers and wives without men! . . . Where are the men? And the people will say, Ja, Morena, it is this bladdy apartheid. It is those puppets . . . together with their white Pretoria masters. They separate us from our wives . . . And the women will say, . . . there is no work in the homelands. There's no food. They divide us from our husbands and they pack them into hostels like men without names, . . . lives.
>
> (p. 60)

And Morena having heard and seen their plight, will be forced to adopt a line of action:

> Come to me . . . We will find houses where you can live together and we will talk to those who you fear! What country is this?
>
> (p. 60)

And the government's response will be swift and typical:

> They'll start surrounding our homes at night. And some of our friends will be caught by stray bullets. There will be blocks at every entrance to Soweto, and . . . life will go on as before.
>
> (p. 37)

All these predictions indeed come to pass. Morena comes to the brickyard, is betrayed by Bobbiejaan, who, having been bribed with a wage increase of ten rands, takes a message to the police on behalf of baas Kom who describes Morena as a terrorist. Morena is subsequently arrested, imprisoned and like a number of people before him, he is soon found dead. *Woza Albert!* ends happily as Morena resurrects, goes to the cemetery and brings fallen anti-apartheid heroes back to life.

In spite of its optimistic and cheerful ending, the select list of fallen heroes – Albert Luthuli, Robert Sobukwe, Lilian Ngoyi, Griffith Mixenge, Hector Peterson, Bram Fisher, Steve Biko, Ruth First, coupled with Morena's experience – aptly underscore the impairment of the psyche of South Africa's political leadership.

Impairment of psyche is indeed the only explanation for Morena's killing as well as the brutalization (in real life) of anti-apartheid activists. After all, a clear-minded, wholesome leadership would realize that neither subtle acts of intimidation, nor brutal practices such as torture and assassinations have served as effective deterrents to massive struggles against apartheid.[9]

Earlier on in this paper, I touched upon the traditional Yoruba notion which maintains that a drunk is more likely to be impaired in his judgement of danger than an insane person. Most of the plays under study seem to contradict this notion. Most of the characters seem totally unable to recognize their limits. As one scrutinizes their world a little further, it is interesting to note yet another dimension to them. Most of the characters are drunk. It becomes increasingly obvious that since they wield absolute power, most of the characters soon become power drunk. We thus have an extremely dangerous combination at work – drunkenness and insanity. It is of little wonder then that none of the aforementioned characters is capable of forming

> harmonious relations with others, participate in the changes in his social and physical environment, achieve a harmonious and balanced satisfaction of his own potentially conflicting drives . . .[10]

One of the Africans' main tragedies is the fact that they continue to be governed by these types. African playwrights deserve credit for their in-depth understanding of the nature of these leaders. It is necessary to stress most emphatically that Africa's contemporary leadership is a cancer, an extraneous, unhealthy growth.[11] The next logical theme for African playwrights should be an examination of the impact of the Lejoka-Browns, the Beros, the Kaminis, the imperialists and neo-imperialists, in other words, the impact of contemporary Africa's warped leadership on the psyche of the people.

NOTES

1 For a more detailed discussion, see Oluremi Omodele, 'Traditional and Contemporary African Drama: A Historical Perspective', Ph.D. Dissertation, University of California, Los Angeles, 1988, chs. 4 and 5.

2 Absorptionists were the advocates of a blending of both traditional African values with the 'good' aspects of western culture to generate a hybrid, superior and new way of life. For further discussion of this notion, see Oluremi Omodele, 'Traditional and Contemporary African Drama', chs. 6, 7 and 8. Also Ugugi wa Thiong'o, *Barrel of a Pen* (New York: New Beacon Books, 1983).

3 Ad'Obe Obe, 'Madness and Magic', *West Africa*, 31 January 1982.

4 Ibid., column 2.

5 J. C. Ebie, 'Why Psychiatry in Nigeria' in *Mental Health in Africa*, ed. A. O. Erinosho et al. (Ibadan: University of Ibadan Press, 1982), pp. 133–64.

6 L. Bloom, 'Lying and Culture: A West African Case Study' in *Mental Health in Africa*, ed. Erinosho, pp. 33–43.

7 The average African still remembers President General Gowon's grandiose, ultra-extravagant wedding which was celebrated at the peak of the blood-bath of the Nigerian/Biafra civil war as well as Soyinka's reaction to that event.

8 Wole Soyinka, 'Preface', *A Play of Giants* (London: Methuen, 1984).

9 Witness the rise in the number and vigor of anti-apartheid uprisings since the Soweto massacre, Steve Biko's assassination and other brutal displays of repression.

10 As cited by Ad'Obe Obe, in 'Madness and Magic', p. 241. This is the World Health Organization's (WHO) definition of a mentally healthy person.

11 Anyone who thinks this is an exaggeration should study Africa's traditional systems of governing particularly as it affects accountability and the people's participation in making political and social decisions. Colins Turbull's book, *The Lonely African* (New York: Simon and Schuster, 1962, rpt. 1987), is recommended.

Madness as a satirical tool in two Nigerian plays

ABIODUN GOKE-PARIOLA

African writing in English reveals a recurring preoccupation with the theme of madness. This is usually madness generated by the alienation of an individual from his society. In Ngugi wa Thiong'o's *A Grain of Wheat* (1968), for example, we witness the psychological disintegration of Mugo who betrays the national cause in order to save himself. Thereafter, he is pursued by voices of guilt and of retribution, voices of his innocent fellow human beings whom his act of betrayal has thrown deeper into suffering, until his mind finally snaps. Bessie Head's Elizabeth (*A Question of Power*, 1973) is tortured by a lack of identity, statelessness, and severe loneliness. In Achebe's *Arrow of God* (1969), the inability or unwillingness of Ezeulu, the chief priest of Ulu, to submit himself to the power of collective wisdom, and the god's apparent decision to side with the community – at least in the community's interpretation of events – results in his madness.

One thing all these characters have in common is that their madness springs from an alienation largely defined by the colonial experience. As noted by Ojo-Ade,

> The master-slave relationship that exists in such a society, a relationship that has been adopted and carried forward into the neo-colonialist structure of the independent society, provides a classical setting for the dissipation of sanity and its replacement by dementia.[1]

The clash of the traditional and the modern in colonial and post-colonial experience also sets the stage for various forms of madness. In a society where art is a function of life, it is to be expected that the madness which permeates the societal structure will be a central focus of drama. We see this in plays by two well-known Nigerian dramatists, Ola Rotimi's *Our Husband Has Gone Mad Again* (1977), and Wole Soyinka's *Kongi's Harvest* (1967).

Rotimi and Soyinka, both of whom are Yoruba, have borrowed ideas from the construction of madness in Yoruba culture to achieve opposite dramatic results: comedy and tragedy. According to traditional Yoruba folk wisdom, there are, broadly speaking, two types of *were* (madness, or, mad people): *were alaso* and *were to ti ja*. Literally, these are, respectively, 'the mad person who is still clothed', and 'the mad person who has run amok on the streets' and is, presumably, naked, or at best, only partially clothed. Our understanding of the two categories of madness rests upon a clear apprehension of the underlying metaphor in their characterization. *Were* of the first category is fully clothed, and it is therefore hidden from immediate observation. There is no way to recognize such persons' madness just by looking at them. The difficulty of recognizing and diagnosing the madness is indicated by the Yoruba proverb, *Gbogbo alangba lo da'nu de'le, a o mo eyi t'inu n run*: 'Since all lizards lie on their belly, we cannot tell which one is suffering from stomach ache.' By contrast, the second type of *were* – *were to ti ja* – is easily recognized: when you see someone walking down the street naked, you know that something is wrong. However, these categories of madness are not in water-tight compartments. Within each there are variations, with some forms being more benign than others. Whether a display of madness is classified as comic or tragic depends on what variant of each category of madness is on display, how benign or malignant it is, and how widespread and serious the negative consequences are on the community.

The more dangerous of the two is the *were alaso*. You live with him every day, unsuspecting, because he looks like a normal person. So, the eruption of his madness catches you by surprise. Also, it has the potential for wreaking more havoc on the community. The other type – *were to ti ja* – is more easily dealt with. As the Yoruba often say, *Igi lango leyin asiwere*: 'cudgels are the medicine for treating a madman'. Alternatively, you may simply avoid his side of the road. Informed by a deep understanding of their primary audiences, both dramatists have employed interpretations of the construction of madness in Yoruba culture to elicit the appropriate responses to the comic and the tragic consequences of the clash of conflicting traditions in their society.

Ola Rotimi's play, *Our Husband Has Gone Mad Again*, was first performed by the Yale School of Drama in 1966, directed by Jack Landau. Set in mid-sixties Nigeria, it is a light-hearted satirical comedy, whose central character is a retired army major, Rahman Taslim Lejoka-Brown, who gets into politics, driven more by vanity than an urge to serve his country. He wants his American-trained wife, Liza, a medical doctor, to be introduced at public functions not as the wife of 'a cocoa farmer', but rather as:

> the one and only Dr the Honourable Mrs Elizabeth Lejoka-Brown, MD (Yale), MSc (Gynaecology), wife of the one and only Federal Government Minister of Agriculture and Housing, Mister the Honourable Major Rahman Taslim Akinjide Lejoka-Brown, ON*, MHR*, Esquire!
>
> (p. 29)

He attempts, unsuccessfully, to adapt to a situation he hardly comprehends, while his predicament is further complicated by his unusual domestic life. Without warning, Liza rejoins him while he is still living with two other Nigerian women with whom, unknown to her, he has contracted marriages. At the same moment, his political inexperience catches up with him as he loses out in a power struggle within his political party. In the clash of two worlds and the feeble attempts of an opportunist to exploit both, we see an image of much of the westernized middle class in Nigeria. In fact, Robert M. Wren quotes Ola Rotimi as describing Lejoka-Brown as 'an ordinary Lagos man who does things our more sophisticated moral inhibitions won't allow us to do'.[2] The 'our' obviously refers to the westernized middle class.

Major Lejoka-Brown is cast as a kind of madman: virtually everything about his appearance, his demeanor, his ideas, and his actions is incongruous. A former army officer, he deals with his house-boy as a soldier and approaches elections as he would a military expedition. In the opening scene, Lejoka-Brown, 'husky, broad-shouldered, barrel-chested and hirsute, [and with] only a loin-cloth on, buttressing . . . the complacent sag of his jumbo-sized potbelly' (p. 4) marches onto the stage like a soldier on parade. A Moslem, he contracts a marriage in court with the Catholic Kenyan–American Liza, then agrees to inherit (marry) his deceased brother's wife, Mama Rashida, and finally, marries a young girl, Sikira, daughter of the President of the Nigerian Union of Market Women. He marries Sikira 'for emergency':

> That woman's [Sikira's] case is only for necessity, anyway – temporary measure. We need women's votes . . . if we must win the next elections.
>
> (p. 10)

And how would he handle his National Liberation Party's election campaigns? He tells the executive committee:

> Gentlemen, our election campaign plans must follow a pattern of military strategy known as surprise and attack . . . From city to city, we run over the whole State with a heavy artillery of campaign speeches . . Abeokuta falls . . . an arm of our propaganda brigade crosses over to Jos . . .
>
> (pp. 50–1)

Although he is not naked and running amok in the streets, Lejoka-Brown straddles the thin boundary line between the benign forms of *were alaso* and *were to ti ja*. Much of the time, his antics are indeed symptomatic of the benign form of *were to ti ja*, since he does not constitute a public danger by wielding a machete and threatening the general public. Only once does he almost cross the line between the two types of madness. Having decided that only by acting like a traditional Moslem husband would he be able to control his independent American wife, Liza, he refuses to allow journalists who had come to interview him at home about his party's election plans to see Liza just returning home from the beach, dressed in a skimpy swimsuit. He orders them all to lie face down and threatens to shoot anyone that dares to look up. However, he concludes the show with a toast and a hymn! This kind of resolution of the potentially dangerous crisis, farcical as it seems, makes it possible for Lejoka-Brown's temporary flirtation with the psychopathic variant of *were to ti ja* to reinforce the comedy of situation in this play. We are still able to apply the proverb: *Were dun wo, ko se e bi lomo*: 'The antics of a madman may create a spectacle that's fun to watch, although it is painful to have one for a child.'

Throughout much of the play, Lejoka-Brown's madness remains benign, and principally affects his image alone. As Alex Johnson has correctly observed, rather than being a threat to society,

> he seems more of a threat to himself. We are invited to laugh at and occasionally with him as he cheerfully extricates himself from untenable positions, gracefully accepting his loss of face and sensibly retreating.[3]

Wole Soyinka's play, *Kongi's Harvest*, is set in an imaginary African country. It is the story of a modern-day leader, not unlike Chaplin's *Great Dictator*. Kongi's harvest is supposed to be the official beginning of the Five-Year (Development) Plan. President Kongi has already placed the spiritual leader, Oba (King) Danlola, under 'preventive detention'. But, not content with the political power he has already usurped, he is determined to assume spiritual leadership also by having Danlola personally present the traditional new yam to him in front of the people. According to Kongi's lieutenant, Secretary,

> Kongi desires that the King perform all his customary spiritual functions, only this time, that he perform them to him, our Leader. Kongi must preside as the Spirit of Harvest, in pursuance of the Five-Year Development Plan.
>
> (p. 20)

In his quest for absolute power, he is very much like Kurtz in Conrad's *Heart of Darkness* (1969), with the predictable consequence of madness. It is Kongi's romance with spiritual and political absolutism that defines the madness in the drama. For absolute power not only corrupts absolutely, but first makes the owner mad. In the process of amassing total power over the country and the people, Kongi is transformed into a classic megalomaniac, going on an image-building trip. Virtually everything in the country is now named after Kongi: Kongi Terminus, Kongi University, Kongi Dam, Kongi Airport, and Kongi Refineries. Of course, huge posters of him dot the whole country. Even the years will now be dated from Kongi's Harvest – AKH (After Kongi's Harvest)!

Kongi's case is typical of the malignant form of *were alaso*. Both in his assault on tradition and his megalomania, Kongi is cast as a madman. In Yoruba culture, the force of tradition is indeed very strong. A member of the society must 'do things as they are done' so that the outcome may be 'as it is supposed to be'. This covers the entire spectrum of social relations, family ties and obligations as well as work ethics. A type of behavior contrary to the norm in any of these spheres may produce unpleasant consequences that threaten the existence of the individual, family, or society. A character who behaves in this fashion, then, may be classified as insane, a *were alaso*, with the degree of insanity depending on how wide the ramifications of the behavior are. This form of insanity may eventually graduate to the public one, in which case, the individual becomes a *were to ti ja*.

In an altercation, Oba Danlola threatens to prostrate himself to one of Kongi's emissaries – a terrible abomination. The servant is alarmed, and pleads with the king not to 'put a curse on him':

> Only a foolish child lets a father prostrate to him. I don't ask to become a leper or *a lunatic*. I have no wish to live on sour berries.
>
> (p. 6)

From this, it is obvious that flouting the tradition may lead to the extreme form of madness. When Danlola again threatens to prostrate himself, the Prison Superintendent forestalls the curse by throwing himself down before the king.

The little drama of the threat of madness here foreshadows the conflict between Kongi and Danlola, between old forms of tyranny and new ones, between tradition and sanity on the one hand, and the assault on tradition and the consequent foray into madness on the other. The servant redeems himself by reaffirming the primacy of tradition; but Kongi insists that the king, and not just any ordinary elder, should prostrate himself before him. Yet, in the words of Sarumi, a junior Oba to Danlola, 'The king is god' (p. 3). The Drummer, a praise-singer to royalty, anticipates and warns of the impending pervasive madness in the society when he sings:

> I saw a strange sight
> In the market this day
> The sun was high
> But I saw no shade
> From the King's umbrella.
>
> (p. 8)

The story of the proverbial monster child is also used to reinforce the image of Kongi as a madman. This is illustrated in the following chant between Ogbo Aweri (Head of the Oba's defunct Conclave of Elders) and Sarumi, the junior king:

Ogbo Aweri.   Observe, when the monster child
                Was born, *Opele* taught us to
                Abandon him beneath the buttress tree
                But the mother said, oh no,
                A child is still a child
                The mother in us said, a child
                Is the handiwork of Olukori.
Sarumi.   Soon the head swelled
                Too big for the pillow
                And it swelled too big
                For the mother's back
                And soon the mother's head
                Was nowhere to be seen
                And the child's slight belly
                Was strangely distended.

(p. 10)

In this classic scenario, the dream world of nightmare becomes reality. The madness of Kongi, the monster-child, turns the world on its head. Kongi's very first appearance on stage only serves to confirm the image of a madman. His megalomania is immediately apparent. He enters the chambers in which his Consultative Council is supposed to be meeting, and finds all the members fast asleep. The Secretary, having failed to wake them up by striking the gong, says 'They are practically dead'. Kongi's response reveals the depth of his insanity:

> Dead? How dead? I don't remember condemning any of them to death. Or maybe I should?

(p. 35)

Consumed by what he believes to be a power that belongs to him alone, the power of life and death over his fellow human beings, Kongi misses the Secretary's figurative use of language. Subsequently, he confirms his usurpation of the power of life and death. When the Secretary says of the chant by Kongi's Carpenters' Brigade (a.k.a. Kongi's thugs) 'It is an invitation to the Spirit of Harvest to lend you strength', Kongi becomes apoplectic at this apparently innocent comment: the Spirit of Harvest cannot be invoked to lend Kongi strength because, in his own words, 'I [Kongi] *am* the Spirit of Harvest' (p. 36). And, to make sure the Secretary never forgets this fact, he repeats it four times. In his dementia, the similarity between Kongi and Kurtz (who is supposed not only to have participated in ritual sacrifices, but had sacrifice offered to him as a god) is again inescapable.

As we move back to Oba Danlola's house, the warning of the final explosion of madness is once again reinforced. Danlola is about to renege on his promise to Prince Daodu, the heir-apparent, that he would attend the Festival because of Kongi's cancellation of the reprieve of five detainees awaiting execution. In desperation, Daodu strikes the king's lead drum, bursting it. His father, Oba Sarumi is horrified at this sacrilegious act, which is tantamount to madness:

> *Sarumi (in a horrified whisper). Efun!*
> *Danlola (shakes his head slowly).*
>   No. Your son has his senses
>   Intact. He must know what he is doing.
> *Sarumi. Efun! Efun!* Someone has done this to him.
>   Some enemy has put a curse on my first-born.
> *Danlola (climbing back to his throne, wearily).*
>   Life gets more final every day. That prison
>   Superintendent merely lay his hands
>   On my lead drummer, and stopped
>   The singing, but you our son and heir
>   You've seen to the song itself. . . .
> *Daodu.* I only want a few words. . . .
> *Danlola.* I know the drums were silenced long
>   Before you, but you have split
>   The gut of our make-believe. Suddenly
>   The world has run amok and left you
>   Alone and sane behind.

                                                    (pp. 60–1)

Danlola's words are very revealing. The world has gone so crazy that insanity now seems to be sanity.

Just before the play's shattering climax, Kongi seems to have succeeded in realizing his wishes in spite of the plan by Daodu and his girlfriend, Segi, to sabotage the Festival. Segi's father, the one of the five men condemned to death by Kongi who had escaped, returns to the scene of the Harvest Festival and is killed by Kongi's thugs. Oba Danlola proceeds to offer the new yam to Kongi, and Segi begins to direct the preparation of the feast.

But all is not well. Kongi has gone completely berserk, even though he is still clothed. In this final scene, he delivers in mime a supposedly four-and-a-half-hour speech, a speech submerged in the noise of the preparations of the feast. It is a speech which has been correctly described as 'pure gesture, devoid of sound, unheeded by the world . . . gestures [which] full of fury only, are those of a man out of all emotional control'.[4] He has practically become a *were to ti ja*.

Kongi's madness has virtually destroyed the society spiritually as well as physically. As Segi prepares to present Kongi with the meal of pounded yam, she begins a chant which reveals the utter madness into which the society has been thrown by Kongi's peculiar brand of insanity:

Ijo mo ko w'aiye o	At my first coming
Ipasan ni.	Scourges all the way

Ijo mo ko w'asiye o	At my first coming
Ipasan ni	Whips to my skin
Igin lehin were o	Cudgels on the madman's back
Kunmo lehin were o	
Aiye akowa	At my first coming
Ade egun ni o	A crown of thorns
Aiye akowa	At my first coming
Ade egun ni o	A crown of thorns
Iso lo g'aka m'ogi	The foolhardy hedgehog
Iso lo g'aka m'ogi	Was spreadeagled on nails
Mo ti d'ade egun	I have borne the thorned crown
Pere gungun maja gungun pere	Shed tears as the sea
Mo ti d'ade egun	I was spat upon
Pere gungun maja gungun pere	A leper's spittle
Omije osa	A burden of logs
Pere gungun maja gungun pere	Climbed the hunchback hill
Won tu'to pami	There was no dearth of yam
Pere gungun maja gungun pere	But the head of the firstborn
Kelebe adete	Was pounded for yam
Pere gungun maja gungun pere	There was no dearth of wood
Mo gbe'gi k'ari	Yet the thigh of the firstborn
Pere gungun maja gungun pere	Lost its bone for fuel
Mo g'oke abuke	
Pere gungun maja gungun pere	
Isu o won n'ile o	
Isu o won n'ile o	
Won gb'ori akobi le le	
Won fi gun'yan	
Igi o won n'ile e	
Igi o won n'ile e	
Egun itan akobi o	
Ni won fi da'na	

(pp. 82–3)

Now the second coming must be a different kind of experience. The madness in the world must be cured. It is time for peace. But, in a world that had gone so mad, what is the recipe for peace? Ironically, the suggestion seems to be a greater madness to be used as a counterforce. This reflects another cultural belief implied in the statement *Were ni a fi n wo were*: A madness is only cured by a greater madness. This explains Segi's action. She cuts off her dead father's head and, in place of the customary pounded yam, she presents this in a copper salver to Kongi. In this climactic conclusion to the Festival – and the play – when Segi opens the lid, revealing the head of the old man, Kongi's mouth opens in speechless terror. We are left to wonder if this apparent display of symbolic madness will finally turn the world back on its feet.

While in Rotimi's *Our Husband Has Gone Mad Again*, Lejoka-Brown is redeemed by experience and a knowledge of when to retreat from disaster,

Kongi is unredeemed in his madness. His psychosis in fact becomes contagious, increasing its potential to destroy the entire community. Before the end of the play, virtually everyone in the community partakes of the madness. In the postscript to the play titled, 'Hangover', the Secretary in a conversation with Oba Danlola describes both Daodu and Segi as 'Roadside lunatics'. Danlola concurs, adding,

> The Strange thing is, I think
> Myself I drank from the stream of madness
> For a little while.

(p. 89)

The madness here fails to elicit humour, except, perhaps, an occasional black humour. Thus, it reinforces the sense of communal tragedy in the play *Kongi's Harvest*.

How do we evaluate the madness at the end of the play? Segi's apparent mad act intended to serve as a counterforce to Kongi's does not seem to have been effective. Kongi would appear to have triumphed over his enemies. Insanity remains the order of the day. Lemuel Johnson claims that, in his handling of this satire on the politics of what he describes as 'the Middle passage' – a politics of villainy resulting from the contact between Africa and Europe – Soyinka makes the climactic pathological dance into a 'choreographed near-literal representation of the cannibalistic implications of political rapacity'.[5] This conclusion confirms Soyinka's pessimistic vision of the cycle of tyranny. For, even though 'Dictators rise and fall, . . . Kongism has never been dethroned in black Africa. Kongism is the dogma on whose altar human beings are sacrificed.'[6]

NOTES

1 Femi Ojo-Ade, 'Madness in the African Novel: Awoonor's *This Earth, My Brother . . .*' in *African Literature Today 10: Retrospect & Prospect*, ed. Eldred D. Jones (London: Heinemann, 1979), p. 134.

2 Robert M. Wren, 'Ola Rotimi: A Major New Talent', *African Report*, 18:5 (September–October 1973), 30.

3 Alex C. Johnson, 'Ola Rotimi: How Significant?' in *African Literature Today 12: New Writing, New Approaches*, ed. Eldred D. Jones and Eustace Palmer (London: Heinemann, 1982), p. 142.

4 Boyd M. Berry, '*Kongi's Harvest* (A Review)' in *Critical Perspectives on Wole Soyinka*, ed. James Gibbs (Washington, DC: Three Continents, 1980), p. 87.

5 Lemuel A. Johnson, 'The Middle Passage in African Literature: Wole Soyinka, Yambo Ouologuem, Ayi Kwei Armah' in *African Literature Today 11: Myth & History*, ed. Eldred D. Jones (London: Heinemann, 1980), p. 65.

6 Kola Ogungbesan, 'Wole Soyinka', in *A Celebration of Black and African Writing*, ed. Bruce King and Kola Ogungbesan (Zaria: Ahmadu Bello University Press; Ibadan: Oxford University Press), p. 180.

Index